MARC DANIEL

THE
GIRL
WHO WENT
NOWHERE

Also by Marc Daniel

ETHAN ARCHER SERIES

The Girl Who Went Nowhere

MICHAEL BIORN SERIES

Shadow Pack

Unholy Trinity

Close Enemies

Into the Woods

Acknowledgements

I must start by thanking my wife, Jasmin. She usually gets the last paragraph of this section for putting up with me on a daily basis and serving as a sounding board, but this time she truly deserves the first place. She accepted to do what nobody should ever have to do; she read the first draft of this novel. Her feedback proved instrumental and saved me a lot of headaches down the line.

I must also thank my most loyal beta readers, Darwin and Katherine, who once again provided invaluable feedback.

Sarah, at Cornerstones Literary Consultancy, worked her magic once again to provide the professional editing touch the manuscript required and for which my readers will no doubt be grateful.

The last few typos were caught by Katherine, my eagle-eyed proofreader and friend. Katherine, I am once again in your debt.

Cover Design: Ivan Zanchetta (bookcoversart.com)

To Caroline and Laura

Prologue

The moon was nearly full in the cloudless sky, but not much of its light percolated through the thick branches of evergreens that dominated the forest.

The child's heart was pounding in her chest, her eardrums pulsing in unison. Though she'd only been running a few minutes, her little legs felt like she'd been at it for hours. Soon they'd betray her; she was sure of it. But there was nothing she could do about it. Stopping wasn't an option. Not now, not ever.

She heard the sound again, the crackling of leaves flattened by a foot that wasn't hers. It was getting closer.

Lungs on fire, she accelerated, giving everything she had left. She never even saw the low branch before it hit her square in the belly and sent her reeling onto her back. She still had the strength to muffle a scream but couldn't hold back her tears any longer.

Lying motionless in the middle of the woods, the nine-year-old felt the frozen ground sucking the warmth out of her. The adrenaline rush had maintained her body temperature within a comfortable range so far, but the frigid December night would soon take its toll on her endurance if she remained lying there.

She sat up and started rubbing her palms together to remove the grit coating them. Mustering all the strength remaining in her young muscles, she got back on her feet and heard a rustling sound directly behind her. It was too late. The fall had robbed her of the precious seconds she'd had on her stalker.

She turned around and there it was, standing between the trees no more than thirty feet from her.

This time she couldn't help but scream as she took off in the opposite direction from the ghost. For it was a ghost, no doubt about it; the whiteness of his skin allowed for no other possibility.

She'd never believed in the old folk tales told by the locals. She'd always thought of them as made-up nonsense designed to scare children and attract tourists. But now she was forced to admit she'd been wrong. The ghost was real, and it had come for her.

She took off, running as fast as her legs could carry her, oblivious to the lactic acid burning inside her muscles at every stride. She could hear his feet hitting the ground behind her at regular intervals. Soon he would catch up with her, soon it would all be over.

She made a sudden left turn into a field of boulders. The trees were sparser, and heat could be felt rising from the ground. She was probably close to the natural hot spring. She'd been there before with her siblings. A hole in the ground in the middle of a clearing. Filled with water warm enough to make you sweat in the middle of the Montana winter.

She could no longer hear the ghost's footsteps; maybe she'd lost him. Maybe he'd been tricked by her sudden change of direction.

Utterly exhausted, she stopped behind a giant boulder and listened intently to the silence of the night before allowing herself a deep breath.

She remained there in a half crouch for a long minute, panting as quietly as she could. When she finally stood up and risked a glance around the boulder, she saw no one among the irregular granite blocks peppering the clearing. She breathed a sigh of relief.

And then she felt a giant hand closing on her shoulder. She spun around, flailing her arms in an attempt to free herself, but only managed to trip on a rock and land flat on the ground.

The ghost was on her in a flash and under the eerie glow of the moon she realized her mistake. With the exception of his hands and head, which were as white as snow and void of any hair, the thing bent over her was covered in a thick fur. This was no ghost at all.

The beast emitted a guttural growl as his enormous paw covered her mouth. She tried to scream, but to no avail. She saw him reaching for something behind his back and his other hand came up holding a strange-looking knife. Its blade was darker than the night.

In that instant she realized this wasn't a beast either. No beast could do this to a child. There was only one creature capable of such atrocities. She no longer had any doubt about the nature of her aggressor. It could only be a man.

As her teary eyes watched the blade fall towards her throat, she decided she had no regret. Running away in the middle of the night might not have been the best of ideas, but it was still better than staying there.

Chapter 1

In a corner of the bar, Ethan Archer sat quietly nursing a glass of mineral water that cost more than a draft beer. Everything considered, he had better than average reasons to indulge in the sauce, but he'd never been much of a drinker and wasn't about to start now. His hobby required a clear head.

The bar was a noisy place with a small, crowded dance floor crammed in a corner. Scattered on the walls alongside car parts and framed jokes of questionable taste were vintage LP record jackets that reminded Ethan of simpler times.

Although the average customer was probably in their low thirties, the establishment's patronage was as eclectic as its decoration. Drunk students in their twenties occupied most of the dance floor, but one could also find a few forty-something women prowling the room in groups of two or three, carefully dodging the occasional retired gentleman still hoping for action.

A casual observer would have thought that Ethan's watchful eyes were paying particular attention to attractive single women, but that observer would have been wrong. Ethan's interest in these women was indirect at best. A means to an end.

He spent most of his evenings in such places, watching, waiting, hoping. Usually for nothing. Most nights he closed the place down and headed home, alone with his anguish. But on rarer occasions he found what he was looking for and got his fix. Afterward he still ended up alone in his San Francisco apartment, but the weight of his existence was slightly more bearable. If he were lucky, tonight would be such a night.

He was currently paying close attention to a ravishing beauty sitting alone at a table. The woman's dark hair and olive skin could have come from somewhere in the Middle East, northern India or Pakistan. But San Francisco was such a melting pot of cultures that her family might just as well have been in the country for generations.

She appeared to be watching the sweaty men and women undulating on the dance floor, but Ethan wasn't fooled. She was really feigning to not notice the handsome man standing alone at the bar. The one who, after eying her for a good five minutes, was now making a beeline for her table.

Ethan had a good feeling about this guy. There was something in his demeanor that felt right, or at least wrong in a good way. Yes... with a bit of luck, this couple could turn a boring evening into a good one.

The man reached the woman's table and introduced himself while extending a hand. At first she acted surprised to see a stranger at her table but quickly recovered and finally shook the offered hand, at the same time flashing a smile meant to be both shy and alluring.

Ethan had witnessed this scene a million times before. He knew where the dance was heading, or at least where these two thought it was heading— a very different place than what Ethan had in mind.

They talked for about twenty minutes, the woman laughing at the man's jokes as if they were the most hilarious things she'd ever heard. They smiled so much their jaws probably ached.

Soon, both glasses were empty, and the man went for refills. The bar was crowded and a couple minutes passed before he was able to place his order, but Ethan's gaze never left him.

As the man returned to the woman's table with the drinks and sat back down across from her, Ethan's grip tightened around his empty glass.

They sipped slowly on their drinks, flirting, chatting. Ethan was too far away to eavesdrop, but the exchange of platitudes mattered little anyway; his mind was already focused on the next step. When the man's hand reached out to the other side of the table to caress the woman's arm, however, Ethan's blood nearly started boiling.

The torture lasted another thirty minutes before the couple eventually got up and headed for the door, the man's arm wrapped around the waist of the woman. She wasn't as steady on her feet as she'd been an hour earlier when she'd first walked into the bar.

Careful to maintain his distance, he followed them outside. The night was still young, the parking lot full of cars but void of bystanders. As he'd expected, the two were heading for the same vehicle. He picked up the pace as he saw the man opening the passenger door to let the woman in. How chivalrous of him...

By the time the man reached out to open his own door, Ethan was right behind him. He grabbed the man by the hair and rammed his head into the top of the sedan a couple of times before spinning him around for a magistral headbutt. He heard the man's nose cracking under the impact. A satisfying sound.

The man was starting to collapse, but he wasn't done with him, not by a long shot. As his knee made contact with the bastard's stomach, he heard the woman starting to scream for help. No surprise there. This was a typical reaction.

"Help! Help! He's killing my husband!" she screamed. But Ethan had already punched the guy in the face a couple more times before his brain finally registered the words. Had she said *husband*?

"Police! Hands up!" he heard a man's voice shouting behind him. The voice was entirely too close for comfort.

Ethan turned just in time to see the Taser's prongs racing towards his chest.

Chapter 2

On the crowded dance floor, Jennifer MacKay was watching Ethan from the corner of her eye. She'd seen him walk in around 10 PM. The fact he'd been alone hadn't surprised her. In the months she'd known him, she'd never seen him with a woman. A bit atypical for a straight man with Ethan's looks, but Jennifer knew why that was. Or part of the story, at least. She also knew there was more to it than what had been in the papers, but she had yet to find out what.

It wasn't the first time she saw him in a bar, though she wasn't sure why he came. Escape the loneliness of his apartment? Somehow, she doubted it... He never talked to anybody and remained sitting by himself, usually at a table against one of the walls or in a corner, like today.

Aside from the waitresses, nobody ever talked to him either. It wasn't that Ethan was unattractive, quite the contrary; shy of six foot and with lean muscles he was in better shape than most of the guys in the joint, but his demeanor broadcasted a stay-away vibe impossible to miss.

The waitress placed a bottle of mineral water and a glass in front of him, but he paid her no attention and continued surveying the room as he took a 5-dollar bill out of his wallet and dropped it on the woman's tray.

Jennifer's attention drifted away from Ethan as she felt a stranger's warm breath on her neck. Before she could step away, an arm wrapped around her waist and the stranger started grinding against her to the beat of the music.

Dancing in a circle with the rest of their girlfriends on the other side of the dance floor, Tabatha was giving her a pissed-off look.

Jennifer turned around to see who she was dealing with and found herself face to chest with a tank. With her 3-inch heels she was 5'8", which made the groper about 6'5". A giant who clearly spent way too much time at the gym and didn't look a day over twenty-one.

With her porcelain doll complexion and her 130 pounds of curves, she attracted this kind of attention on a regular basis, but that didn't mean she was used to it. She was utterly uninterested by what gym-boy had to offer, and the fact she was easily ten years older than him was only the tip of the iceberg.

Before she had a chance to pronounce a word, the guy's hands were on her ass and he was pulling her towards him.

"I'm not interested," she screamed over the thumping bass while pulling the offensive digits away from her body.

The guy gave her a toothy grin that smelled of stale beer and partially digested garlic.

Hoping the message would be clear, she turned her back on him and joined her girlfriends.

Barely a minute had passed before Tabatha gave her a *watch out behind you!* look, but the warning came too late. Before Jennifer had a chance to move, the tank was back groping her, his hands braver than before.

Tabatha's eyes were sending daggers in their general direction and Jennifer wasn't sure if they were meant for her or for the jackass. She was about to tell the guy to fuck off when his left hand landed on her breast.

She took a deep breath to calm herself, but only partially succeeded. She gently turned around to face her aggressor who flashed her another repulsive smile. She smiled back and grabbed his hands before placing them on her ass. He looked at her with a mixture of surprise and delight as her hand slipped first inside his pants and then underneath his boxers. She ignored his half-aroused cock and went straight for the balls. Although partially covered by the deafening beat of the speakers, his scream was music to her ears.

"I need to wash my hands," she told Tabatha as she headed for the restroom, not even glancing at the jackass holding his balls and grimacing on the dance floor.

Ethan's seat was empty by the time she came back out. She surveyed the room, but he was nowhere to be found. Oh well, she wasn't his babysitter after all.

She walked to the bar, ordered a rum and coke, and went to sit at an empty table near the dance floor. Tabatha looked to be in a better disposition now. Good! Jennifer wasn't in a mood for a fight.

She took a sip of her drink as her mind drifted once more towards Ethan. Resting her chin in the palm of her right hand, she began gently massaging her ear lobe between her index and middle finger. A silly habit she'd had since childhood. One that had always helped her focus.

Jennifer wasn't sure how long she'd been sitting there by the time a woman walked up to her table and interrupted her train of thought. "I'm sorry to bother you, but I think we may know each other."

Jennifer looked at the attractive blonde bent over her table for a moment before shaking her head. "I don't believe so."

The woman's eyes were searching hers intently. "I could have sworn…"

"It happens. No harm done," said Jennifer, as she got up to join Tabatha on the dance floor.

From the corner of her eye, she watched the woman walk back to a table occupied by two of her friends. Jennifer could barely hear herself think over her racing pulse. She needed to get out of here now, before the woman called her bluff.

Chapter 3

It was six in the morning by the time Theodore Hansen's car stopped in front of Ethan's apartment.

"Thanks, Theo, I owe you one," said Ethan, one hand on the door handle.

"Actually, you owe me three grand! When can I expect them back?" These were the first words out of Special Agent Theodore Hansen's mouth since he'd bailed Ethan out of jail.

"Three grand? That sounds pretty stiff."

"That's what aggravated assault costs these days. Next time maybe you'll think twice before beating a poor guy to a pulp for no reason. But who am I kidding? We both know you'll do it again. It's just a matter of time before you end up in San Quentin for good."

"Are you done?" asked Ethan.

"Not by a long shot! You know you could do some time for this?"

"It crossed my mind."

"And in addition to the criminal case for which you've already been given a court date, the guy's very likely to file a civil lawsuit. You could be forced to pay a shitload of money in damages. This ain't over, Ethan," said Theo, pointing his finger at him.

They'd known each other nearly fifteen years, but Ethan had seldom seen Theo this upset. The two had met at Ohio State during their freshman year and had become quick friends and wingmen. With a mother of Vietnamese descent and an African American father, Theo's exotic looks had been highly appreciated by their female classmates, and since Ethan wasn't ugly either, the duo had been popular among the fairer sex all the way to graduation.

"I'm telling you that he put something in her drink. I saw it," said Ethan, not for the first time.

"And I'm telling you they're married. Whatever weird shit they're into isn't your problem, pal. If it turns them on to act up their fantasies in bars, it's their right, Ethan. And if they like to get high first, it's their right to deny it when the cops question them after a nut job busts the husband's head open."

"So you think that's what happened?" asked Ethan. The theory wasn't a bad one.

"Hell, I don't know… But it doesn't matter. What matters is for you to stop lurking in all those shitholes waiting for some perv to step out of line. That's not a life, bro. You've got to stop doing this to yourself. I feel your pain, I really do, but that's not healthy!"

"If these two had been normal… If they didn't enjoy putting shit in each other's drinks, none of that would have happened."

"You got to stop telling yourself stories, Ethan. Come back to earth."

Ethan hadn't seen Theo this upset in a long time.

"You want to know the truth?" continued his friend. "I talked to the arresting officer. He spent over an hour with the lady. She wasn't high… Whatever was in that drink, it wasn't a roofie, it wasn't drugs, it wa—"

"The guy picks up his wife in a bar as if she were a stranger? Who does that? Deviants! That's who!" interrupted Ethan.

"Do you hear yourself? You of all people are calling these two sexual deviants? If that ain't the pot calling the kettle black, I don't know what is."

Ethan stared at his friend in silence for a long moment. His pulsing temple vein was a clear indicator of how angry he felt.

"I'm sorry. I didn't mean to go there," backtracked Theo.

"Thanks for the ride," said Ethan as he exited the car and slammed the door hard enough to wake up the whole neighborhood.

As he climbed the flight of stairs leading to his front door, he forced himself to take a calming breath. He simply couldn't afford to go there either. Not tonight. Not again.

Chapter 4

Ethan found Jennifer MacKay sitting behind her desk, a mug of coffee in her hand, when he finally made it to the office at quarter past ten the next day.

After Theo had dropped him off, he'd lain down on his couch for a quick nap before heading for the shower. He'd woken up three hours later with an aching back and a head still pounding from the Taser incident.

"Morning," he said, sitting down at his own desk located at a ninety-degree angle from Jennifer's.

"Barely…"

Ethan ignored his secretary's remark and logged into his computer. The rented office space's only window was directly behind him, and this was the time of day when the sun shone through it, resulting in major glare on his computer screen.

The Archer agency being a two-person outfit, there was more than enough empty space in the 200-square foot office for him to relocate his desk, but that would mean he'd be able to see the window from his new vantage point and he found that distracting. The window belonged at his back, period.

"Mrs. Balden called again," said Jennifer, her Scottish accent rolling off her tongue.

Ethan sighed. Mrs. Balden had hired him to follow her philandering husband around and bring her enough evidence of his misdeeds to guarantee her a four-figure monthly alimony check.

"What did she want this time?" Tailing a cheating spouse was a boring job, but it paid the bills. Besides, interesting jobs no longer attracted Ethan. At least that's the lie he told himself to avoid facing the truth.

"She wanted to know what happened to your face," answered Jennifer.

Ethan stared at his poker-faced secretary. "You're funny, Jennifer. Maybe you can apply for a clown's position once I fire your ass."

"Idle threats… There's no one else out there who'd put up with you, and you know it. You're stuck with me, boss."

She was probably right. In the months she'd been working for him, Jennifer had heard more than her share of profanities and witnessed more than a few of his outbursts. On the few occasions where he'd exceeded her above-average threshold for abuse, she'd told him to go fuck himself before taking the rest of the day off. But she'd always been back the next morning acting as if nothing had happened.

She definitely wasn't the best secretary out there, but she was the best he could hope for. And with her long red hair, perfect ass, and sassy smile, she was easy on the eyes too. He also liked the pallor of her skin, a redhead's trademark he'd never found particularly appealing before, but which suited her perfectly.

"Mrs. Balden still wants to know, boss."

"Tell Mrs. Balden what happened to my face is none of her business," he replied, grabbing his phone, seemingly checking for messages when, in reality, he was using the camera as a mirror.

Here it was, a scrape above the eyebrow and a bruise that was starting to turn purple on his forehead. Probably the place where his head had met the asphalt as a result of his tasering incident.

"Jackass!" said Jennifer, staring at her computer screen.

"You'd better not be talking about me."

"I wasn't," she replied, before adding under her breath, "this time."

"Who then?"

"Allister Woodrough, a senator from Wyoming."

Ethan was familiar with Senator Woodrough. The man had been in the news a lot lately. Usually clamoring about "the recent assaults on traditional family values" and the need to "cure homosexuality once and for all." He was also notorious for his misogyny, but this detail had apparently no impact on his electorate since he'd been reelected three times in a row.

"He wants to pass a law against women in the workplace?" asked Ethan.

"Not yet. He's just pushing for drilling for oil inside Yellowstone National Park." Jennifer's Scottish accent was thicker when she was mad.

"Most of the park is in his state... Why wouldn't he?"

Jennifer gave him a look that told him she wasn't amused.

What had Ethan done to his head? Jennifer hadn't noticed anything in the bar, but it had been dark, and he'd been sitting at the other end of the room. He could also have gotten into trouble after leaving the bar. That wouldn't be a first. He'd shown up to work with bruises on more than one occasion in the short time she'd known him. Short time... nearly a year already.

She vividly remembered her first encounter with Ethan Archer. She'd walked into his office to find him on the phone, laughing. Her first thought had been that he looked better in the flesh than in the interviews with him she'd seen on TV. His athletic built, piercing blue eyes and short raven hair were no doubt popular with women. Straight women, that was, but Ethan was of the wrong gender to suit Jennifer's tastes.

She remembered standing at the door for ten minutes while he rambled on the phone about his *closure rate*. Which was simply the percentage of bad apples he'd successfully helped the cops put away. He sounded so cocky and full of himself that she wanted to slap him.

"I assume you're here for the secretary position?" he'd said as soon as he'd hung up the phone. "I see you brought some references," he'd added, pointing at the large envelope in her hand. "That won't be necessary. I find references a perfect waste of time. You can start tomorrow on a two-week trial period at fifteen dollars an hour. If I'm satisfied with your work, you'll be hired full time."

She'd opened her mouth to reply at the same instant he was answering another call. Within a half-minute, she'd witnessed a wide range of emotions on Ethan's face. The boastful attitude had first turned to perplexity. Concern had come next but had only lasted a moment before Ethan had finally turned livid.

He'd gotten up, grabbed his jacket and headed for the door.

"See you tomorrow. Eight o'clock sharp," he'd said before exiting without

another word.

She'd come back the next day to find the office unlocked and in the same exact state it had been a day earlier. She'd sat down behind the desk that wasn't Ethan's and had started surfing the web to kill time. At five o'clock, she'd grabbed her purse and had headed home, wondering what to do about the situation. She'd returned to the office the next day in the hope her new boss would show up, but he hadn't. This fruitless routine had lasted an entire week.

When Ethan had finally returned to the office, looking like the shadow of the man he'd been some days earlier, he'd been visibly surprised to see her sitting behind her desk. He hadn't said a word or offered any explanation for his prolonged absence, however. He didn't have to. His story had been all over the news for days. Ethan Archer's downfall had been a public one.

Chapter 5

This was Paul Richards' first visit to the de Young. Located in San Francisco, the fine arts museum was famous for its paintings and sculptures from Africa, Oceania and the Americas.

Paul was admiring an African stone mask when he took a step back and bumped into a woman in her early thirties looking at a nearby statue.

"I'm so sorry. I was absorbed by this mask and didn't see you." He flashed the beautiful woman an apologetic smile before returning his focus to the artifact.

"This mask is from Ethiopia. That's where my parents are from," she answered with a smile that illuminated her mahogany complexion.

"Now I can see where Ethiopian artists get their inspiration from," he said, looking at her knowingly.

The line was lame, but the woman blushed all the same. Paul Richards possessed charm and charisma.

No other words were exchanged and they each resumed their visit of the gallery.

Thirty minutes went by before their paths crossed again, this time in front of a painted shield featuring deformed faces that wouldn't have been out of place in a Dali painting.

"I'm glad you didn't bump into me in front of this piece," she said, pointing at the shield. "Your comment about the artist's source of inspiration wouldn't have sounded so good in this instance."

Paul raised an eyebrow and examined the shield a moment before replying, "My line would probably have been received with a slap in the face in this instance."

They spent the next hour sauntering from one piece to the next, sometimes commenting on the quality of the work and sometimes on the artist's lack of inspiration.

Paul enjoyed the woman's company and, based on the way she was looking at him when he was seemingly not paying attention, he was pretty sure the feeling was mutual. No surprise there. His broad shoulders, wavy brown hair and chiseled features usually had that effect on women. And in the few instances where his attractive physics failed to impress, his way with words usually did the trick.

Paul's phone started vibrating inside his sportscoat's pocket and he retrieved it to see a familiar name flashing on the screen. "I completely forgot about this," he said, pointing at his phone. "I was supposed to meet a friend for dinner twenty minutes ago."

"Then you'd better run," answered the woman. "I'm Naomi, by the way. Naomi Berhan." She extended her hand.

"Paul Richards. It was very nice meeting you, Naomi. Enjoy the end of your visit," he replied, letting go of her hand and heading towards the exit in a hurry.

As he climbed into his car, he reflected that asking Naomi's phone number might have been a good idea.

Chapter 6

It was 7:30 PM when Ethan returned home to his apartment carrying a large pizza. He'd wasted his whole Saturday tailing Mr. Balden and had nothing to show for it. The tech tycoon had spent most of the day playing golf at his country club in the company of three distinguished gentlemen before heading home to his wife. Ethan was starting to suspect the fat cat knew he was under surveillance. This wouldn't be the first time Ethan got caught following someone. He wasn't any good at it and didn't really care either.

He'd just been sitting in front of the TV, a slice of pizza in hand, when the doorbell rang. He peeked through the window before buzzing his visitor in.

A minute later, Theo was sitting in his favorite armchair sipping on a cold beer.

"How are you doing?" asked his friend.

"Living the dream."

"You look it too. Have you been served your summons yet?"

"Nope."

"You will. I have it on good authority that the guy you beat up is indeed suing."

Ethan just sighed. He really didn't need that, but all things considered, he deserved it. Fortunately for him, California courts were so busy that his case wouldn't be heard for months.

"I don't suppose you can help in any way?" he said.

"I'm with the FBI, not the mob. I can't make lawsuits go away, Ethan. The criminal case against you has already been filed in court, which means only the DA's office or the judge can drop it at this point. And unless the guy pressing charges decides out of the blue not to testify against you, it's not likely to happen. Plus, I already helped… I bailed you out of jail. Which reminds me that you still owe me three grand."

Ethan walked to the room he'd converted into a home office and came back holding a check.

"And don't go spending it all at once," he said, handing it to Theo.

"Unlike you, I can't afford to, pal."

Theo was mistaken, but Ethan didn't feel the need to correct him. In reality, the day was soon approaching where his finances would be on par with his friend's. He had earned less in the past year than he'd once made in a single month, back when he was the best in the business and clients were just throwing money at him.

Times had changed, though. His current case load barely sufficed to cover Jennifer's salary, and he hadn't paid himself in over six months. He knew this couldn't go on much longer; his savings wouldn't last forever. He needed to get more business.

"It's been a year, bro. It's time to get your shit back together. You can't keep going like thi—"

"Like what?" interrupted Ethan.

"You know what I mean. This isn't you. Tailing guys who can't keep it in their pants isn't your gig. You're only one step away from looking for missing pets. What the fuck are you doing? You're wasting this beautiful brain of yours and it's killing me, bro."

Ethan just looked away. He had nothing to respond to that.

"We could use you on a couple of cases, like in the good old days," continued Theo. "I know we don't pay like your old clients, but we may be able to compete with the cat ladies," he added in a lighter tone.

"I'm not touching another serial killer case. You know that. Go to your profilers; they know their job. I was just an amateur who got lucky a couple of times. That's all."

"FBI profilers are great at profiling. True. But that's all they can do for us. And most of the time it's nowhere close to enough. It's one thing to know what a psycho's supposed to look like in broad general terms and another to know who he is. *The killer's a white male. Probably with a wife and kids and a history of looking normal.*' Great! Now I just need to arrest one third of the country."

"They narrow it down quite a bit more than that," said Ethan.

"Granted… But not the way you do."

"The way I *used* to do. The way I did a couple of times when I was younger and arrogant as shit. I've lost my touch, Theo. That's the truth. And I never want to be responsible for another person's death. I'm done with that crap. Maybe one day, if my brain starts to work again, I'll jump back on the corporate wagon. Help entrap an industrial spy or two, but I worked on my last murder case last year. There won't be another one."

Theo looked him in the eyes, slowly shaking his head, the way a father would show disappointment towards his six-year-old. "You never hurt anyone, Ethan. But let's entertain your delusion for an instant. Let's say you did fuck up and what happened was all your fault. One person died because of you. How many did you save before that? Unless I'm mistaken you helped put away three serial killers and two rapists. Each with a half dozen victims or more under their belt. You saved countless future victims, Ethan. You don't think that's worth one life?"

"It definitely wasn't worth *that* one life! Not to me!"

Chapter 7

Ethan rolled out of bed around 9 AM the next morning and walked straight to the kitchen to get the coffee going. He couldn't recall the last time he'd slept this late. It was Sunday so there was no harm done, but it was still surprising to him. He'd had problems sleeping lately and was usually up at the crack of dawn if not earlier.

Of course, Theo had left his apartment after 3 AM so it wasn't like Ethan had peacefully slumbered for twelve hours straight, but still.

Pouring water into the coffee maker, he reflected on the conversation of the past evening. Theo's heart was in the right place, but Ethan was getting tired of his sermons. To avoid arguing, they'd ended up watching part of a James Bond marathon during which Ethan had found his thoughts drifting to his own Miss Moneypenny: Jennifer MacKay.

Although he hadn't been with a woman in what seemed like ages, he almost never thought about sex. And when he did, the feeling it evoked was more akin to disgust than arousal. But he hadn't thought about Jennifer in a sexual way, he hadn't pictured her naked or coming onto him. He'd simply thought about the woman behind her computer, surfing the internet. With their current workload, she seldom had anything else to do these days.

He realized that keeping a fulltime secretary was an unnecessary expense he couldn't afford, but he wasn't about to lay her off. She was the only person he talked to on most days, and her no-nonsense attitude had often helped him snap out of one of his moods.

He walked to the couch carrying a mug of steaming black coffee and turned on BBC World News. Unlike American news outlets, for the most part the BBC still presented facts at face value: the only type of news Ethan was interested in. He didn't need some journalists with a political agenda to explain to him their own interpretation of things. He wanted to hear the facts and then decide for himself what they meant.

The screen showed a female reporter standing with a microphone in the middle of the woods in front of a rocky formation partially covered with vegetation.

"The cave was discovered a week ago by a couple hiking with their dog," said the woman.

In the background, two men wearing hard hats and headlamps could be seen emerging from a curtain of vines covering the mountain wall. On the screen, it gave the impression that the two speleologists had just walked through the rocky wall.

"The exploration of this newly discovered cave system has only just begun, but it's already clear that the network of tunnels and underground rooms is quite extensive. At least one of the galleries exceeds two miles in length and many others have yet to be explored," continued the journalist, but Ethan wasn't paying much attention to this discovery which had all the landmarks of a speleologist's wet dream. He was back thinking about Theo's words.

It was easy for his friend to give advice and tell him to snap out of it. He wasn't the one who'd screwed up and suffered the consequences. Against his better judgement, Ethan found his mind drifting once again to the fateful evening that had turned his life into a nightmare. Eleven months and twenty-one days had gone by, but every detail of the fifteen hours leading to the phone call was permanently etched into his memory.

The woman had been everything he could have asked for. Attractive in a classy way, curvy in all the right places… Even her conversation was interesting, which wasn't always a given with partners he met in that fashion.

They'd spent most of the night on top of each other, and she'd managed to impress him with her bedroom skills. Not something easy to do given Ethan's extensive experience in the domain. It should have been a red flag right there, but blood hadn't been flowing to the thinking part of his body that evening.

They'd barely slept, but Ethan hadn't minded. He hadn't brought her home to get some rest.

He hadn't been surprised to find her gone by the time he got out of the shower the next morning. And he knew he wouldn't be seeing her again. That was one of the rules. Even if he'd wanted to, he had no way to contact her. That, too, was a rule.

He'd walked into the office an hour later with a big grin on his face, replaying some of the night's greatest moments in his head… and then the phone had rung.

Chapter 8

Paul Richards handed the cashier a twenty-dollar bill to pay for his movie ticket and headed towards the usher in charge of collecting the stubs.

Located in Palo Alto and built in 1925, the Stanford Theatre had become a San Francisco Bay landmark. The venue specialized in the projection of classic movies from the golden age of Hollywood. In this respect, the theater played in a league of its own since it accounted for nearly a quarter of all classic film attendance in the country.

Paul was next in line to give his ticket to the usher when he heard a woman's voice tentatively calling his name.

"Paul?"

He turned around to find Naomi Berhan holding her own ticket. "Naomi, correct?" he said, smiling.

"That's right. That's twice in three days, what are the odds?"

"Pretty low," he agreed, amused.

Underneath her fitted black leather jacket, the woman sported a bright yellow dress which nicely complemented the rich chocolate color of her skin, something Paul noticed approvingly.

"So, you like the classics too?" asked Naomi.

"Best way of killing a Sunday afternoon."

"That's already two things we have in common," she said as they entered the vintage theater.

"Would you like to sit together?" he asked.

"I was about to suggest it."

Soon the lights were dimmed and the red curtain covering the screen was lifted, announcing the previews.

Two hours later, as they headed towards the exit, Paul asked, "What do you think?"

"The same thing I thought the first five times I saw *Casablanca*: amazing!"

"I love the interaction between Bergman and Bogart. It's so…"

"Vivid?" offered Naomi.

"Yes, that's the word."

They were now standing on the sidewalk in front of the theater under a fine rain.

"I hope you won't find me too bold, but I was wondering if you had dinner plans. I'd love to invite you if you don't," said Paul.

"Let me check my calendar." She made a show of going through an imaginary day planner before announcing that she was available for the evening.

"Okay, then, we can take my car or we can stay in the neighborhood. It's your call."

She thought about it for a minute before saying, "If you don't mind driving, I know a quiet Italian restaurant but it's a bit far for a walk in the rain."

"Not at all. I'm parked a block away."

Five minutes later, they were heading for the restaurant aboard Paul's Lexus, and Naomi was appraising the luxury sedan's habitat with an appreciative look. The car had definitely scored a point in Paul's favor.

The atmosphere inside the small family-owned restaurant felt very intimate. Patrons spoke in soft voices that reached the neighboring tables as mere whispers, while Chopin played softly in the background.

"What do you do for a living?" asked Naomi halfway through her chicken Alfredo.

"I work as a developer in an IT startup."

"Interesting," she replied in a tone meant to be sarcastic. "And what does that mean?"

"It means I'm working on an app that will revolutionize your life by making it easier to book flights from your phone and at the best possible price," he said with exaggerated enthusiasm.

Naomi nodded, smiling. She was clearly not impressed.

"What about you? What do you do?" he asked, cutting into his lasagna.

"I work in an art gallery."

"Meaning?" he teased.

"Meaning I do what I love and get paid for it. Do you do what you love, Paul?"

He contemplated the question a moment, staring at his glass of chianti. "I can honestly say that I do. I truly can't think of something that would make me happier."

Naomi seemed surprised by his answer but didn't comment further.

They spent the remainder of the meal arguing about the best classic movies of all time and mostly disagreeing. By the time the check reached the table, the playful banter had ceased, and they were back discussing serious matters.

"Are you seeing anyone at the moment?" asked Paul, reaching for the check.

"Not currently. Are you?"

"No. I *have* been thinking about asking someone out for a couple hours now, but I haven't had the nerve yet."

"I understand... Nobody likes rejection," teased Naomi.

"I've already kicked myself all day yesterday for not asking your number Friday night. I don't think I'd survive making the same mistake twice."

"You probably would, but why take the chance?"

They exchanged numbers and Paul signed the check after adding a generous tip. He was in a great mood.

He then drove Naomi back to the theater and parked behind her vehicle.

She looked very pretty this evening and he wanted her bad, but he didn't want to rush things. He'd learned to appreciate taking things slowly. The longer you delayed gratification the better it felt when it finally came.

He kissed her softly on the lips before saying goodbye. Naomi's eyes searched his own. She seemed to hesitate a moment before finally wishing him goodnight as she exited the car.

He knew what she'd been thinking about and was glad she hadn't invited him in. Paul never had sex on a first date. He was really looking forward to date number three though.

Chapter 9

"Any progress with Mr. Balden?" asked Jennifer as she placed a mug of fresh coffee on Ethan's desk.

"No luck. I'm starting to think he's onto me. That, or he's not cheating on his wife."

"A faithful husband… If that's the case, he belongs behind glass in a museum," said Jennifer, sitting on the edge of his desk.

"You truly think all husbands cheat on their wives?"

"Yep. Pretty much! Why do you think I prefer screwing women?"

The remark took Ethan by surprise. He hadn't seen that one coming. Apparently his gaydar wasn't tuned up to lesbians' frequencies. At least things were clear now. If his libido ever staged a return, Jennifer MacKay wouldn't be playing the female lead in the sequel.

There was a knock on the door. It was unlocked, but Ethan gestured for Jennifer to go answer. They really couldn't afford to lose a potential client at this point.

"I'm looking for Mr. Archer?" said a woman who looked to be in her late thirties.

"That would be me. Please come in," said Ethan, still sitting behind his desk.

The woman stepped into the office, her eyes carefully exploring the room as she walked towards his desk and extended her hand to Ethan. "My name is Gwendoline Thomas." Her blue eyes were searching Ethan's face intently. Searching for what, he didn't know.

"Please have a seat," he answered, shaking her hand and pointing at an armchair across from his desk. She looked vaguely familiar, as if he'd met her recently, but he had no idea where it could have been. "Have we met before?"

"I doubt it. I would remember," she answered, staring at the bruises on his face.

She sat down tentatively and replaced a wisp of blonde hair behind her ear before asking, "You are Ethan Archer, the criminal consultant, correct?"

He saw doubt in her piercing blue eyes: something he had grown used to these past few months. People still had in mind the picture of the man they'd seen on TV. A self-assured 6-foot-tall athlete weighing in at 200 pounds. But today the athlete was nearly thirty pounds lighter, with sunken cheeks, and looked as self-assured as a mouse facing a cat.

"I'm a private investigator who's done some criminal consultancy work in the past." There was no need to add that over the past six months his case load had focused exclusively on chasing after cheating spouses and run-away kids. His prospective client clearly didn't want to be bored with this kind of detail.

She took a deep breath before saying, "I have a business proposal to discuss with you. Is there another room where we could talk in private?"

"Would you mind taking an early lunch break, Miss MacKay?" he said, turning his attention to Jennifer.

Behind the woman's back, Jennifer was shaking her head, eyes raised to the ceiling. "It's only 9 AM, Mr. Archer," she retorted with a grin.

"Then go to the gym. Didn't you tell me you wanted to lose weight?" That wiped the grin off her face. She gave him a look that promised reprisals before grabbing her coat and heading for the door.

"Please come back after lunch," he added as Jennifer slammed the door shut.

"It would seem your assistant has a bit of an attitude problem. She's lucky to have a boss who puts up with it." She'd pronounced the last sentence in a disapproving tone he found a bit irritating. Her designer shoes, her Louis Vuitton purse and, above all, her superior attitude were clear indications that Gwendoline Thomas wasn't hurting for money. And like many people in her position, wealth had come with a sense of entitlement and superiority towards the *less fortunate*.

"Luck has nothing to do with it, Mrs. Thomas. But I'm sure you didn't come here today to talk about my assistant."

She ignored the remark. "Before I say anything, Mr. Archer, I would like your assurance that nothing I share with you today will leave this room. Furthermore, if my offer were of interest to you, you'd be required to sign a confidentiality agreement before I could disclose specific aspects of the case at hand."

This wasn't the first time Ethan had been required to sign a non-disclosure agreement. He'd sold his services to big corporations before. In these instances, he'd typically been hired to help identify moles sent by the competition to steal proprietary information, but not exclusively. He'd also sat in patent litigation proceedings to help identify the weaknesses in the case of the opposite party.

"These terms are agreeable," he replied.

"Very well. Let me start by introducing myself. I am the head of the legal department for Woodrough Oil and Gas. A privately-owned company operating in Wyoming. As such, the valuation of our business isn't a matter of public records but let's just say that we are worth enough to attract some enemies."

Ethan thought that even bankrupt oil companies had more than their fair share of enemies, but he kept the remark to himself.

"In addition, the Woodrough family also owns a large ranch with over four thousand head of cattle," she continued. "The ranch and the oil and gas company are separate legal entities but belong to the same group: Woodrough Enterprise. This means that there is a single CEO for the two businesses. Finally, the two businesses are also somewhat tied together due to the fact employees occasionally move back and forth between companies according to business demands."

"Are you one of these persons?" asked Ethan.

"I am indeed, but for reasons I haven't mentioned yet. I'm not only the head lawyer for the oil business, I am also the daughter of Archibald Woodrough, the group's CEO and one of the two main stockholders."

"I see."

She gave him a look he interpreted as *I doubt it'* but continued. "My father received a disturbing letter a few days ago. A threatening letter."

"Then I suggest you report it to the police as soon as possible," said Ethan, who had no desire to involve himself in any sort of a case where lives might be at stake.

"The threats aren't of a personal nature, Mr. Archer."

"You mean to say that your father is being blackmailed?"

"I suppose that would be one way of putting it."

"Do you know another one?" he asked, reclining in his seat.

"I suppose not," she conceded. "I just don't like the term. It carries such a negative connotation."

"That's spoken like a true lawyer. In my experience, those who have nothing *negative* to hide seldom get blackmailed."

She gave him an irritated look that made her more attractive in his eyes. She was pretty, now that he paid closer attention. Not Jennifer MacKay pretty, but attractive nonetheless. Like Jennifer, she had blue eyes, fine features and a delicate neck, but the resemblance stopped there. The blonde had a significantly darker complexion than the Scottish redhead.

"Let's just say that if our *blackmailer* were to execute his threat, our company would have nothing to fear from a legal standpoint," she said.

"So what's the problem?"

"Our reputation would be impacted, and that's something we'd like to avoid."

"I suppose that you're not ready to tell me what's in this letter just yet?"

"That is correct. Not without a signed contract and a confidentiality agreement in place."

"Have you considered paying your blackmailer off?"

He saw a fugitive smile flicker on the woman's lips before she answered. "This is indeed something we would consider. Unfortunately, the letter doesn't mention a word about money. Which is also why the term blackmail may not be the most appropriate one to use in this instance." She looked very pleased with herself. She probably felt like she'd scored a point. The simple fact she would feel the need to score against him spoke volumes about the woman.

"What is he asking for then?"

"Nothing at all. The letter simply states that certain embarrassing information will be revealed to the press on January 15. Which means we have about a month to come clean."

"Or at least spin your own version of the truth," Ethan replied matter-of-factly.

"We did consider that option," she conceded. "But we would rather identify our enemy and come to an understanding with him before the end of the ultimatum. Which is why I have come to you today."

"Why do you think you're dealing with a man?"

"I beg your pardon?" She looked confused.

"You just said 'come to an understanding with him.' Why *him* and not *her*?"

"I guess I misspoke. It could be a her I suppose, but it's very unlikely. The overwhelming majority of our employees are men. Women working in the oil fields are few and cowgirls are fewer."

Ethan took a moment to think before asking a question that had been in the back of his mind ever since Gwendoline Thomas had sat down in the chair across his desk. "Why did you decide that I was the man for the job?"

"You are famous, Mr. Archer. You're the man who figures things out when others are stumped. The one the police call upon when they have no clue who to arrest."

"That's a significant overstatement, Mrs. Thomas. And I haven't been in that line of work for quite some time. My practice has moved in a different direction over the past few months."

"Are you telling me you're not interested in the job?"

"I'm simply not sure I'm the man you need. Let's say I find your blackmailer. What happens next? I don't want to be involved in any kind of intimidation or anything illegal in any way." This wasn't a lie, but it wasn't the main reason Ethan was reluctant about the assignment either.

The truth was that he had significant doubts about his ability to deliver results. He could no longer do what he used to. He'd lost his gift. He'd tried working on a couple of real cases in the weeks following the worst day of his life, but they'd gone nowhere. He wasn't hiding in hotel parking lots with his camera, hoping to catch cheating spouses red-handed, because he liked it. He did it because he no longer knew how to do anything else and he still had bills to pay.

There had been no method to his past success, at least none he could articulate. He'd just been able to see what others didn't. His extremely logical mind had been able to identify patterns invisible to others. He understood human psychology to some degree—he did have a Ph.D. in behavioral psychology from Stanford, after all—but that only explained part of his success. He'd been a mathematics major as an undergrad and had obtained a Masters in theoretical mathematics before deciding he didn't want to spend the rest of his life staring at a blackboard covered with abstract equations. Apparently, studying mathematics at a high level had rewired his brain to think a certain way. At least that's how he explained it to himself. That's how he was able to pinpoint the slightest inconsistency in a case or in someone's narrative; that's how he'd been able to spot the meaningful lies among the mundane ones. Because if there were one certainty in this life, it was that everyone lied all the time.

"You wouldn't be involved in anything illegal, Mr. Archer. I can assure you of this. Once identified, our enemy would be approached with a generous offer, and if this failed to tame him—"

"Or her," interrupted Ethan.

"Or her... we'd simply leak our own version of the facts to the media before they had a chance to react. I don't need an answer today, Mr. Archer. You can take a day or two to think about it. You should know, however, that your skills and discretion are very valuable to us. We are ready to pay you a non-refundable retainer of $100,000. If you were to spend the whole retainer, a second one in the same amount would be at your disposal. This second one would be refundable, however."

These were serious numbers. In his current financial situation, Ethan could sure use the money. But he was still worried about the case. What if he couldn't identify the blackmailer? What if he sank into one of his moods while on the job? What if he collapsed?

There was another cause to his uneasiness towards the case. Everyone lied all the time... and Gwendoline Thomas was no exception. He was absolutely convinced the woman was hiding something. But he wasn't sure he wanted to find out what it was.

Chapter 10

"How much did you say?" asked Jennifer.

He'd never seen her looking bewildered before, but there it was. She'd come back from lunch around 1 PM and had placed a bag containing two apple-filled doughnuts in front of him. He interpreted this as a peace offering but made a mental note to remain on his guard. He suspected his joke about her weight wouldn't go unpunished.

"One hundred grand. Non-refundable."

"And you didn't say yes right away?"

"I said I'd think about it."

"I'd suggest you think fast, because the last time we got paid was for the Wilson case and it's been five weeks. I'm not in charge of accounting here, but I suspect we must be running low on funds."

"How about you get back to whatever it is I'm paying you for and leave money matters to me?"

She was right, of course. Catching Mr. Wilson in the act had brought in four grand, but the money was long gone. And technically it had been Jennifer's earning. Wilson had recognized Ethan and walked straight up to him on the street to inquire if he'd been hired by his wife. Ethan had played dumb and asked Jennifer to take over with the surveillance. This had been the first and only time she'd helped him out in the field, but she'd done a great job. Within a week, she'd delivered album-quality pictures of the quadragenarian fondling his twenty-four-year-old mistress.

"I'm just leery about getting involved with the Woodroughs. There's something fishy about that business," he said, but received no response.

He looked up from his computer where he was reviewing Mr. Balden's planned itinerary for the afternoon to find Jennifer absorbed by her own screen.

He slowly got up and acted as if he were heading for the coffee maker before suddenly changing direction to glance at her monitor. "Do you really think I'm paying you to read the news?" he lectured her.

"That's definitely what you've been paying me for the past five weeks… But I'd be delighted to help you with Mr. Balden or work on finding us more business. I'm bored out of my mind here, boss."

"I've heard about that cave," he said, perusing the article displayed on her screen. "They were talking about it on TV over the weekend. Something about it being huge."

"I would say so. Some of the experts are already speculating that it might be bigger than Mammoth Cave. They're talking out of their asses, of course… It's way too early to know how long those galleries truly are."

"What's Mammoth Cave?"

"What's Mammoth Cave, he asks…" She was looking at him with something akin to pity, slowly shaking her head. "Only the longest cave system in the US. Almost 300 miles of tunnels buried underneath Kentucky."

Ethan was impressed with the reply. The girl knew her subject. "I didn't know you were so knowledgeable when it came to caves, Jennifer. Though it would explain your skin tone."

"Really? You're going there? After suggesting I needed to lose weight this morning, now you're commenting on how pale I am? Have you ever heard of harassment in the workplace, boss?"

She'd said it in jest, but she probably had a point. He knew he could sometimes be perceived as an asshole, and for good reason.

"You know I didn't mean that, right? There's nothing wrong with the way you look. You're a beautiful woman."

"Thank you, Ethan. But this too could be perceived as harassment, by some—"

"There's just no way to win with women, is there?"

"Just don't comment on their looks one way or another in a work setting and you'll be fine, boss."

He hated when she called him boss. Which was probably why she did it.

"I'm actually an amateur spelunker. I've been in quite a few caves in the US and in Europe," said Jennifer.

"I didn't know that."

"There's a lot you don't know about me," she replied enigmatically.

This was true. They'd worked together for almost a year and he hardly knew anything other than that she'd moved from Scotland to California when she was eighteen and was a half-decent secretary. Today, in the span of a few hours, he'd learned that she was a lesbian and a spelunker. What would she tell him next?

He only had himself to blame; it wasn't as if Jennifer had been hiding things from him, he'd just never enquired about her personal life. His lips slowly parted into a smile as he reflected that, on second thought, rating her secretarial skills as half-decent was maybe a bit generous.

"What are you grinning about?" she asked.

"You don't wanna know," he said, returning his attention to the article. "So, that cave's supposed to be a big deal?"

"It is a big deal! They believe it was sealed for centuries, possibly millennia, and was only recently unsealed by an earthquake."

"When was that? I haven't heard anything about a recent earthquake."

"I meant recent on a geological scale. The earthquake was in 1959. It was a pretty big deal back then apparently, 7.5 on the Richter scale. The epicenter of the earthquake was just north-west of Yellowstone National Park and provoked a massive landslide that rerouted a river and resulted in the formation of a lake. The lake was named Quake Lake and is still around today. It's not a small lake either."

"You've been there?" asked Ethan, walking to the coffee maker, mug in hand.

"Yes, I saw it once. I remember the roofs of houses sticking out from the water. I don't expect many of the people who lived in those houses made it out alive."

Ethan checked his watch. "Shit! I'm supposed to be a few cars behind Mr. Balden's Jaguar right now. Try to find something productive to entertain yourself with for the rest of the day."

"I'll get right to it," she replied sarcastically.

As he ran down the flight of stairs leading to the street, he thought back on their conversation. It would probably be worth his while to spend some time trying to get to know Jennifer a bit better. Could she really help him find more business? The woman was apparently full of surprises. He was also starting to suspect that she was sharper than he'd given her credit for. He pondered the question for a minute as he slid behind the wheel of his car. How smart was Jennifer MacKay?

Chapter 11

From a dark recess void of any light, the ghost observed the three invaders desecrating his cave with their headlamps and sophisticated tools. Scientific tools...

Who'd given them the right to enter his domain, violate his home? The beams of their lamps danced on the rocky walls of the cavern, giving them unnaturally bright hues and casting shadows that did not belong inside the cave. Occasionally, one of the beams would dislodge a few bats from their sleeping quarters and send them flying deeper inside the entrails of the granitic formation. These men had no respect for the creatures that called this place home. They had no respect for him.

He wanted them gone. He wanted to return to the peace and quiet he'd enjoyed for so many years, alone in his stone city. But there was no turning back. Life as he knew it had ended only a few days earlier. All because of a dog...

Safely tucked away behind a thick curtain of vines that had grown along the mountain wall, the narrow entrance of the cavern had remained hidden from prying eyes ever since its creation by a massive earthquake nearly sixty years earlier. Hundreds of hikers and hunters had walked past it over the years, but none had ever suspected the vines covered anything other than the mountain's rocky wall.

The dog hadn't been fooled, however. Probably attracted by the scent of his cousins, the Doberman had followed his nose and walked right through the wall of vegetation and into the ghost's domain.

He'd been there when the pet had emerged into his sanctuary, but the animal hadn't seen him. The ghost could make himself nearly invisible when he had to. When it came to stealth, the training he'd received was second to none: something which came in handy when the dog's owners walked through the foliage covering the entrance in search of their unruly pet a moment later.

He watched them for long minutes as they searched the darkness using the lights of their cell phones, marveling at their discovery. They never suspected that someone else was in the room, watching them from up close. He'd known this would be the case. If he'd deceived the dog's nose, these two had absolutely no chance of suspecting his presence.

For a fugitive moment he considered silencing the couple, but this wasn't the way he did things. This kind of business could get messy, especially with a dog that size involved, and this wasn't a time for messy. He had an important task awaiting him and couldn't afford for cops to come snooping around on his turf. Not now.

The commotion in the cave brought his mind back to the present. The three scientists seemed to be arguing about something. They were too far away for him to hear what they were saying, but even if he'd been closer there was no guarantee he'd have understood them.

A long howling sound came from outside the cave, but the men paid it no heed. It was answered by a series of howls in quick succession an instant later, and this time the scientists took notice. They well should; the wolves didn't appreciate the strangers' intrusion either. This was the pack's cave as much as his, and they didn't look kindly upon uninvited guests.

The howling stopped and the ghost watched the men get back to their snooping, searching in the direction they shouldn't be searching.

He felt a growing sense of unease as they edged closer to the entrance of the hidden gallery. It was starting to look like cops would come sticking their nose into his business after all... What was he going to do if the three men entered the gallery? What would he do if the intruders stumbled upon *their* bones?

Chapter 12

Holding the phone's receiver to her ear, Jennifer sighed silently. "I understand, Mrs. Balden, I will have Mr. Archer call you back as soon as possible. Are you certain you don't want to reconsider? ... Very well, I'll let him know. ... Yes, Mrs. Balden, I'll tell him about the money."

She hung up the receiver and answered Ethan's inquisitive look with, "Mrs. Balden just fired us. And she wants her money back."

"Of course she does. Please tally how much time I spent on the case. I'll cut her a check for what's left of her retainer."

"You've spent just shy of sixty hours working this. Which, at your current rate of $90 an hour, means you owe her $4,600 back."

Ethan looked at his secretary suspiciously. "You had these numbers ready awfully fast."

"It's not like we didn't see it coming, or like I have much of anything else to do, boss."

He'd basically banked five grand on this case, which would barely cover the office's rent and Jennifer's salary. He'd have to live off his savings again this month and with Christmas fast approaching, he wasn't expecting business to pick up anytime soon. There was apparently something about the holiday season that gave people hope. Hope that their cheating spouses would start behaving themselves, or maybe hope that they'd slip off the roof while installing Santa's sleigh and break their necks. Whichever one it was, it was bad for business.

A knock on the door interrupted his train of thought. Before he could react, a man dressed in a Fedex outfit entered the office, a large envelope visible in his hand.

"Ethan Archer?" he asked.

Ethan nodded.

The man handed him the envelope before adding, "You've been served." At the same time Ethan looked up, he was caught by a flash coming from the guy's cellphone. An instant later, the man had disappeared, closing the door behind him.

Jennifer looked at him questioningly, but he offered no explanation. He started reading the document to confirm his suspicion. The court date was set for April 5. Theo's info had been correct. The guy he'd beat up in the bar's parking lot was indeed suing him. Now he had a civil lawsuit to worry about in addition to the criminal charges. No big deal; he simply needed to find a lawyer who'd accept to be paid in smiles and well wishes. Except that Ethan really didn't feel like smiling.

"What is it?" asked Jennifer.

"Nothing you need to worry about."

"If it's impacting how long I'll remain employed, I'd say it's something I need to worry about. How about you give me some credit for once?

Maybe I can help. Maybe I'm more than just a 'beautiful woman' as you so eloquently put it a few days ago."

What did he have to lose? He took a deep breath and started telling Jennifer about the parking lot incident.

"Do you often go around beating up random strangers outside bars?" she asked, in a lecturing voice.

"I only beat up the bastards who deserve it. And definitely not often enough, since you wanna know." He could feel his pulse rising. He needed to cool off. Now wasn't the time for one of his episodes.

"It would appear that this one didn't deserve it," she replied pointedly.

"Honest mistake. He really looked like he did." His reply had been stated a bit louder than intended.

"You're telling me he put something into her drink, but they're both denying it. And the cops claim she wasn't stoned and neither was the guy."

"Yes. Those are the facts."

"And you're positive you saw him put something in the glass."

"I am positive, yes. He had something in his hand and the next thing I know, there's a white powder flowing into the glass."

"In-te-res-ting," she said, stretching out the syllables.

"Do you still think you can help?" he asked skeptically.

"Maybe…"

He didn't believe a word of it but wasn't in a mood to debate.

"But just in case I can't help you out of your lawsuit, maybe you should accept Gwendoline Thomas' offer. It's been four days and you haven't given her a reply yet."

"I'm still thinking about it," he said, heading for the door. "In the meantime, I'm going home. I've had enough for today. If you're done catching up on the news, you should go home too."

He received no answer.

☉

Jennifer watched Ethan exit the office. Wheels were turning inside her head. There were several reasons why one would pour a powder into a glass. A powder dissolved faster and was therefore harder to detect. Or one could have an aversion for pills and prefer dissolving their medicine in a liquid. Jennifer had known at least one person who couldn't swallow the smallest of pills. It was perfectly plausible that the man or the woman suffered from the same issue.

There were also several possibilities as to why they would deny the fact in front of the cops. The obvious one was because they didn't want to get in trouble. If they took street drugs, they were unlikely to confess it to a police officer.

There was a problem with that theory, however. Every officer in the country was trained to spot the signs displayed by people under the influence of intoxicants. And since the cops didn't believe that the couple had been taking drugs, it was fair to assume they hadn't. This left only one obvious reason to lie to the cops, or to anyone else for that matter…

Jennifer was starting to feel she was on the right track. She retrieved the plaintiff's name from the summons papers lying on Ethan's desk and ran a Google search on Shereen and Farzin Kazemi. Five minutes later, she'd found the couple's current address.

She looked it up on Google Maps and searched for neighboring pharmacies. She wrote down phone numbers for the five pharmacies closest to the Kazemis and started dialing, each time introducing herself as Shereen Kazemi.

She found what she was looking for on her third attempt.

It was nearly 8 PM that evening when she rang the door of the Kazemis. A gorgeous Persian woman came to answer and Jennifer felt a twinge of excitement at the pit of her stomach. The woman could give Tabatha a run for her money.

"Shereen Kazemi?" she asked.

"Yes."

"Hi, my name is Jennifer MacKay. I'm sorry to drop by unannounced at this hour, but I couldn't find your phone number in our files and the matter is of an urgent nature. It's regarding your lawsuit against Mr. Ethan Archer." This was probably misleading, but technically not a lie.

"What about it?" asked the woman, looking confused.

"Just a couple of points to clarify before we can proceed. Nothing serious. May I come in?"

Shereen Kazemi led Jennifer to a living room whose walls were lined with very low couches ornamented with a score of colorful pillows.

Mr. Kazemi was sitting in a corner, watching TV. His face was badly bruised, his nose clearly broken. For a second, Jennifer felt ashamed of what she was about to do.

The man presently got up and enquired about their visitor.

"Do you mind if we sit down?" Jennifer asked her hosts. "We'd be more comfortable to go over the details."

They all sat down and she started, "My name is Jennifer MacKay and I'm here to let you know that Mr. Archer feels terrible about this misunderstanding and that in addition to covering all medical expenses, he'd like to offer you $15,000 for the prejudice you've received."

"You never told me you represented the other party," interjected the wife.

"That's true, but it changes nothing to our offer. I have here a cashier's check for $15,000 that I intend to leave with you today. Simply send us a bill for the medical expenses and we'll reimburse you integrally."

"I just need to drop the lawsuit, I suppose?" said the man. He was clearly not happy about her intrusion.

"Yes. That would be expected. And you should also let the DA know that you are no longer willing to testify against Mr. Archer."

"No!" he shouted. "There's no way I'm dropping this lawsuit. That psycho needs to pay for what he's done. People like him need to be behind bars where they can't hurt innocents."

"Believe me when I say that I understand your point of view. But Mr. Archer thought he was doing the right thing. From his perspective, you were about to rape an innocent woman."

The explanation didn't appease Farzin Kazemi, however. He was getting ready to kick Jennifer out of their home when she played her trump card.

"I'm really sorry you're taking it this way, Mr. Kazemi. Our offer would have saved both parties the humiliation of a trial. But since your mind cannot be changed, we'll see you in court."

"What humiliation are you talking about?" he asked as she stood to take her leave. "We have nothing to be ashamed of."

"Of course not. It's just that when Mr. Archer's lawyer asks you under oath why you feel the need to add powdered Viagra to your scotch on the evenings you roleplay in bars with your wife, your answer really won't matter. You know how journalists are…"

Chapter 13

Naomi Berhan opened the door of her apartment to greet Paul Richards. "Please come in. I just need a minute to finish getting ready," she said, disappearing at the end of a hallway.

Paul took a few steps into the living room, surveying the pictures on the wall, checking the books on the coffee table. The place was tastefully decorated, but this was no surprise. Naomi wouldn't have it any other way.

The woman came back a couple minutes later. Much faster than Paul had expected. "I'm ready."

"Let's go then."

They got into his car and Paul was pulling out of his parking spot when he said, "I have two dinner options to suggest."

"Okay," she replied with a smile.

"The first option consists in your choice of restaurant. Any that takes your fancy."

"I have expensive tastes, so this is a dangerous offer," she teased. "What's the second option?"

"The second option is for me to cook you dinner at my beach house."

"You have a beach house? How far is it?" she asked, intrigued.

"About an hour north, but the drive is pretty once we leave the city."

Naomi contemplated the two options a few seconds before answering, "Well, it's not every day someone offers to cook me dinner at their beach house. And it's Friday evening, so I don't have to get up early tomorrow…"

Paul wasn't much of a cook, but he could place a couple of steaks on the grill and make sure they didn't turn black. And since the sautéed potatoes, the kale salad and the macarons he served for dessert were store-bought, in the end the meal was edible. Naomi was even polite enough to compliment him on his culinary performance.

The woman hadn't disappointed him in any way so far. She was smart, cultured and had a genuine sweetness that made her the perfect woman for him.

The dinner over, they retired to the deck with a bottle of wine to watch the moon over the ocean. The patio bench wasn't particularly comfortable, but squeezed against him under a blanket, Naomi didn't seem to notice.

"This is the Taurus," she said, pointing at a series of stars in the night sky.

"I'm impressed. It's the first time I've met someone who can point out something other than the Big Dipper."

"I am full of surprises, Paul. But in this instance, I'm even more full of shit." She punctuated her statement by kissing him on the cheek.

"You made it up?" he said, faking outrage.

She winked and he kissed her lips, softly at first. The following kiss contained more passion and they soon found themselves in the bedroom undressing each other as fast as they could.

"That was amazing!" she said thirty minutes later, lying naked next to him under the sheet. "The first time with a new partner typically isn't great, but this was… whoa!"

"I'm glad to hear we agree on this," he said, gently kissing her small breasts.

Paul stood beside the bed holding a tray with hot coffee and freshly baked croissants when Naomi woke up the next morning. The look in her eyes made him tingle with anticipation, but breakfast came first.

"Did you bake those?" she asked doubtfully, as she bit into the flaky pastry.

"I took them out of the freezer and placed them in the oven. Does that count?"

"Is there another way to bake?"

The breakfast tray was soon set aside as they found themselves heading for a second round of under-the-sheet wrestling which lasted even longer than the first and exceeded both parties' expectations.

"I need to jump into the shower and drop you off at your place," said Paul, heading for the master bath. "I wish I could spend the day with you, but I need to catch a plane early afternoon."

"Where are you going?" Naomi was smiling but her eyes betrayed her disappointment.

"I have a conference to attend in Vegas."

"Over the weekend?"

"That's the only sort I can attend. My boss isn't really willing to let me go to these things on company time."

"That sucks!"

"I'm used to it. It's no big deal," he replied, stepping under the shower.

"I've actually never been to Vegas…"

"We'll need to change that," he replied, knowing that the answer would be disappointing at first but would make her smile later on. He was already talking future plans on the second date.

"Is it okay if I take a quick shower in your guest bathroom?" she asked.

"Sure, go ahead."

He was fully dressed and his suitcase was packed by the time she walked back into the room wrapped inside a towel.

He looked at her in surprise. Her long straight hair was now a curtain of loose shiny curls.

"I can see from your look that I'll need to bring my hair straighteners next time," she said.

"No. I like the curls. I just wasn't expecting them."

"Okay… We'll just say I believe you," she teased. "You have a great house, by the way. I took the liberty to have a quick tour."

He gave her a semi-amused look. Women were so predictable.

He dropped Naomi off at her apartment an hour and a half later and watched her climbing the flight of stairs leading to the front door. The woman really had a great ass.

As he drove away, Paul Richards went through a mental list of everything he needed to accomplish over the next two days. There was no time to waste.

Eyes on the road, he opened the central console located between the two front seats. He removed the box of tissues and other random items meant to hide the bottom of the compartment before his fingers finally found the object he'd been searching for. He wrapped his hand around the hilt of his favorite knife and pulled it out of its hiding spot. He looked at the sexy curves of the dark blade and smiled. This particular weapon was very special to him. They had a lot of history together.

Chapter 14

Ethan was walking slowly, paying close attention to the women lined up on the sidewalk. Some were pretty, others not so much. But they were all united in their misery, though some got paid more for it than others.

He checked his watch. A few minutes past midnight. He'd been roaming the red-light district for over an hour but hadn't found who he was looking for. He never did.

Over the past year, he'd also searched for her in every escort service in and around town, but to no avail. Wherever she was, she clearly didn't want to be found. This was often the case with persons of interest in a murder investigation.

Had his brain been working, he'd have found the hooker a long time ago. But his mind no longer flowed along the logical highways it once so naturally navigated. Nowadays, Ethan had to resort to brute force and spend hours pacing sidewalks under the sickly hue of streetlights.

He crossed the street and ended up on another sidewalk. This one with fewer women—in another block or so, there would be none. As he discreetly surveyed the prostitutes' faces while acting uninterested by their offers, he heard a loud voice coming from an alley. The voice belonged to a man. The words were distorted by the distance, but what Ethan heard next was crystal clear: the characteristic slapping sound of a hand striking a cheek.

He walked towards the commotion; he could already feel his body temperature rising as adrenalin flowed through his veins.

"Ya see what happens to whores that ain't got no protection, sugar? Whoring's dangerous business. Ya need a pimp, love," Ethan heard the man's voice saying as he got closer.

He found the bastard between two dumpsters. He was holding a woman in her mid-twenties by the throat, off the ground and against the wall. Neither her tiptoes nor her 4-inch heels touched the concrete. Ethan wrapped his fist around his brass knuckles as he said, "Pimping's dangerous business too, assface."

The man turned around just in time to receive the brass knuckles on the bridge of his nose. He howled in pain, but only for a second as a blow to the stomach drove the air out of his lungs. The pimp folded in half, therefore placing his head in the trajectory of Ethan's incoming knee. He received it square in the mouth before collapsing to the ground.

The girl was standing still, stuck to the wall, as if trying to blend in with the dirty bricks to become invisible.

The pimp lying on the ground was already a bloody mess, but Ethan still kicked him in the ribs a few more times before finally taking a deep breath meant to calm himself down.

The hooker was starting to move, but he gestured for her to stay put as he rummaged through the pimp's pockets. He found a couple rolls of cash, a gun, a butterfly knife and the thug's wallet. He pulled the driver's license out of the wallet and pocketed it along with the rest of his loot. He then grabbed the man by the hair and made him look at the woman he'd been beating up a minute earlier. The guy's face was covered in blood, his front teeth had been knocked in by Ethan's knee.

"I want you to look at her face, asshole. You see it?" said Ethan. "Now I want you to forget it for good. I have your name, I have your address and I have your gun. If anything were to happen to this woman, anything at all, I'd come for you when you least expect it. And believe you me, I'd be really looking forward to it."

He slammed the pimp's head against the ground one more time to make his point and walked away holding the hooker by the arm.

"What's your name?" he asked as they exited the alley.

"April." She sounded frightened.

"You need to get off the street right now, April. Do you have a place to go?"

"I have an apartment with a roommate outside the city," she replied after a moment of hesitation.

"Does he know where you live?"

"I don't think so."

"Don't go back to that motel. You need to go home right now and stay off the street for a while."

She nodded.

"Do you have a ride?"

"I take the bus, but at this time of the nigh—"

"I'll give you a ride. My car's parked a few blocks away."

April's apartment wasn't at all what Ethan had expected. It looked perfectly normal, ordinary. The furnishing was sparse and second- or even third-hand, but it was clean and welcoming. Which in hindsight wasn't all that surprising. There was no reason for hookers to live in crummy, rat-infested buildings with dildos hanging on the walls for decoration.

"Where's your roommate?"

"She's visiting her folks for the weekend," she replied, placing a cup of steaming coffee in front of him on a table littered with magazines. She had relaxed a bit during the drive and was now more talkative. With her thin lips, petite figure and short dark hair, nobody would have called her a stunning beauty, but she was cute in a mousy sort of way.

"Thank you!" she said, looking him in the eyes. "I don't know if what you did will end up saving me or costing me my life yet, but it could have been bad if you hadn't intervened. That asshole has a reputation for cutting women that refuse to work for him."

Ethan reflected on this for a moment. He'd never considered that his action could end up costing the woman more in the long run. "I want you to put my phone number in your cell. If you ever have another problem with him, you call me. But if I were you, I'd try to find a different job."

She gave him the look a daughter would to her lecturing father. He couldn't have more than ten years on her, but that glance made him feel much older than that.

He pulled the two rolls of cash out of his pockets and started counting. There was almost five grand.

He handed her the cash. "That should keep you off the street for a while."

"Are you sure you don't want to keep the money? You know, payment for your troubles," she said tentatively.

"You need it more than I do. And beating up this scumbag gave me great pleasure. That's just what I needed to keep on going another week."

"I feel like I need to do something to thank you," she said, getting closer to him on the couch.

His eyes were drawn to the revealing cleavage plunging mere inches away.

"You're not wearing a wedding band. Do you have anyone?" she asked.

He remained silent a long moment. By the time he finally answered no, she was unbuckling his belt.

The woman wasn't gorgeous but she had plenty of sex appeal. In another life, he would have been glad to take advantage of the offer, but his last experience with a prostitute had ended up very poorly.

He hadn't known the woman was a professional at the time. He'd only found out when Angus Avery had spilled the beans at the station after his arrest.

"At least you got a good time with the whore for free. And don't lie about it. I know the bitch's good. I gave her a test drive before introducing the two of you," Avery had yelled, as two FBI agents were hauling him towards an interrogation room. Driven to the verge of madness by hatred and sorrow, Ethan would have ripped the man's throat open if Theo hadn't been there to restrain him.

They'd never figured out where Avery had found the hooker. The bastard had been shanked to death in jail within twenty-four hours of his arrest, taking his secret to the grave. They'd never identified his murderer either.

Avery's killing had brought no sense of relief to Ethan; the son of a bitch had gotten off too easily. A year later, Ethan still had recurring dreams of finding Avery alive and taking him to an isolated cabin in the woods. Somewhere he'd be able to teach the killer the meaning of pain.

Avery had outsmarted him. He'd played on Ethan's main weaknesses to rob him of everything he had in life.

Ethan returned to the present moment and looked down at April kneeling in front of him. She'd been trying to arouse him for nearly five minutes, but her expert hands were powerless this evening.

He was attracted to the woman, but something inside him was broken. His desire for her didn't extend to the part of his anatomy that was the most indispensable in this type of situation.

It was pretty clear Ethan wouldn't break his dry streak anytime soon. Three hundred sixty-three days and counting.

Chapter 15

US senator Allister Woodrough sat alone in a Vegas bar. It was unlikely anyone would have recognized him, though. He'd traded his suit for a flannel shirt and a pair of jeans with a belt buckle the size of a hubcap. Complete with a cowboy hat, a fake mustache and alligator-skin boots, the outfit was very convincing.

He'd sent his security detail away for the evening. He had no need for them in a place where nobody knew him, but this wasn't why he'd given them the night off. The truth was that he couldn't afford having witnesses this evening, not if things went his way. If his little secret was leaked to the press, his political career would be over. It wasn't something his electorate would ever forgive.

He'd been invited to Vegas to meet with a number of large campaign contributors and had spent the whole afternoon shaking hands and giving speeches highlighting his commitment to energy independence, overturning the landmark Roe vs Wade ruling and defending the sanctity of marriage, which could only be conceived as a union between a man and a woman. The same kind of stuff he spilled at rallies or every time a camera was in sight. He didn't believe half of it, but that got him reelected term after term nonetheless.

As he ordered his first drink, a young man came to sit at a stool beside him. The senator gave him a surveying glance from the corner of his eye and liked what he saw. On the small side for sure, but fit and athletic, with pale, perfectly smooth skin. The man either shaved extremely closely or simply had nothing to shave. The senator liked that.

"Can I buy you a drink?" he asked before the newcomer had a chance to place his order.

The man appraised the senator a few seconds before answering affirmatively. He spoke in a low whispery hush that the senator found sexy.

They spent the next few minutes exchanging platitudes, but it was pretty obvious neither one was interested in chit chat. Men didn't come to this type of bar to have a nice conversation.

Thirty minutes later, the senator was back inside his hotel suite, waiting for the man to join him. A necessary precaution, as he could scarcely afford to be seen going to his room with a man half his age. This wasn't the type of publicity he needed.

He was checking himself in the mirror when he heard a knock on the door. He opened it, stepping aside to let his visitor in.

As the senator closed the door, he pulled a gun out of his robe's pocket and pointed the weapon towards his visitor. "Please forgive my manners but one's never too prudent," he said, reaching for the metal detector sitting on a nearby console with his other hand and waving the wand around his visitor. The detector went off as it passed above the man's belt buckle and again at his right pocket.

Gun still trained on the man, the senator fished inside the pocket to retrieve a set of keys. "Good. Nothing I need to worry about."

The tension in the young man's face relaxed a bit.

"Once again, I apologize for this unfortunate necessity," said the senator, walking to the bedside table where he locked his gun in a safe commanded by his fingerprints.

"Now we can have some fun! Can I serve you something to drink?" he asked, walking to the small bar located in a corner of the suite's living room.

"No, thanks. That's not why I came."

That voice again; the senator tingled with anticipation. He hadn't fucked a young stud in what felt like ages. He could hardly wait. He hoped the man liked it rough, because the senator knew no other way to have sex.

He served himself a glass of scotch and swallowed it down. He then walked towards the man standing in front of his bed and gently caressed his cheek with the back of his hand before ripping his shirt open in a sudden move. The smile on the senator's lips was that of a sadist unwrapping a new torture device.

His eyes went wide as they dropped to the man's chest to admire the terrain he was about to conquer. He tried to scream, but no sound came out of his mouth. No sound ever would again. In addition to severing carotids and jugulars, the knife had cut deep into the senator's windpipe.

He looked at the black, jagged blade dripping with blood in the hand of his assassin.

As he silently bled to death, hands wrapped over his hemorrhaging wound, the senator saw his killer retrieve the room keycard from the table and walk towards the door. "I need to get a few tools I left in my car, but don't worry, I'll be back." The voice had changed; it sounded eerily familiar now.

As he took his last breath on the bloodstained rug in the middle of the room, one question came to the senator's mind. Why hadn't the metal detector found the hidden weapon?

Chapter 16

Ethan and Theo were sitting in the FBI agent's den. The Hansens couldn't afford living inside the city—other than politicians, nobody on a civil servant's income could. Which was why, one Sunday a month, Ethan drove to San Francisco's suburbs to partake in a real family lunch.

A football game was playing on the 72-inch screen mounted to the wall, but Ethan wasn't paying it much attention. He was watching Theo's four-year-old daughter harassing her five-year-old brother.

There was a time where he'd been thinking about having kids, but Ethan now knew he would never be a father. Even if he got over his issues, even if he somehow found a woman that would put up with his shit, there was no way he'd bring an innocent life into this miserable excuse of a world. He didn't want to be responsible for the pain and suffering of anyone on this most basic of levels.

"How's work?" asked Ethan once the two kids had left the room screaming, the girl chasing the boy.

"You don't want to know," answered Theo, opening another beer.

It was probably true, but he couldn't help himself. A part of him never wanted to be involved in another homicide investigation, but another part craved the rush he used to feel when all the pieces of the puzzle finally came together inside his head, removing the mask the predator had been hiding behind all along. "How many cases are you currently working on?" he asked.

Theo sighed heavily before answering, "Two, maybe three."

"Maybe? How does that work? You haven't found the victims yet?"

"Are you sure you want to talk about this, Ethan? I don't want you to go apeshit on your way home. I need to sleep tonight. I don't have time to come and bail you out of jail at three in the morning."

"I need to sleep too. Last night was… busy."

"I don't want to hear a word about it," Theo said, hand raised preemptively.

"I wasn't going to tell. So, what's your *maybe* case about?"

"We have three victims, but it's still unclear whether they were killed by the same guy. There are similarities, but some patterns don't fit the typical serial killer profile."

"Tell me more." Ethan's curiosity was piqued.

"Three women. All fairly attractive, all sexually abused and tortured, but the way they were tortured was different in each case. They also belong to three different ethnic groups. We have a Caucasian, a Latino and an Asian. As you know sexual predators and serial killers both like to choose their victims within their ethnic group, so this doesn't fit the typical whack-job's pattern."

"Correct, so why do you guys think there's a connection?"

"The women may not look the same, but they're all educated, quiet and they'd each recently started dating a guy that none of their friends had ever seen. And, of course, they were all choked to death by the killer's bare hands."

"Sounds to me like you got yourself a serial killer," said Ethan after a second of reflection.

"That's what I'm afraid of, but in that case it's an atypical predator who doesn't have a specific modus operandi and hunts outside his ethnic group."

Ethan raised an eyebrow, slowly shaking his head. "Or you have a typical serial killer who knows the profiler's playbook and is screwing with you."

"And you say your brain doesn't work…"

"It doesn't. Believe me! My input is just conjectural, baby profiling at best. Look me in the eyes and tell me your experts haven't reached the same conclusion already."

"It's one of the possibilities they came up with," admitted Theo.

"That's what I thought. If it's indeed a serial killer, I suspect your next victim will be black. At which point you'll know for sure he's screwing with you."

"Why black?"

"Because of the statistical odds. Black, Caucasian, Asian and Latino are the four dominant ethnicities in the US. Since you already have one victim for each of the three other ethnicities…"

The game was interrupted by a breaking news report, and the two friends turned their attention towards the TV as a journalist standing microphone in hand in front of a massive casino appeared on the screen.

"Senator Allister Woodrough from Wyoming was found dead in his Las Vegas hotel room an hour ago. Foul play is suspected. The senator was known for his strong stance on—"

"This couldn't have happened to a nicer guy," said Theo sarcastically. "I wonder what went down."

Ethan wasn't listening to his friend, however. He was wondering whether Senator Woodrough was related in any way to Woodrough Enterprise? And if he were, could his death have anything to do with the blackmailing business?

"I'm sure glad I'm not in charge of that investigation. It's going to be a total cluster involving the Bureau, Vegas PD and the Capitol police. A giant pissing contest about who has jurisdiction here. Though I expect Vegas PD will gladly bail out of that mess," continued Theo, but his tirade was interrupted by the cell phone ringing on the coffee table in front of him.

He checked the caller ID before answering. "It's Sunday afternoon, what exactly couldn't wait until tomorrow, Sally?"

Sally's justification must have been a good one because no more objections came out of Theo's mouth.

"Are you sure?" he asked, leaving the room, phone still stuck to his ear.

This was strange. Ethan didn't recall his friend ever needing to take a call in private before. What was going on? Did the call have anything to do with the late senator?

The FBI agent returned a moment later, looking disturbed. "I need to head to the office. Something came up."

"Did they find a fourth victim?"

"No. It's about something else," replied Theo evasively. "I'm sorry but you'd better go home. I need to pa—" He stopped himself in mid-sentence, which couldn't have looked more suspicious if he'd done it on purpose.

"Does this have anything to do with the senator? Are you going to Vegas?"

Theo hesitated a moment before finally answering, "Yes. That's where I'm heading."

"But you specialize in serial killers. They think this is part of a series? Do you have a nut job going around targeting politicians?" Ethan asked, warily eying his friend whose unease appeared to be growing with every passing second.

"We're looking at various possibilities. I can't tell you more at this point. It's an ongoing investigation… I'm sorry, I need to go."

Ethan watched Theo leave the room. Very seldom had he witnessed his friend lie to him before, and never in such an awkward and obvious fashion. He had no idea what this was all about, but one thing was certain: whatever it was that Theo was keeping to himself, it had nothing to do with FBI regulations.

Chapter 17

Jennifer was thirty minutes late when she walked into the office on Monday morning. Ethan, immersed in the summon-to-court papers he'd been served that Friday afternoon, paid her no attention.

"Good morning. How was your weekend?" she asked.

"Probably not as great as yours, based on the fact you were supposed to start work thirty minutes ago," he replied, his gaze still focused on the papers in front of him.

Noticing her boss hadn't bothered making coffee himself, Jennifer went to start the coffee maker, one of her secretarial duties apparently. "I did have a good weekend, thanks. I finally did something I'd wanted to do for a long time."

"You bought yourself a watch?" he asked sarcastically.

"You know, Ethan, most of the time you're not as funny as you think you are. And feel free to dock my paycheck by thirty minutes if you'd like."

"I'd rather you stay late this evening and spend an extra half-hour surfing the web."

She ignored the comment and walked to the bathroom shared by all offices on their floor to wash their two mugs. The smell of coffee was starting to fill the office by the time she came back.

"So, did you spend your weekend thinking about a way to solve my lawsuit dilemma?" he asked.

"It wasn't necessary. I solved that problem Friday night. Did you think about Gwendoline Thomas' offer?"

Ethan ignored her answer as well as her question, and she decided to let it go for now.

She was pouring two cups of coffee when his cell phone rang. She placed one of the mugs on his desk and retreated behind her computer screen, the whole time eavesdropping on the conversation.

"It was my friend, the FBI agent," he said after terminating the call. "His contact at the SFPD just called him. The civil lawsuit against me was dropped over the weekend. And the Kazemis also informed the DA that they wouldn't be testifying against me in court. Which means the criminal case will most likely be dismissed as well."

"Why do you look so surprised? I just told you that I took care of it Friday night," she replied nonchalantly.

That caught his attention. "What do you mean by that, Jennifer? What did you do exactly?"

She told him about her visit to the Kazemis, omitting only the part where she'd given them fifteen grand to drop the lawsuit. The money had come out of her own savings and, since she wouldn't need it anytime soon, she wasn't planning to ask Ethan to pay her back. "You still need to reimburse them for medical expenses, though. The guy looks like he went head-first through a brick wall."

Ethan was flabbergasted. "How did you suspect it was Viagra he added to his drink?"

"That was pretty obvious, really."

"Not to me."

"Well, in that case, maybe you made the wrong assumption."

"What do you mean," he asked, looking confused.

"Maybe you assumed you were the smartest person in this office…" That shut him up for the remainder of the morning.

To thank her for her valuable involvement in his legal problems, Ethan had decided to take Jennifer out to lunch to the restaurant of her choosing. Over sushi, they talked about Gwendoline Thomas' offer and more specifically about Ethan's concerns regarding the case. After doing some research, he'd found out that Senator Woodrough was Gwendoline's uncle and his recent murder was of great concern to Ethan who had absolutely no desire to work on a case potentially linked to a murder investigation. This worried Jennifer more than a bit, but she'd kept her concerns to herself.

They'd been back at the office about five minutes when Ethan suddenly punched his flat-panel computer screen hard enough to make Jennifer jump in her seat.

The screen flew three feet in the air before the power cord stopped its flight, at which point it dropped like a brick and shattered on the plastic-tiled floor. Ethan's face was a mask of rage and pain. He abruptly got up from his chair, grabbed the compact scanner on his desk and hurled it against the wall where it exploded on impact.

Fists balled up so tight his knuckles were turning white, he left the office without a word. Was he tearing up? What the hell was this all about?

As she heard his feet flying down the stairs, Jennifer got up and walked to the window to watch him exiting the building. A minute later, he'd disappeared around the first intersection.

She picked up his monitor and plugged it back in. A move immediately rewarded with the smell of melted plastic. Fearing a fire, she unplugged it right away and placed it aside on a table near the door.

Walking to her desk, she grabbed her own monitor and connected it to Ethan's computer. The desktop's tower located on the floor under his desk had simply been pulled forward by the flying screen incident and was still perfectly functional.

The monitor came to life and she saw a video silently playing in the center. For a second she thought she was looking at home-made porn, but she quickly realized her mistake. The woman tied up on what looked like a torture table was everything but willing. A couple minutes of watching was all it took to convince Jennifer that she had no desire to see how the video ended.

The movie was over three hours long and had been posted online in a private channel whose link had been emailed to Ethan. She had no doubt that tracing the email address would lead nowhere.

Afraid that whoever had posted the video would delete the link before a forensic team had a chance to study it, she scrolled back to the beginning and started recording a copy of the horrific movie on Ethan's remote server.

Wondering if the movie came with sound, she turned on the speakers located on the desk. She switched them back off after a couple seconds; the screams were more than she could take.

Her stomach was churning by the time she returned to her own desk a moment later. The video depicted the rape and torture of a woman at the hands of a psychopath, and from several angles. Jennifer didn't need to watch the whole thing to guess that the movie ended with the execution of the unfortunate victim.

She swiveled in her chair to check the calendar behind her. December 8: the one-year anniversary of her death.

Jennifer knew who the woman was. She'd recognized her right away despite the rictus of terror she wore in the video. The unfortunate victim was a perfect match for the wedding picture Ethan kept on his desk.

The video clearly showed Angus Avery sexually assaulting Amanda Archer, but Jennifer suspected that what had driven Ethan to the edge wasn't simply seeing his wife being raped and tortured.

Avery had died in jail in the hours following his arrest and, although it was conceivable he'd sent the email a year earlier with a delayed delivery option, one thing was certain: he hadn't been the one holding the camera.

Chapter 18

Paul Richards opened the front door of his beach house to find Naomi on the other side holding a bottle of wine. It wasn't a total surprise; she'd called two hours earlier asking if she could drop by.

"Come on in," he said, leading her into the living room. "I didn't get a chance to cook anything, but I picked up a pizza we can reheat in the oven. Nobody delivers around here."

"I'm not surprised. Even the GPS had a hard time finding the place. It first took me to your neighbors three miles down the road. That's where I called you from."

"It would appear that technology has its limitations," he said, smiling as he opened the bottle of wine she'd brought.

They settled next to each other on the couch facing the gas fireplace. The flames leaped over fake logs that produced embers realistic enough to fool the casual observer. The smell of burning wood was the only thing missing.

"How was your trip?" asked Naomi, sipping on her wine.

"Very productive overall. But I must confess that I had a hard time focusing."

"Why is that?" she asked, falsely intrigued, already anticipating what was coming.

"Because I kept thinking about you," he said, just above a whisper.

She kissed him softly on the mouth.

"I'm glad I called. For a while I debated whether I should be old school and wait for your call, but I finally decided I wasn't living in the fifties and picked up the phone."

"I'm very happy you did."

They talked and kissed for another hour before pangs of hunger drove them to the kitchen in search of something to snack on while the pizza warmed up.

"This is such a bachelor's place, your cupboards are nearly empty," she commented, amused.

"Guilty as charged. Maybe next time we can go grocery shopping together so you can show me how it should be done."

"Sounds like a plan," she answered, beaming slightly, as he knew she would.

They found a bag of chips and munched on them until the oven's timer went off, announcing the much-anticipated pizza.

They ate in the den in front of Hitchcock's 1954 *Rear Window* playing on a large-screen TV. Naomi had picked the movie. Nestled against him on the couch, she smelled of jasmine and lavender. The fragrance probably came from her shampoo; it was too subtle to be perfume.

Thinking about what was to come, he felt his penis swelling. Not a full hard on but not too far off either.

Naomi picked up on the mood and they were half naked on the couch by the time the credits appeared on the screen.

"Can you spend the night?" he asked.

"I need to open the gallery at ten tomorrow morning, but that should be no problem. I'll just need to leave from here before eight. I brought some clothes and a toothbrush with me… just in case." She punctuated her statement with a wink. "I'll go fetch my stuff now while I'm still wearing *some* clothes," she added, slipping back into her dress.

She went to her car and came back rolling a small suitcase behind her.

"Looks to me like you plan on staying longer than a night," he teased. She blushed slightly, which looked good on her chocolate skin.

They retired to the bedroom and a moment later they were naked under the sheets, kissing and exploring each other's bodies in new and creative ways.

The love-making session lasted nearly an hour at the end of which Naomi lay on her back, satisfied and exhausted. But Paul was still kissing her breasts, navel, inner thighs and everything else he could put his lips on. She moaned lightly at the attention but nothing like she had a moment earlier. He slipped his arm under her back and, grabbing her by the hip in one hand and by the shoulder in the other, he gently flipped her on her belly before kissing her neck and finally lying flat on top of her.

"Looks like someone isn't done yet," she said, as his cock pressed hard against her ass.

"Not by a long shot," he replied, spreading her legs apart.

"Oops, wrong one!" she teased as the tip of his penis fumbled around her anus.

"That's the one I'm going for," he said in a voice void of any humor.

He penetrated her in one powerful thrust, her scream music to his ears. His eyes captured hers in the mirror he'd mounted on the wall for this sole purpose. This was always his favorite moment. And for one simple reason... they never saw it coming.

Chapter 19

E than still hadn't come back to work by noon the next day and Jennifer suspected he wouldn't show up at all. She'd stopped by his apartment the night before to check on him, but he hadn't been home.

Her phone rang and she answered, "Do you have anything for me?"

"Nothing useful," replied a male voice. "The video was uploaded in a cyber cafe in Santa Monica a week ago. The link was sent through a fake Yahoo account that was never used for anything else. The sender had selected delayed delivery which is why the email only showed up on Monday morning."

"So, there's no way to track down whoever's responsible for this?"

"Not using the means at my disposal," answered her hacker friend.

"Would someone else be able to?"

"Not using a computer," he assured her.

She knew he wasn't being arrogant. She'd met Dennis in college and spent many nights watching him work his magic. She'd warned him numerous times about getting caught with his pants down inside a secured server he had no business exploring, but he'd been able to stay out of jail so far.

"By the way, the file had a timebomb set to activate eight hours after it was first opened, so I made you a timebomb-free copy that won't erase itself. But man, that's really fucked-up shit."

"Thanks, Dennis. I'll come and pick it up later today. I don't want that stuff to hang out on the web more than it already has. See you soon." She hung up, wondering how much of the video her friend had been able to stomach. She'd already made a copy of the file, but she'd been worried she'd missed some type of virus designed to delete any duplicate. Not surprisingly, Dennis had identified the threat and neutralized it.

She decided to spend the remainder of the afternoon reacquainting herself with Amanda Archer's story. She'd read all about it in the weeks following her death, but maybe there was more information to be found now.

Some of the circumstances surrounding her abduction were still unclear to Jennifer. Amanda had been found by a surfer half buried on a beach on a Monday morning. The very same morning Jennifer had first walked into

Ethan's office. As a matter of fact, she'd been with Ethan when he'd received the call asking him to come identify a woman's body.

Now that she knew the edited video of Amanda's last hours was over three hours long, she couldn't help but wonder where Ethan had been during that time.

He'd never been suspected by the agents in charge of the investigation, but Jennifer wasn't certain why. It was true the modus operandi used on Amanda had matched that of an active serial killer, but Ethan had been helping the police on that case and was familiar with all the details of the crimes. Had he wanted to get rid of his wife, it would have been easy for him to play copycats.

As she browsed through old articles, the specific chain of events came back to her mind. Amanda had only been dead four or five hours by the time her body had been found at 9 AM, her head the only thing sticking out from a shallow grave dug directly on the beach. Whoever had buried Amanda hadn't meant to hide her.

The corpse had been unearthed by the Santa Cruz Sheriff's Office. The deputies had easily identified the mark seared onto Amanda's left breast and had immediately called in the FBI. This specific brand—two capital A letters overlapping at the base—was the signature of the serial killer the media had nicknamed the Cowboy.

$$\text{Ѫ}$$

Like the six previous victims, Amanda was a beautiful white woman with long dark hair. Like the others, she'd died of a slit throat after being repeatedly raped and tortured. And just like the others, her body had been doused inside and out with bleach to erase any DNA evidence the killer could have left on his victim.

But this time he'd done a sloppy job. Skin had been found under one of Amanda's fingernails and the DNA analysis of the sample had returned a perfect match for Angus Avery, a parolee who'd spent five years in jail for the rape of a seventeen-year-old.

Amanda had been the killer's last victim. Avery's death in prison had put an end to the killing spree. But now someone had sent Ethan that video, confirming what Jennifer had suspected all along. Avery had worked with an accomplice. A bastard who'd waited a year to let Ethan know he'd been played for an even bigger fool than he'd ever suspected.

Chapter 20

The van turned left, and Ethan followed at a distance. He strongly doubted the driver was onto him, but he took no chances. It was nearing midnight and traffic wasn't particularly heavy this time of the day, which made his vehicle easier to spot in the van's mirrors.

Almost three days had passed since the video had showed up in his email. He hadn't found the strength to watch it past the first few seconds, but the images haunted him day and night nonetheless. Wherever he looked he saw Amanda tied up to a table and Avery towering over her. It was as if the images had been seared onto his retinas.

He hadn't slept in two days and had barely eaten. The deprivation was starting to take a toll on his body, but he didn't give a shit.

Since sleep wasn't an option, Ethan had spent his time roaming bars and clubs in search of a predator to use as a punching bag. Something to release some of the pain and frustration balled up in the pit of his stomach. His quest had lasted nearly sixty hours, but he'd finally hit the jackpot in one of the clubs popular with the younger crowd.

The man he was tailing looked to be in his early twenties. He had a quiet demeanor, a forgettable face, and dead eyes… a sociopath's trademark.

Ethan had first started suspecting the perv when he'd caught him expertly scanning a group of drunken college girls shaking their booties on the dance floor. His suspicion had been confirmed when he'd witnessed the man slip roofies in the drinks the students had left unattended on a table. The girls had eventually come back to their drugged beverages and finished them up under the watchful eyes of the creep.

The man had been too focused on selecting his victim to pay any attention to Ethan sitting at a table twenty feet in front of him.

The predator had walked out of the club twenty minutes later holding one of the girls by the waist. After informing the bouncers to keep an eye on the other roofied girls who were now orbiting aimlessly around their table, Ethan had exited the club in a hurry.

He'd made it to the parking lot just on time to see the asshole driving away in a van, the girl slumped over beside him. Ethan had jumped behind the wheel of his BMW and had been following the van around town ever since.

He hoped beating the van's driver to a pulp would help him sleep a little better, but it was doubtful. The bastard was a predator, but not the one Ethan needed. In order to truly relieve the pressure that had been building inside him for nearly three days, he'd have to put his hands on the motherfucker who'd been holding the camera while Angus Avery had raped, tortured, and eventually killed Amanda.

The revelation had haunted Ethan ever since he'd received the video. He'd never suspected Avery had an accomplice. No one had.

While Ethan had been screwing the whore, basking in the glory of his latest professional victory, his wife was being tortured not by one but by two lunatics. And Ethan was the only one to blame for it. He'd taunted the bastards in front of a room full of reporters and cameras.

The press conference had been for another case—with Ethan's help, the cops had finally arrested the man responsible for the abduction and murder of four teenage boys—but when a journalist had asked Ethan whether he'd been helping the authorities to track down the Cowboy, he'd replied affirmatively before adding that he was already following a couple of interesting leads.

It hadn't taken Avery and his friend long to show Ethan how stupid he truly was. Less than two weeks after the press conference, they'd lured him away from Amanda and killed her.

The van reached an industrial zone where traffic was even lighter and finally stopped in front of a large garage door affixed to a redbrick building. Ethan parked fifty yards away and quietly slipped out of his car.

The man got out of the van to lift the aluminum curtain with the intent of driving the vehicle inside the building and away from prying eyes, but Ethan had anticipated the move. By the time the guy was climbing back behind the wheel, Ethan was on him.

He clubbed the perv on the side of the head with his brass knuckles before pulling him out of the car. But the man still had some fight in him and his fist clipped Ethan in the jaw, sending him to the ground.

The hook had caught him by surprise and Ethan was still down, but he'd recovered enough to block the man's incoming kick aimed at his kidney. Twisting the man's left foot with both hands to throw him off balance, Ethan threw his right heel at the man's balls. He felt his foot crushing soft flesh as the man howled in agony.

Ethan was back on his feet a second later. He'd retrieved his brass knuckles that had fallen to the ground and drove them into the man's ribs a few times before going for the head.

Within a minute the guy was lying on his back, Ethan straddling him, still punching with surprising energy for a man who was sleep-deprived.

Focused on the bloody mess his brass knuckles were making of the guy's face, Ethan never even heard the two men approaching from behind him.

Chapter 21

It was Thursday afternoon by the time Ethan finally made it back to the office with a clearly bruised jaw. Jennifer hadn't seen him since Monday but didn't feel the need to ask him where he'd been. She was actually surprised to see him back already.

From behind her computer screen, she watched him sit down at his desk and then realize that his broken monitor was sitting on a table by the door.

He glanced in her direction but said nothing.

"You can use mine. I brought my laptop today," she said, nodding towards her monitor.

He accepted the offer and was about to plug the cord into his own desktop tower when a man and a woman entered the office without knocking. This wasn't shocking in itself, as half of their visitors didn't bother knocking on the door before walking in. Their business-like demeanor and stone faces were a bit unusual, however.

"Ethan Archer?" asked the woman.

Ethan nodded.

"I'm Detective Lee and this is Detective Maloni. We'd like to ask you a few questions."

"I'm listening."

"Would you mind coming with us to the station? We'd be more comfortable there," said the woman.

"Maybe you would... but I wouldn't. You can have a seat and ask me your questions here or you can head back to your station and close the door behind you." The remark had been stated in a matter-of-fact tone void of sarcasm. Not something Jennifer expected from her boss.

"Very well," said the woman, sitting down in one of the armchairs in front of Ethan's desk, her partner quickly following suit.

"Can I offer you some coffee?" Ethan asked.

"That won't be necessary, thank you," answered Detective Maloni.

"What happened to your face, Mr. Archer? It looks like a nasty bruise," said the woman.

Ethan raised his hand to his jaw. "I'd forgotten about that... What can I say, some women can't take a compliment." Now *that* sounded more like something Ethan would say, but it still lacked conviction.

"We'll get back to this later," said the man. "Where were you last night?"

Ethan contemplated the question for a moment. "I'm not sure it's any of your business, Detectives. Why do you ask?"

"Because a man was beaten to a pulp yesterday evening and is currently in a coma," answered Detective Lee. "He'd probably be dead if two passersby hadn't pulled his aggressor away. They were unfortunately unable to hold onto the attacker and the man escaped in a black BMW. What car do you drive, Mr. Archer?"

"A black BMW, but I suspect there may be another one or two in the city. Do you have a license plate number?"

"No, unfortunately, but the description of the aggressor is a pretty good match for you, Mr. Archer," said the man.

"So you hear about a car similar to mine and get a vague description and you come knocking on my door? That's some impressive police work, Detectives."

"What brought us to your door, Mr. Archer, is what was found inside the victim's van."

"What was it?" asked Jennifer.

The two detectives turned their attention towards her. It was Lee who answered. "An unconscious young woman. She'd been drugged and had no recollection of how she'd gotten there."

"Personally, I think whoever put that guy in a coma deserves a medal," said Maloni, "but we still gotta do our job and try to find the attacker. And since you have a history of violence towards this kind of individual, Mr.

Archer…"

"And since your car and physical description match those of the aggressor…" continued Lee.

"I'm sure my boss would have loved to be the one turning that scumbag into a vegetable, but he was with me all night." As she spoke, Jennifer came to stand behind Ethan's chair and rested her hands on his shoulders.

"Are you certain of this, Miss?" asked Lee skeptically.

"Oh, I'm sure," she said, gently caressing the bruise on his cheek, a half smile on her lips.

The two detectives looked at each other an instant and stood up from their armchairs in an almost synchronized motion.

"In that case, we're sorry to have bothered you, Mr. Archer. Please enjoy the rest of your day," said Maloni. Lee nodded her goodbyes and the two of them were on their way.

Jennifer walked to the window and watched them exiting the building before saying, "I don't think they believed me."

"I'm pretty certain of that, but I don't think it matters. They don't give two shits about catching the guy who put that son of a bitch in a coma. They were just going through the motions."

"I'm glad," she responded, returning to her desk.

"Thank you," he said, looking at her. "But in the future, don't lie to the cops for me. I don't pay you enough for you to get in trouble on my behalf."

"Noted," she said. *You actually cost me almost more than you're giving me*, she thought, remembering the fifteen grand she'd given the Kazemis but keeping that to herself.

"I've decided to accept Gwendoline Thomas' offer."

It was about time.

"I gave her a call an hour ago. I'm meeting her tomorrow to discuss the details of the case and sign the paperwork."

"Great! I think it will be good for you." Jennifer bit her tongue as she pronounced the last words but they were already out.

Ethan gave her a scrutinizing look. His lips eventually twisted into a feeble smile. "Did you check my computer after I left on Monday?"

She didn't try to deny it.

"So you've seen the video?"

"I only watched a fraction of it."

Ethan nodded understandingly. "I need to get out of town. I need to get some fresh air. That's what convinced me to get over my reservations concerning the Woodrough case."

"I think it's a good idea."

He then turned his attention to his computer, and she pulled her laptop out of her backpack.

"Son of a bitch!" he screamed an instant later.

She looked at him inquisitively.

"The video!" he said, frantically clicking his mouse. "It's gone! The link has expired."

He sounded utterly defeated.

"Were you really going to watch it? I'm not sure you should put yourself through that kind of torture," she said hesitantly.

"I was going to send it to Theo and have a forensic team review it for clues about the accomplice." His voice was barely a whisper.

"In that case I may be able to help," she said, placing a flash drive in front of him.

Chapter 22

The FBI's San Francisco field office was a large modern-looking building on Golden Gate Avenue. It was nearing 7 PM and the 9th floor was close to deserted when Theo opened the door of one of the small conference rooms and gestured for Ethan to come in.

"When did you get this?" asked Theo, pushing the flash drive towards Ethan. The agent had locked himself up in the conference room for over twenty minutes, fast-forwarding through the disturbing images.

"I received the email at 5:25 Monday morning, but I only found it early afternoon. I also have it on good authority that it was actually sent with delayed delivery from a cyber cafe in Santa Monica nearly a week earlier."

"Who told you that?"

"Don't ask."

Theo sighed but didn't push the issue. Instead, he jotted down the information on a legal pad which was already covered in notes taken during his viewing of the video.

"Based on the coroner's estimate, 5:25 AM roughly matches the time Amanda was murdered," said Ethan.

"That's what the video's timestamp seems to confirm." Theo sounded very uncomfortable.

"I couldn't bring myself to watch it but there may be some clues hidden in the footage. I need you guys to go through it with a fine-tooth comb and let me know what you find." Ethan couldn't keep the emotion out of his voice. He'd been balancing between tears and explosive rage for days now.

"We'll do our very best, Ethan, but you know I can't keep you in the loop on this."

"Don't feed me that kind of crap!" he screamed. "It's me you're talking to. And this fucking bastard just sent me a video of my wife's execution in all its gory details. You really think you're going to keep me in the dark on this? Really? The Cowboy's not dead! We didn't catch *him* a year ago... we got his decoy."

"We don't know that." Theo didn't appear convinced by his own statement.

"He never got sloppy! He didn't miss the skin we found under her fingernail. He left it there on purpose. He meant for us to arrest Avery. I'm sure the fucker is also the one who got him killed in prison. Avery's death was a hit. Pure and simple."

"But it's Avery who left that club with Am—"

"Don't you fucking say it! Don't you say—" The words choked him as he started sobbing uncontrollably.

Theo placed his large hand on Ethan's shoulder, but there wasn't anything he could do to appease his friend.

"I'll get you some water," he said, once Ethan's tears started to dry out.

He came back a couple minutes later with a box of tissues and a cup of water from the cooler.

"You may be right, Ethan. Avery could have been a front man and not the brain of the operation. But if he wasn't the real Cowboy, why did the killings stop after his arrest?"

Ethan took the glass of water, considering the question. "Maybe the Cowboy wanted to disappear. Maybe he thought he could stop killing and framing Avery as the sole killer was his exit strategy. Or maybe he'd planned all along to send me the video on the anniversary of her death. His final 'Fuck you!' to show me how big of a fool he played me for. The year-long break he took was just to comfort us in our belief that we'd gotten him. If that's the case, you can expect a new victim soon, Theo."

Theo pondered his friend's remark a moment before answering, "We may already have one."

Ethan stared at him, confused. "Who? When?"

"I wasn't planning to tell you about this, but given the circumstances... I might as well."

"Tell me what?"

"You remember that I had to fly to Vegas on Sunday afternoon?"

Of course Ethan remembered. He'd known right away that Theo was hiding something from him, he just didn't know what. "I do."

"I was asked to have a look at Senator Woodrough's crime scene because of some resemblance with a case I'd worked on in the past."

"The Cowboy?"

"Yes."

"What similarities?" asked Ethan, feeling increasingly agitated.

"The senator had his throat slashed very deep, that was the cause of death. He also had a single capital letter A branded on his chest."

"A single one?" That didn't make sense. The throat slashing was a match, but the Cowboy's signature was two capital A's, seared into his victim's left boob, the two letters centered precisely around the nipple.

"Sounds like a copycat," said Ethan. "Serial killers don't suddenly switch to men when they've always targeted women. The signature's wrong too. One A isn't the same as two."

"And the A was branded upside down. In the senator's case, the top of the letter is pointing at the feet, not the head."

"Copycat," repeated Ethan.

"That's also the direction I was leaning in, but now with the video showing up a few days later... I'm not so sure anymore."

Ethan wasn't sure either. He was too distraught and too angry to think things through. He had only one thing in mind at the moment: the Cowboy was back, and it changed everything.

Chapter 23

Paul Richards was contemplating his work. Naomi Berhan lay tied up on the wooden bench he'd specially built for her. Her spirit as broken as her body.

The building of the torture table was a ritual he enjoyed particularly. Mostly because it announced the reward of his efforts. Once the table was built, the fun usually started within a day or two.

Inspired from images he'd found in books on the Spanish Inquisition, every one of his benches was unique. They all came with holes to accommodate chains and slits for the leather straps, but each one had a particular feature serving a specific purpose. This one, for instance, was equipped with a rope that could be passed around the neck of the victim before disappearing under the table. There, a pully system allowed him to strangle his prey with a great degree of control while defiling her in whichever way struck his fancy at that particular moment. Naomi had passed out from lack of oxygen several times already, but he'd always been careful not to overdo it. Killing the victim prematurely was a rookie mistake he no longer made. Where was the fun in that?

He once again congratulated himself for his planning and foresight. It was his attention to details and his constant anticipation of his victims' moves that kept him three steps ahead of them. Just like Saturday morning when Naomi had taken advantage of him being in the shower to go snooping around the house. What if she'd found his homemade torture chamber behind the door of one of the spare bedrooms? Instead, she'd only found a bed and a couple of nightstands. Simply because, like a true hunter, he understood his prey.

Women liked to poke around in other people's business, stick their nose where it didn't belong. Paul had anticipated all that. He hadn't started his little construction project until later that weekend, confident Naomi would soon come running back to him. They always did, each one faster than the last. And why wouldn't they? He pushed all the right buttons, played on their fantasies, desires, hobbies, and insecurities. By the time he arranged the first chance encounter with his future victim, he'd already been secretly observing her for weeks. Learning her habits, placing himself in her head to pinpoint her weaknesses and the best way to exploit them to his advantage.

He called it the prenuptial phase. A solitary period, since he needed to keep his distance at all times, but a highly enjoyable one. Coming up with a novel strategy for each woman was a challenge that stimulated his intellect and made him high with anticipation. An anticipation that kept building up ever higher during the second phase of his campaign. The one he'd nicknamed the honeymoon. A phase that started with the staged first encounter.

The honeymoon always followed a similar pattern. The first contact never exceeded a couple hours and often ended with him leaving without asking for the woman's contact info. The second encounter was designed to last much longer. The goal was to turn their second meeting into their first date, an intense seduction session at the end of which a kiss was exchanged.

The third encounter was the second official date and always ended with sex. Usually great sex for the woman, since by then she was smitten with him and psychologically prepped for it. The fact he could work on pleasuring them until they came, no matter how long it took, had a lot to do with his ability to satisfy them. This was an essential part of the ritual since the endorphins released during orgasm deepened the emotional connection the women felt towards him. Naomi had been easy to please, but he recalled how it had taken him nearly an hour to finally make Andrea Gomez climax, at which point they had both been utterly exhausted. Lasting long under those circumstances was no challenge, though. Unlike some losers who came within seconds of touching a woman, he could only come when sex got rough.

The third official date was always the last one. The funeral phase... By that point, the woman was so head over heels with him, so convinced that she'd hit the jackpot, that she was ready to walk through hell for him. Which was perfect since this was exactly where he planned on taking her.

The sensations running through his body at the precise second his prey first realized she'd been duped couldn't be described with words.

For years he'd raped and murdered his victims on first encounter, but he'd been a fool. The pleasure of raping a perfect stranger was nothing in comparison to what he now experienced with the women.

It was the trust he'd carefully built and their budding, delusional love for him that gave him such a high the moment he flipped the switch and revealed his true self in all its power and glory.

Only then could his orgasms reach a paroxysm as he looked into the terror-filled eyes of his prey. He always made sure to look into their eyes. The battle between delusion, incomprehension, and terror that raged in those pupils was something he now craved like a drug.

He'd been torturing Naomi for three straight days. Three terrifyingly long days for her, but three disappointingly short days for him. The saying was definitely accurate: time flew when one was having fun.

Unfortunately, all good things had an end and it was now time to say goodbye to his playmate. He'd used her phone to respond to her friends' text messages and found excuses for her to not show up for work, but he couldn't keep the charade going much longer. Soon someone would start wondering about Naomi, and he needed to be far away by the time this happened.

Giving Naomi the wrong GPS coordinate had bought him a few days, but no more. This was a precaution he took each time in case the woman decided to tell a friend where she was going.

Giving the wrong physical address would raise all kinds of red flags, but giving incorrect GPS coordinates was always perceived as an error from the GPS itself.

"I want you to know that you're not dying in vain, Naomi. Having you over these past few days has brought me a tremendous amount of pleasure," he said, his fingers already tightening around her throat. "I will miss you."

He'd already cleaned the room thoroughly and incinerated the tarps used to protect the carpet from the blood. Now he simply needed to get rid of the body and come back to finish moving out of the rental.

He pulled the driver's license from his wallet and threw it in the hearth where he watched it first melt and finally burn. Paul Richards was dead. He now needed to choose a new persona from the half-dozen he had in advance, complete with fake social media accounts full of photoshopped pictures.

Chapter 24

Gwendoline Thomas' suite at the St Regis hotel cost 1200 dollars a night and was as spacious as Ethan's apartment.

The woman had suggested they meet there instead of his office for increased privacy. Gwendoline was apparently still concerned about talking in front of Jennifer.

As Ethan sat down on an L-shaped couch facing a large window with a view of Treasure Island, Gwendoline went to answer the door for room service.

The waiter was carrying a tray with a large pot of coffee, a smaller teapot, a plate of scones, and a muffin basket.

She gestured for him to place the tray on the coffee table in front of Ethan as she signed the receipt. She then sent the waiter on his way with a five-dollar tip and sat on the couch at a 90-degree angle from her guest.

"Thank you for coming, Mr. Archer. I was very pleased to hear that you were onboard."

"My pleasure," he replied, serving himself a cup of coffee and offering some to his host.

"First things first. Here's the confidentiality agreement. I would appreciate if you could read and sign it now, so we can get started."

Ethan went through the four-page document in detail before finally signing it.

"We can have the front desk make you a copy before you leave," said Gwendoline, placing the document on an end-table beside her.

"That would be good, thank you. Now let's hear those details. What was in that letter?"

"I'll let you read it for yourself," said the woman, handing him a manila folder containing a single page. "It came by mail and was sent to our main office in Cody. As you can see, the letter was addressed to me and sent to our legal department."

Calling the note a letter was a bit of a stretch. The message was short and to the point: *I know what happened on November 20, 1997. On January 15, the media will too.*

"I assume you know what they're referring to?" asked Ethan, replacing the folder on the table.

"I was eleven in 1997, so when I received this letter I was at a bit of a loss. But I went to my father and he knew right away what this was about." Gwendoline poured herself a cup of tea. "Are you familiar with oil and gas production, Mr. Archer?"

"I understand the concept."

"Good. Well, on November 20, 1997, one of our pipelines carrying crude oil failed due to unsuspected internal corrosion. Because the failure happened in the middle of the night, approximately twelve hundred barrels of oil had been spilled by the time the ruptured line was discovered, and the leak finally stopped."

"That's a lot of oil!"

"For an operation our size, it is, but for our industry in general, it's on the low side."

"Alright, so you had an oil spill twenty some years ago and now someone comes and reminds you of it. I guess that means the spill was never reported to the regulatory authorities, correct?"

"The price of oil was near an all-time low when the spill occurred and dropped further down the following year. Our company was barely surviving the turmoil as it was. The fines associated with such a spill would have bankrupted us. Every employee understood this, and it took little effort to convince them it was in everyone's best interest to keep quiet about the incident. They had mouths to feed at home, so they complied. The disaster was expertly covered up and no outsider ever found out about it."

"But now someone's having second thoughts…"

"It looks like it, and your job is to figure out who that someone is."

"What would happen, from a legal standpoint, if this info was leaked? If regulators learned about this 'incident'?" asked Ethan, placing his coffee mug back on the table.

"Enquiries would be made, but since the statute of limitation has expired, the company couldn't be prosecuted."

Ethan walked to the suite's window, absently peering at the view of downtown San Francisco. He had serious reservations about the case and wondered if he should walk out while he still could. But walking out meant kissing the hundred grand retainer goodbye and he could hardly afford to do that. Worse, he'd have nothing to occupy his mind and distract him from those images of Amanda that still haunted him day and night.

"I was sorry to learn about your uncle," he said, turning back to face the lawyer.

"An unfortunate tragedy." Gwendoline Thomas didn't sound particularly distressed.

"Was he connected to your company's business?"

"He was a board member but wasn't involved in the day to day operations. His contribution was limited to attending a couple of board meetings a year."

"I thought it was illegal for a US senator to sit on a company's board of directors."

"We're privately held, Mr. Archer. This law doesn't apply to us. The queen of England could sit on our board if she so wished to."

He pictured Queen Elizabeth traveling to Cody, Wyoming, to attend a Woodrough Enterprise board meeting, and it brought a faint smile to his lips.

"Do you think your uncle's murder could have something to do with the letter you received?" he asked.

"I strongly doubt there is any connection. As I said, Allister had very little involvement in the company and wasn't more involved in '97 when the incident occurred. Furthermore, the letter doesn't threaten any physical harm to anybody."

"Be that as it may, the timing of the two events seems unfortunate. Your company is blackmailed, and your uncle is killed a few days later…"

"Coincidences do happen, Mr. Archer. I really don't think there's any connection here."

She was probably right. Allister Woodrough had been killed by a serial killer's copycat. It didn't sound like the work of a disgruntled employee.

"I will take on your case," he said finally, "but if future events reveal a link between what happened to your uncle and this case, I will be forced to resign."

Gwendoline looked puzzled. "May I ask why?"

"Because I no longer work on murder investigations, Mrs. Thomas. I make no exceptions."

"Very well. Per the terms of our contract, you would not, of course, be able to keep the retainer in this instance, but I understand your position."

Ethan grabbed a chocolate muffin from the basket on the table and sat back down on the couch.

"I would like to discuss the specifics of your involvement now, Mr. Archer."

Chewing on a mouthful of pastry, Ethan nodded his agreement. The train had left the station, and he was onboard whether he liked it or not.

Given his lackluster investigative track record of the past few months, he had serious doubts about his ability to identify the blackmailer. Something which, thankfully, Gwendoline Thomas ignored.

He'd spent the past year unable to cope with his failure. He'd thought himself so smart, but the Cowboy had played him for a fool and taken the most important thing in his life. And now the bastard was back.

Chapter 25

The life of the ghost had suddenly taken a turn he hadn't anticipated. He'd known change was coming—it had been coming for nearly twenty years—and he'd known the upcoming weeks would be testing his strengths in ways they had never been before, but the discovery of his secret hideout had thrown a serious wrench into his plans.

The scientists had been searching the cave for days when the thing he'd dreaded since their arrival had finally happened. They'd stumbled upon the hidden entrance to the room, to *their* room... And it had changed everything.

The three men with head lamps and fancy tools, who mostly spoke in low voices, had quickly been replaced by a dozen loud-mouthed cops who'd brought in even more tools. The intruders had installed industrial-sized spotlights that projected a light brighter than day inside a cave that had never seen any. The ghost could already see the impact on the walls where patches of strange moss started to appear.

Blinded by the brightness of the lamps, he'd been forced to retreat deep into the cavern where the light couldn't reach him. The bats had done the same. The cave was far bigger than anyone suspected, and far more intricate. It also held many secrets...

He didn't even want to think about what would happen if the intruders discovered the veins of silver embedded inside the rock walls in some of the central rooms. Fortunately, it would require years and serious manpower to explore the entire subterranean complex. This bought him some time.

The cops had closed the cavern's main entrance with wide yellow tape, and it was now under twenty-four-hour surveillance. That didn't stop him from sneaking out under the cover of darkness, though. He almost never got out during daytime anyway; he much preferred the soft light of the moon to the harsh brightness of the sun. The woods were also much safer at night, deserted by hikers and hunters alike. Now he was forced to use a different entrance, however, one nobody knew about. At least, not yet.

"We found another one," he heard a man yelling in the distance, his voice bouncing off the rocky walls in all directions. "That's four already."

"How old?" asked another voice.

"Maybe eight or nine years old. It's impossible to tell from these piles of bones."

The ghost was growing angry. These men had no right to be here. They had no right to rob him of his treasures.

Chapter 26

"Did you sign the contract?" asked Jennifer as soon as Ethan walked into the office.

"I did."

"Cha-ching," she said, pulling the lever of an imaginary cash register.

"That's the good news. The bad news is that your days spent surfing the net are over. I'm going to need you to come with me to Wyoming and help out."

"Meaning?" she asked suspiciously.

"Meaning that your little stunt with the Kazemis proved your talents are wasted sitting behind this computer. And since this assignment will need two investigators, you're getting a promotion. Congrats!"

"It's Gwendoline Thomas who's going to be thrilled to have me around."

"As a matter of fact, when I mentioned I would need to work with a partner, she asked if you'd be suitable before I even had a chance to mention your name."

Jennifer gave him a suspicious look. "Are you pulling my chain?"

"Not even. That's the truth. You'll need to sign her non-disclosure agreement but short of that, you have the all-clear."

"Whoa! I must be even more charming than I realize."

There is some truth to that, he thought.

"Does this promotion come with a big raise?" she asked, leaning back in her chair.

Ethan had to think about it for a moment. He hadn't considered that point. "If your contribution helps me solve this case, you'll get a bonus equal to your monthly salary."

"And if we don't solve the case?"

"Then you'll get a bonus equal to half your salary. Either way, it will be worth your while."

Jennifer considered his offer an instant. "Alright… When are we leaving?"

Ethan internally breathed a sigh of relief. He was really counting on Jennifer's brain on this one. He had clearly underestimated his assistant and, with his recent track record, her presence could make a significant difference. "We're leaving Sunday, I need you to start booking our flights and hotel as soon as we're done here. We'll be gone all the way through New Year's Day, though. I hope that won't be a problem."

"Tabatha won't be happy, but she never is anyway."

"Who's Tabatha?"

"A girl I've been seeing. What exactly will I be doing?"

Ethan sat down behind his desk as he started telling her about the blackmail and covered-up environmental disaster.

"Let me get this straight, our plan is to just show up and start asking questions, hoping the blackmailer will suddenly feel bad and confess?"

"That would be plan B. In plan A, the two of us will pose as external auditors hired to identify inefficiencies in the business. As such, we will have carte blanche to stick our noses in any file we want and interview the employees."

"And just so that I'm clear, why do you need me for this? It's not like I've done something like that before."

"Neither have I, if it makes you feel any better."

"It's not looking good for my bonus," she replied sarcastically.

"I need you because of the timeline we're on. The letter mentions January 15 as the date our blackmailer will leak what he knows to the media. That means we need to have identified him or her by January 10 at the latest to give Gwendoline a chance to approach them with an offer to buy their silence."

"That's just a month away."

"Indeed, which is why I need you out there with me. While I look into the oil business, you'll investigate the ranch."

"Why not the other way around?" she asked, eyeing him suspiciously.

"Because I think those cowboys will be much more likely to confide in you than they would in me."

She gave him a look, but the twinkle in her eyes told him she appreciated the compliment.

"And we're supposed to play auditors through the end of the year? These people don't take time off between Christmas and New Year's?"

"The plan is to interview company employees and sift through paperwork until Christmas. If we're lucky, we'll have found our man by then and we'll be back for the holidays," said Ethan, who wasn't really in a rush to get back to San Francisco. He really needed a break from this place.

"And if we aren't lucky?" she asked.

"Then we're invited to spend Christmas break with the Woodrough family at their cabin in Montana."

"What?! Why should we do that?"

"We're to take part in the yearly Woodrough gathering. Every year, Archibald Woodrough invites family and close friends—which include a number of company board members—to his cabin for a week-long event. We'll still be playing the part of external auditors and can interview board members and the business' upper management."

"Archibald Woodrough suspects the blackmailer could be one of his old friends or family members?"

"He doesn't, but his daughter isn't so sure. She's the company lawyer; it's her job to be suspicious of everyone."

"Oh well, at least we're almost guaranteed a white Christmas," said Jennifer, clearly pleased at the prospect.

Ethan hadn't thought about it, but late December in Montana would indeed be snowy.

They spent the next hour ironing out some details and going over travel arrangements. When Ethan was reasonably certain the important issues had been taken care of, he wished Jennifer goodnight and headed for the door.

This had been a busy day which had left him little time to think about anything other than the case at hand. Alone in his car, however, his demons were back with a vengeance.

Tonight, he wouldn't be drowning his sorrows in mindless violence, though. He didn't intend to go hunt for some random perv. Tonight, his attention would be fully focused on a single individual. Ethan shuddered at the anticipation of the pain to come.

Chapter 27

Theo and Ethan were sitting in the private investigator's living room. Mostly empty cartons of shrimp fried rice, Singapore noodles and eggrolls sat abandoned on the coffee table. The FBI agent had brought the Chinese food over when he'd showed up unannounced a bit after 7 PM.

Ethan had had other plans for the evening, but he was still thankful for the visit, and for the food, too, given that week-old leftover pizza had been the only thing in the fridge up until Theo's arrival.

"The forensic team has only spent a day on the video, Ethan. You can't expect miracles. Give them some time. If there's anything interesting to be found, they'll find it. They know what they're doing. You know that."

"So they found nothing?" Ethan's voice was edgy.

"They found something, just not much yet."

"What is it?"

"They cleaned up the audio and were able to isolate the sound of the sea in the background, waves rolling onto the beach."

"Waves…" repeated Ethan pensively.

"Yes, waves. It looks like Amanda was killed very close to the sea. A boat house, possibly, or more likely a beachfront property. Given the number of beach houses in the area, it doesn't narrow things down too much, but it's something."

Ethan remained silent for a moment, lost in thought. Amanda had been killed in a beach house and found buried on the beach. Could the house be in the vicinity of where Amanda had been found? It would make sense. The killer would have wanted to get rid of the body as soon as possible to reduce the chance of him getting pulled over with a dead woman hidden in his trunk.

"They might find something else. They're just getting started," Theo continued.

Ethan watched him get up and stretch before walking to the window overlooking the street. He stood there silently watching the cars go by until Ethan finally broke the silence. "Anything new with the senator? Are you sure you're dealing with a copycat?" He knew the answer to that question, but he really needed something to hold onto. Some shred of a clue he might sink his teeth into to find his wife's killer.

"We're about ninety percent certain. The branding and the slashed throat are about the only commonalities with our man, and even that isn't a perfect match."

"Meaning?"

Theo looked at him a moment before sighing heavily. "None of this information is public so you keep it to yourself, understood?"

Ethan nodded. Who was he going to tell, anyway?

"I already told you that the branding on the senator's chest was a single letter A instead of two and that the letter was upside-down with respect to the Cowboy's signature."

"Yes..." Ethan was waiting for his friend to get to the point.

"But that's not all. The senator was branded postmortem."

Ethan found this to be a very interesting detail, a definite telltale sign. The killer who branded his victims while they were alive did it because he enjoyed inflicting pain as much as to sign his work. Branding the victim after he or she died, on the other hand, had nothing to do with inflicting pain. They were definitely dealing with a copycat.

"The blade used to slash his throat is also different from the one the Cowboy used in the past. This one isn't even made of metal. Based on the residue they found inside the wound, it looks like flint," continued Theo.

"Why would anyone use a flint blade nowadays? Where do you even buy one?"

"Online, just like everything else. We also think we know why he didn't use a regular knife."

"I'm listening."

"The senator liked to travel with a hand-held metal detector. He used it on his guests to make sure they weren't armed. A flint blade would have fooled the detector."

"That implies the killer was familiar with the senator's habits. That should narrow things down for you. What was his security detail doing while he was being murdered?"

"His bodyguard had been given the night off. We interviewed the guy and it was apparently not unusual. The senator liked his privacy when he was planning to have guests over in his room."

"What kind of guests are we talking about here? Escorts?" asked Ethan, grabbing another eggroll. The night was going to be long, and he'd only nibbled at his food. Theo had done the bulk of the eating for once.

"Even better than that. It would seem that our gay-bashing senator was a bit of a hypocrite..." said Theo with a smirk.

"Call me shocked. I wonder if Gwendoline Thomas knew about this?"

"Who's that?"

Ethan explained who the woman was and how he'd accepted an offer from her company to come and investigate a case.

"You guys think the senator was killed by a man he picked up in a bar?"

asked Ethan.

"It would seem that way. We have the testimony of a bartender and video footage of a guy entering the hotel's lobby that support that theory."

"Do we see his face on the video?"

"No, the killer made sure to keep his head down in front of the cameras. He knew what he was doing."

Theo left the apartment a little after 11 PM, but Ethan wasn't a bit tired. He grabbed his laptop and settled on an ottoman facing the window. He was getting a late start but still intended to do the work he'd originally planned on doing.

He clicked on a folder he hadn't opened in a year and started going through the various files it contained. He needed to reacquaint himself with every detail of the case. He had to find the clues he'd missed a year ago; he had no other choice.

For the next four hours he reread every police report on the Cowboy, reviewed the crime scene pictures and descriptions, and went over every word of the FBI profilers' report on the killer's personality. They, too, had completely missed the fact a second psycho was involved.

The autopsy results were next on his list. He had the autopsy reports of all the victims—all save Amanda. He'd never requested a copy of her file. There had been no need for it since they'd supposedly caught the killer. He was also fairly certain he wouldn't have been given a copy even if he'd requested it. He was a bit too close to the victim to be allowed to work on the case.

Ethan had no documents relating to his wife's murder. Just a clipping of her obituary… utterly worthless.

This wasn't technically true, though. He did have something… Something that could hold the clues he needed to find the man he dreamed of gutting from the inside out. He just didn't have the balls to use the only piece of evidence in his possession.

At 3 AM, he finally went to bed, only to toss and turn underneath the sheet, his mind refusing to relax.

He knew he was simply delaying the unavoidable. He didn't have a choice in the matter. It had to be done, and he needed to be the one doing it.

An instant later, he was back on his computer searching through the files hosted on his remote server. He found the video he'd copied from Jennifer's USB key and pressed play. The image of his wife's naked body tied up to a homemade torture device filled the screen.

Chapter 28

Ethan woke up to the sound of someone knocking hard on his door. He opened an eye and looked at his watch. It was nearly two in the afternoon. He got up and walked to the front door to find Jennifer on the other side.

"Are you okay?" she asked, looking at him with a mixture of worry and repulsion.

"I'm fine, why?" he answered, scratching an itch behind his head. Except the itch was more like a jackhammer attacking what was left of his brain.

"Because we were supposed to meet at the office five hours ago to start researching Woodrough Enterprise. I've been trying to reach you all morning, but your phone keeps going to voicemail."

He just stared at her blankly.

"Have you been drinking?"

He shook his head affirmatively. A stupid thing to do as it kicked his headache into overdrive.

"Go get a shower, you smell like you slept with a pack of street dogs. I'll start making coffee. We've got work to do, boss," she said, pushing her way through the door.

Ethan was still trying to emerge from the booze-induced fog surrounding his memory. What the hell had happened last night? As he walked to the bathroom his eyes fell on the open laptop lying on the floor beside the ottoman. Now he remembered why he'd been drinking.

The smell of coffee filled the apartment and Jennifer had cleaned up the mess in the living room by the time he walked out of the bathroom, refreshed but still seriously hungover.

"How full was this when you got started?" asked Jennifer, holding a nearly empty bottle of scotch.

"It was brand new, I think."

"I didn't know you drank."

"I do now, apparently."

"You picked the perfect moment to start. I'm sure Gwendoline will be thrilled. She's paying you a hundred grand and you show up drunk as a skunk."

"I'll probably have sobered up by Monday..."

"Assuming you don't start drinking again!"

"I don't intend to drink anything for the foreseeable future," he said, rubbing his temples. "I need some water, my mouth feels like I took a nap in the desert."

As Ethan walked to the fridge and poured himself a glass of water, Jennifer's phone chimed obnoxiously.

"What's that?"

"A news alert."

"Lovely! Since when do you receive news alerts on your phone? It makes enough noise as it is," said Ethan, referring to the multitude of text messages she received daily at the office.

"You're just jealous because people actually want to talk to me," she responded with a smirk. "Looks like we have a new serial killer operating in the region," she added, reading from her phone.

"What does it say?"

"That's it. It's just a news alert, not a news report."

He walked back to the living room to grab the TV's remote control. He flipped through a few local channels before finally finding the breaking news report he was looking for.

"*According to a source in the San Francisco Police Department,*" said the anchorman, "*Naomi Berhan is the killer's fourth victim and the second one in the San Francisco area. The first victim was Stephany Pierce, a librarian whose body washed ashore near the Golden Gate bridge in March. Patricia Wu, his second victim, was a Vegas schoolteacher. She was found dead in the desert a few miles outside the city in June. The third victim, Andrea Gomez, disappeared from Albuquerque, New Mexico in September. Her corpse was discovered in the Sandia Mountains nearly a month later. In all instances, the killer seduced his victims and went on several dates with them before finally killing them. Because of this atypical behavior, some media have already nicknamed him Casanova, after the famous eighteenth-century womanizer.*"

"I wonder if Naomi Berhan's black," said Ethan, as the anchorman and his cohost were starting to speculate on when a fifth victim would be found.

"She is. I just found an article with a picture of her. How did you know?" asked Jennifer, staring at her laptop. Ethan hadn't even noticed she'd brought her computer over.

"I had a bet with Theo," he replied.

Naomi's ethnicity confirmed Ethan's theory. Casanova was a serial killer who liked to screw with cops' heads to show how smart he was. Just like the Cowboy had done with him.

"What motivated you to drink this much last night?" asked Jennifer, after it became clear he wasn't going to offer further explanations regarding Naomi Berhan.

He suspected Jennifer already knew the answer to her question, but he humored her anyway. "I watched the video."

"You mean *the* video? Why would you torture yourself like that? I didn't save it for you to watch. It was just to pass along to the cops so they could do their job."

"I was looking for clues."

"You actually watched the whole thing?"

"Twice," he whispered, rubbing his temple.

She gave him an astonished look. "You have issues, Ethan. That's masochism. There's no other word."

"I needed to know what was on it."

"You needed to see exactly what your wife went through so you could have nightmares about it for years to come? Let the FBI do their job. They actually get paid for that shit."

"I don't trust the FBI to solve the case."

"You don't trust Theo? You don't think he's bright enough to figure it out?"

"Theo may be bright, but in this instance, I can't trust him. He's not telling me everything he knows. He's trying to protect me."

Theo had told him that the only useful piece of information that had come out of the recording so far was the sound of the sea lost in the background. But he'd forgotten to mention something nobody could have missed: the second murderer appeared on the video as well. Unlike Avery who wasn't shy about showing his face to the camera, the second killer wore a black leather mask that covered his entire face, but he was there nonetheless. A tall, athletic, Caucasian man with good posture. The video ended with him slashing Amanda's throat while Avery watched from a corner, jerking off.

Chapter 29

The serial killer newspapers had nicknamed Casanova watched the woman get into her car from the corner of the street where his own vehicle was parked. Casanova… he liked the ring of it. It sounded classy. Much better than the Cowboy. He'd always despised the stupid nickname. He'd been so much more than that. Anyone could brand their initials on a woman's chest, but it took skills to make them suffer the way he did. In his own way, he was a true artist. And like most great artists, his work wasn't being appreciated the way it deserved.

The woman's vehicle had long been swallowed by the flow of traffic when he started his car and headed in the direction she'd taken. Night had fallen a few hours earlier, but the streetlamps diffused enough light that he needed to remain cautious and keep his distance. He didn't want his next prey to accidentally see him before he was ready to meet her.

There was no need to hurry anyway. He'd placed a GPS tracker under her car, so he could always keep an eye on her, learn her habits and, most importantly, be able to find her anytime he wanted. This was his strength. Always thinking three moves ahead of his victims… and five ahead of the cops. The thought made him smile.

To date, Amanda Archer's murder remained at the pinnacle of his achievements. The scheme he'd come up with deserved to be featured in behavioral psychology textbooks as an example of perfectly executed manipulation. He'd managed to fool everyone.

The plan he had for his next victim wasn't anywhere as extravagant, but it would still be thoroughly rewarding.

The dot on his GPS tracker stopped moving and he found the woman's car two minutes later parked a block from a club that was the flavor of the moment among millennials. She was nowhere to be seen, so he decided to play the odds and headed for the club.

Once inside, he walked to the bar and ordered a beer from a male bartender who gave him a hungry look. Casanova was apparently as irresistible to faggots as he was to women, but his own interest resided exclusively in the latter.

He found an empty seat against the wall and focused his gaze on the woman who had won the dubious honor of being his next victim.

The club's atmosphere brought back fond memories. Flashbacks of the night he'd snatched Amanda Archer.

He'd been sitting a mere three tables away with his own date when Angus Avery had approached Amanda. He'd recruited Avery specially for this job, and it hadn't been an easy task. Finding an attractive, psychotic rapist whose initials were A.A. had taken some work, but it had been time well spent. Avery hadn't disappointed him in any way. He'd played his part perfectly and two hours later, Amanda had been strapped to a table wondering how the hell things could have gone so wrong so fast.

The fact she was Archer's wife had only made the whole experience more delightful. Of course he would have preferred enjoying the woman's company alone, but this hadn't been an option. Avery still had a part to play in his flawless plan. The part of the sacrificial lamb. And there again his accomplice had exceeded expectations.

As expected, the DNA evidence he'd purposefully left under Amanda Archer's fingernail had led to Avery's arrest in record time. The cops hadn't had much time to interrogate him, though. The two inmates who'd been graciously paid in advance for their services had made sure Avery didn't survive his first night in jail.

In truth, Avery had very little information to communicate to the cops, but keeping him alive had never been part of the plan. As far as the cops and the public were concerned, Avery had been the Cowboy and his death had given him, the real Cowboy, the alibi he needed to fool Archer and the FBI.

In the end, Archer's ego had been his downfall. He'd bragged in front of the cameras and tipped his hand. The prick should have kept his mouth shut. Up to that point the Cowboy hadn't even suspected that Archer was working on identifying him. But since the prick had been kind enough to inform him, he'd been forced to take action to neutralize the threat. He didn't know if Archer was as good as the media made him out to be, but he wasn't interested in finding out. From that moment, the fate of Amanda Archer had been sealed.

As predicted, murdering the man's wife had done the trick. Archer had completely lost it. For all practical purposes, his career had effectively ended with her death.

With Archer out of the picture, he'd been free to move on to greater things. And move on he had. The Cowboy had died with Avery, only to be reborn as Casanova, a better, more efficient predator. One who spent much more time torturing his victims. A definite improvement over the Cowboy's approach. Why should he toy around with his women for a mere hour or two when he could have them to himself for three or four days?

He'd already had tons of fun playing Casanova, but the best was yet to come. His next prey would be much more enjoyable than the last four. He was going to take almost as much pleasure in torturing her as he had with

Amanda.

His next victim's ethnicity didn't fit the pattern he'd followed so far. She wasn't Native American, the fifth largest ethnic group in the country, but it didn't matter. It was good to keep cops on their toes. Let them predict your next move only to hit them with something out of left field.

He watched the woman exiting the dance floor, his eyes following her through the crowd. She had a certain charisma about her. She walked with the assurance of someone who knew what she wanted. He liked that.

She reached her table and sat next to a cute brunette to whom she gave a lengthy kiss on the mouth. He hadn't seen that coming! It definitely threw a wrench in his plan… How was he to seduce Jennifer MacKay if she was a lesbian?

Chapter 30

After a connection in Salt Lake, Ethan and Jennifer landed in Cody, Wyoming, early on Sunday afternoon. They rented a four-wheel-drive SUV at the airport and were checking in at their hotel a short drive later.

"The town looks pretty. Do you want to drop your bag in your room and go for a walk?" asked Ethan. He had his hotel key in one hand and the handle of a small rolling suitcase in the other.

"Give me about fifteen minutes to freshen up. I'll meet you in the lobby," answered Jennifer.

Cody was indeed a cute little town. Ethan, who'd never ventured into this part of the country before, was pleasantly surprised. The Rockies, visible from all around the city, and the picturesque stone buildings lining the streets layered a quaint old-West veneer over the small-town-America atmosphere.

"What do you think?" asked Ethan as they walked down Sheridan Avenue, the town's main street.

"It's nicer than I expected," admitted Jennifer.

"Ever been to Wyoming before?"

"I went to Yellowstone a couple of times, but that's it."

"How's that? I've never been," asked Ethan.

"You're missing out. It's an amazing thing to see. If at all possible, you need to go check it out before heading back to California. Of course, most of the park is closed to traffic this time of the year, but you can go on a snow coach or a snowmobile tour and see what it looks like under six feet of snow. I hear it's quite a sight. And it's only like twenty miles west of here."

"You looked it up?"

She pleaded guilty and Ethan agreed to go. If his Scottish secretary had been to Yellowstone several times already, he owed it to himself to go check it out. It was a matter of national pride.

"So, what's the plan, boss?" she asked, as they entered a city park in search of a bench to rest their legs.

"We split up. You go to the ranch and I'll meet with Gwendolyn here in town. The ranch foreman will pick you up outside the hotel at seven tomorrow morni—"

"Seven?" she interrupted. "Why so early?"

"Because they're cowboys and don't usually sleep till noon. Anyway… you'll be heading straight to the ranch. I need you to ask a lot of questions. Be over the top. They need to be somewhat relevant to the job we're supposed to be doing here, but if you overwhelm them with enough questions, they're less likely to notice a few irrelevant ones thrown in the mix."

"Ask a lot of questions and hope for the best. Got it!" she replied, as they sat down on an empty bench. "I put together a couple of audit folders with a bunch of questionnaires I found online. I thought that would make us look more legit." She stared at a red squirrel chomping on an acorn. The rodent was smaller and cuter than his cousins roaming the streets of San Francisco.

"When did you do that?" asked Ethan, impressed but trying not to show it. He'd never thought of that.

"While you were sleeping your whisky off yesterday morning."

"Good. Well, you know what we're after, so I trust you to figure out a way to get the intel we need."

"I'll do my best. What about you? What's the plan for you?"

"Gwendoline will pick me up at the hotel at 7:30 for breakfast and then we'll head to their office."

"How come I don't get to eat breakfast with my cowboy?"

"Maybe you will. Can we stay focused here?"

She nodded her agreement while rolling her eyes. "When are we going to their cabin in the Madison?"

"What's the Madison?" asked Ethan.

"It's the mountain range nearest West Yellowstone. I assume that's where their cabin is located."

"It could be. She hasn't given me directions to get there yet. How do you know the name of the mountain range?"

"Because, unlike some members of this team, I do my homework before showing up to an assignment," she replied pointedly. "And maybe also because that giant cave they've recently discovered happens to be in the foothills of the Madison range."

"Now *that's* an explanation I can buy! With the amount of time you've spent reading about that cave on company time, you're probably on a first-name basis with its bats by now."

Jennifer gave him a look but said nothing.

"I saw a guy on the plane reading something in the paper about that cave. Did they find bones in it?" asked Ethan.

"Yes. And now it's closed off to scientists until the cops are finished with the place, which could take months at the rate they're going. They won't let us visit it anytime soon."

Ethan didn't share Jennifer's enthusiasm towards spelunking and had no desire to ever visit the place, but he kept it to himself. "So what's the deal with those bones? Are they human?"

"Definitely."

"Do they have a whole skeleton? Did they discover a caveman?"

"They have three skeletons, but they're still looking for more. At this point, they don't know how long they've been there. Carbon fourteen dating takes some time."

Ethan was vaguely familiar with the concept of estimating the age of an object based on the amount of residual radioactivity caused by the carbon fourteen atoms they contained.

"Men? Women?" he asked.

"Kids. Two boys and a girl apparently. Based on the bones' lengths, it looks like they were all under ten."

"And they have no idea who they belong to?"

"Not at this point. The theory of a lunatic targeting kids is favored by the media."

"That would be my favorite as well," said Ethan.

"Something doesn't fit though. With a population density as low as it is in the region, someone would have noticed if three kids had gone missing," pointed out Jennifer.

"And nobody has noticed, I assume."

"Nope."

Ethan agreed it was odd, but it didn't rule out a serial killer. He could have been killing over decades, in which case the disappearance would have seemed unrelated. He could also have abducted the kids from various states and brought them to the cave to hide their bodies. The sad truth was that kids went missing every day across the country.

Ethan was sitting on his bed, back against the headboard, his laptop propped open on his lap. He'd been doing online research on the Woodroughs and their businesses but hadn't found anything remotely suggestive of an oil spill around 1997. He hadn't expected to find anything, but he still had to check. If the blackmailer had gotten his intel online, the task of identifying him would have been nearly impossible.

His eyes went to the clock in the corner of his screen: already 10:23 PM and he still needed to shower before going to bed. He was about to shut his laptop when a headline at the bottom of his search engine page caught his eye.

The year 1997 was definitely in the title, as was the name Woodrough, but the article had nothing to do with their businesses.

Ethan clicked on the link and spent the next ten minutes reading a Yahoo News article that had been published December 30, 1997.

The article related the mysterious disappearance of Myriam Woodrough, the nine-year-old daughter of Archibald and Vivian

Woodrough.

The family had been spending the holiday season at their chalet in the Madison mountain range—something they did every year—when the drama had occurred.

The mother had kissed the young girl goodnight in bed around 9 PM on December 27, but when the girl's sister had come to check on Myriam the next morning, her bed had been empty. The house and the woods surrounding the chalet were thoroughly searched, but the girl had never been found.

The picture attached to the Yahoo article showed a smiling little girl with blonde braided hair wearing a baby-blue dress.

Ethan spent another hour searching the web for any articles concerning Myriam Woodrough's disappearance. He found a few, but none offered any explanation as to what had happened to the girl. There had been no arrest in the case. No one was even mentioned as being a person of interest during the police investigation, despite the Woodroughs' political clout.

This was highly unusual in Ethan's experience and spoke volumes as to how clueless the investigators were about the whole thing. They truly had no idea what had happened. The little Myriam had simply vanished. Vanished a month after the oil-spill cover up. Could this be a coincidence?

As Ethan stepped under the shower, he wondered if Myriam's body had spent the past twenty years buried in a cave, only to be unearthed in the past few days.

Chapter 31

Clive Thomas, the ranch foreman, had picked Jennifer up in front of the hotel at 7 AM sharp. An hour later, she'd been riding a horse nearly as tall as she was alongside him. It hadn't taken Clive long to mention he was Gwendoline's husband. And even less time for him to point out he hadn't gotten the job thanks to his wife; he'd already been running ranch operations by the time the two of them started dating.

"When did you start working for the Woodroughs?" asked Jennifer conversationally.

"When I was twenty-five."

This wasn't nearly as informative as a secret investigator would have wanted.

"In 2001, if that's what you were trying to figure out. Which means I wasn't around in 1997," he added with a big grin.

Jennifer feigned incomprehension.

"My wife told me what you and your associate are really here for. Don't worry. Your secret is safe with me, I wouldn't dare piss off my boss."

"Is Mr. Woodrough difficult to work for?"

"I was talking about Gwendoline. Archibald's a teddy bear in comparison." Clive was clearly enjoying himself. Apparently, Gwendoline had married a comedian.

"This is going to make my life a lot easier," said Jennifer. "Since you know the truth, maybe you can help me with records from that epoch and point me towards employees that were working either in the oil field or at the ranch at the time of the incident."

"That should be no problem. We're a family business and our employees usually stick with us until they retire. Mr. Woodrough pays good wages and decent benefits. Cowboys don't easily run from that kind of treatment."

As they reached the edge of a cliff, Jennifer's eyes opened wide. Three or four hundred feet below, thousands of cows were spread out all over the valley.

"Careful not to get too close to the edge. We don't want you to go dying on your first day. You're doing great with that horse, mind you."

"I used to ride quite a bit when I was a kid, but it's been a long time since I've been on one."

"I didn't realize they rode horses in Scotland. That's where you're from, right?"

"It is. And we do have horses. You may be surprised to learn that we have color TV, too."

"And sexy accents," he said winking at her.

Was Clive Thomas flirting with her? Fit and muscular with a mane of short brown hair, the man wasn't unattractive by any definition. She guessed he was a tad over six feet which made him slightly taller than Ethan, and just as handsome. But Jennifer wasn't interested.

They led their horses away from the cliff and galloped down the hill.

"What do you know about the spill?" asked Jennifer once they reached the bottom.

"Nothing at all. I heard about it for the first time from my wife a week or so ago. None of the cowboys have ever mentioned anything about it. Not even those who worked in the oil fields at the time. Everyone did a great job keeping their mouths shut."

"That's surprising. People usually like to gossip," said Jennifer.

"Cowboys are a loyal bunch. They don't bite the hand that feeds them."

"Could we see those records? I need to find out who was employed at the time and where they are today."

"Alright, let's head to the office then. We can finish the tour tomorrow."

Jennifer agreed and soon they found themselves galloping along a creek with pristine water. Its width varied from ten to about fifteen feet depending on the section. Trout and perch could be seen swimming between the rocks.

Jennifer missed all this. As far as cities were concerned, San Francisco was one of the prettier ones, but she wasn't a city girl at heart. She was all about nature and wildlife and felt in her element on the ranch.

She heard the rushing water before she saw it. "What's that?" she yelled over the drumming sound of the hooves hitting the ground.

"You'll see for yourself in a minute," Clive yelled back.

They continued following the creek and soon Jennifer was able to see a point where a stream of water about three feet wide connected with the creek in the distance.

As they got closer, she noticed that the water from the smaller stream was steaming slightly.

"What's that. Is this hot water?"

"It's about ninety degrees by the time it connects with the creek."

"Where does it come from?"

"From the oil field. We're only a couple miles away from the closest well pad."

"What are they using the water for?"

"For nothing. It's produced water. It comes along with the oil. They separate the two liquids before releasing the water to the surface."

"Is the water clean enough?" she asked, surprised by the practice.

"See for yourself."

They reached the intersection of the two streams and Jennifer noticed something strange about the smallest of the two. The water was not only turbid, it also had a slight brownish tint to it.

"Is this crude oil mixed with the water?" she asked.

"It is."

"And that's legal?"

"As long as the concentration doesn't exceed fifteen parts per million. That's the legal threshold for surface release in Wyoming. If your water contains more oil than that, you need to keep cleaning it or reinject it in the ground."

"But the water's brown."

"I know. At the legal concentration the oil is still visible in the water."

"It's disgusting. What if animals drink it?"

"Keep your opinions to yourself around the Woodroughs, or anyone else other than me, for that matter. I'm with you, I find it gross, but Wyoming doesn't get nearly enough rain to support the ranching industry. Cattle need the water from the oil fields, that's why the regulators allow such a high concentration of oil in the water. Without this water, the cows wouldn't have enough to drink."

"But we end up eating those cows!"

"That we do. And they taste good too!" said Clive with a big grin.

Jennifer made a note to steer clear of red meat for the entire trip.

"How can we be certain the amount of oil in the water doesn't exceed the legal limits?"

"The producers must measure it before releasing it."

"And who checks that they're in compliance?"

"The regulators audit the fields from time to time, but it's mostly based on the honor system. If your water's dirty, you shouldn't be sending it to the rivers."

Jennifer wondered how many oil producers sent water dirtier than it should be down to the rivers. And she also wondered if Woodrough Oil & Gas was one of them. That water was really brown... But if they were indeed actively breaking the law this way, surely the blackmailer couldn't know about it. Why would one rely on a twenty-year-old cover up that could no longer be prosecuted if one had evidence of an ongoing infraction that could have potentially been going on for decades?

Jennifer needed to ponder the question carefully. She had a bad feeling about this.

Chapter 32

The air felt frigid on Ethan's face. The temperature had dropped forty degrees overnight. He clearly hadn't packed for Wyoming weather, an oversight he was already regretting. He was almost glad for the hard hat and coveralls he'd been given to visit the Woodroughs' oil field.

"What's this?" he asked, pointing to a large cylindrical vessel.

"How many oil fields have you audited?" asked Derrick Elliot suspiciously. The facility engineer—a title which meant little to Ethan—had been assigned as his tour guide by Allan Woodrough, the production superintendent.

From what Ethan understood, Allan was the man in charge of the oil operation. He was also Archibald Woodrough's first-born, and Gwendoline's brother.

"This is my first one," answered Ethan honestly. There was no point in trying to fool the old-timer. "It's not necessary to be well versed with oil production for the type of work I'm doing here, Mr. Elliot."

"That's a separator," replied Derrick without questioning Ethan's statement. "It's designed to separate the oil from gas and water."

"Where does the water come from?"

"You do understand that oil is generally found in deep subterranean reservoirs together with gas and water, correct?"

"I do now..." said Ethan.

"Alright, we'd better go over a few basics before we continue our visit... An oil well almost always produces a mixture of oil, gas and water. But we're only interested in the oil and in some cases the gas. The water needs to be removed once the fluids reach the surface. That's done in vessels like this one," said the man, pointing at the separator.

Ethan nodded; the intricacies of oil production were of little interest to him. He'd never been in an oil field before and watching the beam pumps going up and down to extract the oil from the ground had only been entertaining a few minutes.

The landscape was nice to look at, though. Snow-covered mountains surrounded the field, which was itself a vast expanse of reddish dirt covered with saltbush shrubs, sage brush and other wild bushes unfamiliar to Ethan.

"Once the oil has been separated from the gas and water, it's sent through a pipeline to wherever it needs to go," continued Derrick.

"What happens to the gas?" asked Ethan, trying to look interested.

"It depends on the field. If it makes economic sense, the gas is sold and exported out of the field. But very often it's simply reinjected into the ground or burnt."

"Burned? Isn't this a huge waste?" asked Ethan, surprised by the answer.

"It's a waste from an energy standpoint, yes, but we're in the business of making money. If there's no infrastructure available to export the gas, it's usually cheaper to burn it as it's being produced than to develop the pipeline to sell it. All the gas we produce is burnt in our field. It's called flaring."

Ethan gave him a bewildered look.

"I can assure you that's common industry practice, Mr. Archer, including on massive off-shore platforms. Our small operation is just a drop in the bucket. To give you an idea, there's enough gas flared in the Permian basin alone to power the entire state of Texas." Derrick Elliot punctuated his statement with a half-smile, as if it were a source of pride.

Ethan was speechless. He'd known for a long time how wasteful society had become, but this revelation put things in perspective. He'd significantly underestimated the extent of the waste.

"But we're getting off topic here," said his guide, heading for the pickup truck.

They climbed inside the vehicle and headed for the next stop while Derrick Elliot continued his oilfield 101 lesson.

Their next destination turned out to be just as fascinating as the previous one and Ethan found himself wishing he'd gone on the ranch tour and left the oil field to Jennifer.

"How long have you been with the company?" asked Ethan.

"Nearly forty-five years." There was pride in the man's voice. "Aaron Woodrough was still running the show when I joined."

Ethan knew that Aaron was Archibald's father, Gwendoline Thomas' grandfather.

"That's impressive, Mr. Elliott. Forty-five years working for the same employer, that's quite an accomplishment. Few employees have this kind of loyalty nowadays."

Derrick's face lit up at the compliment.

"I guess that means you were here in '97," said Ethan.

"I was…" The man's smile had evaporated instantly. He looked more guarded now.

"I mean when Archibald's little girl went missing. I just stumbled across the news last night while looking up the town's history."

"Yes, I was here when it happened. We stopped production that day and the whole crew drove to the Woodrough's cabin in Montana to go look for her in those damn woods." The old-timer appeared more relaxed now that he knew Ethan wanted to talk about Myriam. If Derrick Elliott hadn't been one of those cleaning the 1997 spill, Ethan was ready to eat his hard hat.

"How far of a drive was it to the cabin?"

"About five hours, I reckon. We took the shortcut through Yellowstone."

"The park wasn't closed for the winter season?" asked Ethan, remembering what Jennifer had told him the night before.

"We didn't enter the park through the Cody Entrance. We drove to Cook City and then on to Gardiner. That's the only road in Yellowstone that remains open year-round."

"I didn't know that," said Ethan, acting like he actually knew something about the park. "The girl was never found, correct?"

"Nah. 'Twas a sad business. That poor family is cursed," said Derrick.

"What do you mean by that?"

"First the little Myriam goes missing and now Mr. Allister is murdered in his hotel room…"

"You're talking about Senator Woodrough?"

"Who else? He was probably killed by someone who didn't like his ideas. The senator wasn't afraid to stand for his convictions. He was good for Wyoming. Good for business, because he knew what he was talking about. That's him who ran Woodrough Oil and Gas before Mr. Archibald took over. And now it's Archibald's son, Allan, who's in charge."

"When did Archibald take over the oil business?"

"Must have been around the year 2000. When Mr. Allister was elected senator, he had to give up his position. And then a year later Mr. Aaron died and Mr. Archibald became CEO of Woodrough Enterprise."

That was interesting. Ethan needed to corroborate Derrick's recollection with other sources, but if the man wasn't mistaken about the year, that would confirm that Gwendoline had lied to Ethan on at least one point. She'd told him that her uncle was already no longer involved in the business back in '97 when the spill had occurred. What reason could she have to lie about this?

"What was Archibald doing before he took over the oil operation?" asked Ethan.

"He was running the ranch. After Mr. Allister became senator, he ran both businesses for a while. Technically Mr. Aaron was still in charge during the first few months, but he was too sick to be bothered with any of it by then. In fact, Mr. Aaron hadn't really been involved in the business's operations in quite some time. He pretty much stopped caring back in the mid-90s when he first got sick."

"Did Senator Woodrough completely detach himself from the business after his election?"

"Hardly," answered Derrick chuckling. "It wasn't like him to just let someone else run the show and decide how to grow his money. He still owned fifty percent of the company, you know, and he gave his brother hell anytime he could."

"The two of them didn't get along?"

"Only when it came to running the business. Otherwise, they were two peas in a pod. The Woodroughs have strong family values. They stick together through thick and thin. Always spend Christmas vacation together and all. How many families do that nowadays?"

"Have you ever been invited to their cabin?" asked Ethan.

"No. The only time I went there was to look for little Myriam. After that I wouldn't have gone even if they had invited me."

"Why's that?" asked Ethan, surprised by the man's categorical tone.

"I want nothing to do with those damn woods. There's something evil that lives there. Everyone knows it. I don't know why they don't sell the cabin and buy one somewhere else. Especially after what happened to the kid."

"What do you mean by 'something evil'?"

"There's a presence in those woods. I didn't know back then, but I know now. I talked to folks who live over there. It's not a secret for any of the locals. They all know those woods are cursed."

Chapter 33

I t was a starless night, but the ghost required no light to see. He stood enveloped in the darkness of the woods, peering at the cave's entrance from a distance.

After days spent poking their noses where they didn't belong, the police had finally deserted his domain. A large warning sign forbidding unauthorized visitors from entering the underground network had been posted directly in front of the wall of vines hiding the cave's entrance.

The three teenagers he'd seen walking into the cave shortly before nightfall hadn't seemed deterred by the warning, though. He even suspected the sign had been the only thing pointing them towards the entrance in the first place. Without it, they'd still be feeling their way around cluelessly.

He could hear them talking inside the cave. The girl's high-pitched voice carried particularly well. It bothered him intensely. He wanted to be alone. He needed silence to properly grieve for his loss.

It had taken the cops three days, but they'd finally found all the children. They'd placed the bones in individual boxes and had taken them away from him. All of them. Even hers…

He'd felt such anger as he watched the officers carry the boxes one by one out of the cave. What gave them the right to rob him of his friends? These children had kept him company for so long… and now they were gone forever. Reminiscing on his loss brought the thought of another child to his mind. The child who would soon have to die… But the bones of that one would never come to the cave. There was no room for him in the ghost's sanctuary.

He heard laughter coming from inside the cave and decided he'd had enough. There were no more child remains to be found in the underground network, but it still held many secrets. Secrets that required protection from the likes of those three teenagers. It was time they learned that their actions had consequences.

He felt a presence behind him and slowly turned around. He wasn't surprised to find his companions gathered at his back. Obeying his silent command, they noiselessly converged towards the cave's entrance. The night was quiet, but the teenagers' screams would soon change that.

Chapter 34

At Ethan's request, he and Jennifer had dined in the hotel restaurant. The thermometer had dropped another twenty degrees since the afternoon and Ethan had no desire to go out in subfreezing temperatures if he didn't have to. He wasn't made for this type of crazy weather. It seldom got hot in San Francisco, but it never really got cold either.

They'd started discussing their findings over dinner, but neither of them had the slightest clue yet as to the blackmailer's identity.

Jennifer had a theory that the blackmailer either no longer worked or had never worked for the oil company itself, based on some oil-tainted water she'd seen getting into the river. She was convinced that the blackmailer would have been using this as leverage against the company instead of the twenty-year-old spill if he'd known about it.

A farfetched theory in Ethan's opinion, but he kept his view to himself. He didn't want to discourage his assistant. Not when he himself had found precisely zero leads to follow. Worse, he wasn't at all convinced he'd be able to recognize a valuable piece of information if it slapped him in the face.

He wasn't worried about missing obvious evidence, he wasn't that thick yet. But Gwendoline Thomas hadn't called on him to draw obvious conclusions. She was paying him handsomely because she expected Ethan to see things others would miss.

Dinner over, they headed to the reception area which was roomier and cozier than either one of their rooms.

"What's the plan for tomorrow?" asked Jennifer, as they sat down in two adjacent armchairs in front of a gas fireplace. There was no one to be seen behind the reception desk and the lobby was equally deserted.

"More of the same, I guess. We'll need to start interviewing the employees one on one to try to learn something useful. We also need to look at the finances starting from 1995."

"I'm not sure I'm qualified to look at a company's finances," said Jennifer. "I'd be hard pressed to tell the difference between a healthy company and a bankrupt one."

"I know you're not, and neither am I. Take pictures when nobody's looking. I have a guy I use to analyze financials. He's not cheap, but he's a genius in this particular area."

Jennifer nodded, but he could tell she was no longer listening to him. Her eyes were focused on the television hanging from the wall.

"Is that the cave you were talking about?" asked Ethan.

The local news channel was showing crystal-clear images of a cavern. Some had been taken from the outside in broad daylight while others, artificially lit, showed the inside of the cave.

Jennifer didn't answer but walked to the screen and turned the volume up as the image faded out to reveal a news desk with two journalists.

"*Patty, please tell us what we know so far about this disturbing discovery?*" said the anchorman.

"*What we know for certain, Dennis, is that a newly discovered cave turned, in only a few days, from a fascinating scientific discovery into a disturbing mystery when the skeletons of eight children were found hidden in one of its galleries.*"

"*Should people be afraid, Patty? Are we dealing with a serial killer?*"

"*The investigation is just starting and it's much too early to know one way or the other at this point, Dennis. For one thing, we don't know how long these skeletons have been there. In the past, certain Native American tribes used caves as sepulchers for their dead.*"

"*So this could be some kind of crypt?*"

"*It could be, although the fact that only children's remains were found seems suspicious.*"

"*Do we know how old these children were? Do we know how they died?*"

"*Based on the forensic evidence collected so far, the youngest was about seven or eight while the oldest was closer to ten or eleven at the time of their death.*"

"*I understand there was only one female found among the remains, is this correct, Patty?*"

"*Yes, absolutely. The bones belong to seven males and one female. None of the skeletons show signs of blunt trauma, but that doesn't mean the deaths were accidental. They could have been poisoned, suffocated or killed in a number of ways that the bones wouldn't necessarily reveal.*"

The two journalists continued speculating for a good fifteen minutes at the end of which Ethan got Jennifer back.

"Eight kids…" she said, shaking her head. "I wish the asshole had found a different hiding spot for his victims. It would have been nice to have a look at that cave while we were in the area. But now…"

"Yeah, you'll probably be old before they open it back up to the public. Maybe even dead."

Chapter 35

It was the middle of the night, but Ethan lay wide awake after tossing and turning for a good hour. He hadn't slept much, and the little sleep he'd gotten had been filled with nightmares involving a cave and a serial killer, one targeting a ten-year-old version of Amanda.

At three in the morning, he finally gave up on getting any meaningful rest and turned on his computer. He needed to do something to busy his mind. This wasn't the city; he wasn't going to find a way to release the pressure building inside him in the middle of the night in a place like this.

Lost in the Rockies' foothills and with a population under ten thousand, Cody was the largest city within a hundred miles. And it wasn't likely to be a predator's hot spot.

He sat down at his hotel room's desk and started doing research on the late Senator Woodrough to try and get Amanda out of his head, but to no avail. He kept picturing her tied up on a wooden table, tortured by Avery and his masked accomplice.

He took a deep breath and suddenly got up. He needed some fresh air. He got dressed and a minute later he was walking the town's deserted streets.

The thermometer had dipped below zero, but for once he welcomed the feel of the frigid air on the exposed skin of his face and hands. A thousand ice needles gnawing at his lips, fingers, and ears. The sensation was so ridiculously unpleasant that he couldn't think of anything else. This was precisely what he needed.

His purifying walk lasted only ten minutes, but it was enough. By the time he sat back down at his computer with a cup of freshly brewed coffee from the lobby's Keurig, Amanda was no longer front and center in his mind.

Ethan had two good reasons to focus his research on the senator. The first had to do with the amount of information readily available on the man; Allister Woodrough was a public figure and there were hundreds upon hundreds of news articles available about him. The second reason was the coincidence—or lack thereof—of the timing between his death and Gwendoline's reception of the letter. A coincidence that Ethan had to consider in a new light now that he knew the senator had owned fifty percent of Woodrough Enterprise.

He started by looking up Allister's family tree and quickly found what he was looking for. The senator had only been married once, and the union had produced two children. Sadly, the senator's wife had died in a tragic boating accident in 1998, leaving him alone to raise their son, Matthew, and daughter, Emily. The late 90s hadn't been kind to the Woodroughs. The family seemed to be *cursed* indeed, as Derrick Elliot had put it earlier that day.

After graduating from Princeton Law, Matthew Woodrough had served as his father's chief of staff for a number of years but had resigned his position six years ago to focus on a more lucrative career as a lobbyist.

The senator having two children, his shares of the company would probably be split between Matthew and Emily, along with everything else. Unless stipulated otherwise in Allister Woodrough's will, of course.

Two more hours spent staring at his screen only confirmed what Ethan already knew about the late senator's public views on guns, gays, family values, energy independence, abortion, and a slew of other subjects.

Not looking for anything in particular, he next sifted through hundreds of pictures of Allister Woodrough doing what politicians typically do on the campaign trail: shaking hands with farmers, kissing babies, visiting an orphanage, and other things along the same lines.

The same orphanage was showcased in a number of pictures supposedly related to the senator, some of which featured kids with sad smiles and no senator at all. Ethan found it odd at first, but the explanation soon became obvious when he found out that the Woodroughs were among the orphanage's main benefactors.

Ethan didn't find any allusion to Allister Woodrough's secret sex life. No articles, no suggestive or even ambiguous pictures, nothing at all. That wasn't particularly surprising. One didn't become senator without paying off a few enemies, and a paparazzi's price was probably a bargain in comparison to the types of bribes congressmen typically dealt in.

No, it seemed the senator's sexual orientation was a well-kept secret. And yet he'd been killed by a man he'd picked up in a bar. A man who had carefully premeditated the crime. A man who had therefore known his dirty little secret... How interesting.

Chapter 36

Jennifer was finishing applying eyeliner in front of the wardrobe's mirror when her phone chimed on the bedside table. She looked at the screen and immediately turned on the TV.

She flipped through all the local channels but didn't find what she was looking for. Frustrated, she tried the national news networks without any more success.

She was getting into a pair of jeans when the local channel she'd left on in the background finally broke the news she'd seen on her phone.

On the screen she could see police cruisers parked on a small hiking trail parking lot. Their spotlights were moving back and forth in an effort to penetrate the thick wall of evergreens but were no match for the dark trees.

Between the cars parked on the edge of the woods, a crying mother was being protectively steered away from the cameras by her husband.

The image then focused on two ragged teenage boys with muddy faces and torn clothes. They were being interviewed by a sheriff's deputy holding a small notepad.

Within a few minutes, Jennifer had a clear picture of what had happened. Three teenagers had gone to the cave at night despite the interdiction and had been attacked by wolves. The two boys had managed to escape but had gotten lost in the woods. They'd walked around for hours before finally picking up a cell network and calling for help.

Their friend, a sixteen-year-old female, had been right behind them as they'd ran out of the cave, but she hadn't been with them by the time they'd finally managed to shake the wolves loose. Search parties had been organized to go look for the girl, but so far she hadn't been found.

The whole story bothered Jennifer. With the rare exception of rabid individuals, wolves almost never attacked humans. And when they did, it was always in self-defense. A pack of unprovoked wolves attacking a group of three grown humans was simply unheard of in recorded history.

Chapter 37

Casanova checked his phone one more time, but nothing had changed. The blue dot indicating the location of Jennifer MacKay's car hadn't moved in three days and he was growing impatient. Where had she gone? The fact the car was sitting in the long-term parking lot at San Francisco International did little to appease him. She could be gone for weeks for all he knew.

He'd checked on Archer at his office and apartment, but the prick's car hadn't been parked in front of either in days. With the end of the year still two weeks away, it was unlikely they'd taken off for their respective holiday destinations, which meant they were probably on a business trip together. He hadn't bugged Archer's car—a mistake in retrospective—and couldn't confirm it was also parked at the airport, but it was a fair assumption.

He'd been under the impression the woman had only been Archer's secretary, but if he was taking her with him on a business trip, there was maybe something else going on between the two. Wouldn't that be something if he was fucking her? Casanova felt his skin tingle at the idea of robbing Archer of his wife's replacement. But then he remembered Jennifer kissing that woman in the club and tempered his hope.

Maybe MacKay was bisexual… In which case, it would make things easier for him. It was much easier to seduce someone with some inclinations towards men than to try and pick up a dyke.

Casanova had seen Jennifer for the first time ten days ago. He'd been sitting in his car a half block from Archer's office, hoping to catch a glimpse of the prick's face soon after he'd received the video of his wife, when he'd seen him come out of the building with a gorgeous redhead. He hadn't known who the woman was at the time, but when the two of them had returned together an hour later, Casanova had made up his mind: he would have her.

The bitch was decidedly hot, but it had nothing to do with his urge. He wanted to be inside her, hurt her and eventually kill her, simply to rub it in Archer's face. He was genuinely looking forward to inflicting more pain on the man who'd thought himself smarter than him. And sending the prick the video of his wife had been a good start.

He'd still been around to witness Archer stumbling haggard onto the sidewalk ten minutes after returning from lunch. The prick looked so pissed off, so distraught, it had been a scene to behold. The man was pathetic.

It hadn't surprised Casanova in the slightest, though. He'd profiled the expert much better than the expert had profiled him. He'd known exactly which buttons to push to get what he wanted from his nemesis. Nemesis… Archer hardly deserved the title. He was more like a trained chimp who could give the illusion of having a brain when asked to perform some simple tasks for which it'd been trained.

His initial plan had been to send the video a few weeks after Avery's death using an email manager that allowed delayed deliveries. A sort of *fuck you* from the grave Avery would have supposedly arranged prior to being caught. In this scenario, the video would have been edited to make it seem like Avery had been the only man present.

But he'd given up on this plan when he'd witnessed Archer's unravelling. The death of his wife had completely unhinged the prick. Sending the video at this point would have done no good at all; Archer had already hit rock bottom.

That's when he'd opted to wait for the one-year anniversary of her death to send it. Give the guy some time to recover so he could feel fresh excruciating pain and despair all over again. By then Casanova had decided to show himself in the video. He couldn't let Archer think he'd won. He needed his enemy to realize his wife's killer was still alive and had played him like a violin.

Casanova had always understood people much better than they understood themselves. He'd been a student of human emotions for as long as he could remember. As a toddler, he'd learned from the other kids his age when to cry and when to look happy. He'd had to learn to emulate most emotions for the simple reason that he never felt any of them.

In his whole life, he'd never experienced anything that wasn't a variation of anger, impatience, or desire. The notion of empathy was completely foreign to him. He knew the word and its definition but was unable to make any sense of it. When relating to this kind of emotion, he felt like a blind man asked to imagine nuances between colors. He had absolutely no point of reference.

His strongest, most powerful feelings had always been those of lust and anger. Feelings he expressed best one on one with his victims.

Vengeance was also a powerful motivator to him. His first victim had been killed out of revenge. He'd been nineteen at the time and out of high school for two years when he'd finally gotten even with his eighth-grade English teacher. A chubby but attractive blonde, who always had it in for him.

He'd followed her around for weeks, observing her from a distance. His opportunity had come one evening when she was grocery shopping late at night.

He'd parked his rented van beside her car and waited for her return. He'd clubbed her on the head and thrown her unconscious form into the van. Half an hour later, he was having his fun with her in the woods. She almost managed to escape him afterward, but he was faster and had caught up to her with his favorite knife. A messy business, but he'd learned from his mistake and had gotten much better with time.

This had been his first time with a woman, too. He'd had a few *girlfriends* before that but had never gone all the way with any of them. With the exception of Suzy Vickers, they'd all turned him down, claiming they weren't ready. Suzy had been ready, though. She was no prude, that one.

He hadn't been able to perform, however, and it had been her own damn fault. The little cunt couldn't make him hard. At least not while they were dating. She eventually succeeded a few years later on a deserted parking lot. He'd come all over her, but she had never noticed. He'd already killed her by then.

Chapter 38

Jennifer and Ethan eventually found the restaurant they'd been looking for. It was literally in the middle of nowhere and would have been impossible to locate in the dark without GPS. The road didn't even have light poles.

They parked on the nearly deserted lot across the road and got out of the car. They'd been in Wyoming for eight days and tomorrow they'd be heading to Montana to continue their investigation among the Woodroughs' close friends and relatives.

To celebrate their last evening in the nation's least populated state, they'd decided to treat themselves with a nice steak. Twenty miles later, they were entering one of the most interesting venues Ethan had ever seen. The place where the locals went to satisfy their carnivorous instincts, according to the hotel clerk.

Just like in old Western movies, conversations stopped abruptly as soon as they entered the saloon and seven pairs of eyes turned towards them. In this instance the saloon was supposed to be a restaurant, but it wasn't obvious from the way it looked. To Ethan, the place had the appearance of a dodgy red-neck hangout for non-recovering alcoholics. The only indication that the place actually served food was the empty plate abandoned on one of the crummy bar tables.

In the past, Ethan had spent a fair amount of time giving interviews and speaking in front of cameras at press conferences, but never had he felt this uneasy with an audience. All eyes were turned towards them and no one spoke.

"Are you still serving dinner?" he asked, though it wasn't eight o'clock yet.

"Yeah, but you'll have to eat in the bar, we don't open the restaurant room on Mondays," replied the woman behind the counter, nodding towards a closed door.

"That will be fine."

"What do you want to drink?"

Ethan ordered a beer and Jennifer an orange juice.

"Can I see some IDs?"

"You need my ID for an orange juice?" asked Jennifer.

Realizing the bartender's unwavering gaze was the only answer she would get, she pulled her driver's license out of her purse.

"California! You two are a long way from home."

"You're tree huggers?" slurred a man sitting at the bar two feet away, who was missing more than a few teeth.

"I like trees, but I don't usually hug them," replied Jennifer, in her rolling Scottish accent.

Ethan was pretty sure she'd laid it on extra thick on purpose.

"We're working for the Woodroughs. You know them?"

The bartender nodded and the atmosphere immediately relaxed. "Sit where you want. I'll bring you menus in a minute."

They sat down at a table in the middle of the empty room, which meant only fifteen feet from the bar where the locals had resumed their discussion interrupted by the arrival of the West Coast hooligans.

"I feel like I walked onto the set of *Deliverance*," said Jennifer in a voice low enough to not be overheard.

The reference to the iconic 70s movie featuring Burt Reynolds made him smile. "I can see that…"

True to her word, the bartender brought menus along with their drinks a moment later.

"Let's try and sum up our findings," said Ethan, after they'd placed their order.

"That shouldn't take long."

He agreed. For a week's worth of snooping around and interviewing workers, they had little to show for it. "We know that the Woodroughs have loyal employees. Both at the ranch and on the oil side of their business. I didn't hear a single negative thing about them the whole time I was there."

"Neither did I, but I'm not sure that means a whole lot. Would you badmouth your employer in front of the consultants they supposedly hired to boost efficiency?" Jennifer remarked. It was a valid point. "Did you hear back from your guy about their finances?"

"Yes. He called me this morning. The finances look legit for both companies, though he was surprised they were still in business."

Jennifer raised an eyebrow.

"Their operation went through a rough patch in the late 90s," said

Ethan, as their food was brought to the table. "The price of oil was extremely low and they were losing money hand over fist. The ranch should have been doing well, but it wasn't. Probably due to poor management."

"What does it mean?"

"It means they should have gone under, or at least gone through massive layoffs."

"But they didn't."

"Nope. They survived to thrive today."

"How?" asked Jennifer. She'd just bitten into her steak when she remembered the crude-contaminated water cattle drank around here. But the steak was so good she decided to forget about it for now.

"Private cash. Archibald and Allister each forked millions into the business."

"Daddy's money?"

"I don't think so. Aaron Woodrough was still the sitting CEO back then, but he was already really sick. His money was being administered by his second wife who didn't like the two sons much from what I gather. She had power of attorney over her husband's estate at the time and wouldn't have loaned them a dime. They only got their inheritance after his death in 2001."

"How old were they to have all those millions already?"

"Early thirties. That's old enough for them to have been multi-millionaires based on salary and their gifted company shares acquired as minors, except that they both got out of school at the time the price of oil tumbled by more than fifty percent. And it hadn't recovered by the time they forked all that money out of their private accounts either."

"And how is this helping us with our blackmailer?" asked Jennifer.

"I don't know that it does," admitted Ethan.

The steaks had been worth the drive and they'd just ordered dessert when the conversation at the bar got animated.

"She was seven," said the guy with no teeth.

"No! Was older than that. At least eleven she was," said the bartender.

"Nine. She was nine when she gone missin'. I went looking for her with the guys the next day. Drove all the way to Montana." The man who'd spoken looked to be in his early seventies.

"Sure as not that's her bones they found," said a woman who hadn't spoken since the two of them had arrived.

Ethan returned his attention to Jennifer. "Were they able to date the skeletons they found in that cave?" he asked in a whisper.

"They figured out the age and approximate year of death for the girl, but they're still working on the boys. She was about eight and died between 1995 and 2000. They can't be more accurate than that with the current methods. And that's lucky already, it's only in 2012 that a researcher came up with a way to apply carbon dating to recent skeletons. Up to then it was useless for anything more recent than the 1500s," replied Jennifer, who was still fascinated with anything related to that cave.

"You sure know a lot about that stuff," Ethan said, surprised.

"I would hope so, I spent enough time studying it."

"You studied carbon dating?"

"I studied anthropology."

Ethan raised an eyebrow at the announcement. The woman really was full of surprises. "We'll need to talk about that some other time. I think our friends sitting at the bar are talking about Myriam Woodrough. Based on what you just told me, they could be right; the skeleton in that cave could be hers."

"Who's Myriam Woodrough?"

Ethan related what he'd read about the kid online, and what he'd learned from the oil field workers.

"And she disappeared just weeks after the spill?" asked Jennifer.

"Yes, but it's more likely to be a coincidence than anything else."

"And now you've got those wolves going around attacking kids," they heard the bartender saying.

"It's them woods," said the old-timer who'd worked for the Woodroughs. "They're cursed. Weird things happen over there."

"Do you know what they're talking about?" asked Ethan.

It was Jennifer's turn to explain about the three teenagers who'd trespassed into the cave at night only to be chased out by a pack of wolves.

"Did they find the woman?" asked Ethan.

"Yes, they found her in the woods a few hours after she was reported missing."

"Dead?"

"No. She barely had a scratch."

"That's weird."

Jennifer gave him a questioning look.

"Weird that the wolves didn't kill her, I mean."

"I find it perfectly normal. It would have been weird if they had. Wolves almost never attack humans. They would need to have rabies or be starving. And since we're only at the beginning of winter, it's doubtful they're starving."

"So now you're a wolf expert too. Let me guess, you were a double major. Anthropology and zoology?"

"I wish! I just know a few things about wolves. But I've trained a lot of dogs and I understand them well. In the end, wolves aren't that different."

"Well, I *trained* dogs too when I was a kid," he replied, putting air quotes around trained, "but I'm pretty sure it taught me nothing about wolves."

"And may I ask how many of the dogs you trained were seen performing in commercials or in a major Hollywood production?" She was smiling but didn't appear to be joking.

"You mean to say that you *actually trained* dogs for the movies and such?"

"Indeed. Anthropology is fascinating, but unless you're a professor, it doesn't pay the bills. And since I'm not... I had to find a job after school.

I was always good with animals—back in Scotland I used to volunteer at a zoo—so I thought I'd give it a try and it worked. I was a dog trainer for about eight years before I got let go."

"What happened? Hollywood was no longer making money?"

"Something about my attitude. Some people really can't take a joke, let's leave it at that."

Ethan stared at his dog-training anthropologist of an assistant a moment before asking, "How many secretarial positions did you hold before working for me?"

"None. This is the first one."

That explained so much…

He just shook his head in disbelief. He truly knew nothing about the girl.

Chapter 39

Snow had started to fall two hours into the trip, and they'd been forced to slow down quite a bit. Neither Ethan nor Jennifer had much experience driving in this type of weather. But after six and a half hours on the road, they were finally getting close.

"Make a turn here," said Jennifer, pointing at the incoming intersection.

"You're sure?"

"The GPS seems sure. Do you see another road?"

Ethan didn't so he turned off the highway and onto a narrow mountain road bordered with giant Douglas firs on each side. It was covered with snow, and they were caught by surprise when the asphalt ran out and the path turned to dirt.

"I wonder what that road's gonna look like in a couple hours if it keeps snowing like this. I hope the Woodroughs are prepared for this eventuality," said Jennifer.

"If they've been coming here for decades, I suspect they are. They probably have snowmobiles or the like."

"Yes, but we don't."

"It doesn't matter, we have nowhere else to go for the next week anyway. We need to make the best of our time here because so far we have very little to show to justify our handsome retainer."

Ethan had said it in good humor, but it did worry him. This was precisely what he'd feared. His brain just didn't connect the dots. He'd talked to everyone working for Woodrough Oil and Gas and Jennifer had related all the conversations she'd had with the ranchers. Despite all this, he still had no clue about the blackmailer's identity, their motivations, or why they'd waited twenty years to send that letter.

The list of suspects wasn't even that long. The envelope containing the letter had been found at the front desk with the rest of the mail, but the stamp showed no postmark. Which suggested the letter had never been sent. Someone had simply placed it with the mail in a half-ass attempt to hide that fact. Therefore, the blackmailer had been in the company's office building.

"Here, Ethan! Turn here," said Jennifer, pulling him out of his reverie.

"Sorry, I was thinking about the lack of a postmark on that letter."

"You mean the detail that was supposed to help us out..." she added lightly.

Gwendoline had mentioned this detail during their first meeting and it had been one of the reasons Ethan had hoped to be able to find the man or woman responsible.

"Someone put it there while the receptionist went to the bathroom. That's the only possibility," said Jennifer.

"There is a small chance it was actually delivered with the mail."

"So you think the mailman did it? That's almost as farfetched as the butler."

"I meant there is a chance the letter went through the mail, but never got stamped. I have received one or two of those in the past. They just get through the postal service's cracks and get delivered without a mark."

"How often does that happen?" Jennifer sounded more than skeptical.

"Seldom for sure, but it does happen."

"And you think this is one of those rare occurrences?"

"No, I don't. The coincidence would be amazing. I think someone waited for the receptionist to leave her desk and dropped it on top of the mail," he admitted.

"Which means it had to be someone in the office."

The mail had been delivered shortly after lunch and distributed by the receptionist an hour later. In the meantime, only two workers had come in and out of the office, according to the receptionist. Ethan had interviewed both and doubted either one of them was involved.

"Then we're dealing with only four suspects, but we've talked to them all and it led nowhere at all," he said.

"Four? You're counting the receptionist and Gwendoline as suspects? I can see the receptionist, but Gwendoline is the one paying us a hundred grand to figure out who sent the letter. I doubt she's doing it just to cover her tracks."

This was a valid point, but Ethan had seen weirder things.

"I still think someone came in while the receptionist went to the bathroom, dropped the letter off and was out of the office before anyone noticed," said Jennifer.

The office was located on the edge of the oil fields. Anyone had access to it, but it wasn't on a main public road. Getting there required driving on the lease roads for a good five minutes and anybody not belonging there would likely have been spotted.

"If the blackmailer came in and out, he had to be watching the receptionist from outside, waiting for her to leave her desk," he said.

"Or maybe the receptionist lied when she said she was only gone five minutes. Maybe she's in the habit of taking long breaks and everyone in the company knows about it. That's something we should ask Gwendoline."

The snow-covered road finally led them to a clearing of about an acre where a few cars were parked on the side of a massive chalet. Ethan had never seen anything like it. By the look on Jennifer's face, neither had she.

The two-story log cabin covered at least a quarter of the clearing.

"That's a castle," said Jennifer. "I wonder how many bedrooms this place has."

"We'll be snowed in by the time we wake up. Wanna bet?" said Ethan, parking their rented car between two large pickups.

"No thanks. I'm pretty sure you're right."

They stepped onto the wide wooden porch surrounding the entire lodge and rang the front bell.

The door was answered a minute later by a man in his sixties wearing a dark brown corduroy suit, a white shirt and a short black tie. He had piercing eyes and thinning gray hair that gave him a distinguished look.

"Please come in. The other guests are in the billiard room. Who should I announce?" asked the man in a professional voice.

Apparently, butlers still existed... Maybe Ethan should get one to clean up the mess in his apartment.

They followed the man who'd introduced himself as James Travis as he led them through the house. It had an interesting floorplan. A massive fireplace surrounded by a vast expanse of open space stood at the center of the cabin. Comfortable-looking couches and armchairs were arranged all around the hearth. All the rooms on the first floor were located on the periphery of the large open space while two sets of stairs, situated on opposite ends of the cabin, led to the second floor.

The billiard room occupied the southwest corner of the house. Gwendoline and Clive Thomas were playing pool at one of the two tables while two men Ethan didn't know racked the balls at the other. Another three guests were sitting in armchairs arranged in front of the large windows, chatting with drinks in their hands. Kids could be seen playing in the snow outside the windows.

"Mr. Archer, Miss MacKay, I'm so glad you could join us," said Gwendoline, as she walked towards them. "Let me introduce you to our other guests."

They went around the room with their hostess and were first presented to Garett Springer and Blake Jones. The two men interrupted their game of pool to shake hands with the newcomers. Springer appeared to be in his late fifties. With his slightly curved back, sunken cheeks, and vanishing hairline, he reminded Ethan of a cartoonish turtle.

"I understand the two of you are here to help Archibald with the business?" said Blake Jones. "Let us know if we can assist in any way."

Blake was an inch or two shorter than Ethan but stood very erect, which made him appear taller than he was. He had short wavy brown hair, green eyes, and a smile that women probably found charming.

"Blake and Garett sit on our board of directors," explained Gwendoline.

Blake seemed a bit young for a board member; Ethan guessed he was somewhere in his late thirties.

They were then introduced to Tiffany Springer, a pretty little thing who couldn't be more than half her husband's age. The slim brunette's smile looked as fake as her large breasts, but that didn't appear to deter any of the men in the room who glanced in her direction on a regular basis.

"And this is my cousin Emily Jones who also happens to be Blake's wife," said Gwendoline as Emily got out of her seat to shake hands.

"And these are the kids," said Emily, pointing through the window at three girls and a boy playing outside in the snow. "The youngest and oldest girls are mine. The one sticking a carrot into the snowman's head is Gwendoline's, and the boy is Allan's, Gwendoline's brother."

Ethan could see a family resemblance between the two mothers. Both were blonde with blue eyes, had fine features and straight noses. Gwendoline's stomach was a bit flatter than Emily's, however, and her muscles a bit more toned. Possibly the difference between one and two pregnancies.

"Allan won't arrive until later this evening. His son drove up with us to get a head start on the fun before it gets dark," explained Gwendoline.

The discussion was interrupted by a woman in her early sixties wearing a white apron. She carried a tray covered with a variety of refreshments.

"Thank you, Mrs. Travis," said Gwendoline. "Mrs. Travis is the wife of our groundskeeper. The man who answered the door when you arrived," she added for Ethan and Jennifer's benefit.

Ethan gave Jennifer a discreet look and she replied in kind. Where the hell had they landed?

Between the billiard room, the butler and the maid, Ethan had the feeling he'd walked right into an Agatha Christie novel. The only thing missing was a body.

Chapter 40

The ghost had his eyes on the boy who'd ventured to the edge of the clearing. The girls were still playing with snow on the other side of the house, but the boy had gotten bored and left them to their games.

The snow hadn't yet covered the ground under the trees, and the kid had no problem finding the small rocks he hurled at the birds perched high up in the branches.

The ghost was only a few yards away, but the boy had no idea. To the child, he was simply invisible. He was invisible to most adults as well. It took a keen eye to spot him in the woods he called home: an eye few people possessed. And those who did spot him never agreed on what they'd seen. Some saw a bear, others a beast they called sasquatch, but those who saw a ghost were the closest to the truth. This was the best description their minds would ever come up with, for their lack of imagination forbade them to grasp the much simpler truth of his identity. To them he was a shadow, a rustling of the leaves, a quickly forgotten hallucination. And that's the way he liked it.

The boy heard a noise and turned his head, looking right past him, oblivious. The ghost hadn't been spotted, but he still felt uneasy.

He'd managed to stay away from the log cabin for so long… But today he was back, driven by necessity. Back where it had all started.

He'd known kids would be here. There were always children visiting the house this time of the year. And they were often left playing outside on their own, the adults confident in the safety offered by the cabin's isolation. No evil could reach them here in the middle of the woods, so far from the dangers of modern society.

But they couldn't be more wrong. The rumors were true, these woods were cursed. And the very isolation of the cabin was what made it so dangerous. Out here, no one came to one's rescue.

A cat meowing caught the boy's attention, and he dropped the rocks he'd been throwing at trees—the birds had long fled from their persecutor.

"Kitty, kitty, kitty," said the boy, kneeling under a lodge pine, one hand extended towards the approaching cat. "That's a pretty kitty. Come here, kitty, you look cold."

The cat cautiously approached the boy, stopping every few steps to reassess the situation and meow some more. The animal eventually closed the distance and the boy caressed him with one hand for a few seconds. When it started purring, the boy grabbed him by the scruff of the neck and lifted it up in the air. The cat went wild, hissing and meowing, thrashing as hard as he could, but his claws and teeth were facing away from the child who firmly held it, arms extended in front of him.

He walked with his capture back to the edge of the clearing where a half-foot of snow had already accumulated on the ground and buried the cat's face in the icy powder. The cat's cries were now muffled by the snow. Its paws were pushing against the ground in an attempt to lift its head and breathe some fresh air, but the boy was pressing his entire body weight into the poor creature.

A minute later, the cat was still attempting to fight off his assailant who was getting tired. That's when the boy's hand slid around the pet's neck and started squeezing.

"What are you doing, Gregory?" asked a girl's voice, but the ghost couldn't see to whom it belonged from his vantage point. He couldn't risk moving without betraying his presence among the trees. The girl appeared a moment later. She looked about five or six, her nose and cheeks red with cold.

"What you're doing, I said?" She was getting closer.

"Nothing! Go away, Clara," he said, getting back up. He was keeping his body between the dead cat and the girl as if to hide his kill.

"What d'you have there?" she asked, pointing at the ground behind his feet. "Did you kill another squirrel? I'll tell your dad and you'll get in trouble."

"Go away, Clara, it's a rat and it will bite you if you get too close!"

Clara made a disgusted face and headed back in the direction she'd come from. The boy watched her a few seconds before returning his attention to the dead animal. He never saw his cousin turning around and sneaking up on him.

"Oh my god! You killed Mr. Travis' cat! You're going to get in sooo much trouble."

"It was already dead," the boy said.

"Liar! I saw you pushing it under the snow. I thought you were burying a squirrel you hit with a rock."

"You're not gonna tell Clara."

"Yes I will!" said the girl, as she started running towards the house. A moment later, her cousin was upon her and it was her head buried under the snow.

"Kids! It's time to come back inside. We're going to be serving dinner soon." The woman's voice had come from the front of the house.

The boy lifted the girl's head out of the snow. She was sobbing heavily. "Tell anyone about the cat and I promise I'll kill you. You hear me? Now stop crying like a baby. It's Christmas Eve, you'll soon get your presents."

The ghost watched the two of them disappear around the corner of the house before closing his eyes for a moment. He took a deep breath and reopened them. He felt at peace.

Chapter 41

Dinner had been served in a dining room large enough to accommodate the entire party, which had grown significantly since Ethan and Jennifer had first arrived. Archibald Woodrough, the group's CEO, presided at one end of the massive table. With a thick mane of white hair, an authoritative demeanor, and a tenor voice that carried to the other side of the table, he looked every bit like the clan patriarch he was.

Ethan had met Archibald at his office a week earlier. A ten-minute meeting organized by Gwendoline. The man had been courteous but appeared fairly uninterested by what Ethan was doing. It had clearly not been his idea to get him involved.

Archibald's wife sat to his left. She was a skinny scarecrow of a woman with haunted eyes who reminded Ethan of a submissive pet. He wondered if she'd always been that way or if the submission had been beaten into her after marrying her husband. She'd likely been an attractive young woman, but the years had not been kind to her.

"Your name sounds familiar, Mr. Archer. Where might I have heard it before?" asked Matthew Woodrough who was sitting at Ethan's right. The late senator's son was a likable guy who looked nothing like his father.

Matthew didn't look like Ethan's idea of a lobbyist either.

Just like Allan, Archibald's son, who was currently sitting next to his father at the other end of the table, Matthew had thick brown hair and a slightly cleft chin overlooking an athletic body. The family resemblance between the cousins was once again unmistakable but the two weren't twins. The senator's son was quite a bit handsomer than Allan.

"I'm not sure, Mr. Woodrough, I guess it's a pretty common name," replied Ethan.

"Please call me Matthew. Given the number of Woodroughs in this room, it's going to get confusing really fast otherwise."

"Very well, Matthew. Please call me Ethan."

"You used to be a criminal consultant, weren't you, Ethan?" asked Sheriff Oliver Bradford who was sitting at Jennifer's left, directly across from Ethan. The sheriff had been introduced as an old family friend.

"That's correct, Sheriff, but those days are gone. Now I use my brain to identify inefficiencies in businesses and suggest ways to correct them," he answered, hoping the sheriff wouldn't pursue this line of questioning further.

The lawman was about to say something else when Jennifer placed her hand on his forearm and asked him about his most dangerous law-enforcing experience. Ethan would have to thank his assistant for that later.

"What do you do, Mr. Clifford?" Ethan asked his neighbor on the other side.

"I'm retired, Mr. Archer. I used to run a boys' orphanage, but we were forced to close it down a few years ago due to lack of funds."

"How unfortunate."

"It really was. My friends Archibald and Allister helped financially as much as they could but, in the end, even their help didn't suffice. I'm not complaining, though. I'm enjoying retirement quite a bit to be perfectly honest, so there is a silver lining."

Not for the kids, thought Ethan, but aloud he said, "I thought orphanages were a thing of the past and all orphans were now placed with foster parents?"

"This is true for the majority of the kids. And all public orphanages have indeed been closed for decades, but there are still some privately-owned ones operating in most states today."

The grandfather clock rang midnight and all the kids got up from their seats at the other end of the table and ran towards the Christmas tree located in the vast open space the Woodroughs called a lounge. This announced the end of the meal and everyone followed the children out of the dining room.

The unwrapping frenzy was over and the four children played with their new toys amidst the wrapping paper detritus covering the floor. Adults for their part were enjoying various spirits while conversing in small groups on the couches surrounding the fireplace.

Jennifer and Ethan were sitting side by side respectively talking to the sheriff and Matthew. The lobbyist was explaining to Ethan the intricacies of fostering relationships with congressmen from both sides of the aisle in order to serve his customers' best interests, but Ethan was only half listening. From the corner of his eye, he was watching the kids. The dynamic between the youngest girl and the boy was peculiar. She seemed to avoid him while he appeared to go out of his way to play close to her. Ethan didn't like what he was seeing. The girl's mother had noticed too. Emily's eyes didn't leave the boy.

Guests were moving around the room, finding new things to discuss with new people. Ethan and Jennifer were talking with Gwendoline's husband now. It was the first time Ethan met the ranch foreman, but he immediately liked the guy. Unlike his wife and her cousins who'd been born into money, Clive Thomas had worked his way to the position he occupied today, and that gave him a different outlook on life. Salt of the earth was a good way to describe the rancher.

The patriarch's booming voice soon declared that it was time for the children to go to bed: an announcement that was met with sighs and protests from the clan's offspring.

"Can we have milk and cookies first?" asked Allan's boy.

"Your cups are already waiting for you in the dining room," announced the grandmother.

The kids headed for the kitchen followed by Gwendoline who was to supervise and prevent any trashing of Mrs. Travis' domain.

"It's a family tradition. Each kid gets two cookies and a cup of warm milk before going to bed. They even have their own personalized cups with their names painted on. It was already like that when Gwendoline was a kid," said Clive.

Jennifer commented on the priceless memories such traditions fostered, but Ethan was only discreetly listening. His attention was focused on Archibald, the sheriff and the retired orphanage director who were talking in low voices in a corner of the room.

They were much too far away for Ethan to hear anything, but something had suddenly shifted the patriarch's mood. Archibald Woodrough didn't look pleased at all.

Gwendoline came back from the kitchen a moment later and was immediately summoned by the trio. After a short exchange during which Gwendoline appeared to be chastised by her father, the four of them left the room.

Whatever had caused Archibald Woodrough's mood to swing, his daughter was taking the heat for it.

There were dynamics within this group that would take a while to figure out, but Ethan suspected he already knew the cause of Archibald's anger.

Chapter 42

The next morning's sun had been up a couple hours when Ethan got out of the shower feeling refreshed. He had slept through the night, something he seldom did lately. The six-hour drive and the lengthy evening had no doubt contributed to this small miracle.

Ethan heard a gentle knock on the connecting door between his bedroom and Jennifer's. The door was unlocked, so he simply told his assistant to come in.

"My room's bigger than yours," she bragged, taking the tour of his sleeping quarters. "Your bathroom's nicer though. I don't have a jacuzzi in mine. Should we head down for breakfast?"

"Sure, let me put my shoes on and I'm ready. Do you have cell reception?"

"No, nothing. But I suspect we aren't the only ones. The mountains probably block the signal, which explains those." She pointed at a corded landline phone on the bedroom's desk. "I have one in my room too."

Ethan hadn't even noticed the presence of the device before she pointed it out.

"Did you learn anything interesting last night?" she asked.

"Other than Blake Jones wouldn't mind getting in your pants, not really. At least nothing that would help us identify the blackmailer."

"Because Blake trying to get in my pants is useful in that matter?" she teased. "He's not bad looking, but I don't think I'm interested."

"Yeah, not really your type…"

"How do you know what's my type?" asked Jennifer, one hand on the door's handle.

"I thought you preferred women, and that doesn't fit Blake's description. Plus he's married…"

"I don't broadly reject men, Ethan. I'm usually more attracted to women, but I don't see myself as a hardcore lesbian. I'm open to trying new things."

Good to know.

As if reading his mind, she added, "Just not with you…" She flashed him a smile and exited the room.

They found Gwendoline and Emily having their breakfast in the dining room along with their respective husbands and Tiffany Springer, the trophy wife. Garett Springer could be seen smoking outside. He was in the middle of a discussion with Archibald Woodrough. Some business matters, probably. They were bundled up in winter jackets and vapor almost as thick as Springer's cigarette smoke was coming out of their mouths as they spoke.

"How cold is it out there?" asked Ethan.

"Probably around zero," ventured Clive. "We've had a cold front coming down from Canada over the past few days. It probably won't get better anytime soon."

"We also had a snowstorm overnight," said Emily. "Two feet of powder on the ground. If it wasn't Christmas, we could go skiing," she added, sounding disappointed.

Children's squeals were heard from the outside and Ethan suddenly tensed.

"It's just the girls playing in the snow," said Emily, who'd noticed his reaction. "A mother learns to recognize the different types of screams. We get plenty of practice, believe me!"

"Plenty!" acquiesced her husband.

Ethan had caught Blake staring at Tiffany's ample cleavage when they'd walked into the room, but Emily's husband had now turned his attention to Jennifer once again—albeit in a more subtle way than he had under the influence of alcohol the night before.

"Is Gregory playing with them?" said Jennifer, just as Ethan was about to ask the same question.

He wondered if his assistant had also noticed the boy's peculiar attitude of the previous evening.

"No, I think he's still in bed," said Gwendoline.

Breakfast over, Ethan spent the next couple hours mingling with the guests gathered around the fireplace. They seemed like a surprisingly tight bunch, but something felt odd about the atmosphere. Something Ethan couldn't explain.

Gregory still hadn't been seen by the time Mrs. Travis announced that lunch had been served.

"I'll go check on my son. Don't wait for us," announced Allan as the others followed their noses to the origin of the mouthwatering aroma.

The hungry guests had settled down in their chairs, and dishes were passing from hands to hands when Allan returned, looking flushed.

"Gregory's dead," he announced.

"What did you say?" asked Vivian. The color was already starting to drain from the grandmother's face.

"I said he's dead, Mother. Gregory's dead in his bed."

As the shockwave of his announcement traveled through the room, Allan stood at the door looking more dumbfounded than upset. This wasn't the reaction one would have expected from a grieving father. On the other hand, Ethan knew that different people grieved in different ways. Maybe Allan would start bawling his eyes out once the realization of his son's death sank in. The first stage of grief was denial after all.

Emily and Vivian were the first ones to cry, but their tears were contagious and within a minute Mrs. Travis had joined in. The rest of the audience did their best to keep it together, but the sadness was palpable in the room. The death of a twelve-year-old tended to have that effect on people.

Archibald seemed strangely immune, though; his stoical behavior was bordering on callousness as he rounded up his son and the sheriff to go check on the body. As the three of them headed upstairs, Ethan followed and nobody objected.

They made it to Gregory's room and quickly confirmed that Allan hadn't been mistaken. The boy appeared to have died in his sleep. His face was as white as snow, but he looked at peace.

Rigor mortis had already set in, which suggested he'd been dead several hours already.

"I don't understand how it's possible," said the dad. "He's just a kid, he's perfectly healthy." The man looked bewildered, but still not distraught.

"It doesn't make any sense," said Archibald, lifting the sheet and cover to examine his grandson. But there was nothing to discover, the boy's pajamas showed no trace of blood.

"Do you want me to call it in?" asked the sheriff nervously.

Archibald gave him a look. "Obviously! What else is there to do at this point, Oliver? We're not going to keep the body in here through the holidays."

The sheriff picked up the phone sitting on a nearby dresser and started dialing. He replaced the receiver, shaking his head, a few seconds later. "The line is dead. The storm must have taken it out. We'll need to go to town to get an ambulance."

Archibald sighed heavily before exiting the room. They followed him downstairs and the sheriff volunteered to go get some help.

Through the window, Ethan and Jennifer watched him get into his car and drive away.

"Do you want to get some fresh air?" asked Jennifer.

Ethan agreed and they went to retrieve their respective jackets from the coat rack.

"What happened to the kid?" asked Jennifer once they were outside.

The air was frigid, but Ethan barely noticed. "I don't know. Maybe a heart attack or an aneurism. There is no sign of foul play. He seems to have died in his sleep, without a care in the world."

"He was only twelve." Jennifer looked more distraught than the kid's father.

They'd slowly walked a full circle around the house by the time the sheriff's car returned.

"What happened?" they asked as the man stepped out of his vehicle.

"A tree fell across the road."

"Do you need help?" offered Ethan.

"What we need's a miracle, or at least a chainsaw and some shovels, because it's a big one and it's buried in snow."

The whole household was informed of the situation and Mr. Travis went to the tool shed. He came back a moment later carrying an axe and a shovel. "That's all I have in working order. The chainsaw needs a new chain," he said apologetically.

"Looks like we're going to be stuck here for a while," said Ethan to Jennifer. He was starting to have a really bad feeling about the whole thing.

Chapter 43

J ennifer had retreated to the billiard room with Ethan to give some space to the grieving family. They were soon joined by Blake Jones.

"That's going to douse down the Christmas spirit a bit," said Blake, sitting down beside her. "How can such things happen?" he added, shaking his head.

Whatever Gregory's death had done to the Christmas spirit, it apparently hadn't tempered Blake's interest in her person. Something Ethan had noticed as well, given the look her boss was currently giving her.

She was starting to wonder whether Ethan saw more than a coworker in her. She'd never done anything to lead him to believe she wanted more than a professional relationship with him, but men didn't always need encouragement.

"I'm going to see if I can be of any use out there," said Ethan, leaving her alone in the room with her new friend.

"Your boss seems to be all work and no play."

"How do you know he's my boss?" she asked, not joking.

"I'm sorry. I clearly made an incorrect assumption. Probably because I'm a chauvinistic pig…"

"That's all right. Your assumption was correct. I just wanted to know what made you think I wasn't his boss. But your explanation sounded pretty convincing so I'll let you off the hook this time," she teased.

"What's his story? Last night at dinner he looked uncomfortable when the sheriff started telling people what he used to do for a living."

"I don't think he was uncomfortable. That's a part of his life that's over. Now he's doing other things and I think he's happy with the change."

"If you say so…" he said, brushing her arm with his hand as he grabbed the cup of tea on the coffee table in front of them.

She gave him a look meant to convey that she'd not been fooled by the maneuver.

"I suppose your loyalty lies with your boss. I can understand that. I don't want you to tell me anything about him you're not comfortable with," he continued.

Jennifer wasn't sure what the man was after, but if he'd come to her for intel on Ethan, he was going to be direly disappointed.

"Have you seen a cat?" Mr. Travis asked Ethan as he stepped out of the billiard room.

"I can't say I have. There are none in there," he replied, pointing to where he'd come from.

"That's odd. Nobody's seen him today and he didn't come home last night. He hasn't touched his supper. That's not like him." Travis looked worried.

They walked back together towards the lounge and ran into Emily and her daughter Clara.

"Mr. Travis, I have more bad news, I'm afraid. Clara says Gregory killed your cat yesterday."

And now the kid is dead... Karma truly is a bitch, thought Ethan.

The groundskeeper's face had turned two shades paler. "What? Why would he do that? Why didn't you call me?" he asked Clara.

The kid was crying, her sobs making her answer impossible to understand.

"Because he threatened to hurt her," interpreted her mother.

"Where's the cat now?" asked Mr. Travis.

"Outside in the snow," Clara managed to say between two sobs.

She led them to where Gregory had left the cat's body, but they found no sign of the animal.

"The snow must have covered it," suggested Emily.

Ethan went to fetch shovels as the older man knelt down in the powder and started digging with his hands.

Ethan came back with two shovels, and the men dug silently in search of the poor animal. As they did, Ethan's mind drifted to the articles he'd read about Myriam Woodrough's disappearance.

The nine-year-old had vanished from this very house twenty-two years ago, nearly to the day. He seemed to recall she'd gone missing on December 27. And now, her nephew had been found dead in his bed, maybe even in the same room the girl had been occupying back then. Was this a coincidence? And was the fact the boy had died a few hours after his cousin had witnessed him killing the groundskeeper's cat a coincidence too?

After thirty minutes of efforts, they eventually stopped digging. If the cat's body hadn't been carried away by a fox or a coyote, it had been buried somewhere else.

They headed back to the house in silence. The wheels were turning in Ethan's mind. Strange things were going on in this place.

The thought reminded him of the conversation he'd overheard the night they'd been dining at the steak house. These folks had seemed convinced that the woods were cursed. That evil lived there.

Ethan didn't believe in the supernatural. He didn't believe in curses. But he believed in evil. He had looked evil straight in the eyes.

The old folk tales about this forest were perhaps true, after all. Maybe a monster did dwell here. But if that were the case, one thing was certain: the monster was human.

Chapter 44

As was to be expected, Christmas dinner had been a depressing one. Few words had been exchanged and it was obvious based on the general mood that nobody wanted to be here anymore. It was particularly evident among the friends of the family who would have paid a lot of money to be able to hit the road and leave the Woodroughs to their grief. What was one to say to a father who'd just lost his son?

Interestingly enough, Allan didn't appear to be grieving all that much. He seemed annoyed and angered as if his son's death was an inconvenience he didn't need, but he didn't look particularly distraught. Talking to no one in particular, he simply kept repeating that he didn't understand what had happened. In that respect, he wasn't the only one.

Ethan kept replaying in his mind the sequence of events that had led to the morbid discovery of the morning, but he had yet to pinpoint anything suggesting foul play. Until proven otherwise by an autopsy, Gregory appeared to have died of natural causes. At any rate, the fact it might not have been the case didn't seem to have crossed anybody else's mind yet.

The puny fire burning in the hearth was a reflection of the energy level in the room. Nobody was even thinking about adding more wood to it.

"Did you find the cat?" asked Matthew to Ethan. The lobbyist looked somber, more affected by the tragedy than the boy's dad.

"No, we didn't. Some scavenger probably got to it."

"Are you okay, Jennifer?" asked Matthew.

"I'm fine. It's just a headache," she replied. Her eyes were closed, and she was rubbing her temples.

"You're sure you're okay?" enquired Ethan.

"Yes. I just need a minute. It happens sometimes." She sounded slightly ticked off by the repeated questions and Ethan decided to drop the issue.

The fire had nearly completely died now. Only a few embers could still be seen among the ashes. That's when the lights went out—immediately followed by a child's scream. This time Ethan was certain fun hadn't been the motivation for the scream.

"Clara! Clara, where are you?" he heard Emily say as she stumbled around between the furniture, searching the darkness for her daughter.

Soon Ethan's eyes grew accustomed to the dark, but the glow of the dying embers didn't cast enough light to see anything outside a three-foot perimeter surrounding the fireplace. The rest of the room was pitch black.

"James went to check the breaker." Mrs. Travis' voice was coming from somewhere behind him. She'd probably been in the kitchen when the power had gone out.

"Thank you, Mrs. Travis," said the grandmother as the lights returned.

The faces around the room were still as grim as they'd been before the power outage, however.

"The main breaker had tripped, everything's back to normal now," declared Mr. Travis, returning from the electrical panel.

Gwendoline entered the room a moment later to announce that the kids' milk and cookies were ready. It was only half past nine, but the ritual was probably meant to infuse a sense of normalcy into an otherwise very disturbing day for the children.

The three girls headed for the kitchen and a few conversations picked up here and there.

Vivian Woodrough seemed to be the most affected by the death of her grandson.

Speaking in a whisper, Ethan asked Matthew, "Did Gregory have a mother?" The two of them shared the same loveseat, while Jennifer sat alone in an armchair at their side.

"No. She passed away a few years ago," murmured Matthew.

"How did she die?"

"She drowned trying to cross a lake. A tragic story."

Tragedies seemed to strike the Woodroughs at a particularly high frequency. The senator had been murdered, his wife had died in a boating accident, Allan's wife had drowned, Gregory had died in his sleep at the age of twelve, and Myriam had disappeared when she was nine, never to be seen again.

Ethan's reflections were interrupted by a gasping sound coming from his right. Allan appeared to be choking. Jennifer was on her feet in an instant to administer first aid, but it became clear very quickly that Allan's problem wasn't limited to lack of oxygen. His whole body started seizing but it only lasted a few seconds. Before anyone could grasp what was happening, Allan Woodrough slumped from his seat onto the floor.

Jennifer checked his pulse and was about to administer CPR when Ethan pulled her away. "Don't put your mouth on his," he said with authority. "He displays all the signs of acute cyanide poisoning."

Allan's name could be added to the list of Woodroughs having met an untimely death, but in his case foul play wasn't even a question. Allan Woodrough had definitely been murdered. And by someone standing in this very room.

Chapter 45

With the exception of Emily and Gwendoline who'd taken their daughters upstairs, everyone stood in a circle around the body lying on the floor.

The sheriff took charge. "What makes you say that, Mr. Archer? What poisoning signs are you referring to?"

"Breathing distress, seizures and cardiac arrest are all signs of acute cyanide poisoning, Sheriff. Allan only choked for a few seconds, which means he didn't die of lack of oxygen. Asphyxiation by choking would have taken closer to a minute. And his son dying in his sleep last night... that's just too big of a coincidence."

"Are you suggesting the boy was given cyanide as well?" asked the sheriff.

"I don't think it was cyanide, but I suspect he was poisoned, yes."

"He makes some good points, Archibald," said the lawman, looking to the patriarch for guidance. "Something's not right here. We need to call the authorities."

"You're the sheriff, god dammit! Do your job," answered Archibald.

The room was as silent as a tomb; the sadness and general discomfort that had weighed over them since the death of the boy had been replaced with genuine fear for their lives. And Ethan was convinced they should be. A killer was hiding among them, he was certain of it. The tree blocking the road, the dead phone line and now a second body all pointed to the actions of a lunatic. Though in the back of his mind he suspected they wouldn't be that lucky. The perfectly organized and methodical nature of the crimes wasn't pointing towards a madman but a very methodical individual.

He started to look at his companions with a very different eye. The eye of a hunter tracking a dangerous predator.

"We need to get to town and make some calls. We must clear the road. Maybe we can pull the tree away with the trucks if we put chains on the tires. Whoever isn't helping must stay in this room. Staying together will lower the chances of another tragedy," said the sheriff.

"We were all together when Allan was poisoned. That didn't stop whoever did this," pointed Clive Thomas.

"But now we're watching each other," replied the sheriff. "It will make a difference."

"Are you saying that one of us killed him?" asked Tiffany, the trophy wife.

The sheriff looked uncomfortable. "It's a possibility we must consider, ma'am."

Before anyone had a chance to react to his statement, the sheriff enrolled the help of the retired orphanage director, Matthew and Clive and headed for the door.

"How do you think Allan was poisoned?" the patriarch asked Ethan.

"Most likely in his drink. Someone must have slipped a solution of sodium or potassium cyanide into his scotch when he wasn't paying attention."

"Maybe the killer took advantage of the power outage," suggested Blake.

"If that's the case, whoever put the poison into the drink may still have the vial with them," said Jennifer.

This was worth a shot and Ethan congratulated himself for bringing her along. A thought he immediately regretted when he realized what it meant. By bringing Jennifer to the cabin, he'd placed her in harm's way.

"Jennifer's making a good point," he said. "Everyone should empty their pockets and have their neighbor pat them down thoroughly."

Nobody protested Ethan's suggestion, which wasn't a good sign. If someone had been carrying something incriminating, they wouldn't have subjected to the search so willingly. They went through the motions anyway, only to find out that no one in the room had a vial in their possession.

"It must be one of the men who left with the sheriff," suggested Tiffany.

"Or the killer already got rid of the vial," replied Ethan.

The four men presently returned from outside looking even grimmer than when they'd left.

"All vehicles have been disabled," announced the Sheriff. "The tires have been slashed and the brake lines severed."

"What about the snowmobiles?" asked Archibald.

"We tried starting them, but the tanks are full of dirt or some type of sand," answered Matthew.

"Let's search their pockets," said Tiffany. But this time the suggestion was even more futile. Had the killer been among them, he'd have had plenty of opportunities to get rid of the evidence while outside. Nonetheless, the four men were told the procedure and they subjected to it with only minor protests from the sheriff who deemed himself above any possible suspicions. As Ethan had predicted, no vial turned up.

It was decided that the room should be searched next, and they ransacked the place for a good fifteen minutes before agreeing that the vial couldn't be found.

"What about Emily and Gwendoline? They haven't been searched," pointed Tiffany.

"Gwendoline was in the kitchen preparing the girls' hot cocoa when the lights went out, and if Emily had been the one pouring the poison, she'd have had twenty minutes to get rid of the vial by now. There's no point searching her," said Ethan, who'd already considered the possibility.

The others seemed to agree with his conclusion as an uncomfortable silence settled upon the room.

"It doesn't look like we'll solve anything here tonight and we all need some rest," said the sheriff. "I would advise we all head back to our rooms and barricade ourselves in for the night."

"What do we do with Allan?" asked Vivian, who was still silently crying by her son's body.

"Leave it there, Vivian. He doesn't give a damn about it anymore," was her husband's reply as he headed to his bedroom.

Archibald Woodrough was showing even less emotion over the death of his son than Allan had over Gregory's. In what kind of vipers' nest had Ethan landed?

Their respective doors locked and secured with heavy chests of drawers, Jennifer and Ethan met in Jennifer's bedroom to regroup.

"What do you think? Are we all going to get targeted one after the other?" she asked.

Ethan considered her question for a moment before answering. There was no point lying to Jennifer, she'd see right through him anyway. "It depends what type of killer we're dealing with. If it's a lunatic acting out a fantasy, it's likely that nobody's safe. But I don't think that's who we're dealing with here. I think whoever's behind this has a bone to pick with the Woodroughs. So far, the killer has only targeted family members."

"Do you think it's the work of our blackmailer?"

"It's possible. Maybe the letter was just to get Archibald's attention. Make him anxious, get him to worry ahead of the true ultimatum."

"Which would be murdering his whole family in the middle of the woods with no way to run?"

"Something like that…"

"That sounds cheery. I have to say, Ethan, that bonus of yours is looking pretty crappy right now. I'm starting to think that screwing Tabatha in front of *How the Grinch Stole Christmas* would have been a tad more fun."

"I'm glad you haven't lost your sense of humor."

"What about the senator? Do you think it's the same psycho who killed him?"

"I don't know. There's something about the way the senator was killed that doesn't fit what we have here."

"What do you mean?"

Ethan decided that, given the circumstances, he could trust his assistant with the details Theo had provided. "This is confidential information you must keep to yourself, Jennifer, but the senator was killed by a Cowboy copycat."

"His chest was branded with two capital A's?"

"No, only one, but the throat slashing is also a match."

"Why do you think it's a copycat? Maybe it's the original killer back for round two. He did send you that video, didn't he?"

Ethan hadn't thought about the video all day, for the first time since he'd received the link.

"I don't think so. I don't see him branding his victim post-mortem, that's not the type of thing he'd find satisfying. This is a different guy."

They sat on her bed in silence for a moment.

"Any idea who's behind it?" asked Jennifer after a while.

"No. I've been trying to replay the evening in my head, especially the minutes leading to Allan's death, to see who could have been close enough to his glass to poison it, but it's not an easy exercise."

"And memories are tricky, I saw a documentary on the subject. Our minds will make up memories and trick us into believing they're authentic."

"I'm aware of this, but let's not worry about it at the moment. Let's try and rearrange the room with everyone in it."

"Alright. Let's say the fireplace is the center of a clock dial. You and Matthew sat on the loveseat located at twelve o'clock while I sat in the armchair at one o'clock."

"Allan sat on the edge of the loveseat located at three o'clock. Who was sitting between the two of you?" asked Ethan.

"Emily was, sometimes, but she moved around the room quite a bit over the evening."

"She was definitely sitting there when the lights went out, though. I heard her getting up to go check on her daughter."

"You think she could have done it then? I mean pour the poison into his drink?" asked Jennifer.

"It's possible, but she would have needed to know where the glass was precisely, whether in Allan's hand or on the end table between their two seats. She'd also have had to act very fast because she was kneeling with the kids by the time the lights came back up."

"If the glass was on the end table, she would have just needed to extend her arm."

"Assuming she already had the poison in hand and was ready to pour. That would imply she knew not only that the lights would go out but precisely when," said Ethan.

"And unless she has amazing telekinetic powers and flipped the breaker with her mind, that would mean she had an accomplice flipping the switch for her."

"Who wasn't in the room when the power went out?"

They both sat thinking an instant.

"The Travises weren't, but they're almost never with the guests anyway," said Jennifer.

"Gwendoline was in the kitchen working on the kids' milk and cookies."

"Where was the retired orphanage director? I don't recall his name."

"Sam Clifford, I believe. I can't picture him in the room either at that time. He moved around over the evening as well. At times he was talking with the sheriff and Archibald, who were sitting side by side at nine and ten o'clock respectively, and at others he was talking to Gwendoline and Clive, who were sitting on the couch at six o'clock."

"What about Emily's husband, Blake?" said Jennifer.

"He was sitting next to Vivian on the ottoman at eight o'clock. Mostly staring in your direction."

Jennifer ignored the comment. "Who was sitting on the other side of Allan at the four o'clock position?"

"I don't believe there was anyone in that chair all evening," answered Ethan.

"Which means someone could have approached Allan's glass in the dark from that side without being noticed."

"His glass could even have been on the end table to the left of his chair, making things easier for anyone coming from that direction."

"This is a fun exercise, but I'm not sure it's leading us anywhere," said Jennifer.

"Agreed. It would seem Emily had the best opportunity to act but she would have needed an accomplice."

"She would also have needed a motive to get rid of Allan and maybe even his son, if it turns out Gregory was poisoned too. Can you think of one?"

"Nothing obvious comes to mind. Money doesn't seem to be relevant here since she wouldn't be inheriting anything from Allan. Unless, of course, he specifically stipulated in his will that he left money to his cousin Emily because they'd had such great fun together as kids…"

"Not likely, I agree."

"It's approaching midnight, we'd better get some sleep. Tomorrow's going to be an interesting day," said Ethan, getting up and heading for the door leading to his room. "Make sure your windows are closed and don't open the door for anyone. And come and get me if you hear anything suspicious," he said from the door.

In return he received an ironic half-smile and a "Goodnight, boss."

He exited her room, pulling the door shut behind him.

He was in bed ten minutes later thinking about potential motives. Emily had no obvious reason to kill Allan, but Ethan hadn't forgotten what he'd seen on Christmas Eve. The way Gregory had been acting with Clara and the way the girl had responded to his behavior. Clara had looked uncomfortable, scared even. And Ethan hadn't been the only one to take notice. Emily had seen it, too, he was sure of it.

Chapter 46

From his vantage point a few feet outside the perimeter of the clearing, the ghost saw the last light go out inside the cabin. They'd all turned in for the night. He doubted they'd be getting much sleep though. They'd be too scared for that.

The second victim had lifted the veil of denial from their eyes. That, and finding their sabotaged vehicles. They now knew without the slightest doubt that they were dealing with a killer.

He wondered if they'd already figured out that the phone line and fallen tree hadn't been accidents. They were trapped with nowhere to run. Trapped in his woods.

He hoped they felt fear. He wanted them to experience the paralyzing terror of a mouse cornered by a cat. He wanted them to feel what it was like to be facing an enemy far stronger than they were.

Arrogance wasn't in his blood, however. He knew that a cornered snake was twice as dangerous, and he wouldn't make the mistake of getting within striking distance until the enemy had no force left to fight.

He mentally went over the chronology of future events. The next kill would be a tricky one. There'd be no poison involved this time. But just like with the first two, they'd never see it coming.

He needed to take his time, though. He couldn't take the risk of ruining everything by rushing things. But he had no concern in this regard; he had the skills required for the task. Patience had never been an issue. He'd already been waiting so long for this.

Chapter 47

Morning came and by nine o'clock everyone was assembled in the billiard room at the sheriff's request. The lounge would have made for a more convenient room to accommodate all the guests, but its centrally-located fireplace would act as a divider and the lawman didn't want that.

Ethan sat between Jennifer, to his right, and Matthew to his left. Blake had managed to grab the chair to Jennifer's right: an obvious move by Emily's husband that annoyed Ethan.

The sheriff spoke. "Thank you for joining me this morning. I know some of you felt like they didn't have much of a choice in the matter, and I apologize for this, but we are facing an extraordinary situation that requires extraordinary measures."

He paused and looked into the individual faces in the room. "With two cases of poisoning within twenty-four hours, it should be evident to everyone that the consumption of food and beverages has become a major concern to all of us. Unfortunately, we do need to eat and drink to survive long enough to find a way out of this trap. For make no mistake, this is a trap. A trap cleverly designed by a lunatic who's more than likely hiding among us."

"How do you propose we solve this problem?" asked Garett Springer. The turtle was clearly not used to being told what he should and shouldn't do. Businessmen like him were usually in a position of power and gave orders, not the other way around.

"Until further notice, Mr. and Mrs. Travis will be the only ones allowed in the kitchen. Anyone other than these two found wandering in the kitchen will have to answer to me," said the sheriff.

"What about the children?" asked Gwendoline.

"No exceptions. I count on you and Emily to make your daughters understand the situation."

"This is ridiculous," said Emily under her breath, but loudly enough for the whole room to hear.

"Mrs. Travis will prepare the food and bring it to the dining room escorted by her husband. She will serve everyone herself, starting with her husband and ending with her own plate. The two of them will eat before us all and it's only once their plates are empty that the rest of us will start eating. I believe the reason for these proceedings will be obvious to everyone."

People nodded in agreement.

"From now on, we will only drink from unopened bottles and cans. Water should be taken straight from the tap or from a brand-new plastic bottle. I would advise carefully examining the bottle for any trace of puncture that could be the result of tampering with its contents. Is this clear to everybody?" asked the sheriff.

Everyone agreed but the tension in the room was palpable. The trust they'd enjoyed twenty-four hours earlier had been replaced by suspicion and fear. All it would take was the right kind of spark for the whole room to explode into uncontrollable panic.

"May I add something to this?" asked Ethan.

Sheriff Bradford gave him a wary look before nodding in acquiescence.

"Several of us had scotch last night, but only Allan was poisoned. This implies that Allan's drink was poisoned in his glass, not in the bottle. This means that people should at all cost avoid leaving unfinished glasses lying around. Keep your glasses with you until they're empty and don't refill them. Go get a new glass for a refill."

"This is a good point, Mr. Archer. Thank you for bringing it up," said the sheriff.

"Maybe we should ask Mr. Archer why he felt the need to bring it up?" said Tiffany Springer.

"What do you mean?" asked Archibald Woodrough in a tone that showed his patience was running thin.

"I mean we've all known each other for years with the exception of Mr. Archer and Miss MacKay. They're the only strangers among us. Nobody ever died before they showed up."

Archibald gave Garett Springer a look that Ethan interpreted as *'Tell your wife to shut the hell up,'* before saying, "And what would be Mr. Archer and Miss MacKay's motivation here, Tiffany?"

"I don't know, Archi, maybe they're just crazy," she replied, unfazed.

"First of all, *Tif*, don't call me Archi. Second of all, Mr. Archer isn't truly here to try and improve the efficiency of our business. He's a renowned criminal investigator I hired at Gwendoline's suggestion to sort out a sordid blackmailing issue."

The announcement was met with displeased stares, but nobody dared complain about the deception to the patriarch.

"And finally, Tiffany, you've only been here twice before, so you hardly qualify as family or close friend yourself," Archibald concluded.

The woman turned a dark shade of red and kept quiet from then on, her eyes throwing daggers in turn to the patriarch and her husband who hadn't said a word in her defense.

"What's this blackmailing business about, Uncle? Could it be related to what's happening now and Dad's murder?" asked Matthew. The lobbyist was raising a very good question.

"It's about some incident most people here are familiar with and that doesn't need to be mentioned at this point. And I have no clue whether Allister's death is related to any of this."

"Are we even sure Gregory's been poisoned?" asked Clive Thomas.

"The coincidence would be monumental, Clive. I believe it's fairly safe to assume that Gregory was murdered." The sheriff had pronounced the last few words in a lower voice as if the three girls playing outside—but plainly visible from the billiard room's large windows—could overhear him.

"Maybe Gregory's body will show signs of poisoning now that we know what we're looking for?" suggested Jennifer.

Ethan doubted it but didn't want to contradict his assistant in public.

"It's worth checking, I suppose," said the sheriff after a moment spent considering the question. "If you wouldn't mind staying in this room while I go upstairs to have a look at the boy. Mr. Archer, would you mind assisting me?"

Ethan had apparently been promoted to medical examiner, a title for which he had absolutely no qualification. He voiced no protest, however, and accompanied the sheriff to the boy's bedroom.

The cold air hit them as soon as they'd entered the door.

"Who opened that window?" asked Ethan.

"Mr. Travis. It's to slow down decomposition."

The idea wasn't bad. With the sub-zero temperature outside, the room had been turned into a walk-in freezer.

Ethan walked to the window and closed it. "Just until we're done here. I'm from California, not used to this kind of weather," he said apologetically.

The sheriff removed the sheet covering Gregory's body and the two men stared at the corpse in silence for a while.

"Do you see any sign of poisoning?" asked the sheriff, eventually.

"I'm not seeing anything obvious, but I don't know what to look for either."

The sheriff slowly shook his head, sighing. "Neither do I…"

"Do you smell something?"

"Yeah. Looks like he's decomposing pretty fast despite the temperature."

"That's odd," said Ethan, taking a few steps back. "The smell is really getting worse now."

"How can it be? He's only been dead a day and the temperature in this room's near zero."

Ethan went down on his knees. "The smell's worse down here. I think it's coming from under the bed."

The sheriff looked as concerned with the revelation as he was. Whose body were they going to discover now?

They lifted the bed skirt and found themselves staring at a very dead cat.

Chapter 48

The discovery of the dead cat did little to lighten the mood in the cabin. As Ethan had expected, it had been the Travises'. After retrieving his decomposing pet from under the bed, James Travis had buried it in the woods. A tough job given that, even under the forest's canopy, the frozen ground was covered with over a foot of snow.

"Someone knew about the cat," said Matthew to the others who had once again assembled in the billiard room, with the exception of Gwendoline who was keeping an eye on the girls playing in the lounge. The precaution was as much to keep the children safe as to prevent them from eavesdropping on the grownups. The three girls had already been through enough trauma for a lifetime and didn't need to hear anything more about murder.

"Someone must have seen Gregory kill it and retrieved the body after the boy went inside the house," continued Matthew. "Probably the same someone who killed Gregory."

"Who would kill a boy over a cat?" asked Clive.

"It could only be the pet's owner," said Tiffany, always quick to point fingers.

Travis was helping his wife with lunch arrangements and wasn't present in the room at the moment, which made him a perfect scapegoat.

"Why would Travis kill Allan in that case?" asked Ethan. He was certain Travis hadn't poisoned the boy in reprisal for his cat's death. It wasn't that he believed the groundskeeper incapable of killing the boy, but simply because he'd seen the distress in the man's eyes when Clara had told him about his cat's fate. Ethan didn't think the groundskeeper was this good of an actor.

"If not Travis, who else?" asked Tiffany.

"We're assuming the cat's death and the boy's are related, but maybe they aren't," said Jennifer, who'd seldom spoken publicly over the past couple of days.

"Jennifer could be right. Maybe Gregory hid the cat under the bed himself so that it wouldn't be found," suggested Emily. "He was the type to do such things." She'd lowered her voice to pronounce the last statement as if ashamed of speaking ill of the dead boy, but she still attracted unfriendly looks from Vivian. The grandmother had red, puffy eyes, a sign she'd spent a good part of the night grieving over her son and grandson. Surprisingly enough, she seemed to be the only one in the family to do so. Even Gwendoline, whom Ethan had seen at breakfast, displayed little distress over her lost brother and nephew.

"We need to get some help from the outside. We're not going to all wait here for a lunatic to do us in one by one. This isn't a horror flick, we have options," said Blake.

"What are you suggesting?" asked the sheriff, who was starting to look out of his depth in this whole situation. "We have no cell phone reception, the landline is down—which means no DSL—all vehicles are trashed and the only road out of these mountains is barred by a giant tree."

"Someone needs to go by foot. Someone everyone trusts isn't the killer," answered Blake.

"Have you been outside lately?" asked Clive. "With the windchill the temperature's well below zero. It's also fifteen miles to the main road with two feet of snow on the ground."

"It would be shorter if one cut through the woods. No more than ten miles… With less snow on the ground and better shelter from the wind thanks to the trees," replied Blake.

"Are you volunteering?" asked Clive.

"If everybody's fine with it, I'll go," said Blake.

"I'm not comfortable with it," said Archibald. "I don't trust you, Blake, or you, Clive, or you, Matthew, or any of you for that matter." The patriarch had taken off the gloves.

"What about Mr. Archer? Don't you trust him?" suggested the retired orphanage director.

Archibald Woodrough kept silent an instant, considering the question. "Mr. Archer would be acceptable," he concluded finally.

"Ethan, would you accept the responsibility?" asked the sheriff.

Ethan agreed readily enough. He didn't like the idea, but he had no other way to prevent another murder. They needed to contact the authorities and bring a proper forensic team to investigate. He'd been thinking about the problem from all angles and had come up with nothing. He couldn't identify any pattern that would make sense and point to the killer. Maybe he was simply lacking some key information, but it was equally likely his brain was incapable of inferring the logical connections necessary to unveil the killer among them.

"Anyone has an objection to Mr. Archer going?" asked the sheriff.

"I do!" said Jennifer.

Ethan looked at her, surprised, and then realized that him going meant leaving her behind with the killer.

"It's a death trap, Ethan. This isn't a walk in the park. The conditions out there would be dangerous for an experienced woodsman. You know nothing about the forest and even less about the cold. You have a fifty-fifty chance of dying before reaching the road. Don't do it."

He was athletic and in good overall shape, but Jennifer wasn't wrong. Even if he wasn't afraid of jogging an hour on the hilly streets of San Francisco and had plenty of experience with bar fights, this situation was totally different. And he was smart enough to recognize he was lacking the experience necessary for the task. But what alternative did he have? He didn't trust Blake any more than Archibald did… mostly due to the man's interest in Jennifer, of course, but not only. At least, that's what he told himself. And even if someone else felt like volunteering, they wouldn't dare going against Archibald.

"I'll be fine, Jennifer. Don't worry about me," he said with more confidence than he felt.

"No, you won't be!"

"Are you offering to go with him?" asked Tiffany.

Jennifer hesitated an instant.

"No. She's not," said Matthew. "But you can go with him if you want,

Tiffany. I don't think anybody's suspecting you either. You're too dumb to pull something like this."

This time Garrett Springer came to his wife's defense and a three-way shouting match ensued, soon broken off by Archibald who'd lost patience with his guests.

It was finally decided that Ethan would go alone, equipped with warm gear, snowshoes and a compass to keep his aim true through the woods. He'd also be given a backpack with some energy bars and a few bottles of water.

"I'll go get dressed," he said, leaving the room and heading for the closest staircase.

"I'll help you get ready," said Jennifer, following suit.

"We need you to stay here with us, Miss MacKay," said the sheriff. "Nobody's to wonder alone in the house."

"Gwendoline's alone and so are the Travises, Sheriff," she said, as she exited without waiting for an answer.

Jennifer followed Ethan to his room where he put on the warmest clothes he'd brought with him and a triple layer of socks.

"Come back at the first sign of trouble, Ethan. It's really not worth dying out there for these people."

"I'm not doing it for them. We're all in the same boat. You and I aren't any safer than they are. We need a way to get out of here. We're just sitting ducks in this cabin."

"Promise you'll turn around and come back if you feel like you're not going to make it."

He looked her in the eyes. She appeared genuinely concerned, scared even. More scared than he'd ever seen her. Was she worried about him or about being left by herself with the Woodrough clan and the killer?

He opened the nightstand drawer and pulled out his gun. He handed it to her, saying, "Keep it with you at all times."

"I didn't know you'd brought a weapon on this trip."

"It seemed like a good idea at the time. Now I'm very glad I did."

He'd half-expected her to protest and tell him he needed it more than she, but instead she took the weapon and placed it in her pants' waist band under her sweater. That answered part of his question; Jennifer was afraid for her own safety at least as much as his. He didn't blame her.

"You're smart enough to survive this, Jennifer. Don't worry, I'll be back with some help."

"It's you I'm worried about. You don't know what it's like out there."

"I hadn't realized how much I meant to you," he teased.

"You do. If anything happened to you, I'd be out of a job… And finding another one where I get paid to surf the internet all day wouldn't be easy," she replied, stone-faced.

Ethan shook his head in disbelief and put on the winter coat and boots Clive had given him. The boots were slightly too large, but they'd have to do. "Okay I think I'm all set," he said, heading for the door. "Aren't you going back downstairs?" he asked, as Jennifer showed no signs of following him.

"No. I've had all I can take of that bunch at this point. I'm going to stay in my room for a while."

"I thought you'd come and kiss me goodbye at the door, just like in movies."

"You're mistaken about the nature of our relationship, boss. I'm sure you can find the door by yourself. But if it makes you feel any better, I'll wave from my bedroom window…"

"Looking forward to it!"

Chapter 49

Even with the hat he'd borrowed and the thick scarf wrapped around his head, the cold was worse than Ethan had anticipated. Clive's fur gloves did a great job protecting his fingers, though.

He turned his head one more time towards the cabin only to see that Jennifer was indeed not waving him goodbye at her window. She'd said it in jest and it really shouldn't have bothered him, but it did.

He followed the snow-covered road for about half a mile before his compass told him to make a right into the woods. The half-mile walk had taken him nearly thirty minutes; walking with snowshoes in fresh snow wasn't easy and he'd had no practice.

But Blake had been right, things got easier once he started moving under the forest's canopy. Ethan wasn't going any faster, but this had more to do with dodging fallen trees and keeping an eye on the compass than it had with the snow on the ground which didn't exceed three or four inches in places.

They'd expected him to reach the road in about ten hours, but at his current pace, he might actually make it faster than that. A good thing, since he was unlikely to get cell reception there either. He would need to stop a car or walk until the coveted bars appeared on his phone's screen.

His thoughts drifted once again towards Jennifer. He was starting to wonder if he wasn't developing something other than simple physical attraction for his secretary. He seemed to have grown fonder of her lately. He wasn't sure why.

Was it the fact she was so much smarter than he'd given her credit for during all these months, the fact she'd gotten him out of trouble with the Kazemis, or the way her cute little mouth smirked at him when he got on her case? Probably a combination of all these things. Whatever it was, he had no use for it. She wasn't attracted to him; she'd made that point plenty clear on several occasions.

At first he hadn't believed her when she'd said she wasn't a true lesbian. He'd thought she was just playing with him. But he'd seen her eyes drift to Matthew Woodrough when the lobbyist wasn't looking. He wasn't surprised; Matthew was attractive and charismatic, even Ethan could see that. At least it wasn't Blake Jones, thank God for small mercies.

The cold no longer bit his face the way it had when he'd first left the cabin, but he didn't know whether that meant he'd grown accustomed to it or his face was frozen solid.

He heard a sound behind him. He turned around to check it out but saw nothing. He'd completely forgotten about the woods' reputation up to that point, but the stories he'd overheard since he'd arrived in the region suddenly came back to him in a hurry.

Alone in the middle of the forest, unable to move faster than a couple miles per hour, he suddenly felt very vulnerable. He reminded himself that he didn't believe in the supernatural, but that didn't help a whole lot. The remains of eight children had been found in a nearby cave, and they hadn't gotten there of their own accord. Evil was real and it was possibly haunting these woods.

He'd barely covered a mile when he heard the first howling. He was no expert, but he was pretty sure he knew which animal the sound came from. He reached for his gun inside his pocket and remembered he'd left it with Jennifer. A grand gesture he might come to regret much sooner than he'd expected.

According to Jennifer, wolves very seldom attacked humans, so what were the odds they'd attack him? That was the spirit... Nothing was going to happen to him. The wolf was simply calling on his friends to go on a hunt and he had no reason to believe he'd be playing the part of the prey.

The second howl did make him pause, though. It came from a different direction. More to his left while the first one had come from his right.

As he continued forward in the direction indicated by his compass, he started searching around for something he could use as a weapon in case of need.

A branch protruding from the snow eventually caught his eye. Ethan grabbed it and immediately realized it was still attached to a downed tree buried deep under the snow. It took some work, but he finally managed to break it free form the trunk and ended up with a relatively straight walking stick about two and a half inches in diameter. The wood was light enough to be wielded at an attacker in case of need and strong enough not to break at the first impact.

A few minutes later, Ethan's path met again with the winding road. He followed it for a couple hundred yards before stopping dead in his tracks. This stretch of road was perfectly straight and the shape he perceived cut against the snowy background a couple hundred feet in front of him was definitely not a dog.

The wolf appeared to see him at the same time and let out a long howl that was answered in rapid succession by three or four more.

Ethan estimated the cabin was maybe a mile and a half behind him, which meant the main road was still eight or nine miles away. Under those circumstances, the decision was easy to take. It was time to turn around. He had the feeling the beast in front of him hadn't heard of Jennifer's theory about wolves not attacking humans, and he had no desire to be the one explaining it to him up close and personal.

He reentered the woods where the trees would make it harder for the wolves to see him and started walking at a brisker pace than he had previously. A brisk pace with snowshoes was still excruciatingly slow, however.

Behind him, the howling continued. He couldn't tell for certain whether the beasts were getting closer but the howling frequency was definitely increasing. The wolves were calling out to each other, enquiring about the position of their prey, his position.

He'd walked back on his track about a half mile when a large white wolf appeared between the trees fifty feet in front of him. Its fur blended perfectly with the surrounding snow, which explained why he hadn't spotted it earlier.

The wolf was staring at him and Ethan stared back, trying to not show fear as he bent down to pick up a fist-sized stone protruding from the thin layer of snow at the base of a pine tree.

He took a few more steps towards the animal before hurling the stone at it. The aim was good, but the wolf dodged the projectile and took off running in the opposite direction.

The trick bought Ethan a few minutes, but the howling soon returned, the sound coming from behind him this time.

He picked up the pace, thinking about how ridiculous his situation would have sounded a mere week ago. Ethan Archer hunted down by a pack of famished wolves in the middle of Montana. *Doesn't sound so absurd now,* he thought, looking at the piece of wood in his hand, a feeble excuse for a weapon.

On more than one occasion he felt a presence close to him, something watching. But nothing was there when he would turn around to check.

He estimated his position as a half mile from the cabin when he spotted another wolf, a gray one, between the trees, twenty yards to his left. It was stalking him at a distance but showed no desire to get closer. Ethan understood why a few minutes later when he heard a rustling sound coming from his right. Two wolves had been slowly sneaking up on him, the closest one a mere thirty feet away.

He searched the ground for stones, but the snow cover, deeper in this part of the woods, had swallowed all potential projectiles.

The wolves growled as they inched their way closer to their prey. His knuckles white around his improvised weapon, Ethan was starting to have a really bad feeling about this. Jennifer's prediction of him dying in the woods was about to realize itself. But it wasn't the cold that would claim his life, it was the wolves that, according to her, never attacked humans. How was that for irony?

Within minutes, Ethan found himself at the center of a triangle with a wolf at each of its vertices. The triangle quickly morphed into a pentagon when two more wolves joined their brothers for the kill.

Ethan was keeping them at a distance by wielding his stick around him as fast as he could manage which, with his snowshoes hindering his moves, wasn't very fast.

The white wolf suddenly lunged at him, its teeth closing on the sleeve of Ethan's parka, missing the arm by a hair. Before he had a chance to bring his weapon down on the animal, a second wolf was on him and he fell to the ground. The remainder of the pack moved in for the kill.

Ethan was drenched in sweat, his throat so tight he could barely breathe. This was it. In a minute they'd have torn him apart. It definitely wasn't the end he'd expected, but it was the end nonetheless.

From a distance came a loud howling sound. Ethan heard it but his conscious mind didn't register it at first. It took him a few seconds to realize that the wolves had stopped their assault and were now retreating

He got back on his feet to see them disappearing between the trees. What had just happened? Why hadn't they killed him? He'd been at their mercy, utterly defenseless.

He started heading towards the house once again, hoping he'd get there before the beasts returned, and was shocked to see the cabin appear between the trees two minutes later. The attack had taken place only a couple hundred yards from the clearing.

Chapter 50

Up in a tree, the ghost was looking at the three men and the woman staring at the paw prints on the fresh snow. They had no idea he was there. So close and yet invisible.

The man who'd been chased by the wolves was pointing at the spot where he'd fallen. The fresh snow told the story of his struggle as well as he could, but these people didn't know how to read the signs. And so the man spoke, while the others listened to his tale with a mixture of concern and perplexity.

Hopefully his misadventure would serve as a lesson to them all. Nobody was to leave the cabin. There was no escaping their fate. That one had been lucky to survive, though luck was maybe not the proper word.

There was a plan and the ghost wouldn't allow it to be changed. A certain chronology was to be respected, a certain timing, too. They weren't supposed to die in random order, and they wouldn't die all at once. The psychological aspect was important. They needed to know their end was coming and that there was nothing they could do about it but wait for their turn.

"I'm glad you believe me now," said Ethan to the sheriff as the two of them

walked back to the house accompanied by Clive and Jennifer. He had a hard time hiding the bitterness in his voice; the holes in his parka's sleeve hadn't sufficed to convince the others of his story. The paw prints and signs of struggle on the ground had done the trick, though.

"That's still strange. I've never heard of wolves attacking humans," said Clive, as they reached the clearing.

"I have!" said Ethan. "Some kids were attacked by a pack of wolves a few days ago around that cave that's been in the news."

"I was involved in the search for the girl," confirmed the sheriff. "It took us a few hours to find her lost in the middle of the forest, but all her bruises and scratches came from her running and falling in the woods. The wolves never actually bit her. To be honest, I was skeptical about the whole story. I thought the kids made it up. But now… I'm not so sure anymore."

"You think these could be the same wolves? How far is that cave?" asked Jennifer.

"The entrance is about fifteen miles away," answered the sheriff.

"That would be a stretch for a pack to have a territory this large, but it's possible," commented Clive. The rancher knew something about wolves. "Maybe this pack has lost its fear of humans, in which case we should expect more attacks to come."

"We'll need to remind the wolves why they should be afraid," said the sheriff, tapping his jacket pocket where he'd placed the gun he'd retrieved from his car's glovebox. "I'd be happy to add a few more pelts to my collection."

Ethan was wondering how many more people were packing in this house. Now that he thought of it, this was Montana, so there was a chance they all were. Even Tiffany probably had a cute pink automatic hidden between her fake boobs.

"You collect pelts?" said Jennifer, looking slightly disgusted.

"I sure do! I shot myself two nice wolves a couple years ago, not twenty miles from here. A male and a female."

"It was most likely a breeding pair, the female was still nursing," added Clive, who didn't seem to approve.

"Maybe the wolves who attacked me were their offspring?" said Ethan.

"Not likely. They wouldn't have survived long without their mother's milk," said Clive.

They headed back to the cabin, eager to warm themselves up by the fire.

"What do you think of your theory about wolves never attacking humans now?" Ethan asked Jennifer as the group entered the house.

"I think since you don't have a scratch, it still stands. Sounds to me like they just wanted to play and you misinterpreted their intention."

He knew she was joking, but he also suspected she believed it to some extent. Somehow, it bugged him that she would side with the wolves that had nearly killed him.

Nearly… Why had they spared him at the last moment when he'd been on the ground, defenseless? They had answered a call, but something had been strange about that call, so close and yet... different from the others.

They found the rest of the guests assembled around the fireplace where a fire was roaring. Some of them held bottles of water, not daring to set them down on the side tables peppered between the seats.

A few were watching television with the kids in a den adjacent to the lounge.

"Do you have a satellite dish?" asked Ethan, wondering how the house had TV reception but no functioning landline, internet connection or cell phone reception.

"Yes," said Gwendoline, "but the internet connection is DSL, in case you were wondering."

Ethan had assumed as much since it had gone down with the landline. He was just thinking about the irony of the situation. They received live news from around the world but were unable to communicate with the closest town located thirty miles away. A satellite phone sure would have been handy right now, but hindsight was always twenty-twenty.

"Blake, come check this out," called Emily from the TV room.

As Blake got up to answer his wife's summons, Jennifer and Ethan followed him to the den.

"They found a large lake in that cave." Emily was pointing at the TV.

"I thought they'd closed it for the investigation," answered her husband.

"They reopened it to scientists a couple days ago apparently. A team went down one of the unexplored galleries and after a couple of miles that's what they found."

The images on the screen were dark, but one could clearly see a vast expanse of water surrounded by rock walls. The water appeared black on the screen but was probably as clear as tap water in reality.

A rock landing led to the edge of the lake. The darkness made it difficult to guess the actual size of the cavernous room, but it appeared gigantic. There was a sort of bluish quality to the light inside the cave which the scientist on TV explained as coming from bioluminescent glowworms previously unknown in the US but similar to a species that had been found in a New Zealand cave.

"Can we go see it, Dad? The lake even has fish in it," said Clara. "We could camp inside. The man said it has everything someone needs to live. We wouldn't even need to go outside to eat. We could fish in the lake." The six-year-old sounded excited.

"It's closed to the public right now, honey, but we'll go when they open it up for everyone to visit."

"You promise?"

"Promised," answered Blake.

But Ethan wasn't convinced the father would be able to keep his promise. A thought that had to be in everybody's mind.

"Jennifer wants to go visit too," Ethan said to Clara. His assistant was glued to the TV screen.

"Now more than ever," she said with a smile.

The adults returned to the lounge and Ethan asked Emily if the journalists had mentioned anything new about the kids' skeletons.

"They think they were between seven and twelve at the time of their death. The oldest one has been dead nearly thirty years. And they said about ten years for the most recent one."

"Another psycho targeting children," commented Tiffany.

Ethan thought about her words for a moment. *Another psycho…* The cave was only a few miles away. What if it wasn't another psycho? What if it was one and the same?

Chapter 51

The gunshot woke up the entire house a little after six the next morning. A moment later, Ethan was pushing open the door connecting his room and Jennifer's to find her standing on the other side.

"Was that a gunshot?" she asked. She had a shallow pillow mark on her left cheek.

"It definitely sounded like it."

"What do we do? Go out and have a look?"

Ethan was contemplating their options when they heard voices coming from the hallway. After a brief consultation with Jennifer, he opened his door and stepped into the hallway, draped in a robe, to find Matthew and Clive discussing what they'd heard.

Everyone agreed it had been a gunshot, but no one knew where it had come from.

Jennifer stepped out of her room a moment later wearing workout leggings and a black tank top that highlighted both her cleavage and the paleness of her skin. Even fresh out of bed, Jennifer MacKay looked stunning.

Ethan suggested that they should maybe go investigate. The others agreed and the group started heading towards the end of the hallway where the Springers and Gwendoline were coming out of their rooms.

"Did you find out what happened?" asked Gwendoline to her husband.

"Not yet."

"Vivian! Vivian! Open your door," they heard Archibald Woodrough yelling from somewhere on the opposite side of the house.

By the time the group reached Vivian's bedroom, they found the rest of the household waiting in front of it while Archibald banged on the door in his pajamas.

"She won't open the damn door," said the patriarch, sounding more irritated than worried.

Ethan discreetly counted the guests only to confirm that only the kids and Emily were missing. The woman had probably stayed in her room with her two girls.

"Where's your daughter?" he asked to Gwendoline.

"She's still sleeping. The shot didn't wake her up."

"Maybe you should go back to your room and keep an eye on her until we figure out what's going on," he suggested to the mother.

Only then did Gwendoline seem to realize the potential danger of the situation. She nodded and headed back towards their bedroom at a brisk pace.

"When did you leave your room?" asked Ethan to Archibald.

The patriarch turned towards him with the look of someone who didn't understand English. "What do you mean? When I heard the shot, of course..."

"Your wife and you sleep in different rooms?"

"Obviously!" The man was looking at him as if he were a complete idiot.

Vivian's bedroom didn't connect with any other and her solid-wood door had been locked and barricaded from the inside. As a result, it took tools and a good thirty minutes before they could breach the fortified door and discover the mess awaiting inside.

Vivian Woodrough was lying on her bed in a puddle of blood. Her brain was spattered across the walls. The gun she'd used to shoot herself was still in her mouth.

Chapter 52

"Are we sure she committed suicide?" asked Jennifer to Ethan after they'd regained their rooms to freshen up. They were both standing in the middle of Ethan's bedroom.

Jennifer was even paler than usual; the grandmother's death seemed to be affecting her more than the previous two, and Ethan worried that the constant stress of their situation was getting to his assistant. How many more deaths could Jennifer take before losing it for good? How many more could *he* take for that matter?

"The sheriff seems to think she killed herself and I would tend to agree with his assessment."

"She left no suicide note," said Jennifer.

"Not everybody writes a note before killing themselves. She had showered and dressed, and she was shot sitting on the edge of her bed. It doesn't look like murder. Now if you factor in the barricading from the outside and the closed shutters on her windows, I don't see how anyone could have gotten inside her room."

"And the gun belongs to her husband? You don't think that's weird?" she asked, as Ethan pulled the rocking chair from a corner of the room where it rested against the wall.

"Not particularly. If she doesn't own a gun and she knew he kept one in his bedside table, that's where she'd have gone to get a weapon," he said, sitting down.

Jennifer's eyes were glistening and for a moment he wondered if she was going to cry. But she didn't and regained her composure.

"What do you make of it, Ethan?"

He noticed that she hadn't called him boss this time. "We need to get out of here. That's all I know. I have no idea what's going on in this house, but whatever it is, it's bad. It's not only that people keep dying, it's also that no one seems to care about those who died. Archibald is reacting to his wife's suicide the same way he reacted to his son's and grandson's deaths. Irritation and a bad mood. Normal people cry and feel pain, but not him. And he's not the only one to act strangely. Blake seems more worried about getting in your pants than figuring out who's behind this, and Gwendoline was roaming the house where a gun had just been fired while leaving her kid sleeping alone on the other side of the cabin."

"I think everyone's starting to lose their nerves."

"Maybe," he said, unconvinced. "But I need you to remain cool, Jennifer. I need your help. I wasn't entirely candid with you when I asked you to accompany me on this trip."

Jennifer moved the armchair that stood by the window so it would face Ethan and sat down. What was he talking about? "Okay… I'm listening."

"When I asked you to come with me it wasn't simply because I needed you to investigate the ranch while I was looking into the oil side. It was part of it, but it wasn't my only motivation."

He paused, looking uncomfortable.

"Go on," she encouraged.

"There's a reason I no longer work murder cases, kidnappings, serial rapists and the like."

Jennifer was pretty sure she knew why that was, but she didn't interrupt.

"It's not simply that I don't have a taste for it after what happened to my wife. It's not that I don't want to have the death of another victim on my conscience if I fail to identify a human predator. It's that I no longer have the brains for it, either. I haven't been able to solve anything more meaningful than a cat's disappearance in a year."

This was the first time Ethan had brought up his wife in front of her. Jennifer had pieced the story together from news articles and his behavior, but he'd never once mentioned Amanda.

"I saw the way you figured out that what Farzin Kazemi had been putting in his glass was Viagra and I realized I had significantly underestimated you. You can do what I used to be able to do. You can take isolated pieces of information and weave a web, linking them to get to the true story."

"I got lucky with the Kazemis, Ethan. My brain's nothing special. I'm just a secretary, remember."

"False modesty isn't helpful right now. Until we find a way to get out of here, our best chance of stopping the killer is to figure out who he or she is."

"You think it could be a woman?"

"Anyone can poison someone, Jennifer. It takes no particular strength or special skills. A child could have done it."

She knew all that already but wasn't interested in discussing the recent murders at the moment. What she wanted was an answer to the riddle that had been bugging her for months. And now was as good an opportunity as she'd ever get. "Can I ask you a question?"

"Sure," he said.

"I never dared ask before but there's something I've been wondering for a year. And since you brought up the subject of your wife…" She saw a shadow fall upon Ethan's face, but she'd said too much to stop there. "What exactly happened the night your wife died? From what I could piece together and, let's be honest, some eavesdropping on your conversations with Theo, it looks like your wife willingly followed Avery out of that club. Why?"

He remained silent for so long that she no longer expected an answer when he finally spoke. "Because of me."

Perplexed, she repeated, "Because of you?"

"My wife and I were swingers. We'd go to clubs and parties that specialized in that sort of thing and find a couple to our liking. Then we'd split and most of the time I'd take the woman home while Amanda ended up at the man's place."

Jennifer hadn't seen that one coming. She'd been convinced Amanda was unfaithful and had been seduced by the wrong guy. She'd never imagined Ethan had willingly loaned his wife to the bastard who'd raped and killed her.

"That look in your eyes right now, that barely veiled disgust. That's exactly the way I've been feeling about myself for the past year," he said, getting up from his chair.

But she stopped him, gently pushing down on his shoulders until he sat back down. "I feel no disgust, Ethan. That look was surprise, not judgement. There are no rules when it comes to sex between consenting adults, no matter what society says. You did nothing wrong, and fuck the prudes and hypocrites who think otherwise. You're not responsible for what happened to your wife, Ethan."

"But I am," he said, exhaling deeply. "I'm the one who got her into that stuff in the first place. She wasn't thrilled about the idea initially. She eventually said she'd give it a try, but it was just to please me, not because she really wanted to. After our first swinging experience, she claimed to enjoy it and even bragged about it to her friends, but deep down I always knew she was doing it for me."

"Did she tell you that?" asked Jennifer.

"She didn't have to. I just knew."

"You *just knew* because she was a woman and women can't enjoy this sort of thing? You'd be surprised, Ethan. Men have all kind of preconceived ideas when it comes to women and sex, but the truth is that we love sex as much as guys do, and for some of us even more. We don't show it the same way and we don't brag about it because, once again, society wouldn't approve… but we enjoy kinky stuff too, as long as it's wrapped in the right package."

Ethan was now looking at her with a strange expression. A mixture of doubt and perplexity.

"If I wanted to make you blush," she continued, "I'd just have to tell you some of the stuff Tabatha and I are into."

This time he gave a tentative smile. "Maybe someday you will."

"Maybe…" she replied, winking at him teasingly. "But for now we need to figure out how to solve our little problem, and don't count on me to do all the thinking. I'm not the one with the fancy math and psychology degrees."

Once again surprise registered plainly on his face. "How do you know that?"

"How do you think, boss? Google, of course… You graduated Summa Cum Laude from Ohio State as a math major, before obtaining a Masters in theoretical mathematics from Berkeley and finally a PhD in behavioral psychology from Stanford."

He just stared at her; for once, Ethan Archer appeared to be speechless.

"Don't look at me like that. Background checks work both ways. I like to know who I'm working for."

"Impressive memory," he said finally. "You have everything it takes to make a great detective. Why did you ever want to be a secretary?"

"I can honestly say that I never did. But stop complimenting me or else I'll think you're trying to pull a Blake Jones."

"Pull a Blake Jones?" he asked confused.

"Get in my pants! I thought you of all people would get the reference. Anyway, what do you plan on doing on your side while my brain is doing the thinking?" she teased. "Will you try to go back out there and hope the wolves won't find you this time? That's probably what Blake's going to suggest…"

"He can go himself. I'm not stepping back into those woods any time soon."

"Those wolves really freaked you out, didn't they?"

"The wolves are only one of the reasons I'm not going back out there."

"What other reasons do you have?"

Ethan looked her in the eyes an instant before looking away towards the window. "The wolf call that got them off my back, for one."

"I'm not sure I'm following you."

"I realize it's going to sound crazy but… I'm not sure the howl came from a wolf. There was something odd about it. I think it could have been a man."

"A man who would rule over the wolves? Is that what we're talking about here?"

"Something like that..."

"Interesting theory," she said, not trying to hide the sarcasm in her voice this time.

Chapter 53

E than and Jennifer found people dispersed in small groups throughout the house by the time they finally made it downstairs. The sheriff's idea of keeping everyone huddled together to prevent future catastrophes had apparently died with Vivian Woodrough.

Maybe the sheriff was simply too overwhelmed by the situation to try and coerce the guests into following his orders at this point, or maybe he knew something the others didn't. The gun that had killed Vivian had been Archibald's, after all, and the friendship between the two men went way back.

"The snow has finally stopped," said Clive, looking through the window.

Ethan hadn't even noticed it had started snowing again, but when he joined the others in front of the massive sliding door in the dining room, the snow on the ground was a half-foot higher than it had been the day before.

"We should try and see if anything can be done about the cars," said Clive. "Maybe we can repair one of them. The brake line shouldn't be that hard to fix and we may be able to use the vehicles' spare tires too."

The idea was worth trying, and the most technically-inclined men gathered outside to try and duct-tape a running vehicle. Ethan knew precisely nothing about cars, but he tagged along to get some fresh air and discreetly observe his companions' behavior.

Within a few minutes, Clive Thomas, Blake Jones, Sam Clifford and the sheriff were outside wading through two feet of snow while Ethan watched them from the porch. Despite the warm gloves and hat he'd borrowed from Travis, he still felt a thousand tiny needles pricking at his hands and ears.

The men went from vehicle to vehicle to retrieve the spare tires from their trunks and brought them all to the porch.

There were all kind of sizes in the lot, but there was a chance they could find a set of four that would more or less match.

"Assuming we can fix a car, what do you guys plan to do about the snow on the road?" asked Ethan.

They all looked at each other as if the idea hadn't occurred to them before he mentioned it.

"Travis has a snowplow on his truck inside the barn. If we can't find four tires to fix his truck, we can maybe mount the plow on one of the others," said Clive, who appeared to be the most familiar with the place.

He'd been married to Gwendoline for eleven years and had probably spent every Christmas at the Woodroughs' cabin since.

They all headed to the barn, which looked more like an oversized garage with four rolling doors than Ethan's idea of a barn. The metallic walls had been covered with siding on the outside and painted brown to help the monstrosity fit better in with its surroundings, but the attempt had failed miserably.

After a few minutes spent tinkering around the groundskeeper's vehicle, it became obvious that there wasn't a set of four tires that would fit Travis' old pickup. They therefore started to explore the possibility of transferring the plow to a different truck or maybe even an SUV. With three pickups to choose from and five SUVs, there was a chance they would get lucky.

They worked through the remainder of the morning, Ethan even helping from time to time when an extra pair of hands was required. By 1 PM, when Travis came out to announce that lunch was going to be served, they had managed to mount three tires on Clive's F-150 and were well on their way to successfully rig a fourth one. With a little luck and another couple of hours of work, the plow would be transferred to the F-150, and the brake line would be fixed.

Ethan hadn't noticed any strange behavior or anyone trying to sabotage their progress, which suggested the killer was probably inside the house and not working on the trucks. But would the man be stupid enough to tip his hand if he were? It was doubtful. Whoever the killer was, he'd proven himself smart and organized.

"Let's make sure nobody comes out of the house to ruin our work while we're having lunch," said the sheriff, as they stepped inside the cabin.

"I'll drink bottled water to that," said Blake, in an attempt at humor that fell flat with his audience.

They walked back inside, and Ethan went straight to Jennifer to enquire whether anything noticeable had happened in his absence. The answer was no. Sticking to their plan, she'd always avoided being left with fewer than two people in any room while maximizing her roaming in order to keep an eye on as many guests as possible.

They all sat down at the dining room table and, following the sheriff's orders, the Travises quickly swallowed their meal under the watchful eyes of the others.

Satisfied the elderly couple hadn't died in their plates, the rest of them started eating.

Lunch was simple but tasty, especially considering that it had been made exclusively from canned goods to avoid any risk of poisoning.

It was a quarter past two when the five men returned outside to finish fixing Clive's truck.

"Son of a bitch!" yelled the sheriff as soon as they'd passed the corner of the cabin.

In front of them, the F-150 had three flat tires and the fourth one they'd been trying to mount was in no better shape.

"Who in heaven's name did that?" asked Blake, addressing no one in particular. "I thought everyone was in the dining room."

"Everyone was," said Ethan, who was thinking about the howl he'd heard the day before. The one that had drawn the wolves away from him. Someone was out there. Someone who wasn't a friend. Once again, the stories he'd heard in Wyoming about the woods being haunted came back to his mind.

"Who could have done this," said the sheriff as they reached the pickup. All the tires displayed large laceration marks. There was no fixing them at this point.

"If I get my hands on the man who did this, I'll strangle him with my bare hands," said Sam Clifford, looking at the forest. The rictus on the man's face wasn't pleasant. The orphanage director was revealing a new side of himself.

"Show yourself, you bastard," he screamed at the woods.

A second later, Ethan saw something shoot straight out of the forest, immediately followed by a wet squishy sound.

It's only when Sam Clifford collapsed backward into the snow that he noticed the arrow buried in the man's chest.

Chapter 54

They all ran for cover, leaving the dead Sam Clifford lying on his back, his blood staining the immaculate snow carpet around him as it seeped from the wound.

"What do we do?" asked Blake, who had taken shelter behind one of the SUVs along with Clive.

Ethan and the sheriff were hiding behind another. The lawman was breathing hard. He was no youngster and wasn't used to moving this fast anymore.

"We need to get back inside. We're sitting ducks out here," said the sheriff.

"What about Sam?" asked Clive, his voice shaking.

"He's dead. There's nothing we can do about him right now," replied the lawman categorically. "On my count we all run to the house. One, two, three!"

They all sprinted for the cabin's porch with the exception of Ethan who crawled as fast as he could toward Sam Clifford's body.

His eyes hadn't deceived him; there was indeed something attached to the arrow. A roll of paper about 4 inches wide was wrapped around the shaft protruding from the dead man's chest.

Nervously surveying the section of the woods where the arrow had come from, Ethan worked on untying the piece of string securing the message to the shaft. But his fingers, numbed by the cold and shaking with fear, weren't working as fast as he wished.

He eventually managed to loosen the string and unrolled the piece of paper which wasn't a message at all, at least not a written one. It was an old photograph.

Ethan stuffed it into his jacket pocket and started crawling towards the porch. Not daring to get back up, he continued crawling through the snow until he reached a patch that hadn't been trampled by anyone. The powder was much too soft for him to crawl on top of now; he no longer had a choice.

He quickly got up and started running, the knee-high snow slowing his escape to the point that he might as well have been walking.

He was shocked to make it to the porch and around the corner of the cabin without being shot in the back. At the same time, shooting a bow through a forest of trees left the archer with limited options.

He made it inside the house to find the others assembled in the foyer, talking all at once. Clive had already broken the news, and they were all debating the implications.

"What were you doing out there?" Jennifer looked upset.

The whole room turned towards Ethan, awaiting an answer.

"I saw something on the shaft of the arrow, and I went to retrieve it."

"What was it?" asked Gwendoline.

"This," he answered, pulling the picture out of his pocket and unrolling it for the others to see.

"It looks like a picture of Sam in front of his orphanage. The kids surrounding him are some of the orphans," said Gwendoline.

Sam Clifford looked about fifteen years younger in the picture. A half dozen boys stood on either side of the director. The youngest one looked to be six or seven while the oldest was probably thirteen or fourteen.

"Let me see," said Archibald, reaching for the picture.

Ethan handed it over, and the patriarch examined it closely for a moment. "What does it mean? Why would that picture be attached to the arrow that killed Sam?" he asked finally, as he stuffed the picture inside his pants pocket.

"Could I get it back? I wasn't done with it," said Ethan, extending his hand towards the older man.

Archibald fished the picture out of his pocket and handed it to Ethan, an icy look in his eyes. "Have at it, Mr. Archer. If you think this picture's the key to stop this ludicrous joke, be my guest."

"It may not be the key, Mr. Woodrough, but it could be an important clue. We haven't found many of those so far," replied Ethan. "Maybe we can sit down and discuss all this?"

Archibald didn't look pleased with the idea, but Clive, Blake and the Springers seconded the motion.

Everyone moved to the billiard room for another round of questioning. This time the exercise was led by Ethan, albeit under Sheriff Bradford's watchful eye.

"Have any of you seen this picture before?"

Nobody had, but Ethan found some answers more convincing than others. Archibald's belonged to those that weren't.

"Do any of the kids look familiar to you?" Ethan continued.

"Maybe, maybe not. It's hard to say." Mrs. Travis usually kept silent and Ethan was surprised to hear her speak up. "He's brought so many over the years. These could have come with him before, but I don't have a good memory for faces and they could have been younger or older then too."

"You mean Sam Clifford came to visit with kids?"

"Yes, he'd bring one or two over for the weekend or during the holidays. When we were kids, we used to play with the orphans when they visited," said Gwendoline.

"And you don't recognize any of these?"

"No. Not particularly," she replied.

The answer was disappointing, but he still felt he was onto something.

"One thing's certain," said the sheriff. "The enemy's out there, not in this room. It's not one of us doing all this."

Ethan wasn't certain of that just yet though. "Where's the main breaker?" he asked.

"It's in the vestibule by the door on the south side of the house," answered James Travis.

"Can you show me?"

Travis led the way and Ethan followed him to the electric panel. He tried the door beside the panel, and it swung open.

"Is this door ever locked?" he asked.

"We lock it at night and when we leave the cabin."

"I suggest we keep it locked at all times from now on," said Ethan, heading for the lounge where Allan had been poisoned.

Using his phone as a timer, he estimated it took about sixteen seconds to walk from the electric panel to the chair Allan had been sitting in. He then returned to the others in the billiard room.

"Your conclusion, Detective? Could Sam's killer have come from the outside to poison my poor cousin, or does he have an accomplice among us?" asked Matthew, who'd guessed what Ethan had in mind.

"Someone could have come from the outside. That person could have flipped the breaker and walked to the lounge in the dark if he knew where he was going. Coming from outside his night vision would have been at its best and the few embers burning in the foyer could have given him enough light to find Allan's glass and pour the poison into it. That would also explain why we didn't find the vial when we searched the room."

"So you think that's what happened?" asked Tiffany Springer hopefully.

"It's a possibility, but it doesn't mean that's what happened. For one thing, the man would have had to retreat before Travis made it to the breaker box, which would have left him very little time to do so."

"He could also have hidden inside the house and taken advantage of the commotion generated by Allan's death to sneak out unnoticed," suggested Jennifer.

"So what you're saying is that you don't know if we have a killer among us," said Archibald dryly.

"I don't, but I can assure you there's at least one waiting for us outside. And I don't think he's your average killer either," said Ethan who was once again thinking about the strange howling he'd heard.

"What do you mean?" asked the sheriff.

"I didn't have much time to observe it, but the arrow that killed Sam Clifford seems strange to me. Home-made, if you know what I mean. I think it's worth getting a second look at it."

"Are you volunteering for the job?" asked Archibald.

"There are plywood panels in the garage, we could use them as shields to go out there," suggested Travis.

They considered the idea for a while and decided it was a good one.

"Maybe it's time to get the guns out of the safe?" said the sheriff, looking at Archibald. His voice was hesitant.

The patriarch sighed. "We're getting three guns out: one for you, Oliver, one for Archer and one for Clive. That's it. And the guns are going back inside the safe as soon as you guys are back."

It was now clear who had the patriarch's trust and who didn't.

"Why do they need guns?" asked the little Clara who'd sneaked in on them unnoticed.

"They're going to see if they can hunt something we can eat, honey," replied her mother. Satisfied with the explanation, the girl returned to her sister and cousin in the other room.

The wood panels were retrieved from the garage and the maneuver practiced a few times inside the spacious lounge. Six men would go out. Three would be holding the wood panels in a protective fashion and three would be covering them with the guns. They couldn't afford trying to drag Clifford's body inside the house, the maneuver would expose them too much, so it was decided that they'd just pull the arrow out and return to the cabin immediately after.

A shotgun and two rifles were retrieved from the safe along with ammunition, and Archibald handed the weapons to the three men composing the armed escort.

The party then exited the house through the garage.

The operation went more or less as planned, and they were able to retrieve the arrow and return to the cabin without anyone shooting at them.

True to his word, Archibald collected the guns as soon as they came back in, while the others gathered around Matthew who was holding the arrow in his hand.

The shaft was perfectly straight, but it was clearly made from a branch. The fletching was fashioned from a bald eagle's feather and the head was black flint. It looked like a Native American arrow from pre-Columbian times.

"It's the ghost. He's returned," said the quavering voice of Mrs. Travis.

The woman was standing by the door leading to the kitchen. All color had drained from her face.

Chapter 55

The dinner was over and the guests were talking in small groups scattered around the fireplace when Ethan signaled Jennifer to keep an eye on the guests as he discreetly exited the room.

He found Mrs. Travis clearing the table in the dining room as he'd expected.

"Can I talk to you a minute?" he asked.

"I have work to do, sir. I can't stop for a chat."

"Then we'll talk while working. Let me help you."

Ethan ignored the woman's protests and started transferring dirty plates and dishes to a serving trolley.

"Who's that ghost you mentioned this afternoon?"

Under the pretext of needing some fresh water, Mr. Travis had quickly ushered his wife into the kitchen after her revelation. The woman had indeed looked sickly, but Ethan suspected her husband's move had been intended to shut her up more than anything else.

"It's old wives' tales, Mr. Archer. I shouldn't have brought it up. All this nonsense is making me lose my nerves."

"You and everyone else, Mrs. Travis. Which is why I need to hear what you know if I'm to try and stop this madness. Old wives' tales have a kernel of truth in them sometimes…" He paused for effect. "Who is that ghost, and where have you seen him before?"

"I don't know who he is," she whispered. "I only saw it once. A long time ago. But others have seen him roaming the woods."

"What does he look like?"

"Nobody knows what's his true form. People say he's not human. Some people call him sasquatch, some call him the devil, but they all talk about the same thing."

"How do you know?"

"I just know. They all describe him evaporating into thin air, as if absorbed by the woods."

"That's what you saw?"

She nodded slowly. "A minute he was there standing a few feet under the trees at the edge of the clearing, by the road. He looked at me and I screamed for James to come out, and then he was gone."

"What did he look like?" Ethan was intrigued by the woman's story.

"His face was very white with no hair on it. No hair on his head either. But his body was covered with a thick black fur."

"Was he tall, short? Are you sure it was a male?"

"He looked like a man, but not really. I don't know how tall he was—at least my height, I reckon."

"Why do you say no one knows his true form, if you've seen him?"

"Because what I've seen isn't what others who've encountered him describe. At least not all of them. Sometimes he's short and sometimes he has no fur at all, just a very white hairless body. But nobody ever gets a good look at him, he's there an instant and he's gone the next, like a shadow you see from the corner of your eye. Like a ghost..."

Ethan had no doubt Mrs. Travis was telling the truth. At least what she thought to be the truth. These were the same rumors that had spooked the oil field workers sent to look for Myriam after she'd vanished.

But Ethan believed neither in ghosts nor in a polymorphic big foot. There had to be a logical explanation and the most obvious one was that they were dealing with more than one individual. Maybe the one Mrs. Travis had seen was the real thing—whatever it might be—and the other sightings were cases of mistaken identities. Teenagers playing tricks on their friends, or campers who'd had one too many drinks.

"Do you remember when you saw it?" he asked.

She nodded again. They'd cleared the whole table, but Mrs. Travis no longer appeared concerned with the work awaiting her in the kitchen. "It was about ten days after the little Myriam disappeared."

"It had to be in January of '98 then?" The specter of the little girl was pointing its nose once again. Ethan was starting to have the strange feeling that her disappearance and the current situation were somehow linked. But how?

"It was. I knew right then that it was him who'd taken her away. I don't know how he did it, but he came and stole her from her bed that night. I'm sure that those bones they found in that cave were hers."

There had been eight skeletons discovered in the cave, but only one had belonged to a female. And according to Mrs. Travis, it was Myriam's.

"Did you know Myriam well? What kind of kid was she?"

"She was the sweetest of them all, even sweeter than Gwendoline. And a hundred times sweeter than her brother, but that's easy."

She seemed to regret her last statement as soon as it had escaped her lips. "I mean, Allan wasn't a bad kid. He was just a boy and boys like to get in trouble."

He was pretty certain this wasn't the way she'd meant it but didn't push the issue. "What else can you tell me about Myriam?"

"Let see... She liked animals a lot. Especially dogs and horses. They used to bring trailers with horses to the cabin back then and go on long rides in the woods."

"This is very useful information, Mrs. Travis. What else can you tell me about her?"

"Myriam was smart. Very smart."

Ethan smiled; it sounded like the description of any kid made by a loving relative or friend.

Mrs. Travis must have read his mind because she added, "I mean *really* smart. Mrs. Vivian got her tested to jump grades and the psychologists said she was a genius. I don't remember her scores on the QI test but it was very high."

"She took an IQ test?" asked Ethan, tactfully correcting the acronym.

"Yes. They said she was smarter than everybody else in her school. Smarter than ninety-nine percent of people. Mrs. Vivian was real proud of her daughter. Myriam could have been an astronaut, or a doctor, even."

He wondered how truly smart Myriam had been and whether it ran in the family. "Do you remember the day Myriam disappeared? Can you tell me exactly what happened that day?"

"We weren't here when she was taken. My husband and I had been given the week off. We only came back when we heard the news. To help with the search, you know."

"They'd given you some time off during the yearly family gathering?" asked Ethan, surprised.

"Yes, that year they did. And a couple more times after that. They used to give us our weekends off too when they would come to visit. I guess they liked their privacy and that was all the better for us, because we didn't have to cook and wait on the whole bunch."

"I guess Aaron Woodrough was still in charge back then?"

"No. Aaron was already sick. He and his wife stopped coming to the cabin in the early 90s. Misters Allister and Archibald were the masters of this place by then."

"How did Mr. Archibald react to Myriam's disappearance?"

"Oh, he was very upset. Always yelling and in a terrible mood."

"Did you ever see him cry or looking sad, maybe when he thought he was alone?"

She paused to think about it for a minute before answering, "Not that I can recall. Mr. Archibald isn't one to show his feelings. He keeps everything bottled up inside."

This was one possible explanation for the man's behavior, but Ethan doubted it was the correct one. He had a much more satisfying theory to explain Archibald's strange comportment. One that, if proven correct, would be a lot more concerning for everyone involved.

Chapter 56

Everyone had retired to their bedrooms and barricaded themselves in for one more night in the cabin that had become their prison.

"Archibald Woodrough's hiding something, and he's not the only one," said Ethan to Jennifer.

The two of them were meeting in Jennifer's room this time. He'd already related his discussion with Mrs. Travis and Jennifer had reported what had happened in the lounge in his absence, which amounted to nothing of interest.

"He definitely knows something about that picture." Ethan pulled the photo out of his pocket and stared at it one more time. "It's a message and he understood it, but he's not talking. And there's nothing we can do about it."

"Or maybe he truly has no clue, and you misread his behavior. He seems to me like a regular asshole," said Jennifer.

He decided not to tell her about the mental tally he was keeping on Archibald until the patriarch scored above a certain threshold. Jumping to a conclusion could be very damaging in this kind of situation and Ethan needed to go by the book with this. "But that's the thing, Jennifer. There seem to be two Archibalds. In the oil field everybody seems to have his back. He's described as a good boss by his employees and the company has a very high retention rate. People working for him don't want to quit their jobs."

"How much interaction does the CEO get with his workers? Maybe he's an ass to his close collaborators and nice to the people he talks to once a year." Jennifer cracked open a fresh bottle of water and took a sip.

It was a possibility he hadn't considered. "Maybe," he admitted, "but he was also a decent guy with his guests until people started dropping dead."

"Then maybe it's the stress of the situation that brings out the jerk in him. Maybe he's not always like that."

They dropped the matter; neither one of them was going to come up with an answer to that question tonight, and at this point it probably didn't matter anyway. Unless Archibald Woodrough were a world-class actor, he wasn't the one behind the killings. But of course, if Ethan's suspicions were correct, the patriarch's acting skills were likely to be far above average.

"If the picture's a message, maybe we missed others," said Jennifer. "Maybe there was a clue left with Allan that we overlooked… or with Gregory. Something left on the kid's dresser or in a drawer in his room. And maybe the message becomes clear only when the clues are assembled together."

"It's possible," replied Ethan thoughtfully. "Let's just hope we won't have to wait for everyone to die before understanding the clues."

For the next minute, each remained absorbed in his own thoughts.

"What if the cat had been the message?" said Ethan finally.

"What kind of a message would that be?"

"What if the killer or killers were justifying their actions with the clues?"

"You really think there may be more than one killer?"

"Don't you?" he asked, but received only a shrug for an answer. "Whether Sam Clifford was shot by Mrs. Travis' *ghost* or someone else, one thing is certain: it wasn't one of us. There's definitely a killer hiding in those woods. But there's still a good chance he has an accomplice inside this house."

"You say that because of Allan's poisoning, I suppose. You don't think someone from outside would have had time to come in, poison the drink and disappear before the light came back on?"

"It's a possibility, but I find it unlikely. What makes me lean towards an accomplice is actually Gregory's poisoning, though."

Jennifer looked at him questioningly. "We don't even know how he was poisoned."

"We don't, that's true, but what are the odds he was poisoned while playing outside? Pretty slim if you ask me. The ground's covered with snow, there are no fruits or nuts on any of the trees, and if a stranger had offered him something, he was old enough to say no and let his father know about it."

"So you think that he was poisoned by someone he trusted. Someone inside the house."

"It's the most logical explanation. My money is on the hot cocoa he drank before going to bed. Clive was saying that each kid had their own mug. It would have been easy to selectively poison one of them."

Jennifer nodded her agreement as she walked to the ottoman and sat on it.

"Okay. So we probably have two killers on our hands. But why would they feel the need to leave clues to justify their crimes?"

"Serial killers sometimes do that. Some of them see their victims as deserving their fate. That's why prostitutes are among their favorite targets. The murderer justifies killing them because they're supposedly deprived of morals. It's not unusual to find bible verses beside the bodies of prostitutes, for instance. All relating one way or another to the divine punishment of sinful women. And of course, they make particularly easy prey too…"

"So the killer would be justifying Gregory's murder because the boy killed the cat? That seems a bit extreme…"

"We're dealing with a lunatic here. His reactions are extreme and irrational by definition."

"What about Allan? What message could we have missed?"

"I'm not sure," admitted Ethan. "It may be worth having another look."

"Now?"

"Why not? Everyone's in bed. I can go to his room and search for clues without anyone ever needing to know."

They discussed the idea for a few minutes before deciding they had little to lose by trying.

Ethan placed his holstered gun inside his waistband and dropped his shirt on top of it. "Don't open your door to anyone while I'm gone. And lock the door between our bedrooms."

"That goes without saying, boss."

He stepped into the deserted hallway using his cell phone as a flashlight, the only thing the device was good for in the absence of a network to connect to. He headed cautiously towards Allan's bedroom, making sure to walk along the walls where the hardwood floor was the least likely to creak.

He made it to Allan's door and slowly turned the handle. It was unlocked. He let himself in, silently closing the door behind him.

Allan's body had been transported to the barn for preservation, and the air inside the room felt stuffy but not nauseating.

The room was pitch black, but Ethan didn't dare flip the switch for fear that someone would notice the light under the door from the hallway. Still relying on his cell phone for illumination, he started thoroughly searching the room.

He'd been at it a few minutes when he noticed a cheap disposable phone hidden among Allan's socks. An interesting discovery, but he doubted it was a clue left by the man's murderer. He pocketed the burner phone and continued his search, before finally giving up twenty minutes later.

"Any luck?" asked Jennifer when he made it back to his room.

"Nothing that could be construed as a clue… but I found this," he said, pulling the burner out of his pocket.

"A flip phone? Why would Allan have one of those?"

"For calls he didn't want traced back to him, of course."

"Did you look inside?"

"It's out of battery and I couldn't find the charger."

"Well, unless you still need me, I think I'm going to go to bed, boss. And you should do the same," she said, yawning.

"I'm not quite ready for bed yet. There's still one relevant place we didn't search for clues," he added enigmatically before heading for the door one more time.

Chapter 57

Casanova had eagerly awaited Jennifer's return for more than a week. Awaited in vain. Driving by her empty apartment and Archer's equally empty office, he'd felt his frustration growing day by day. He'd have paid good money to find out where the bitch had gone.

When he'd finally given up on her coming back anytime soon and had headed to his usual holiday retreat, he'd been shocked to find Jennifer and Archer among the guests.

Who could have foreseen something like this? The coincidence was so enormous that at first he'd thought Archer was onto him.

Casanova had never bought the story about the two of them auditing Woodrough Enterprise and was relieved when Archibald had finally revealed the true purpose of their presence. A purpose which had nothing to do with him.

Now, he needed to reexamine his whole strategy concerning Jennifer MacKay. Although he wanted her more than ever and couldn't wait to force himself inside her, he could no longer use his Casanova approach on her. That ship had sailed the minute Archer had seen his face. How could he secretly seduce Jennifer behind Archer's back now? The odds she would end up mentioning dating him to Ethan were much too high. He simply couldn't risk it. He was going to have to come up with a whole different approach, one he hadn't yet thought through in detail.

She could of course fall victim to that mysterious ghost everyone was worried about, but where was the fun in that? Ethan needed to know she'd been targeted by a sexual predator. Finding his dear assistant poisoned in the study or shot in her bedroom wouldn't have the same psychological impact on the prick. That wouldn't do.

What he needed was a new creative way to kill the bitch. But there would be time to think about that later. For now, he wanted to stand back and enjoy the show. Three days at the cabin and already three bodies; the holiday season was more exciting than it had been in many years.

As he often did at night, Casanova was roaming the cabin's hallways, eavesdropping on conversations he wasn't meant to hear, when he saw Archer quietly coming out of Jennifer's room.

He stepped back around a corner and held his breath as the man started heading in the opposite direction.

What was the prick up to now? Looking for more *clues*?

He'd been amused by how adamant Archer had been about the picture being a clue. He was right, of course. The picture *was* a clue, an obvious one for those in the know. Which meant the prick would probably never understand its meaning since the clue wasn't meant for him.

He waited a few seconds before following his favorite nemesis at a distance. Ethan was already outside and halfway to the barn by the time Casanova reached the back door of the house and slipped out.

They had moved all the bodies to the barn under cover of darkness a few hours earlier to avoid the smell of decaying flesh spreading through the house. Keeping the windows opened in the deceased's rooms was no longer an option now that it was clear a lunatic was roaming outside the cabin.

In the pale light of the moon, he saw something in Archer's hand. He was keeping it by his side against his leg, but Casanova was pretty certain the prick was holding a gun. A useful piece of information to have for future reference.

Archer was almost constantly checking his surroundings, but Casanova was invisible behind one of the porch's pillars. When Archer finally reached the side door of the barn and disappeared inside, he went for it, making sure to step in the other man's footprints so as not to betray that he'd ever been there.

He reached the barn a few seconds later but didn't dare to open the door. The risk was too great that Archer would be alerted by the noise. Instead he went to one of the windows on the side of the building just as Archer flipped the switch to illuminate the inside of the structure. This was going to make his spying a lot easier.

Through the window, he observed Archer bent over Allan's frozen body, going through his pockets. It didn't take long. A moment later, the prick was holding an empty vial and a blue necklace. A necklace Casanova immediately recognized.

Chapter 58

A t breakfast the next day, Ethan told the others about the necklace and vial he'd found in Allan's pocket. The news was received with skepticism by a few, and suspicion by a couple, but overall he felt like the majority believed him. What reason would he have to lie about this anyway?

"What does it mean?" asked Gwendoline, returning from putting the kids in front of the TV. The three girls were spending their days in the den and would soon go nuts if they remained locked up in this house, just like the adults for that matter.

"The necklace I found in Allan's pocket was a message, just like the photo attached to the arrow and maybe even the cat under Gregory's bed," said Ethan.

He repeated the theory he'd expressed to Jennifer the night before, but the group appeared unconvinced.

"With the exception of the dead cat, I don't know what these clues mean. But I suspect some of you do know and if you want to get out of this nightmare alive, I'd suggest you tell me about it so I can try and figure this out."

"It's kind of you to try and help, Mr. Archer, but this isn't the job I'm paying you for. Sheriff Bradford is in charge of figuring out what the hell is going on here and any useful information one might have should go through him, not you," said Archibald, who couldn't have looked guiltier if he'd been wearing an orange jump suit and hand cuffs.

The sheriff, for his part, looked taken aback by the remark and tried to recover with an unconvincing, "That's right. You come and find me if you recognize that necklace or know what this picture's about."

Before anyone could respond, a loud thud was heard coming from outside. As if someone had kicked the front door.

"Travis, go see what that is, but be careful," said Archibald. As if being careful was going to save the old groundskeeper if someone was waiting for him on the other side of the door.

"I'll come with you, Mr. Travis," said Ethan, getting to his feet.

They went to the front door, followed at a distance by all the others.

"Wait here and don't open it before I tell you it's safe," Ethan told Travis before heading for the side door by the electric panel. Once there, he drew his gun out of its holster and cautiously stepped outside into the frigid morning air.

He went quietly around the corner of the house to check the front porch and the surrounding clearing, but no one was there. He was about to return inside the way he'd come when he saw it. He quickly ran to the front door and knocked for Travis to open; the old man did so, and a moment later Ethan was inside with the arrow he'd pulled out of the wooden door.

The projectile was of the same construction as the one that had killed

Sam Clifford. And just like the other one, this arrow had a message wrapped around its shaft. Not a picture, but a piece of animal skin with three words traced in blood:

Harm and Disserve.

They just stared at each other silently.

"These clues are becoming more and more cryptic. What's that one supposed to mean?" said Gwendoline.

Nobody had the slightest idea and, for once, Ethan had the feeling they were telling the truth.

"It's time to start playing offense," said the sheriff, surprisingly pumped up all of a sudden. "We know there's a jackass out there with a bow and an arrow who wants to kill us. We have eight men and plenty of guns in your safe, Archibald. Let's go get this son of a bitch. What do you say?"

The patriarch thought about it for what seemed like an eternity but was only a few seconds. "Let's do it! I have two shotguns and four rifles in the safe. That should give the bastard something to think about."

Ethan wasn't convinced this was a great idea, but he didn't have a better one, so he went with the flow and grabbed the shotgun Clive handed him. He would be teaming up with Blake. Clive would accompany Garrett Springer. And the third group would be composed of Matthew Woodrough and the sheriff. Archibald and Travis would stay at the cabin to protect the women. At least that was the way the patriarch put it.

Ethan took Jennifer aside and discreetly handed her his sidearm. He had very limited trust in Archibald Woodrough.

Hidden in a Douglas fir, the ghost heard his enemies come out of the cabin before he saw them spreading between the evergreens twenty feet underneath him. He'd been waiting for that.

He identified his target and patiently waited for the group to move deeper inside the woods before coming down from his tree.

His enemies had started a slow game of cat and mouse, but they were mistaken about who played what role. These were his woods.

The men fanned out between the trees in smaller groups. But the deeper they moved into the forest, the farther apart they became. This was exactly what he'd been waiting for.

The woods were silent but strong and their strength inhabited him, he who knew how to listen, how to live in harmony with the land. His foes were many, but he was far from alone.

He pulled the object out of his pocket and double checked it. Reassured, he resumed the stalking of his prey.

The lawman and the senator's son were at least three hundred yards from any reinforcement. A distance the ghost judged sufficient for the task at hand.

Carefully he got closer to his target. Slowly reducing the distance between them from a hundred feet to eighty, and then to sixty. He probably could have dropped the man at this distance, but the trees were thick in this part of the forest and he still needed to get closer to play it safe.

He was only thirty feet behind the two men when he pulled his favorite weapon from his back and hurled it at the senator's son.

The projectile hit him square in the back of the head and the man fell to the ground unconscious.

As the ghost pulled an arrow from his quiver, he saw the sheriff's eyes drop to the weapon lying near his friend's head.

Moving at a speed the ghost hadn't expected from the older man, the sheriff dived to the ground and fired in his enemy's direction as the arrow flew above his head, missing it by mere inches. But the lead pellets didn't miss their target. The ghost felt them shredding through his insides with the efficiency of a thousand tiny piranhas.

He fell backward, his bow lying a few feet to his right. He just had the time to reach for the object inside his pocket before the sheriff was over him, the cannon of his shotgun pointing straight at his head.

The ghost didn't understand the words the man spat at him as the sheriff depressed the trigger of his weapon. He heard the detonation and felt a couple of pellets grazing his cheek and forehead, but nothing else. The shot had wildly missed him, and he knew who to thank for this miracle.

Focused on his target, the sheriff had never noticed the wolves sneaking up on him. A mistake he was now paying for with his life as the beasts tore him to pieces.

Chapter 59

The snow around the sheriff's head was a bright shade of crimson. His throat had been ripped open by the beasts. That's what had killed him, the massive blood loss from the severed neck arteries. As indicated by the lack of deep wounds anywhere else on his body, this hadn't been a predatory attack. This had been an execution and the wolves were the weapon.

Ethan and the others had heard the gunshots, but the sound had been bouncing off the mountains, rendering the pinpointing of its origin impossible. A sea of trees lay between the groups, and none had the faintest clue where the other two were. It wasn't until Matthew had regained consciousness and called for help that they'd been able to locate the sheriff's lifeless body.

The numerous marks imprinted on the snow all around his corpse left little doubt as to what had happened. The sheriff had definitely been killed by wolves.

Only a few feet away from his body, another puddle of blood helped complete the picture. After Matthew had been knocked out, the sheriff had turned around and shot their attacker, as indicated by the damaged tree right behind the second blood puddle. The pine's trunk showed characteristic buckshot marks.

"Where did he go? He was clearly injured," said Clive, but no one had an answer for him.

The snow showed that their enemy had gotten back up and taken a few bloody steps to a patch of bare ground void of snow under a massive tree, and then nothing. It was as if the ground had swallowed him whole.

They carried the sheriff's corpse back to the cabin, a difficult task given the snow and the weapons they carried. The group kept together this time, four of them serving as an escort while the others carried their fallen companion.

They finally reached the house and were welcomed with the avalanche of questions one could expect in this type of situation.

"That's what knocked me out," said Matthew in answer to one of them as he pulled something from under his jacket. "I found it in the snow beside me when I woke up."

The object in his hand looked like a tomahawk. A rounded stone secured to a strong wooden handle by thick leather straps.

"It would seem our friend has a thing for Native American weapons," said Matthew, who still looked slightly woozy.

Ethan wondered if the lobbyist might be suffering from a concussion in addition to the pigeon-egg bump on the back of his head.

"Are there any Native Americans in the region?" asked Jennifer.

"A few, but no reservation or anything. This used to be Shoshone territory, but that was long before I was born," said James Travis.

"Why would Native Americans come after us? To take back their land? Sounds unlikely..." said Archibald.

Ethan admitted that it did sound unlikely. Their homicidal stalker was more likely a lunatic who liked to play cowboys and Indians. He was a very skilled and very dangerous lunatic, however. One who'd already killed twice. Possibly more if he was also behind the two poisonings.

"Did he leave a message?" asked Emily.

"None that we found, but he probably didn't expect to be shot. That surely modified his plan a bit," said Clive. "He may have forgotten about any message he'd meant to leave us in his haste to get away with a belly full of lead."

Ethan had thought about this on their way back to the house. He'd come up with a different hypothesis, however. Maybe the message had been sent ahead of time. Maybe the cryptic words written in blood on a piece of hide had been the clue justifying the sheriff's execution. Put in this perspective, one couldn't help but notice the similarity between *Harm and Disserve* and the *Protect and Serve* motto placarded on every law enforcement vehicle in the country.

"If nothing else, this should buy us some time. The asshole was shot with a 12-gauge, he's not likely to come after us anytime soon," said Clive.

The others approved the statements as Mrs. Travis announced that lunch was ready. They all headed toward the dining room, but in his mind Ethan was staring at the sheriff's bloody corpse. Hadn't the lawman bragged about killing a pair of wolves a few years back? Karma truly was a bitch, quite possibly literally in this case.

Lunch was long over and, after two hours of debates, there was still no agreement on what their next step should be. Some of the men wanted to go back out there and look for the ghost, but Ethan had pointed out that it hadn't turned out so well for them the first time around. It was getting increasingly clear that the ghost wasn't the only enemy they needed to worry about. The wolves were an integral part of the equation.

"I'm not worried about the wolves," said Blake, who, like most men of the Woodrough clan, was an avid hunter.

"Sheriff Bradford wasn't either," answered Ethan pointedly.

"Is Matthew still sleeping?" asked Gwendoline. Her cousin had excused himself before lunch and retired to his bedroom to nurse the massive headache caused by the tomahawk.

"I think so. I haven't seen him since," said Emily.

She'd barely finished her sentence when a loud engine sound came from outside. A moment later, a snowmobile flew in front of the window heading for the road.

"Who's that?" exclaimed Gwendoline, jumping to her feet.

Nobody had an answer. Clive, Blake and Ethan ran to the barn to check on the snowmobiles, only to be confronted with the obvious: one of the bikes was missing.

There was sand on the ground and the other snowmobiles had been tinkered with as well—partially taken apart. Someone had successfully cleaned one of the tanks and had gotten a bike running using parts from the others.

They walked back inside the house to relate their findings as Emily was coming down from the second floor. "Matthew's room is empty. It doesn't look like he was ever in bed," she said, looking panicked.

"The little prick! What does he think he's doing?" said Archibald.

From the corner of his eye, Ethan saw Jennifer discreetly walking up the stairs and heading for her room. He excused himself and followed her a second later.

"Are you okay?" he asked.

She hadn't heard him coming and she jumped in surprise in front of her window before turning around to face him. "You scared me!"

"Sorry, I didn't mean to scare you. Are you alright? You seem distraught."

A tear fell on her cheek and she quickly wiped it off with her sleeve. "I'm starting to have enough of this, Ethan." She gave him a contrived smile. "I want to go home, all these deaths… I thought I was tough, but I'm not."

"Why now, all the sudden?" he asked, trying to understand.

"Because now you have killer wolves on the loose, and a rogue cousin that's probably an accomplice to all those murders... That's just too much to take."

"Why do you think Matthew's an accomplice?"

She rolled her eyes, slowly shaking her head. "Isn't it obvious? The ghost could have killed him out there. If he could knock him out with a tomahawk, he could have shot him with an arrow just the same... But instead he decided to go for the sheriff and spare Matthew. Why would he do that? And now that the ghost has been injured, Matthew magically manages to fix a vehicle and takes off without telling anyone about it. Do you really think those are the actions of someone with a clear conscience?"

Ethan had carefully listened to Jennifer's arguments and he agreed with her on at least one point. There was something strange in the facts she just mentioned. But what bothered him the most in the whole thing had nothing to do with Matthew Woodrough.

Chapter 60

After tinkering with the engine for nearly three hours, Matthew was finally able to start the snowmobile on his fifth try.

At the sound of the engine coming to life, he rushed to the wall and pressed the button opening the garage door. He then grabbed one of the helmets, put it on, and jumped onto the snowmobile. He didn't have a second to waste. He needed to escape before anyone realized what he was up to.

The snowmobile skidded loudly on the barn's concrete floor, but the ruckus stopped as soon at the bike reached the snow.

He saw Gwendoline standing in front of the billiard-room's windows from the corner of his eye and knew he had succeeded. They wouldn't be able to stop him now.

He sped up across the clearing and entered the road a bit too fast. He lost control of the snowmobile for an instant and nearly collided with one of the trees lining the left side of the road, but he regained control at the last minute and returned the snowmobile to the center of the road, albeit at a less risky pace. It wouldn't do him any good to crash the bike before he was out of the woods, literally and figuratively.

The next couple miles went smoothly. He had made his escape.

Suddenly the snowmobile's engine started sputtering. Panic set in, but he did his best to ignore it. Perhaps some sand he'd overlooked had made its way to the fuel line and was now partially blocking it. The bike coughed and erratically jumped forward for an additional two or three hundred yards before finally dying.

He was almost three miles from the cabin and still twelve miles from the highway. A perilous position, especially considering that he'd taken no weapon with him. Being seen walking from his room with a rifle would have been a bit too suspicious.

He jumped off the bike and removed his helmet to have a better look inside the tank. He saw nothing but darkness.

Then he heard it! A howl. Quickly answered by several others.

Swiftly, he disconnected the end of the fuel line going to the engine. Only a few drops of gas dripped from the hose. This suggested the blockade was either in the line or at the tank outlet.

He tried to squeeze the line a few times but it didn't budge. The reinforced rubber was too stiff to be compressed by his quickly numbing fingers.

Placing his lips around the hose, he sucked gently, hoping to purge the blocked line, but to no avail. The howling sounds were getting closer now.

He then tried blowing into the line and heard air bubbling inside the tank. He continued blowing as hard as he could before alternating sucking and blowing on the line.

Finally, he managed to dislodge the blockage and spat out a mouthful of gas. His heart jumped into his throat a second later. A wolf was running between the trees towards him. The beast was less than two hundred feet away.

Hurriedly, he reattached the line to the engine, spilling gasoline on the snow in the process. He jumped back on his bike just as a wolf emerged from the trees followed by two more.

The engine started on Matthew's first attempt as the lead wolf lunged at him. He kicked out with his right leg and caught the beast square in the chest before speeding away.

The snowmobile was running smoothly again, but he knew he wasn't safe yet. As long as the bike behaved, the beast wouldn't catch up with him, but if it died again…

There was also the tree across the road ahead of him to worry about. He would lose some precious time navigating around the obstacle.

As he'd predicted, the massive Douglas fir came into view a moment later. There was no pushing the darned thing with the snowmobile, that was for sure.

He gave a quick glance behind him to find five wolves chasing the bike. They were about six hundred feet away, perhaps closer.

He came to a stop fifteen yards from the obstacle, looking for a path between the surrounding trees that grew particularly thick in this part of the woods.

He identified a potential way and engaged the snowmobile between two large evergreens bordering the right side of the road.

The progress was steady but slow. The wolves were rapidly catching up. They were only a couple hundred feet away by the time he finally got around the downed tree and started working his way back to the road. But it was easier said than done. The thicket was simply impenetrable in places and the stress made an already tricky situation even harder to manage.

Just as he was about to emerge onto the road, he felt teeth ripping into his right calf. He didn't look down, that would do no good. He needed to outpace his attackers.

The second wolf went for his right arm, but his thick winter jacket partially protected the limb. As the bike finally climbed back onto the road, Matthew pressed down hard on the throttle.

Their bodies flailing around in the snow, the two beasts hung onto him for a good hundred feet before eventually releasing their hold.

His leg was hurting and he was losing blood, as evidenced by the red spots dotting the path of the snowmobile, but he had to focus on the positive: he was safe... for now.

Chapter 61

"The son of a bitch won't get away with it," said Archibald, as Ethan and Jennifer rejoined the others around the pool tables. They'd been gone nearly thirty minutes, but the discussion hadn't evolved much.

"Where have you two been?" he asked suspiciously, as they entered the room. The man was displaying increasingly obvious signs of paranoia. Not a good thing given the circumstances. Paranoid personality disorder could have tragic consequences if the paranoia became too serious; Timothy McVeigh's Oklahoma City bombing was only one example of how dangerous these people could be.

"In our rooms. We needed a break from all this," answered Ethan.

"Don't we all?" Tiffany Springer chimed in.

"Have we decided anything?" asked Ethan, walking to an empty chair facing Blake Jones who was once again furtively looking at Jennifer when nobody seemed to be paying attention to him. Ethan wondered if Emily had any idea about her husband's philandering tendencies. Ethan had no proof of this, of course, but he'd spent enough time tailing unfaithful spouses over the past few months that he'd developed an eye for the guilty ones.

"We've decided nothing! We're completely helpless here. This is just unbelievable!" Tiffany threw her glass against the hardwood floor but failed to shatter it. The woman was quickly moving from abrasive to unstable.

"Handle your wife, Garrett," said Archibald, which started an all-out shouting match between him and Tiffany, and threw the bimbo's husband into the unfortunate role of a referee too overwhelmed to count the points.

The confrontation ended with Tiffany storming out of the room. Her husband followed closely behind her, looking utterly defeated.

It was barely four in the afternoon but the light outside was already starting to dim. Soon the night would be back, and with it all their fears would be multiplied.

Blake had suggested that Matthew might have gone to get some help, and that he hadn't warned anyone about his plan because he didn't know whom to trust.

The idea had merit—Ethan had considered the possibility almost as soon as he'd seen the snowmobile fly by through the window—but Archibald was, of course, not convinced and nobody dared going against the patriarch after the invectives he'd recently exchanged with Tiffany.

Throughout the discussion Ethan kept trying to understand the meaning of the clues left by the killer. He was convinced he lacked context to understand the significance of the orphanage picture and the necklace found inside Allan's pocket, but the cat and the message shot at the front door were more accessible. He was pretty sure he knew what the *Harm and Disserve* message had meant; now he needed to find out to what extent it was true.

Dinner had once again been a quick affair made of canned goods. Mrs. Travis hadn't been as inspired this time, but not even Archibald had felt like mentioning the fact to the cook. Garrett Springer had come down for dinner, but Tiffany had remained in their room, no doubt simmering.

They all retired to the lounge where the fire burning in the hearth was all but out.

"Travis, put some logs on those embers. We don't want a repeat of what happened the last time this fire went out," said Archibald, referring to Allan's poisoning.

Travis nodded and bent down to retrieve some logs from the storage space under the fireplace.

"I don't understand," he said, getting back up. "There are none left, but I restocked it yesterday."

At that moment a loud thud came from the front door. This time everyone knew precisely what it meant. Not only was the ghost still kicking despite being shot, he'd sent them a new message.

They all stared at each other, no one daring to move.

"Maybe we should see if the arrow came with a note," suggested Ethan to break the silence.

"And get shot as we open the door? Be my guest, Mr. Archer, go check," said Archibald.

Ethan got up and they all followed him. When they reached the front door, he made sure nobody stood directly behind it and swung it open away from him, using the wall as a shield.

"There is a message," he said, staring at the arrow planted a few inches left of where the first one had landed.

"What does it say?" asked Gwendoline.

"I don't know," said Ethan, who was thinking about a safe way to retrieve the message wrapped around the shaft without exposing himself to the archer.

All the sudden, the light in the foyer went out and the kids started screaming, quickly followed by the sound of the door closing. The light returned a moment later as Jennifer flipped the switch back on. "Sorry about that, but I thought I'd make a harder target in the dark," she said, showing them the message she'd retrieved from the door. She unrolled the piece of paper and showed it to the others.

The message only contained two words: *wrong door.*

A second later the lights went out in the entire house and this time no flipping of the switch brought them back on.

"He's in the house, he came in through the side door," said Clive, as Gwendoline and Emily were calling frantically for their respective daughters.

Ethan remembered that the side door was right next to the electric panel which aligned with Clive's theory about the ghost's position.

The house was pitch black and once again the only light came from the dying fire. Under other circumstances, everyone would have pulled out the flashlight on their cellphones, but all mobile devices had been left in the rooms. What was the point of carrying your phone around in a house with no Wi-Fi and no cellular network?

"We need to find him," said Archibald, who was holding a gun in front of him. It was too dark to tell for sure, but Ethan suspected this was the very gun his wife had used to shoot herself.

"You're the one with the gun, Archibald," said the turtle.

"We need to get some light back on," said Jennifer. "We won't find him in the dark and we're making perfect targets all standing in the only room that has any type of illumination. We can't see him but he's probably staring at us right now."

Jennifer was very likely to be right. Once again, the situation was favoring the enemy.

"What do you suggest?" asked Clive.

"Gwendoline and Emily should take the kids to the den on the opposite side of the house and keep them safe," Jennifer answered in a whisper that was nonetheless loud enough for everyone to hear since they were all huddled together. "Ethan and Mr. Travis will fetch some snow from outside to put out the fireplace. As soon as it's dark, Clive and Blake, run to your rooms upstairs for distraction. During that time, I'll sneak outside and go around the house to the side door where I'll flip the breaker back on."

"Out of the question. What if the ghost is waiting for you near the breaker?" said Ethan.

"Then I'll shoot him," she answered, pulling his gun out of her hoody's pocket.

"How about I take the gun and the two of us go together to the electric panel as soon as I'm done dealing with the fire?" Ethan said.

"Fine, now let's move," said Jennifer.

The two mothers ran with their kids towards the den while Travis and Ethan gathered armfuls of wet snow from outside which they used to douse the fire. The puny thing died with the sound of hissing steam, immediately followed by the running steps of the two brothers-in-law heading upstairs.

Ethan made it outside first and started silently moving towards the side door without waiting for Jennifer. He didn't need her for this particular task and wanted to spare her the risk associated with it.

"You were supposed to wait!" she whispered in his ear a moment later as she caught up with him.

He ignored her and they soon reached the side door. It was wide open. Ethan listened for signs of life but heard none. He decided to go for it. In a fluid motion he slipped inside the house and reached for the main switch. He found it after three or four excruciatingly long seconds fumbling around in the dark.

The lights came back on throughout the house, but the vestibule was completely empty.

"He's not here," screamed Ethan to let the others know before heading for the lounge, gun in hand.

He reached the group as Garrett and Clive were coming back down, each holding their cell phone set to flashlight. Blake also held a handgun now.

"Let's sweep the house. All those with guns should lead the way. Archibald, that means you too," said Ethan to the patriarch who was sitting in an armchair. "Archibald?"

The man was perfectly immobile. His unblinking eyes were fixated on a point far in front of him.

Ethan walked to the armchair and checked the man's pulse. He had none. What Ethan did find was the handle of a paring knife protruding from the base of Archibald's skull.

Chapter 62

The sweep of the house turned up no intruder; the ghost was already gone. Ethan was starting to understand the nickname. The man was like vapor, nearly invisible, impossible to catch, and those who tried burned themselves.

At Ethan's suggestion, they'd searched Archibald's pocket for a clue and found a dirty rag that had once been a small stuffed bunny. As usual, nobody knew what it meant or recognized the object.

This was precisely the reaction Ethan had expected, which was why he'd been paying close attention to his companions' facial expressions. It had been a good idea since he was fairly certain it was recognition that he'd seen flashing in Mrs. Travis' eyes as she'd stared at the raggedy bunny. He wasn't about to confront the cook in front of the others, however. This was the type of matter better handled in private.

"What now?" asked Gwendoline, who'd joined them in the lounge. Emily was keeping an eye on the girls who were watching TV in the den. Ethan wondered how badly this weekend was going to mess those kids up.

"It's nearly nine o'clock. I suggest everyone turns in for the night. Barricade yourselves in your rooms, and it wouldn't hurt to sweep your bedrooms one more time for potential intruders before locking the door," said

Ethan.

There was a short discussion regarding the helplessness of their situation, but in the end nobody had anything more productive to propose so they followed his suggestion.

The whole house woke up around midnight to the sound of a large diesel engine.

Within seconds, Jennifer was in Ethan's room wearing nothing but cotton panties and a white tank top. "What's that?" she asked, as he tried not to stare at her boobs, clearly visible through the thin fabric.

"I don't know. It's coming from outside," was all he managed to say.

They walked to the window but saw nothing at first. The night wasn't as dark as it should have been given the thick cloud cover, however; something was emitting light near the clearing.

"Let's check my window, it has a view onto the road," she said, already heading for her room.

From Jennifer's window, one could see a ramp of light through the trees. It was moving forward on the road at a slow pace, sometimes stopping and backing up before moving forward again.

"Is this what I think it is?" asked Jennifer.

"I think so..."

Five minutes later, a V-shaped snowplow pushed by something resembling a bulldozer was emerging from the road and onto the clearing. It was quickly followed by a half dozen police vehicles from the Sheriff's Office. Matthew Woodrough had returned, and he'd brought the cavalry with him.

Chapter 63

By 7 AM, the nine sheriff deputies who had guarded the house overnight had been joined by the state troopers who'd brought in some detectives. The state police asked a few questions and quickly decided that, given the magnitude of the mess, the FBI should be called in on the basis of the potential connection with the assassination of Senator Woodrough.

After the initial relief caused by the unexpected rescue, the mood of the survivors of the ordeal switched when they were told that they couldn't leave the premises until the FBI had arrived and everyone had given their statements.

None of this surprised Ethan. Five people had been murdered and it wasn't completely clear whether the lunatic looming in those woods had been responsible for all of them or whether he'd had some help from the inside.

The FBI resident agent dispatched from Bozeman arrived around 11 AM, but the forensic team and other reinforcements he'd called in from the Salt Lake City field office weren't expected until later in the afternoon.

The mood of the guests lit up a bit when the landline was reestablished and with it the return of the DSL connection. Everyone jumped onto the network at once, like famished hyenas discovering a carcass after days of starvation. Of course, this sudden interest immediately brought the network to a crawling pace that reminded Ethan of the era ruled by dial-up modems.

He was eventually able to connect his cell phone to the DSL network and was surprised at the number of new voicemails and texts he'd received over the past few days.

All but a couple were from Theo who was asking Ethan to call him back with an increased sense of urgency as the messages went by. Ethan gave up after the fifth one and decided to save some time by calling Theo directly.

His friend picked up on the second ring. "Where the hell have you been?"

"Hi, Theo. I'm doing well, thanks. How are you?"

"You're okay? I was worried sick. I've been trying to reach you for three days and all my text messages came back as 'not delivered.' I was starting to think the other psycho got you."

"He nearly did, but not the psycho you're thinking about."

Ethan spent the next twenty minutes telling Theo about the nightmare of the past days. A mere ninety-six hours that had felt like an eternity.

"That's crazy, bro. You need to get your ass back to civilization. We've got plenty of nut jobs here in the city. No need to go to the boonies to get whacked by some hillbilly who thinks he's Crazy Horse."

"Given the major cluster this turned out to be, I think I'm going to be stuck here a few days. I have to give my statement to your colleagues, for one thing, and they have yet to show up."

"I haven't heard anything about it yet, so I guess that means I'm not getting assigned to the case." Theo sounded almost regretful.

"Count your blessings. Whoever lands this one is getting a doozy. They're already organizing a search of the forest. They're planning to go at it with dogs and a couple hundred armed men, but I'll be shocked if they catch the guy."

"You seem almost an admirer." Theo sounded concerned now.

"I don't think that's the word. But I wouldn't make the mistake of underestimating the enemy. If he's the man the locals call the ghost, he's been roaming those woods for decades. He could very well be responsible for the deaths of those kids discovered in a nearby cave last week."

"What would he be doing going after adults now? Serial killers don't change their M.O. this drastically."

"The first victim of the killing spree was a kid named Gregory. But I agree with you, he would need a good reason to start targeting adults."

"Talking about serial killers… There was a reason I was trying to get in touch with you in the first place."

"I'm listening." Ethan was suddenly very serious.

"We found something of interest on the video."

If Theo was about to tell him that there was another guy there, Ethan was going to get mad.

"Based on the sound of the waves, the house has to be a beachfront property. One with single-paned windows."

"That's your news?"

"Let me finish! We roughly knew Amanda's time of death and what time she was discovered on the beach. That gave us a driving radius for beach-house properties to look at."

"One with a few thousand houses, I would imagine."

"Correct, but if you narrow it down by looking only at the ones that are fairly isolated, relatively old—"

"Why relatively old?" Ethan interrupted.

"Because most modern houses in the area would have double-paned windows, Ethan. Then we narrowed it down further by looking only at rental properties. Don't ask why. It was just a hunch from one of the guys on the team."

"You're killing me here. What did you find?"

"We found the house where Amanda was killed. It was vacant so it was easy to organize a visit by acting like a potential customer. She was killed in one of the guest bedrooms. They'd moved all the furniture out, but the walls are identical and so is the flooring."

"Was it rented at the time of her death?"

"Don't get too excited, bro. It was rented but to someone who died five years ago. Obviously, the ID was stolen, and the picture isn't that of our killer either. It matches the name on the driver's license."

"How did he pay the landlord?"

"Cash. In advance for a six-week lease that ended a week after Amanda's death."

"Maybe he killed other victims in that house. Maybe he'll come back," Ethan said, not truly believing it.

"We're already following that trail, but so far nothing."

Although this was much more information that he'd been hoping to get from the video, Ethan still felt terribly frustrated. The bastard had underestimated the FBI's resources, but so far it hadn't been enough to get to him.

"I gotta go. Thanks for the news, Theo, and call me as soon as you have something else for me. No matter how small it may be. You hear me?"

As he hung up, Ethan felt a presence behind him. He turned around to find Blake leaning against the wall five feet away, checking his cell. How long had he been standing here? And why did it bother Ethan? Even if Blake had eavesdropped on the entire phone call, how could it matter?

"What's this room? I don't think I ever noticed it before," he said, pointing at the door to the right of Emily's husband.

"That's Aaron's old study. The senator sometimes used it as his office when he came to the cabin. It's just a spare room now, I guess," answered Blake, putting his phone back in his pocket.

What had attracted Ethan's attention were the initials on the door: A.W.

for Aaron Woodrough. But there was something strangely familiar about those initials.

"Do you think someone would care if I had a look?" Ethan said, placing his hand on the door handle.

"I think the only one who might have cared died last night."

Ethan pushed the door open and found himself in a dusty office furnished with large wooden bookshelves and an antique desk the size of a small car. On the walls were pictures of cows and cowboys taken at the ranch. Like the rest of the cabin, the decoration was Western art. Antique guns, an old lasso and some branding irons also hung from the walls.

He was about to leave the room when one of the branding irons caught his attention. It took him a second to realize what he was looking at. When he finally understood why the brand looked so familiar, he almost screamed.

Chapter 64

The ghost sat against the wall of the cave surrounded by his wolves. They knew they would soon lose their friend. They could sense his weakness. They could smell his blood.

His head slowly pivoted, his eyes taking in the room in its entirety. The phosphorescent glowworms provided more than enough light for him to see through the cave's darkness. This room wasn't the largest one of the vast subterranean complex, but it had always been one of his favorites, one he visited on a regular basis.

What better place could he choose to exhale his last breath than in a room filled with the bones of the dead? Hundreds of skeletons lay assembled in neat little piles all around him. He'd known the exact number at some point, when he'd still kept track. But he no longer did. What was the point? This was the end.

The thought brought sadness to his heart. Not because he was going to die. Death didn't scare him. He knew he had nothing to fear from it.

He was sad because this cave would soon be empty. The wolves would still use it as their lair, but it wasn't the same. He had so many memories of this place, fond memories.

He coughed some blood and the alpha came to rest his head on his extended legs. It was for the wolves that he felt the worst. Who would protect them once he was gone?

He heard footsteps coming towards him. Few people would have been able to hear such soft sounds, but a life spent in almost permanent darkness had sharpened his other senses.

He smiled at the man as he entered the dark room but received a somber look in return. He wasn't surprised.

The man had found him unconscious, bleeding at the base of the tree and taken him back to the cave. He'd been careful to erase the tracks left by the snowshoes as the ghost had taught him to do, but his intervention had been against his better judgment. He'd been forced to get involved, he who had wanted nothing to do with the ghost's crusade. And he wasn't pleased with the way things had turned out.

The ghost felt exceedingly weak. One person was still missing, but he knew this was all the company he would get to accompany him to the other world. It wouldn't be long now.

Chapter 65

E than took the branding iron off the wall and stared at it a long moment. A capital A and a capital W joined together by the continuation of the bar crossing the A.

$$A\!\!\!\!W$$

This bar was the reason they'd misread the branding marks left by the Cowboy on his victims' breasts. The two A's had never been A's in the first place, it had been a W all along… One they'd been reading upside down.

$$\Lambda\!\!\Lambda$$

He pulled his phone out of his pocket and opened a measuring app. He then took the exact measurements of the W to compare it with the actual brand on the victims, but he already knew it was a match.

He hadn't seen the A branded on the senator's chest so he couldn't confirm it matched the one he was currently holding, but he'd be surprised if it didn't.

Someone had separated the two letters from a similar iron and used the W to sign his victims. That someone was the man who'd killed Amanda. The real Cowboy.

The A branded on the senator's chest, apex pointing towards the victim's feet, had been a clue. One meant to let the investigators know that the Cowboy's signature had been a W all along. One branded in the same position and with the same orientation as the A on the senator's chest.

This meant their copycat wasn't a copycat at all. It was someone who knew the real killer…

Ethan took several pictures of the branding iron before replacing it on the wall. He then exited the room in search of Gwendoline.

He found her with her daughter in the den. The two of them were watching cartoons with Emily's kids but Gwendoline's unfocused eyes were a clear indication that her mind was somewhere else.

"Can I see you for a moment, Mrs. Thomas? I need to ask you something."

She got up from her seat, intrigued. "What's going on, Mr. Archer?"

"It'll be easier if I show you," he said, leading the way to Aaron's study. "What is this?" he asked, pointing at the branding iron on the wall.

"A branding iron," she answered, looking at him questioningly. "Where does it come from?"

"It's our old brand. That's how we used to mark our cattle before my father changed the brand to make it his. The new one is still made of an A and a W but the overall shape is different now."

"So, this is the one and only original iron from your grandfather's time?"

"It's the last one. Where are you going with this?"

"There were other irons identical to this one?"

"Over the years? Sure, a few. I remember that one got lost, one broke... and these are only the ones I know about."

"You say one got broken? How? I mean, where was the break?"

"What's going on, Mr. Archer? Why are you asking all these questions about an old branding iron?" Gwendoline was looking at him suspiciously now.

"It's very important, Mrs. Thomas, believe me."

"Does this have something to do with what happened here? My parents' and my brother's death?"

"No. It has nothing to do with that," he said to reassure her, although he had no idea. This question would need to wait. He'd just noticed something he'd completely overlooked before. He'd been so focused on the murders and Archibald's odd reactions to his son and grandson's passing that he'd paid no particular attention to Gwendoline until now.

She'd looked sort of upset after her mother's passing, but the emotion had only showed on her face for a few hours. In the space of four days, she'd lost both her parents, her brother and a nephew, and had displayed as much grief as a rancher butchering a calf.

"So why do you ask?" she said vehemently.

"Alright... It may be related to what happened here over the past few days, Mrs. Thomas," he said, affecting reluctancy. "It's just too early to tell at this point. Please, answer my question. In which way was the iron broken?"

She thought about it a moment before answering, "It's been so long I can't remember for sure, but I think half of the W broke off."

"Thank you, Mrs. Thomas. This is very helpful information," said Ethan. And he meant it.

It wasn't what he'd expected to hear—he'd suspected the break had been a clean cut between the A and the W, something that would have made more sense based on the iron's design—but it had been very informative, nonetheless.

Gwendoline had clearly been lying, but people didn't lie for the sake of it. They did it when they had something to hide.

Chapter 66

For the first time in ages, Casanova had been caught by surprise. Technically, it was the Cowboy, his other persona, who'd been caught with his pants down, but it made little difference. Whether Casanova or the Cowboy screwed up, he was the one who'd pay the price.

He'd never known another copy of his favorite branding iron had been hanging on the wall in Aaron's study. This was a major disaster. It wouldn't be long before Archer put two and two together. The way the prick had been staring at the damn thing and playing twenty questions with Gwendoline was more than concerning.

Casanova boiled on the inside. Had he known Archer was going to put his hands on such a compromising piece of evidence, he'd have killed him days ago. He'd have been one of the first ones to die. The only one who truly needed to, as far as he was concerned. The recent murders had made an otherwise boring vacation fun, but he'd had no qualms over the victims. He even had a certain affinity for a couple of them, although their deaths had been of no consequence to him.

Killing Archer now was no longer an option, however, not with a house full of suspicious cops. The involvement of the man they'd nicknamed the ghost was a given fact, but they were still fishing for an accomplice.

Casanova couldn't afford to attract any attention to himself right now, but he couldn't afford to delay silencing Archer, either. The prick would want to share his discovery with his FBI friends as soon as possible.

Fleeing was an option, but not a good one. It would immediately bring him under suspicion, and there was no guarantee he'd succeed in getting away.

He only took calculated risks. That's what made him so good at what he did. Rushing into a half-assed retreat would be a mistake. There might soon be a time where he wouldn't have a choice in the matter, but not just yet. Archer might even have believed Gwendoline's story about the broken iron... The prick wasn't too sharp.

He took a deep breath and went to sit in one of the chairs by the fireplace. As he did, he smiled at a cute female deputy carrying evidence bags. Even in situations like these, he remained a predator first and foremost, and women had always been his favorite prey. He'd killed men too, of course, sometimes you couldn't afford to be picky, but it never brought him the same thrill. There was something about a woman's screams when he applied the red-hot iron to her naked boob that a man simply couldn't compete with. This thought gave him the answer to his problem. It was so obvious he couldn't believe he hadn't thought of it right away. The iron was the answer. He simply needed to plant his own iron in Allan's stuff for the cops to find.

A dead man made for the perfect scapegoat. And of those who'd been killed over the past few days, Allan was by far the best candidate for the job.

He just had to retrieve the branding iron from the dungeon and hide it in Allan's belongings without anyone noticing. In a house swarming with cops, that was easier said than done.

Chapter 67

The two dozen cops who'd been searching the woods came back to the cabin a couple hours after nightfall with nothing to show for it. Even the dogs hadn't picked up any scent. The search would be resumed in the morning with numerous reinforcements from the state police, but Ethan doubted they'd have more luck the next day. He had a feeling the ghost wouldn't be found.

Under normal circumstances, the survivors would have been encouraged to leave the premises to preserve the crime scenes, but the circumstances were far from normal and the crime scenes had already been trampled so many times by so many people that it hardly mattered at this point. As a result, the guests had been asked to await the arrival of the FBI team dispatched from Salt Lake City before taking their leave. The Feds should have already been here, but they'd been delayed due to a mechanical problem with their plane.

This suited Ethan just fine. Now that they were no longer in danger of being murdered by an elusive killer, he wanted to spend some time investigating the connection between this place and the Cowboy.

The first order of business was to figure out what he, Ethan, was doing in this house.

Gwendoline had hired him to investigate a simple blackmailing incident. Could it be a coincidence that a branding iron nearly identical to that used by his nemesis was present in the family's cabin? It was doubtful. Did the killer himself arrange for him to be involved? Was Archibald the killer? Or was it someone else entirely who was behind his hiring? Only Gwendoline could answer that question and, based on her reaction in front of the branding iron, it was doubtful she'd tell him the truth. She definitely knew something, but she wasn't talking.

The next question was whether the man responsible for Amanda's death was also the one behind the killings of the past few days.

Until proven otherwise, Vivian Woodrough had taken her own life, but her husband, son and grandson had been murdered. With Sheriff Bradford and Sam Clifford, it made for five murders and a suicide in four days. This had to be some type of a record.

The sheriff, the patriarch and the retired orphanage director had been killed by the man Ethan had come to think about as the ghost, but it wasn't obvious whether Gregory and Allan had also been poisoned by him or if someone else was involved. Ethan's money was on the ghost working with an accomplice in the house.

Assuming this was correct, was the Cowboy the ghost's accomplice? And if so, had he recruited the ghost to use him as a scapegoat just like he'd done with Avery?

The other possibility was that the ghost worked alone. In which case, if the Cowboy had been in the house in the first place, was he even still alive or had he fallen victim to the murderer?

Ethan didn't really see the sheriff in the role of his nemesis, but the retired orphanage director, Allan and his father could all fit the Cowboy's profile. The three of them had ample opportunities to travel and be away from home for extended periods of time. Each could have been living a double life with no one the wiser.

His head was starting to hurt. He would never get any answers to his questions without further information. Not the way his brain had been working lately.

Ethan heard Jennifer getting out of the shower in her room and gave her a few minutes to get dressed before knocking on her door.

There was a pause between his knock and her "Come in."

When he finally entered her room, he found her fully dressed and lacing her hiking boots.

"Are you going somewhere?" he asked, confused, as it was nearing eight in the evening.

"I need to get out of here. I can't take it anymore. This atmosphere… I need some fresh air." She'd spoken softly, almost whispering, as if pronouncing the words out loud would somehow make her feel worse. He could tell from her reddened eyes that she'd been crying.

"Are you alright?" he asked, not knowing what else to say.

"I'm fine. I just need to get out of this house for a while."

"But we don't have a car…"

"I'll go for a walk."

"That's not a good idea, Jennifer. There's still a killer on the loose out there."

"The cops spent the afternoon searching those woods. I doubt the killer will be back this evening with the ground still teeming with Sheriff Bradford's deputies. I'll be fine."

"I can't let you take the risk. It's just not safe out there. Tomorrow we'll be able to leave this house, but you'll have to put up with it one more night."

"Fine, but I need to be left alone, Ethan. We'll talk in the morning."

"Okay. I'll leave you alone. You know where to find me if you need anything. Or if you just want to talk."

She thanked him and he left her bedroom through the connecting door. He heard the lock sliding in place as soon as he closed the door.

He was feeling bad for her. She was tough, but the stress of the past few days had finally gotten to Jennifer. He worried about the lasting trauma the ordeal might have caused.

He heard a knock on the door leading to the hallway a few minutes later and opened it to find Gwendoline standing on the other side.

Chapter 68

Walking nonchalantly from room to room, Casanova was mentally mapping the position of everyone currently on the first floor. His timing needed to be perfect; nobody could see him sneak out of the house or he'd have some explaining to do. The kind of explaining he didn't need.

Fortunately, most of the guests had already retired to their rooms. Mostly because they didn't want to hang out on the first floor with the six sheriff deputies tasked to spend the night.

The cops were officially there to protect them, but he had little doubt they'd also been told to keep an eye on the guests and make sure no one left the premises.

He completed his tour and concluded he was screwed. The cops were watching every door. Sneaking out unnoticed wasn't an option. For a moment he considered leaving through a window but decided against it. It would look very bad if he got caught. Not a chance he was willing to take.

He finally went straight to the front door and had one hand on the handle when one of the deputies called out to him from across the room, "Where are you going, sir?"

"I'm going to get a steak. You want one?"

"Thank you, sir, but nobody should leave the house right now. It's not safe out there."

"I'm not crazy enough to leave on foot, officer. I'm just going to the walk-in freezer in the barn. I'll be back in a minute. You can even come with me or watch me from that window right there if that makes you feel better."

"Okay, go ahead," said the cop, sounding uneasy. "But hurry back, sir."

He exited the cabin and headed straight for the barn. Good thing the cop hadn't called his bluff and accompanied him. The officer was standing behind the window, though.

He entered the barn using the side door and locked it from the inside. He grabbed a box full of venison steaks from the walk-in freezer and placed it in front of the barn's door as a reminder not to leave without them.

He then went back to the freezer and rotated the thermostat in the manner one would the dial on a safe, a few degrees to the right, a few to the left, then right again. A low clunk soon came from the freezer.

Inside the massive refrigerated unit, one of the metallic floor panels had popped open, revealing a steep metallic staircase he quickly descended.

At the bottom, he entered a six-digit combination on a keypad on the wall and the trapdoor closed above him at the same moment lights came on in the basement.

The space had about half the footprint of the barn itself, which made it a very respectable basement. A cage similar to the prison cells one sees in Western movies occupied a quarter of the room. Inside were a few old mattresses and a bucket that served as a toilet.

What the hell? he thought, his eyes focused on the floor in a corner of the cage. Two Latina women lay there, immobile. They looked to be in their late teens, pretty despite the filth covering their faces.

He opened the prison door using the set of keys hanging on the wall and cautiously walked toward them. He wasn't afraid of screams, the basement was perfectly soundproof, but he wasn't sure whether the women were trying to play a trick on him.

He crouched next to them and felt for a pulse on their necks and wrists. Nothing… This was such a waste. He could have had some fun with these two if only he'd known they were here. But he hadn't known and now they were dead. They'd run out of water and died of dehydration. It was recent, too, as the stench of decomposition was totally absent. Oh well, there was nothing to do about this mess at the moment.

He walked to a shelf littered with all sorts of souvenirs taken from those who'd had the unfortunate privilege of spending some time in the cage. Dozens and dozens of clothing articles, worthless trinkets, and other crap.

This was where the ragged bunny found in Archibald's pocket had come from, but few knew that. The blue necklace Archer had retrieved from Allan's corpse had not come from this pile, however. Which was why more people should have recognized it. Gwendoline in particular… It was her necklace, after all.

Right in the middle of the macabre keepsakes, underneath a red sweater torn at the elbow, was the Cowboy's branding iron. A large W with a horizontal bar in the middle. What those idiots at the FBI had taken for two A's.

Their mistake had bothered him at first, but he'd quickly decided it was a good thing after all. Let them search for a meaning to those two A's… Morons!

He put his gloves back on and went up the staircase.

Once in the barn, he wiped the branding iron using a clean rag he'd found on a nearby workbench before walking to the bodies lined up on the floor. Luckily for him, the FBI's forensic team hadn't showed up yet and the corpses hadn't been moved.

He placed the iron in Allan's hand and closed its fingers around the handle a few times. Rigor mortis had already disappeared, which made the task easier than he'd expected. He repeated the operation along the shaft of the iron until he was confident that he'd left enough incriminating prints to satisfy the cops.

He slipped the handle inside the left sleeve of his jacket and closed the thick parka back up. The W, squarely resting on his shoulder, made a slight bulge, but it was unlikely anyone would notice.

He walked to the door and picked up the steaks before exiting the barn.

Careful not to drop the iron hidden under his clothes, he walked back to the cabin under the watchful eyes of the deputy who was still staring at him through the window.

He was just a few feet from the front door when it opened and Jennifer MacKay came out, wearing warm hiking clothes.

"Going for a walk?" he asked with a smile.

She nodded silently.

"Don't go too far, those cops would come after you like there's no tomorrow."

She ignored his remark and started heading for the road.

This was interesting. Maybe he should join her on her walk and see where that led. Killing her here and now wasn't an option, but they could still get to know each other a bit. That could always come handy in the future.

He made up his mind and hurried inside. He needed to go hide the iron in Allan's bedroom and then he'd catch up with the beautiful Jennifer. The woman truly was gorgeous, just the way he liked them.

Chapter 69

As Gwendoline exited his room, Ethan reflected he had no idea what to make of the woman. Half of her family had just been murdered and had yet to be buried, and she'd come to ask him whether he'd made any progress on the case for which he'd been hired.

Apparently blackmail trumped mass murder in her book. There was no longer any doubt in his mind, the whole Woodrough clan was composed of nut jobs.

He grabbed his laptop from his backpack and turned it on for the first time since they'd arrived at the cabin. With the internet down he'd had little use for the device, but now the connection was reestablished and there were more than a few things he wanted to look up.

He started a search by combining the words *orphanage* and *Sam Clifford*. A few thousand entries popped out. Way too many to sift through. He added the query *Montana* and focused on articles published before 2010 since the orphanage had closed in 2009.

A few hundred results remained, and he started clicking on the most promising ones.

He spent the next thirty minutes browsing through a variety of articles about the orphanage's history, its staff and its director, Sam Clifford.

The private orphanage had opened its doors in 1978 and had been on the verge of bankruptcy when Clifford had taken over as director in 1993. He'd been praised for turning the place around and bringing it back from an all but certain death.

Under his leadership, the establishment had grown, with up to thirty-eight boys living on the premises at one point. His success as an administrator had been mostly due to his fund-raising abilities. Although numerous local businesses had supported the orphanage, Woodrough Enterprise had been the largest benefactor of the lot by far.

Everything had come to a halt in 2008 for no immediately obvious reasons. By February 2009, the place had closed for good.

The nineteen boys who'd still called the orphanage home at the time of its closure had been sent to foster families with the exception of a few who'd ended up in another private orphanage in northern Montana.

Digging further, Ethan identified that things had started to go south in early 2008. It took him another twenty minutes of snooping to stumble upon an article that explained why.

In December 2007, a boy named Pete Rogers had gone missing from the orphanage and had never been found. The boy had been seven at the time. Old enough to run away but much too young to survive alone in the outside world.

A thorough police investigation had been conducted, and the entire staff had been under scrutiny. In the end, the police conclusions were that the boy had probably run away and bumped into problems of some sort. He was expected to be dead, but a body had never been found.

The skeletons discovered in that cave came back to Ethan's mind. The boy's age was a match for some of the remains.

Although the staff had eventually been exonerated of any wrongdoing, there had been enough questions around the kid's disappearance that a number of benefactors had pulled their support, leaving the organization in a precarious financial position.

The orphanage had survived another year but had eventually closed due to insufficient funding.

None of the articles he'd read had shown pictures of the young Pete Rogers, but Ethan suspected this wasn't out of respect for the kid. A more likely explanation was that nobody at the orphanage had given the journalists a photo of the boy. Whether it was because such a picture didn't exist or because the staff had been forbidden to do so was anyone's guess.

Curious as to whether the kid's body had eventually surfaced somewhere, Ethan ran another search using the boy's name and narrowed the timeframe to search results between 2008 and 2012.

This search only returned a few dozen results, and Ethan quickly found a headline that caught his eyes: *The case against Sam Clifford three years later.*

The article was dated from 2011 and was written in an accusatory tone. While showing little evidence to support his allegations, the journalist was plainly accusing Sam Clifford of knowing what had happened not only to Pete Rogers but also to Caleb Stensen, a nine-year-old boy who had gone missing a few years earlier and whose disappearance had been allegedly covered up by the sheriff's office. A quick search informed Ethan that the sheriff the article referred to was no other than the now deceased Oliver Bradford.

Ethan knew he was on the right track. Both men had been murdered over the past couple days and a picture showing Clifford surrounded by his orphans had been left on the director's body. This simply couldn't be a coincidence.

Eager to share his discovery, he knocked on the connecting door, but Jennifer didn't answer. Could she be asleep? Unlikely, it was barely half past nine. He was starting to have a bad feeling about this. He tried the handle but it was locked. He walked to the hallway and found her bedroom door unlocked, but the room was empty. When had she left? He hadn't heard a thing.

She'd wanted to be left alone so he doubted he'd find her downstairs shooting the breeze with the deputies on surveillance duty.

He put on some boots, grabbed his jacket and ran downstairs.

"Has anyone seen Jennifer MacKay? Redhead, in her thirties...?" he asked the cops.

"She went out a while ago," answered a female deputy. "I told her she shouldn't, but I couldn't hold her in against her will. She can't have gone far by foot."

Ethan headed for the door.

"You should wait for her here, sir," said the deputy.

Ignoring the woman's advice, Ethan rushed outside.

The snow in the clearing had been trampled by so many feet by now that it was impossible to tell which direction Jennifer had taken, but he quickly noticed two sets of tracks heading for the recently plowed road.

The tracks continued on the road itself, albeit not as deep and harder to read. The two sets were far enough apart to suggest that the two individuals hadn't been walking together. One set was also significantly larger than the other. A man and a woman most likely.

It was impossible to tell whether one had been following the other or if the tracks had been left hours apart, but Ethan didn't like what he was seeing. In his mind the killer had followed Jennifer and already caught up with her. The deputy had said she'd been gone for a while. Why hadn't she come back yet? What was she doing out there when he'd expressly asked her not to go out?

He was running down the road now but only realized it when he slipped on a patch of ice and went flying. He got back up, brushed the snow off his jacket, and was about to start running again when a sound caught his attention.

He held his breath, listening intently for any noise rising above the silence of the night. He heard it again, a moment later. A faint voice.

He walked quickly towards the next bend of the road. By the time he reached it, he saw them. Chatting and walking back towards the house at a leisurely pace. Jennifer and Clive Thomas. Was Gwendoline's husband after Jennifer now too? What a family!

Chapter 70

The FBI investigators made it to the house early the next day and by three o'clock the guests had been excused and allowed to go back to their respective lives. The disabled vehicles had been tended to by an army of mechanics called to the rescue, and by 3:30 PM the majority of the guests had left the cursed cabin. This included Jennifer, who'd insisted on getting out of there as soon as possible.

Ethan, for his part, wanted to stay in Montana a couple more days to continue his investigation. He could have used Jennifer's company, but he understood her position. The whole story had taken a toll on his assistant as indicated by the dark circles around her eyes and her moodiness.

"Mrs. Thomas, may I have a word with you in private?" Ethan indicated Aaron's empty study.

The woman gave him an appraising look. "Regarding?"

"Regarding the matter for which I was hired."

They headed for the study and Ethan closed the door shut behind them.

"You found out something about the blackmailer?" she asked, surprised.

"I believe so, yes. But before I can be certain of anything, I need to ask you a couple questions."

"Go ahead," she said, sitting down in a swiveling leather chair behind Aaron's desk.

"Why me? Why did you come to me?"

"Because of your reputation, Mr. Archer. You're supposed to be very good at what you do. Aren't you?"

"But that's the thing, Mrs. Thomas. I'm not that good anymore these days. You no doubt know that I lost my wife last year. The story made national news for a week."

"I'm aware of the fact, yes," she admitted.

"And if you know this, you also know that it took a toll on me. This too has been in the news, and at any rate, someone in your position doesn't hire someone like me without doing their homework. You must have looked into my background before approaching me and this would have come up."

"What's your point, Mr. Archer. I'm not sure I understand." She sounded defensive now.

"My point is the following: why did you offer a hundred grand retainer to a has-been?" Ethan couldn't believe he'd only just now come up with this realization.

"I obviously ignored that you weren't worth anything anymore when I hired you, Mr. Archer. But I've been suspecting it for some time. And now that you've confirmed the fact, let me ask you this: why did you accept my money when you knew you couldn't deliver on the job?"

"It turns out I did deliver, Mrs. Thomas. I know the identity of your blackmailer."

"Please do tell. Don't keep me waiting," she said sarcastically.

"The blackmailer is *you*, Mrs. Thomas. You placed the letter on the receptionist's desk yourself, that's why there was no postmark on the envelope."

"This is preposterous!"

"Your office is the closest to the reception. You simply needed to wait for the receptionist to use the restroom to go and drop the letter. It wouldn't have taken you more than fifteen seconds to carry out the deed."

"That's what I've been paying you for?" Gwendoline sounded utterly pissed off now.

The move had been a gamble, but it had paid off. It was the most logical explanation, but Ethan hadn't been certain that was the way things had happened before confronting her. Now he was sure, though. Her outrage looked fake, and she was panicking. Not the reaction of an innocent woman. A casual observer might have been fooled, but not Ethan. He'd been trained to recognize the signs.

"I know it was you. What I can't figure out is why. Why would you blackmail your own company?"

"You're insane," she replied, slowly shaking her head.

"Am I? At least this explains why you hired me. You wanted it to look like someone was looking into it, but you didn't want them to find anything. Hence hiring the has-been detective."

"I've heard enough. Don't expect any reference from me, Mr. Archer." She left the room, flustered and red in the face.

How many Gwendoline Thomases were there? The woman who'd hired him and the one who'd just left the room, he could reconciliate easily. But the Gwendoline he'd gotten to know over the past few days had been a different woman. She'd been courteous to him and Jennifer, the strangers among the lot. She'd also been cooler-headed than average under the extraordinary circumstances they'd all been subjected to. Of these two personalities, which one was the real Gwendoline?

Ethan needed to have one more conversation before leaving the house. He found Mr. and Mrs. Travis in the kitchen doing the lunch dishes.

"May I interrupt you a moment? I have a few questions to ask you."

James Travis eyed him suspiciously. "What about?"

"About those instances where the Woodroughs gave you some time off and gathered at the cabin in your absence. For Christmas break and the like."

"This hasn't happened in a long time. It's been at least fifteen years since we were given the Christmas holiday off," said Mr. Travis, looking uneasy.

"I want to know whether you've ever observed something strange when you got back from such vacations."

Mr. Travis shook his head. "Never noticed anything unusual. They're all good people. I don't understand why someone would go and kill them like this."

"When was the last time they gave you some time off because they wanted the cabin for themselves?" asked Ethan.

But James Travis was apparently done talking. He was furiously drying the clean dishes his wife handed him while acting as if Ethan weren't in the room.

"A couple of weeks ago," answered his wife eventually.

"And you noticed absolutely nothing out of the ordinary when you returned?"

"Nothing," said the husband, but Ethan wasn't convinced.

"And the other times?"

"Tell him, James," said Mrs. Travis in a low voice. The remark drew a dark look from her husband, but he said nothing.

"Mr. Travis, Archibald is dead, his wife is dead, their son is dead, their grandson is dead; who are you loyal to? I'm trying to figure out who killed them here. I'm not the enemy."

"Isn't that the police's job?"

"Tell him about the truck tracks, James," said Mrs. Travis, who'd stopped cleaning the dishes entirely.

"What about them? Everyone drives pickups around here," answered her husband.

"You know they were left by no pickup. They belonged to a bigger truck. Something like a medium-sized U-Haul."

"And those tracks led to the cabin?" asked Ethan.

"To the barn. The truck went inside the barn."

"When was that?"

"The last time they gave us a weekend off. Two weeks ago," said the husband, who'd recovered the ability to speak.

"Do you know what was in this truck?"

"Probably some food delivery for the holiday," said the man. But he didn't sound like he believed it himself.

"It wasn't food, James. We're always the ones receiving deliveries, and there was no more food in the house or the freezer when we came back than when we left. And there was also that shoe you found."

"What shoe?" asked Ethan.

It was clear the man wouldn't say a word, but he didn't object when his wife started telling her story.

"Some years ago, James found a shoe in the snow. A ragged tennis shoe. A kid's shoe."

"Couldn't it have been one of the girl's or Gregory's?"

"It was before they were born. And Mrs. Gwendoline and the others were already in their twenties. There were no kids around the house at that time."

"Do you know who the shoe belonged to?"

She shook her head.

"We have no reason to believe the Woodroughs had anything to do with that shoe," said Mr. Travis.

"But it still bothered you enough to notice it and remember it years later," Ethan pointed out.

Having exhausted this particular line of questioning, Ethan brought up the ragged bunny they'd found on Archibald after his death. "It seemed to me like you recognized the bunny when Clive pulled it out of Archibald's pocket. Was I mistaken?"

"I can't be sure. It could have been the same, but it's been so long…" said Mrs. Travis.

"The same as what?"

"Don't go and tell stories if you aren't certain, Gladys," said her husband.

"Oh shush, James!" replied his wife. "It was probably twenty or so years ago. Mr. Clifford came to visit, and he brought a couple of his orphan boys with him to spend the Saturday afternoon. He did that sometimes to get them out of the orphanage. A kind of distraction…" She trailed off.

"And?" Ethan encouraged.

"And one of the orphans was carrying a ragged bunny like the one in Mr. Archibald's pocket. I remember because it had a hole in it and was losing its stuffing. I sewed it back together for the boy. Very grateful he was."

Ethan, who'd spent some time staring at the ragged animal, had noticed stitches on the bunny's belly. "Do you remember where the hole was?"

"Not really. His back maybe, or perhaps his belly. It's been a long time."

"Did you ever see this boy again after that day?"

"No. Mr. Clifford seldom brought the same kids twice."

The Travises had no more useful information to offer so Ethan thanked them and took his leave.

In the lounge, he bumped into Special Agent Melany Parker, an old acquaintance.

"Ethan Archer! What are you doing here?" said the woman, looking puzzled.

"Hello, Melany. Long time no see."

"Long time indeed, but that doesn't answer my question."

"I was here for the holidays…"

She gave him a questioning look. "You're not kidding, are you?"

"Nope. I was right here when everything went down."

"Talk about being in the wrong place at the wrong time."

Their conversation was interrupted by an FBI agent Ethan had never met. He was carrying a duffle bag. "Look what I found, Melany," he said, showing her something inside the bag while making sure to block Ethan's view. "Looks familiar, doesn't it?"

"What is it?" asked Ethan, intrigued.

"Nothing you need to worry about, sir," answered the man as he was closing the bag.

Following an uncomfortable silence, Melany and Ethan stared at each other.

"Show him," she told the other agent after a few seconds.

"But Mela—"

"This is Ethan Archer, Agent Norton. He has the right to see what's in that bag. Where did you find the object?"

"In Allan Woodrough's bedroom," he replied, unzipping the duffle bag and showing its content to Ethan. A branding iron with a large W, divided in its center by a horizontal bar. A perfect match for the mark the killer had left on Amanda's chest.

Ethan felt the blood rushing to his head along with the anger. There was no longer any doubt possible. The Cowboy had been in this very house all along.

Chapter 71

The road conditions weren't what Ethan was used to, but the rental's studded tires handled the packed snow adequately as long as he drove significantly under the speed limit. On the plus side, the roads were virtually deserted. Not particularly surprising for mid-afternoon on New Year's Eve in central Montana.

According to his GPS, he only had five miles to go. This had been a busy day already, but he was nowhere close to done.

After a night spent in a motel that barely deserved its two stars, he'd spent the morning visiting with Phil Clarkson, the journalist who'd written the article entitled *The case against Sam Clifford three years later* back in 2011.

Ethan hadn't learned a whole lot more than what the article already stated, but he'd obtained the address of one of the kids who'd lived in the orphanage at the time. That's where he was heading now.

He'd also checked on Jennifer by phone and although she'd assured him being back in San Francisco was doing her a lot of good, she hadn't sounded her peppy self.

Ethan worried about her. He wished he could be by her side right now, but that simply wasn't an option. For one, he had the feeling she didn't want his company at this time. For two, he needed to figure out the connection between the Woodroughs and the Cowboy. This had become his top priority now that he knew he'd spent nearly a week locked up in a house with his wife's murderer.

The branding iron found in Allan's belongings had been covered with fingerprints. Now the million-dollar question was: to whom did they belong? Because he was pretty sure they couldn't be Allan's.

The house appeared on the white horizon, isolated in the beautiful vastness of the mountainous landscape. A moment later, Ethan was parking in the driveway.

He rang the bell and the door was opened by a woman in her fifties.

"Good afternoon, ma'am. My name's Ethan Archer and I am looking for Kyle Vickers."

"Kyle!" she called, inviting Ethan inside.

A man in his early twenties appeared, wearing blue coveralls stained with white paint.

"Kyle? I'm Ethan Archer. We talked on the phone this morning."

"I remember."

"Would you like some coffee, Mr. Archer?" asked the woman.

"That would be great. Thank you very much."

Kyle ushered Ethan into a small den. The room was simply but tastefully furnished.

"What's this about? You mentioned the orphanage on the phone?"

"That's correct. I talked to Phil Clarkson this morning and he suggested I talk with you."

"Was that the journalist?"

"Yes, he's a journalist."

"I haven't seen him in years. I'm surprised he still has my number."

"Do you mind if I ask you a few questions about the time you spent at the orphanage?"

"Sure. That's why you drove all the way here, isn't it?"

"It is… You have a lovely home by the way."

"It's my mother-in-law's. We're living with her until we have enough money to buy our own," he explained. "What'd you want to know about the orphanage?"

"Did you enjoy your time there?" This was a weird question, but Ethan didn't really know how to approach the subject.

"As much as any orphan likes spending time in an orphanage, I guess… 'Twas probably better than some foster homes and worse than others…"

"Phil Clarkson is under the impression that weird things were going on over there. He found the disappearances of Pete Rogers and Caleb Stensen particularly troublesome. Do you remember what happened back then?"

"I wasn't around when Pete disappeared. I left the orphanage in 2005. Was moved to a foster home. But I remember Caleb. It was weird how he left. One day he was there and the next he was gone. We were told he'd been adopted, but usually there are signs something like that's happening."

"And in this case there were no signs?"

The mother-in-law returned with two mugs of coffee she placed on the table between the two of them.

"No, nothing. And later on there were rumors that he hadn't been adopted. That he'd run away."

"This was the only time it happened during your years in the orphanage?"

"There was one other boy, Tommy something, who was *sort of* adopted but I don't remember the details… 'twas a long time ago."

Ethan pulled up a picture on his phone and showed it to Kyle. It was the photo that had been attached to the shaft of the arrow responsible for Clifford's death. Ethan had snapped the picture before turning the original over to the FBI investigators.

"Do you recognize any of the kids in this picture?" he asked.

"Sure. The smallest one here is Pete," Kyle said, pointing at the photo, "and this was Mark, Alex, KC, and Chip. I don't remember this one's name. He arrived not long before I left."

This was useful information on its own. The journalist hadn't been able to identify anyone in the picture. He'd never met any of the kids. But Kyle had confirmed that Pete Rogers was among the kids. This suggested that the man who'd killed Clifford saw him as responsible for Pete's disappearance. Or at least used it as an excuse to justify killing the retired director.

Ethan considered his next question carefully. There was no easy way to ask this.

"Did you know Sam Clifford well?"

"He was the director. Everybody knew him."

"What did you think of him?"

"Nothing much. He was okay, I guess."

"His behavior with the children was… appropriate?"

"You want to know if he was a pedophile?" asked Kyle, cutting to the chase.

"Something like that…"

"Not that I ever noticed. He never touched me and I never saw or heard him touching other kids."

"So there was nothing unusual going on in your opinion?"

Kyle sipped on his coffee before answering, "I don't know that everything over there was *usual*, as you put it. A couple of times, the last year I was there, some foreign kids would show up for a night and they'd be gone the next day."

"How did you know they were foreign?"

"They spoke Spanish, and they looked darker than the average Montana boy. Sometimes there were young girls, too, and since it was a boys' orphanage, that was extra weird…"

"Did you ever talk to them?"

"No. They always kept them separate from the other kids."

"And they never spent more than a night at the orphanage?"

"No. Sometimes less even. Just a few hours."

"How did they leave the next day? Someone came to pick them up?"

"I guess. Most of the times they were just gone, we didn't see them leave. Once a police car came to pick them up."

A cop? Now that was interesting. Ethan wondered… He grabbed his cell phone and, after a quick online search, turned the screen towards Kyle. "Was that the guy who came to get them?"

Kyle looked at the photo for a while. "It's been a long time and he was younger then, but I think so."

The picture on the phone had been taken from the Madison Sheriff's Office's website. Sheriff Oliver Bradford's picture.

Ethan was backing out of Kyle's driveway when his phone rang.

"Hey, Theo. What's up?"

"I got some good news and some bad news for you."

Ethan didn't like the bad news part, but Theo didn't sound particularly worried about it so it was probably fairly minor. "Does this have something to do with the Cowboy?"

"Nothing. It's about the guy you put in a coma."

"I didn't put any guy in a coma. I spent that whole evening with my assistant Jennifer. You can ask SFPD."

"Yeah right. Well, the good news is that he's no longer in a coma. The bad news is that he died in the hospital without regaining consciousness."

"Does that mean the cops are going to be looking for his attacker a bit harder now?" asked Ethan, concerned.

"It's possible, but since it wasn't you…"

For a few seconds nobody said anything. It was Theo who broke the silence. "Don't lose sleep over it. The bastard's DNA was run into the database and he's responsible for at least a half dozen rapes according to my contact at the SFPD. And that's only the women who reported their assault in time to get a rape kit done. That means he's probably raped dozens more. I don't think the cops are going to be spending too much time trying to find this scumbag's killer."

"Now that's a relief… for his killer, I mean."

"Right!"

"I wanted to ask you something while I have you," Ethan said. "Could you please let me know as soon as you have ID'd the fingerprints on the branding iron?"

"I don't think I can do that, Ethan," said Theo reluctantly. "I don't want you to overreact and go kill someone based on some fingerprints that may have been planted there in the first place. Whatever that mess is that you got yourself into, that's some fucked-up shit."

"You owe me that, Theo." Ethan was suddenly very serious.

"I don't owe you shit, Ethan! But I'll think about it."

"Thanks." Ethan knew what it meant. "I got to go, I need to go look at some prime real estate," he added cryptically.

"Wait! There was another reason I was calling you."

"I'm listening."

"I have the feeling SFPD might come ask you some questions in the near future. Not about that serial rapist you didn't put into a coma, about something else. I just wanted to give you the heads up."

"That's all the details you have?"

"That's all the details your lying ass deserves. But I'll tell you what I know anyway, because I'm a nice guy."

"You *really* are. So, what's that all about?"

"My SFPD contact told me he'd seen your name come up in another case they're actively working. The murder investigation of a hooker."

"And they think I killed her?" Ethan asked skeptically.

"Nah! They know you were stuck in Montana when she was murdered. But your number was in her cell and according to her phone records she tried to call you a half dozen times in the two days preceding her death."

Ethan searched his memory and came up with only one possibility. "Do you know the girl's name?"

"April Steiner or Steimer… Something like that."

Ethan felt his heart sink when he heard the name. *April…* poor girl. She'd reached out to him for help and he hadn't even known. And now it was too late.

He clearly remembered what she'd said to him that night after he'd escorted back to her apartment: *"I don't know if what you did will end up saving me or costing me my life yet, but it could have been bad if you hadn't intervened."*

Now she knew the answer. His intervention had cost April her life. He was sure of it.

Chapter 72

Jennifer was walking on Crissy Field South Beach, enjoying the contrast between the cool morning breeze and the warmth of the sun on her face. From time to time the waves would reach her bare feet, submerging them up to her ankles. She liked the walk. It was peaceful, relaxing. Just what she needed. In front of her, a ferry full of tourists was approaching Alcatraz Island and its famous museum prison.

She'd been back in San Francisco two days, but her mind lingered in Montana. The assignment had taken an unexpected toll on her. She'd always known the trip would present numerous challenges, but what had happened over the past week had far exceeded her worst nightmares. Now she needed to come to peace with it, for there was nothing else she could do. She really wished she'd never gone to that godforsaken cabin.

Ethan was still over there, investigating. She was thankful for that. She needed the break his absence was providing. She needed to be alone right now. She hadn't even told Tabatha she was back in town.

The beach was virtually deserted at nine in the morning on this second day of January, and she sat down to stare at the sea for a while. She took a few deep breaths, exhaling slowly in an attempt to calm her mind, but there was no peace to find. And then her phone rang in her pocket. There was no need to check the screen, only one person was assigned this particular ring tone. "Morning, Ethan."

"Good morning. How are you feeling today?"

"I'm fine. Is that why you're calling? To check on me?" She didn't know whether to be irritated or pleased about it.

"In part, yes."

"Well thank you, boss. But no need to worry about me, I'm doing alright."

"Did you get your suitcase back?"

"No. It's still missing. It's been more than forty-eight hours and according to the airline lady I talked to, that's not a good sign. It's unlikely it will be found at this point. The one time I stick my purse in my suitcase, it gets lost…"

"I'm sorry about that."

"Don't be. It's not your fault and everything in it is replaceable. What's the other reason for your call?" she asked, digging her fingers into the cold sand.

"I need you to do some research for me. Could you look into the deaths of the senator's and Allan's wives? The first one supposedly died in a boating accident and the second one drowned in a lake. The coincidence is interesting as is, but I'd like you to really look into it. Find out if there was anything suspicious about either death?"

"Alright, I'll get to it as soon as I get to the office."

"Where are you now?" Ethan sounded surprised.

"I'm sitting on the beach, I felt like I deserved a bit of time off."

"You absolutely do, it wasn't a criticism. I just want you to be careful. I have the feeling things aren't quite over. You should be safe in San Francisco, but one's never too cautious."

"I'll keep an eye open. I promise, boss," she said, in the way teenagers talk to overbearing parents.

"There's something else I'd like to ask you, but it's a bit more…"

"More what?"

"Illegal…"

"Now you have my attention."

"You mentioned you had friends who could do things with computers."

"You need someone to fix the screen you punched?" she asked, knowing full well this wasn't what he was asking about.

"Not quite, I need someone to pull some telephone records."

"Can't Theo do that for you?"

"He can, but he won't. That would be illegal."

"I may know somebody… Whose records do you have in mind?"

"Archibald and Allan Woodrough to start, and I'd also need Sam Clifford's as well as Sheriff Bradford's, both business and personal lines. I can give you the numbers—do you have something to write them down with?"

"Yes, go ahead."

He dictated the phone numbers, but Jennifer didn't feel the need to write them down. She would remember, she always did.

"This will probably take a few days," she replied.

"Really? Okay… well, do your best."

"I always do, boss. Why do you need those phone records? What did you find?"

"Not a whole lot yet, but I can tell you one thing, our dear sheriff lived in a very nice house. I drove by it yesterday and let me tell you, I'm impressed. I also checked his salary since it's public record, and he definitely didn't pay for that house with it."

"Maybe he inherited money. Or maybe his wife comes from a wealthy family," offered Jennifer.

"I'm still looking into it, but I doubt that's the explanation."

Jennifer doubted it too. She doubted it very much.

Sitting on a bench fifty yards away, Casanova was observing his next victim. He'd devised a plan to kidnap Jennifer MacKay and had already rented the house where he'd be enjoying her pale skin from up close. Her skin and her screams.

Chapter 73

Night had fallen by the time Ethan walked out of the newspaper office and headed back to his hotel. After spending the previous day locked up in his room browsing through thousands of web searches, he'd spent today hunched over the screen of a microfilm reader at the archives of the largest newspaper in southwestern Montana. And all he had to show for it was a body that ached from the neck down. He needed to find some food; he was starving.

He'd been looking for names, or at least potential names, to associate with the skeletons discovered in the cave. With the exception of Myriam Woodrough, Pete Rogers, and Caleb Stensen, there had been no unsolved disappearances of children in the region over the past thirty years. He'd extended his search radius to northwestern Wyoming and a couple Idaho counties, but to no avail. His search for a "Tommy something," the third orphan Kyle Vickers had mentioned, hadn't been any more fruitful.

This meant at least five of the skeletons had belonged to kids abducted elsewhere, and that was assuming the cops had found them all, which was far from certain. For all they knew, there might be a dozen more skeletons waiting to be found somewhere in the giant cavern.

Ethan didn't consider his time wasted, however. The fact the kids had been brought here to die was meaningful in itself. It suggested the geographical area had some appeal to the killer. The question was why? Why would someone go through the trouble of bringing kids from out of state to kill and bury them in the middle of nowhere?

Overall, he didn't feel any closer to answering the most important question: who had killed those kids?

Whoever it was, it was someone intimately familiar with the woods. Someone who knew about the cave long before its public discovery a few weeks back.

The man Ethan had come to think about as the ghost was an obvious culprit. He had clearly demonstrated a willingness and an aptitude to kill.

But if the ghost was truly a wild man of some sort, as the locals believed, he wasn't likely to travel out of state much. It was also not fitting the typical serial killer profile. The skeletons all belonged to children, seven boys and a girl. This was the work of a child killer, someone who got his kicks murdering and most likely molesting helpless kids. But the ghost had gone after adults over the past few days.

Gregory had been a kid, of course, but Ethan wasn't convinced the ghost had been the one killing him. His poisoned-hot-cocoa theory suggested an inside job, not the work of a deranged killer living in the woods.

Spending the day plowing through old newspaper articles had also helped Ethan paint a clearer picture of Myriam Woodrough. The kid had truly been as remarkable as Mrs. Travis had described her. The girl had been tested at age eight with an IQ of 160, the same as Albert Einstein. She could have grown up to be anything she wanted. The sky was the limit for someone with such intellect.

As is often the case in child disappearances, the family had been heavily scrutinized, but nothing incriminating had been discovered. It just looked like the girl had gotten up and left the cabin on her own in the middle of the night.

Had she gotten lost or attacked by animals, her body would have been found by now. And maybe it had… if the female skeleton discovered in that cave belonged to her. Maybe she'd run away for her own reasons and bumped into the wrong individual. This could explain why there was a single female skeleton in the cave. Boys may have been the killer's favorite prey, but would he have passed on a nine-year-old girl throwing herself in his arms in the middle of the night?

Ethan drove past a small diner on the way to his hotel and turned the car around. It wasn't going to be gourmet cuisine, but that would do just fine.

He sat down at a table and ordered a cheeseburger and a chocolate shake; he was in a diner, after all, so why do things half-ass?

The restaurant only had three other customers, a family sitting at a nearby table, and Ethan wondered how places like this remained in business. He was wondering the same thing about Woodrough Enterprise. Where had Allister and Archibald found the private money that kept the company running through the oil crash of the 90s? Ethan had asked his 'financial analyst' to conduct an in-depth investigation on the matter, but he had yet to hear back from the guy.

His phone rang as the waitress was coming back with his order.

"Can this wait? I'm about to clog my arteries with a pound of cheeseburger," he said, answering the phone.

"Sure, but don't start yelling at me for not delivering the news right away when you finally hear what I have for you," replied Theo on the other end of the line.

That got his attention. "Shoot, I'll chew silently."

"We made some progress on the beach-house front."

"The guy with the fake ID rented it several times?" Ethan was getting excited.

"No. We're not that lucky. But we started looking at rental beachfront properties that were both isolated from neighbors and rented out on short-term leases when the Cowboy's victims were abducted."

"And?"

"And we found two more houses that fit the criteria. We're still looking for more, but even if we don't find any, it's still something."

"Who rented these?"

"Fake IDs again. Different pictures than the one used to rent the house where Amanda was killed, but similar build and height, same brown hair, early thirties."

"What are the heights and weights?"

Theo listed the vital statistics listed on the three drivers' licenses and Ethan concluded that the descriptions fit Clive Thomas, Blake Jones, and Matthew Woodrough equally well.

"Any chance you could email me those fake IDs so I can have a look?" he said.

"The men are all dead, so I suppose it can't do much harm. I'll send them to you as soon as we hang up."

"Thanks! Do you have anything else for me?"

"Not at the moment, but we're still looking. I thought you'd be happy with that."

"It's good stuff, Theo. But that's far from enough to make me happy. Me happy won't happen until my fingers choke the life out of the bastard."

"We'll pretend you didn't just make that comment to an FBI agent."

"Talking about FBI agents, did your guys ID the fingerprints on the branding iron?"

There was a pause on Theo's part, which Ethan interpreted as a yes. "Whose are they, Theo? Tell me."

"The prints belong to Allan Woodrough," said Theo reluctantly.

"Son of a bitch!"

Chapter 74

Back in his hotel room, Ethan was replaying Theo's phone call in his head. Amanda's killer had finally made a mistake. Two actually... He'd technically made his first over a year ago, but it was now going to come back and bite him in the ass. Shoot him in the head, even, if Ethan managed to find him before the cops.

Based on the fake IDs Theo had just emailed him and the branding iron found in Allan Woodrough's belongings, the list of suspects was seriously narrowing down. If the killer had been one of the guests present at the cabin, it could only be one of four men and only three of them were still alive: Clive, Blake, and Matthew.

Ethan instinctively wanted to remove Clive Thomas from the list. As a ranch foreman, the man was unlikely to travel extensively for work, and since most of the Cowboy's victims had been killed in California, that placed Clive out of the picture. He'd need to double check this, of course, but his money was on the others.

Ethan needed to figure out why he'd been invited to the house. He was convinced this was an important aspect of the mystery, a vital piece of the puzzle. Had this truly been Gwendoline's idea or had the Cowboy been the one behind the invitation? Was Gwendoline somehow involved with the Cowboy, or was it serendipity that had brought Ethan and his wife's killer together under one roof over the holiday?

The timing was also suspicious. Gwendoline had hired Ethan at the exact time the Cowboy had sent him the video... after laying low for a whole year. Could it be another coincidence? That seemed highly unlikely, but on the other hand the video had been sent on the first anniversary of Amanda's death.

That's when Ethan realized something he hadn't thought of before. The Cowboy had been a prolific serial killer. A new victim had been found dead every few months all the way till Avery's arrest. And then the killings had stopped. Which made sense at the time since Avery had been presumed to be the only killer. But knowing what Ethan knew now, it no longer made the slightest sense.

Serial killers didn't simply stop killing. It was a compulsion. They couldn't help themselves. If anything, the killings usually accelerated until the perpetrator finally got caught.

Ethan refused to believe that the Cowboy was an exception. Which meant he'd kept killing over the past year. He'd just changed his modus operandi to slip under the cops' radar. He no longer targeted the same profile, no longer left the same mark on his victims' breasts, but he still killed. Ethan was sure of it. The man was a master in the art of deception. Deception... An idea had popped up in his mind. It was nearly 10 PM but he didn't care. He grabbed his cellphone and called Theo back.

"What?" answered his friend, TV and kids blasting in the background.

"Talk to me about that case you're working. The one where every victim belongs to a different ethnic group."

"Casanova? Why?"

"When was the first victim killed?"

"March."

"Three months after Amanda's death..."

"Where are you going with this?"

"Can you extend your beach-house search to periods where Casanova's victims were found?"

"You think there's a link between the two killers?" asked Theo.

"I think there's only one killer."

"I don't understand. You think the Cowboy and Casanova are the same person?"

"I think it's a distinct possibility, yes. I'll explain later. Right now, I need to warn Jennifer, I think she may be in danger."

Chapter 75

Jennifer watched her boss nearly colliding with Blake Jones as Ethan walked into the office around a quarter to noon. The two men exchanged greetings that sounded less than heartfelt, and Emily's husband exited the office, closing the door behind him.

"What's he doing here?" asked Ethan, as Blake could be heard going down the flight of stairs leading to the street.

"He was in town on business and wanted to know if I had lunch plans," she said, hands joined against her chest as she sighed like a smitten teenager.

"In town on business, huh? How convenient. And what did you tell him?"

"That I had a lot of work to do and that I'd already made plans to go out with a friend."

"You have?"

"No! But he doesn't know that."

Ethan appeared to relax and smiled for the first time since he'd walked into the office.

"How was your flight? Are you coming straight from the airport?" she asked.

"Can't complain. It didn't crash. And no, I stopped by home on my way here."

"Why are you still carrying a suitcase then?" she asked, pointing at the carry-on he'd left by the door.

"That's for you. It's to replace the one the airline has lost. I assume they still haven't found it?"

She shook her head. "They haven't, but you didn't have to do that. I could have bought myself a new one."

"Your luggage got lost on a business trip, it's only normal your employer should get you a replacement."

"Thanks a lot. It's much nicer than my old one," she said, rolling her new luggage to her desk.

"You should open it."

She did and found a gorgeous purse inside the suitcase. "Now you really shouldn't have. It must have cost you a fortune."

"Nothing's too good for my assistant. Do you like it?"

"I love it," she said, caressing the leather. She was genuinely touched by the attention. She gave him a warm smile and asked, "Anything new since last night?" He'd called her after 10 PM to let her know she might be in danger and needed to be extra careful, especially if approached by any one of the survivors of last week's nightmare. As if she hadn't figured that one out on her own.

"Nothing. What about you?" he said.

"I got the phone records you requested. And I'm about done looking into the senator's and Allan's deceased wives."

"Anything there?"

"Nothing I could find. There was a brief investigation on the drowning, which suggests the cops may have suspected wrongdoing, but the investigation concluded to an accidental death, even though she was a strong swimmer... The way I see it, they found no evidence of wrongdoing, but they didn't buy the accidental death."

"What about the senator's wife?"

"There was never any investigation there, but I suspect Senator Woodrough had enough political clout to make sure nobody looked into it too closely."

Her cell phone started vibrating on the table. She reached for it and quickly read the message before making it disappear from the screen as Ethan approached her desk holding a cup of coffee.

"Can I get those phone records?" he asked, sitting down on the corner of the desk and sipping from his mug.

She handed them to him, and he skimmed over the few pages distractedly.

"Did you look at these? Did you notice anything interesting?" he said.

"I only got them this morning, and I wasn't really sure what you were looking for, boss."

"Okay. I'll need to have a good look at them and try and see if they have any secrets to reveal."

"What are you looking for exactly?"

"I'm not sure... I'm still trying to figure out how the oil business didn't go bankrupt in the 90s. I heard back from my guy and the money angle isn't leading anywhere. The trail is too cold. The World Wide Web didn't exist back then, which means bank records are a lot harder to access. Five grand well spent..."

"And you think phone records from now are going to answer that question."

"You just never know..." he said enigmatically. "And before I forget, I got you something else." He pulled a small rectangular box out of his jacket pocket. It was wrapped in gift paper and had a bow on it.

"What's the occasion?" she asked suspiciously, handling the box with two fingers as if it were something dirty.

"Do I need a reason to buy my assistant a gift? I placed you in danger last week and I really feel horrible about it, so the gift is to help appease my conscience."

"Thanks, Ethan, but that truly wasn't necessary," she said, unwrapping it.

"I disagree," he answered, as she pulled out a Taser from the box.

"Really, Ethan?!"

"Don't go anywhere without it. Especially not now that Blake Jones is in town."

"Is he on your list of suspects?"

"What do you think?"

She didn't bother answering his rhetorical question.

"I'd also appreciate it if you could install a GPS tracking app on your phone and pair it up with mine."

"You're joking, right?"

"Not even a little."

"No, I'm telling you! You *are* joking. I'm okay carrying the Taser around a few days if it really makes you feel better, but you're not tracking my moves, no way."

"Suit yourself! I've got to go now. Watch your back when you leave the building and please call me when you get home tonight."

She sighed heavily as Ethan left the office, phone records in hand.

As she heard his footsteps on the stairs outside the door, she went back to the message she'd received a moment earlier.

It was a good thing Ethan hadn't seen it. She'd purposely excluded the sender of the message from her phone's contact list to avoid the possibility of Ethan seeing his name lit up on her screen in such an event, but the precaution had been for nothing, the idiot had signed his text:

Just landed. Tell me where to go and I'll see you there.
Clive

She read Clive Thomas' message again and felt a slight relief. This wasn't exactly the reunion she'd hoped for but given the circumstances she needed to be satisfied with what she was getting. Beggars couldn't be choosers. She typed the address of a restaurant she liked and sent it to Gwendoline's husband. She was already starting to feel guilty.

From the driver seat of his vehicle parked a quarter block away, Casanova watched Archer exit his office building. The prick never even looked in his direction as he climbed into his car and drove away.

Now that Archer was out of the way, he could give the beautiful Jennifer the attention she deserved.

Chapter 76

Ethan walked into a phone repair store on Valencia Street and waited his turn as the only attendant was in the process of replacing a busted screen under the watchful eyes of the device's owner. The process only took a few minutes and the patron was soon on his way.

"You came to pay me?" asked the store owner and sole operator, an Asian woman with short blue hair in her late twenties. Ethan had been using her services since she was a teenager.

"That, and also to ask you a couple more favors, Suzy."

"Do we need to go to the back?"

"Yes."

Suzy got up, flipped a sign on the store's window that read *Back in 10 minutes*, and locked the front door.

Ethan followed her through a small storage room located at the back of the shop and into an even smaller room. An entire wall was lined with computer screens while the other three were covered with shelves littered with all kinds of phones and communication devices.

"I take it you got my email?" she said, closing the door behind them.

"I did, thanks. Those files have already proven very useful and I'm not even done studying them. I need a couple more things from you though."

She nodded, sat down at a desk hosting no fewer than four desktops and a couple laptops, and waited to hear his shopping list.

"For starters, I would need four cloned phones answering to those numbers," he said, putting down a folded sheet of paper on which were listed the cell phone numbers of Allan and Archibald Woodrough as well as those of Sheriff Bradford and the retired orphanage director.

"Shouldn't be a problem. What else?"

"I would also need to track four cell phones from my own device."

"I assume you don't have the serial numbers?"

"That's correct. Is that a problem?"

"No, but it's a pain in the ass. I'll need to hack the network provider's database to get the phone's serial number before I can do anything. And that's for every device… What are the phone companies?"

"The first one is AT&T for sure. The second one is most likely going to be Verizon since it's by far the best network in the Rockies, but you may have to try a couple more if that doesn't pan out. I don't have a clue for the other two."

"That's a lot of work. That's going to cost you, my friend."

"Shocking! How long do you need?" he asked.

"If I don't get customers, I'll be done with the clones in an hour. The GPS tracking will be longer to set up, especially if one of the devices is an iPhone. Hacking into the Track My Device app is tricky."

"But you can do it?"

"Of course, I can do it!" she said, sounding offended.

"When?"

"I'll have it done by tomorrow morning at the earliest, forty-eight hours at most."

"How much?"

"Six grand," she said, without missing a beat.

He pulled out a wad of $500 bills and pulled twelve of them out. "Do your best. There's an extra grand in it for you if you get it done today."

"Not gonna happen, Ethan. But thanks for the incentive."

He'd started walking back towards the front of the store when he suddenly turned. "I almost forgot, I need a charger for this, too." He pulled a flip phone out of his pocket.

"Where the hell did you find that?" she asked.

"Hidden among a dead man's socks."

Chapter 77

Ethan didn't go back to the office after leaving Suzy's store but went straight to his apartment. He had some thinking to do and wanted to be alone.

He pulled the charger she'd given him out of his pocket and plugged it into the outlet under the bar separating the kitchen and the living room. He then connected the phone. The device came to life a moment later.

He'd hoped to see some messages or voicemails come up, but there was nothing. The phone had no numbers in memory and the history showed no past calls. It was as if the device had never been used.

Ethan felt a pang of hunger. Not surprising given it was nearly 3 PM, and he hadn't eaten anything since breakfast at the hotel. He placed a TV dinner in the microwave and went to the couch to peer over the phone records. Those records posed a conundrum. He'd expected to see a particular number, one with a Mexican prefix, but that number was nowhere to be found in the transcripts Jennifer had handed him. Why was that?

The microwave's timer interrupted his train of thought. He walked to the kitchen to retrieve his food and grabbed a beer from the fridge.

Back on his couch, feet propped up on the coffee table, Ethan started chewing on his salt-loaded Salisbury steak while mentally summarizing the current state of his investigation.

He'd been suspecting the Woodroughs of being involved in some type of illegal activity ever since he'd noticed the massive amount of cash Archibald and his brother had poured into their business in the late 90s. The exact nature of those activities had been a mystery at the time but not anymore. The clues left behind by the ghost, and Ethan's subsequent discussions with the Travises and Kyle Vickers had shed some light on the question. Ethan was now strongly suspecting that Archibald and Allister had been involved in child trafficking.

His working theory was that the Woodroughs had used Sam Clifford's orphanage as a front to *legally* bring children over to Montana from out of state. Sheriff Bradford, for his part, had been graciously paid to make sure the transfers went smoothly and guarantee that the authorities didn't stick their noses in the shady business.

Ethan's phone rang and he answered. "That was fast!"

"I only have the clone ready, Ethan. I didn't even get started on your little tracking project," said Suzy on the other end of the line.

"You said 'clone.' I asked for four of them?"

"I rerouted the four numbers to the same device. Do you really want to be carrying an extra four phones around?" she asked skeptically.

"I didn't know you could do that. It will still work the same way?"

"Exact same way. All calls placed to these numbers will be directly rerouted to your device. You'll also be able to place calls from these numbers and fool the recipients into thinking they're being called by the legitimate owners."

"Perfect. You're a genius. I'll stop by to pick it up within an hour," he said, before hanging up.

Now that he would essentially have access to the lines of Archibald, Allan, Sheriff Bradford and Sam Clifford, Ethan hoped to confirm his child-trafficking theory. With some luck, one of the numbers would be receiving a call related to their shady dealings, either from someone upstream in the supply chain—calling from Mexico maybe?—or from a client looking for a child to molest.

Had Allan been involved in the sordid side of his father's business? The fact he'd been murdered alongside Archibald and his presumed associates over the past week suggested as much. Ethan still wasn't quite clear on how involved the rest of the family was, though. What about Gwendoline, Matthew, and Emily? What about the women's husbands, Clive and Blake? Had their lives been spared because they'd been perceived as innocents by the ghost, or had the killer simply run out of time when Matthew had returned to the cabin with the cops?

There was of course a point that seriously stressed Ethan's theory. One for which he didn't have any answer yet… If he were correct in his assumption that the ghost had been punishing the child traffickers, why had Gregory been killed? But maybe a better question to ask was by whom?

An unfamiliar phone ringtone interrupted his train of thought, and it took him a second to realize that the sound came from the burner sitting on the kitchen's bar.

He hurried to the flip phone he'd found hidden in Allan's suitcase and answered, "Yes?"

"I need to place an order," said a man's voice on the other end.

"I'm listening," replied Ethan in a hushed voice. He would never sound like Allan Woodrough, but the caller would be less likely to realize the difference if Ethan kept his voice at a whisper level.

"I need a girl. Fifteen or sixteen. Pretty. Brown hair, light skin."

"Delivery, takeout, or is it for enjoying on our premises," asked Ethan, who had no idea whether these options even made sense.

"I didn't know you delivered," said the man reflexively. "No, I'll consume on the premises, it's safer that way."

"We've recently expanded our operation and offer facilities in several locations, would you—"

"I want the usual place, the cabin in the Madison mountain range. I like the features it offers."

"Very well, how quickly would you like this to be arranged?"

"Would this coming Monday work? Say 8 PM?"

"It shouldn't be a problem. What name should I put on the reservation?"

"Amadeus."

An alias, no doubt. Who would have named their kid Amadeus in the twentieth century?

"Very well, we'll be waiting for you on Monday," said Ethan.

He terminated the call and placed the phone inside his pocket.

This was the call he'd been waiting for. It hadn't been placed to one of the cloned numbers, but it confirmed his theory nonetheless. It also proved Allan Woodrough's implication in the trafficking operation, which apparently wasn't limited to children…

He needed to let Theo know about this. Human trafficking across state boundaries definitely fell in the FBI's jurisdiction, and they were immensely more qualified than he was to deal with it. It would have been a different matter if Ethan had thought the trafficking had anything to do with the Cowboy, but he doubted it. If the Cowboy was linked to the Woodroughs' shady dealings, it was indirectly at best. The operation displayed the landmarks of a lucrative business run by heartless bastards catering to sexual deviants. It had nothing to do with the Cowboy's way of doing things.

He picked up his cell resting on the coffee table and dialed Theo's number.

Chapter 78

Ethan pulled the cloned phone and the burner out of his pockets and placed them on Theo's desk. He'd swung by Suzy's store on his way to the Federal building on Golden Gate Avenue to pick up the cloned device.

"What's that?" asked the FBI agent, who was sitting on the other side of the desk.

"Something to help you build a case against the Woodroughs."

Theo gave him a questioning look. "For what? Harboring a notorious serial killer among their ranks?"

"We don't know for a fact that the Cowboy's a Woodrough. Only that he has a connection to the family. They may have no idea about the man's secret hobby."

"My question stands. What are we supposed to be investigating here?"

"Child trafficking."

"You're telling me that Senator Woodrough's family are human traffickers?"

"Some of them at least, yes. And I suspect they've been doing it for a while."

Ethan narrated to Theo the succession of events that had led him to suspect the Woodroughs' criminal activities, before recounting the phone call he'd received from Amadeus an hour earlier.

"The senator couldn't possibly be involved," said Theo, warming up to Ethan's theory.

"Maybe he was and maybe he wasn't. I've never met the guy so I can't tell how big of a dirtbag he truly was. But I'm pretty sure Allan Woodrough was involved up to his neck, given that the order I just received was placed to a burner phone I found hidden in his suitcase after he died. And since he apparently uses the Woodroughs' cabin for his shady business, I'd be shocked if nobody else in the family was involved."

"Okay… Let's step back a minute here," said Theo, getting up; this was starting to be a lot to digest for the agent. "You're telling me that Allan and possibly his father and uncle were human traffickers. And that's on top of the family's connection to the Cowboy? What are the odds, bro?"

"I know what you're thinking, but it's not as unlikely as it seems. The Woodroughs had very interesting eyes…"

"What's that supposed to mean?"

"It took me a while to figure out what was bothering me about those guys but when the murders started occurring and none of the people closest to the victims showed normal reactions, I realized what had bugged me from the beginning. It was their eyes. Archibald and Allan had dead eyes. They never betrayed the slightest emotion."

"You mean like sociopaths?"

"Probably even worse than that. I started applying the psychopath checklist to Archibald, but he died before I could complete the psychological assessment."

"So you don't know for sure?"

"No. But given how high he was already scoring and the way he reacted to the death of his wife, son, and grandson, I'd bet my apartment that he was at least a sociopath. And Allan was too, I suspect."

"What makes you say that?

"The way he took his son's death. It just pissed him off. He displayed no sadness in response to losing his boy, just anger and incomprehension."

"And that's a sign?"

"Yes. Psychopaths don't feel pain or grief, but they're total control freaks. The idea that someone other than himself would have killed his son would deeply anger a psychopath. He'd have seen himself as the only one with rights of life and death over his offspring."

"So Allan wasn't sad about the death of his son, but pissed off that he hadn't been the one deciding it?" asked Theo.

"Pretty much."

"That's fucked up!" Theo's face betrayed a mixture of disbelief and disgust. "So what's your plan now?"

"I have no plan. You're the FBI… But if I were you, I'd start by organizing a sting operation at the cabin to grab our Amadeus on Monday night. And I would also wait for one of these phones to ring." He pointed at the clone and the burner on the desk.

"You found the burner among Allan's belongings, but where does the other one come from?"

Ethan explained the purpose of the clone and how it might prove handy to go after bigger and smaller fish in the sex-trafficking ring, while Theo just stared at him.

"Do you know how many laws you're breaking simply by carrying this thing around?" asked Theo.

"Of course I do, which is why I'm handing it to you."

"I'm not touching that phone with a ten-foot pole. At least not until I have some paperwork signed by a judge stating I can. You're gonna have to hold onto it for now. As a matter of fact, you should also keep the burner in case Amadeus calls back. We don't want him to talk to yet another version of Allan Woodrough."

Theo had a point, so Ethan nodded and returned the two devices to his jacket pocket.

"I need some coffee. Do you want anything?" asked Theo.

Ethan could use some caffeine as well so the two of them walked to the vending machine located at the end of the hallway.

"I have an offer for you. We'd like you to start consulting for us again. You're pretty much doing it already anyway, so you might as well get paid."

Ethan considered the idea while the machine brewed him a double espresso.

"I don't need an answer today. Just think about it, Ethan. I have reasons to believe your mental faculties are doing much better than you claim," added Theo, as he pressed the latte option on the selection panel.

The FBI agent's enigmatic statement had caught his attention. "Is there something you need to tell me?"

Theo simply grinned and headed to his office with his latte.

Ethan followed him and shut the office door before sitting down in front of his friend. "What's up, Theo?"

"It looks like you were right about Casanova and the Cowboy being one and the same."

"Are you positive?" This was good news, but Ethan needed absolute certainty.

"It sure looks like it. We found beachfront properties rented out with fake IDs for periods corresponding to the abductions of at least two of Casanova's victims. The IDs belonged to two men who died in their mid-thirties, just like the ones the Cowboy had used. The chances of this being a coincidence are close to zero. You see! When you try a little… The inference wasn't obvious, or else I'd have made it myself."

"My deductive skills have been improving a bit over the past few weeks, I'm not back to where I was, but I might be on my way," conceded Ethan.

"Glad to hear it. I still can't believe the jackass continued renting beach houses to murder his victims under his new Casanova persona," said Theo, sipping on his latte.

"I suspect he can't help himself. He's probably reenacting some twisted memory every time. Maybe he killed his first woman on a beach, or maybe he was first turned down by a girlfriend in a beach house, who knows… What matters is that we have a serious lead on him and he doesn't know a thing about it," said Ethan, tapping his index finger on the desk for emphasis.

"You seem pretty convinced that Allan Woodrough isn't our man."

"Amanda's killer is still alive. I can feel it. Call it intuition." Ethan wasn't being entirely candid with his friend. Intuition had nothing to do with it. He'd gone through Allan Woodrough's room after his death in search of a potential clue left by his murderer. The branding iron hadn't been among Allan's belongings then, Ethan was sure of it. He wasn't likely to have overlooked a two-foot-long piece of metal hidden in the man's duffle bag. Someone had planted it there, someone who knew about the identical iron Ethan had discovered hanging from a wall in Aaron's study. Someone who wanted to use Allan as a scapegoat, just like he had Angus Avery a year earlier… That someone was the real Cowboy.

"Just in case your intuition turns out to be correct and the Cowboy's still alive, we've already started looking through currently rented vacation homes in hope of catching him before he kills again."

"Could you give me the fake names the killer used on the rental applications under his Casanova persona?" asked Ethan.

"What are you going to do with those?" Theo was staring at him suspiciously.

"I just want to see if there's some type of pattern he's using to pick his fake identities. And could you also let me know if you find out that he's currently renting a beach house?"

"I suppose I can do that but sifting through those listings is a daunting task. For one thing, a house we check today could become rented tomorrow and we wouldn't know about it until we go down the entire list and start over at the top. At which point it could be already too late."

Ethan knew all this and hoped he wouldn't have to rely on the beach-house angle to find Amanda's killer. His own strategy was likely to bear fruit a lot faster than the FBI's, but he wasn't planning on mentioning this to his friend. He didn't want the cops to find the Cowboy before he did.

Chapter 79

The sun was nearing its zenith when Ethan rang the bell of the small apartment the next day. He hadn't committed the address to memory, and it had taken him nearly an hour to find it in a part of town where all the buildings looked alike.

The door was opened by a plain-looking woman in her early twenties who eyed him suspiciously.

"Good afternoon. My name is Ethan Archer and I was a friend of April." He let the information sink in for a second before adding, "I am very sorry for your loss. Your roommate didn't deserve dying like this."

The woman continued staring at him with an obvious lack of trust, "Nah, she didn't... What d'you want, Mister?"

"I was wondering if I could come in and ask you a couple questions about what happened."

"What did you say your name was?" The woman looked concerned.

"Ethan. Ethan Archer."

"I'll be back," she said, shutting the door on him. Ethan wasn't really sure what to make of her.

She came back a minute later holding the business card he'd given April after rescuing her from the pimp. "I knew your name sounded familiar. But I don't think I should be talking to you, mister. I don't want to end up like her."

"I understand. Are you in the same line of work as she was?"

"No. I work in a clothing store at the mall."

"In this case, I doubt you could be in much danger. I just need some answers so I can make sure whoever did this to April never hurts anyone again."

The woman still looked hesitant. "April tried to call you a bunch of times. You said you'd help her out... but you didn't. And now she's dead."

"I spent the holidays in a house in the mountains. There was no cellular network. I didn't get any of April's messages. I assure you I'd have come back to help her if I had. Why do you think I'm here now?"

The woman opened the door wider and let him in.

The inside of the apartment was the way he remembered it. Small, but clean and welcoming. They sat down one at each end of the couch, turned to face each other.

"I need you to tell me everything you know. I'm trying to figure out precisely what happened."

The woman nodded. "After the day you rescued her from that creep, April didn't go back on the street. She started looking for a job at the mall and in other places. I think she got lucky because it was just before Christmas and stores were hiring extra workers for the holidays. Anyway, she found a job in a department store. She looked happy about it but one day, I think it was the day after Christmas, she came back home crying."

"What happened?"

"She'd gotten a phone call from one of the hookers she knew, a friend of some sort. She warned April that a pimp had been asking about her and was trying to track her down. He'd even offered a cash reward. That got her real scared. That's when she started calling your number."

Ethan nodded somberly. He could feel his anger rising quickly, but this wasn't the place to express it. "What happened after that?"

"Two days after the warning, two men came to the apartment and grabbed April. The next day she was found dead," said the roommate, crying quietly.

"How do you know that two men grabbed her?"

"Because I was here that evening. I was in the bathroom when I heard the commotion. I stayed hidden until they were gone and then I called the cops."

"What did you tell them?"

"That April had just been kidnapped…"

"Did you tell the cops who'd done it?"

She shook her head slowly. She looked ashamed. "I was afraid the men would come after me… I told the police that I'd only heard men's voices from the bathroom."

"But you actually saw their faces too, didn't you?" asked Ethan gently.

She nodded. "The bathroom door was cracked open… Two guys, tall, mean-looking. One was white, the other looked Hispanic."

Ethan put his hand in his pocket to fish out the driver's license he'd stolen from the pimp's wallet and showed it to the woman.

"That's one of them," she said, giving him the confirmation he'd been seeking.

"Thank you. You've been most helpful."

Chapter 80

The cabin's porch was lit, but no other light was visible inside the house. Standing in the dark behind a window facing the small dirt road, Ethan, Theo, and Special Agent Melany Parker watched the Chevy Tahoe slow down to a crawl as it approached the cabin. The vehicle slowly entered the clearing and came to a full stop in front of the house. The beams from its headlights delineated the massive rectangular shape of the barn in the distance.

The burner phone rang in Ethan's pocket, and he quickly answered. This was his only job, the sole reason he was a part of the sting operation in the first place.

"This is Amadeus. I'm at the cabin but the barn's doors are closed. Where should I park?"

"Inside the barn. We'll open the doors for you," answered Ethan in the same hushed voice he'd used the first time he'd talked to the perv.

Melany grabbed her radio and gave quick instructions to her men hiding inside the other building. A second later, the silence of the night was broken by the sound of an iron curtain rolling open.

Ethan, Theo and Melany retreated to one of the upstairs bedrooms that had been converted into a command center for the occasion. Inside the room was a bank of twelve monitors displaying video feed from specific angles of the clearing, the inside of the barn, and a number of rooms inside the cabin. All locations had also been bugged with microphones that allowed the hidden agents to follow the action in real time.

Staring at the monitors, the trio saw Amadeus driving his vehicle inside the barn where he was met by an undercover agent who escorted him to the cabin. The perv was then directed towards Archibald's office where two more undercover agents were waiting for them. The male was sitting behind Archibald's desk while the woman stood in a corner behind her partner. She was wrapped in a silk kimono and was doing a great job at looking terrified.

"You guys are new? I've never seen you before," said the perv, sounding suspicious.

Amadeus appeared to be in his fifties and was about as large as he was tall… a human cube. Despite the freezing temperature outside, beads of sweat were visible on his furrowed brow.

"We've been around," answered the male agent in a dismissive tone.

"You've changed the way you operate? I've never been inside the house before," said the perv, still looking uncomfortable with the situation.

What is he talking about? wondered Ethan, who was following the action from the command center. If the clients never came inside the cabin, where were they abusing the victims? Inside the barn? That seemed unlikely. Was there a hidden room outside the house? Maybe buried in the woods?

"We change things a bit from time to time. We have our reasons, don't you worry about it. One thing that hasn't changed is the price," answered the agent behind the desk.

"Of course… That's the girl?" said Amadeus, pointing at the female agent. The perv's words made the woman flinch like a scared puppy.

"That's her. Where's the money?"

"I asked for a fifteen-year-old, sixteen top. That one looks at least twenty. That's not right." The perv was getting bolder.

The man behind the desk inhaled deeply, as if to calm down. He let out a loud exhale while staring at the perv who lost a bit of his confidence. "What's your age, sweetheart?" he asked his undercover partner.

"Seventeen," she answered in a whisper, just as they had rehearsed. The woman was actually closer to twenty-five. And although the makeup artist had managed to make her look a few years younger, she hardly looked like a teenager.

"That's the closest we could find on such short notice. Next time place your order well in advance. That's all we have for you today, take it or leave it but stop wasting my time." The agent's voice had a threatening edge now.

"I'll take her but I want a discount. Twenty percent off the usual price."

The agent appeared to consider the offer a moment. "In which shape are you planning on returning the merchandise if I give you a twenty percent discount?"

"The same as usual," said the fat man, looking hungrily at the woman in the corner. "In pieces…"

The woman collapsed to her knees and started whimpering loudly. The act brought a sardonic smile on Amadeus' lips.

"Shut the fuck up!" yelled her partner. The woman flinched at the words and immediately toned down the drama, sobbing more quietly. She was a talented actress.

"Then no deal. It's full price or nothing."

"Fine! I'll pay. But you can tell your boss than I'm not pleased with this arrangement," said Amadeus, adopting a look of resigned dissatisfaction.

"I'll be sure to mention it to him," answered the agent sarcastically. "Now let's proceed with the payment."

Amadeus pulled his cell phone from an inside pocket of his jacket and started typing.

"Are you sending the wire?" asked the agent matter-of-factly.

"Yes, you sh—"

"Hold on, we've set up a new account for this type of transactions. The old one was starting to attract unwanted attention." The agent handed the perv a post-it note with a routing and account number.

Amadeus sighed loudly, grabbed the note and entered the banking information into his phone. "Done!" he said, replacing the device into his pocket. "And now, sweetheart, you and me are gonna have some fun," he told the woman.

The female agent got back up on her feet and smiled at him before unwrapping her kimono. Underneath she wore a navy-blue tee-shirt with FBI spelled out in big yellow letters.

The perv turned around to run but three agents were already blocking his retreat, their weapons pointing at his chest.

"Sir, you are under arrest," said the woman as another agent placed handcuffs around the man's wrists. "You have the right to remain silent. Anything you say can and will be used against you in a court of law. You have the right to an attorney. If you cannot afford an attorney, one will be provided for you. Do you understand the rights I have just read to you? With these rights in mind, do you wish to speak to me?"

Amadeus didn't wish to speak to her or anyone else for that matter. A shame since he could have provided useful information regarding the sex-trafficking operation.

"The bastard won't say a word," said Theo to Melany and Ethan as the three of them came out of the command center and headed downstairs.

"Not until the DA offers a deal to his lawyer. And the asshole can afford a good lawyer, too, based on the two hundred grand he just dropped into our account for the right to kill his sex toy," answered Melany.

"Where do you think the pervs take the girls if they don't abuse them in the house?" asked Ethan. But the two others had no answer. "I think we should look for hidden basements under the house and the barn. We should also search the surrounding woods for a concealed trapdoor."

"I'll request a ground penetrating radar," said Melany, grabbing her cell phone.

"Ask for a cadaver dog too," said Ethan. "If the vics are being killed here, the easiest way to get rid of the bodies would be to bury them in the surrounding forest."

Melany nodded and started dialing.

Ethan suddenly wondered if the kids' skeletons that had been found in a nearby cave had started their journey somewhere in this clearing. But if that were the case, how had they ended up in a cavern located more than fifteen miles away?

Chapter 81

The ground penetrating radar showed up at the cabin early the next morning. By then, Amadeus had long been placed into custody and taken away. He hadn't pronounced a single word through the process.

The radar technicians had been scanning the barn's concrete floor for thirty minutes when they called out, "We have something here and it looks massive."

Ethan, Theo, and Melany went to check it out and were shocked by the size of the hidden basement. The barn's underground cellar covered an area at least half as large as the barn itself.

"How do we get in?" asked Melany to the technician.

"I don't know. There doesn't seem to be any hatch in the barn itself, so the entrance is probably outside."

They spent the next hour looking for an entrance but, in the end, they resorted to a jackhammer to break through the barn's concrete slab.

By the time the underground basement was finally accessible, the cadaver dog had arrived. Melany told the dog's handler to search the clearing and the surrounding woods before calling for a ladder to lower inside the basement.

A couple of agents went down the ladder and explored the secret room methodically before returning to the barn's ground level with their report. "The basement's clear but we have two bodies," said the taller of the two.

"Let's go have a look," said Melany. "Are you coming, Ethan?"

Ethan didn't care much for the bodies, but he wanted to see the basement for himself. Just in case it contained anything that could point him in the direction of Amanda's killer. The Cowboy, or Casanova as the media now called him, had been in the house a week earlier. Maybe he'd also been in the secret basement.

The dungeon was composed of two rooms separated by drywall and an access door. The largest of the rooms had a built-in prison cell. That's where the badly-decomposed bodies of the two women were located. They'd been dead over a week, based on the stench and bloated aspect of the corpses. Ethan wondered if the women had already been here while Jennifer and he had been staying at the cabin.

The trio walked to the smaller room which was furnished with a bed and a sort of operating table affixed with various restraints. A shelf on one of the walls was covered with sex toys of all kind. Torture devices guaranteed to make the victims' last moments on earth a living hell lay on the shelf below. The complexity of some of the abject tools was a terrifying testimony to the evil that lived hidden inside some people.

They went back to the main room and started exploring it in more detail. There, discarded on another shelf, they found a pile of children's toys and other random trinkets. Mementos taken from victims, Ethan suspected.

"Have a look at this," said Theo, standing in front of an opened filing cabinet, flipping through a manila folder. The word *Einstein* had been written on the file's cover: presumably another alias.

"A personal file. Looks like an in-depth background check with other personal information. Address, phone number, email… It also has detailed family intel," said Theo.

"Based on the number of files in this cabinet, it looks like they might have one of those on every one of their deviant clients," said Melany. "That's going to come in very handy…"

Apparently, the Woodroughs liked to thoroughly vet their customers. A good business practice in their line of work. They also liked paper. In the age of computer hacking and cyber security breaches, Ethan didn't blame them. A filing cabinet locked up in a secret basement was far more secure than any computer for the storage of sensitive information.

Some of the files they found dated back to the mid-90s. The bastards had been running their sordid business for a long time.

In a desk drawer, they discovered a list of phone numbers and associated code names. Several of them started with 52, the country code for Mexico. These were the men upstream in the supply chain, Mexican human traffickers who brought children and women from Central and Latin America for distribution within the US. Ethan's conviction was supported by one of the numbers on the list. He'd seen it appear several times on Allan's and Archibald's personal cell phone records, always as an incoming call. Even more interesting was the fact that, whomever the number belonged to, the individual had only started calling the two men after their deaths. The same Mexico number had also been found among both the incoming and outgoing calls placed from Allan's burner. Although the disposable phone's calling history had been deleted, the FBI communication experts had been able to retrieve it fairly easily.

Ethan suspected that the Mexican contact, having obtained no response on the burner phone, had taken it upon himself to call the Woodroughs' personal cell phones, probably to ask for payment or to arrange a delivery.

Ethan heard the ladder creaking behind him and turned around to see a young field technician walking down the aluminum steps.

"The dog has found something, ma'am," said the man to Melany.

They all went back upstairs to find the dog's handler, leash in hand, following her black Labrador through the trees surrounding the clearing. The snow on the ground didn't seem to impact the dog's sense of smell in the least.

"Astro's already identified two locations. We've started digging at one of them, but with the snow and the frozen ground, it will take us a while," said the field tech.

"We have a third site here," yelled the handler, waving a hand. She was standing twenty yards inside the woods delineating the clearing.

Ethan had the feeling they'd be finding a lot more bodies before all this was over.

Chapter 82

The television was on inside the rented house, but Casanova was paying little attention to the news anchor running his mouth. He was in a foul mood. Things had taken an unexpected turn for the worse.

The FBI had somehow found out about the secret room hidden under the barn and had been asking questions of the whole family. Fortunately, no one had any useful information to provide since all his business associates had been killed. So, where had the cops gotten their information? Nobody left alive knew about the room aside from him and the clients who'd used the facility in the past. And it was highly unlikely one of the pervs would have found religion and suddenly felt the need to confess his rapist, pedophile or murderous tendencies to the cops. So, who'd led the Feds to the hidden basement? Could one of the surviving Woodroughs have known about the sex-trafficking operation? Had the Travises witnessed something they weren't supposed to? The question was driving him insane.

He walked to the window, reflecting on over two decades of a very lucrative venture. He hadn't been around to witness the beginnings of the sex-trafficking ring, but he knew very well how it had started. It had all begun with three men sharing a common unwholesome interest in young children. Two of them were brothers and the third was a man they'd met in pedophile circles. A man by the name of Sam Clifford.

After a very costly evening spent molesting a couple of young kids in an isolated warehouse outside Las Vegas, the three of them had reconvened at the bar of their hotel where Clifford had brought up the idea of getting into the business themselves. It seemed idiotic to be spending the kind of money they were on their hobby when they could be the ones getting paid for the service and still be able to sample the merchandise for free.

Archibald and Allister had jumped on the idea and pulled some strings to make it happen. Within a year, Sam Clifford had become the new director of a small boys' orphanage located fifty miles from the Woodroughs' family cabin. It had been Allister's idea, and a great one too. Clifford's position had secured a vital part of the supply chain while minimizing the risks of scrutiny. People didn't typically have much interest in orphans.

The local sheriff's help had also proven instrumental in the success of the enterprise. Sheriff Bradford hadn't been a pedophile himself, but the brothers had essentially bought his election to office, and they had enough dirt on the crooked cop to send him behind bars for a lifetime and a half. As a result, the lawman proved very cooperative.

The money had quickly started pouring in and, within a few years, the sex-trafficking ring was cashing in multi-million-dollar profits on a yearly basis.

The operation had evolved and expanded its offerings over the years to reach a market larger than just pedophiles. People could come to the cabin's secret underground dungeon to assuage their most perverted fantasies on victims of all ages. Sometimes the vics survived the ordeal, and sometimes they didn't, but this was built into the price, as was the disposal fee. But now, with the cops digging in the woods around the cabin, there would be a lot of questions to answer.

Unlike the others, he himself had never cared for sampling the merchandise. He didn't like his prey served on a silver platter. That was too easy. He preferred working for his reward and enjoyed the thrill of the hunt. Which was why he'd always played a relatively passive role in the sex-trafficking ring up to now.

With Allan and the others out of the picture, things were going to change, though. He would need to play the central role from now on and would reap much greater benefits for it. He'd been thinking about it a lot these past few days, but the cops' discovery of the underground basement had significantly dampened his enthusiasm. He had the contacts he needed to restart the operation once the dust had settled, but for now it was safer to keep a low profile.

He heard a familiar voice coming from the television and turned towards the screen to find Archer standing behind a pulpit, answering questions at a press conference. Two FBI agents stood beside him.

Why was the prick back in the news? What the hell was going on?

He sat down on the edge of the couch and turned up the volume as a journalist was asking, *"Are you back working with the FBI, Mr. Archer?"*

"On a limited basis."

"And what was your involvement in this particular case? How did you figure out the family of late Senator Woodrough was involved in sex trafficking? And do we know if the senator was implicated?" asked another journalist.

"This is an ongoing investigation and we cannot divulge more than what has already been stated at this point," said the man standing next to Archer. *"But let me assure you that Mr. Archer was absolutely instrumental in this case. He didn't only*

break it; he actually brought the case to us."

Casanova recognized the agent who'd spoken. He was one of the prick's close friends. The same agent who'd been in charge of arresting the Cowboy. That didn't speak much for the man's intellect since the Cowboy was currently watching him from this very couch.

He was boiling with anger. Not only was the prick back working with the FBI, he'd been the one responsible for busting the Woodroughs' lucrative operation. And now he came to taunt him on TV! He grabbed the glass of gin from the coffee table and sent it crashing against the wall.

Archer probably thought himself safe from his nemesis because the branding iron had been found in Allan's bag… He thought his wife's killer dead, but he was mistaken. There was nowhere for the prick to hide from Casanova's wrath now, and Jennifer MacKay would be the first one to pay the price.

He'd meant to deal with her much sooner but had run into a snag. Someone he'd recognized on the street. Someone who shouldn't have been in town… And then the whole fiasco with the barn had hit him like a train and he'd been playing defense ever since. But the cops had absolutely nothing on him. As far as they knew, all those involved in the sex-trafficking operation were dead. And they were almost correct in that respect.

He got up from the couch and went to serve himself another gin. Seeing Archer parading on TV had helped him make up his mind. He'd waited too long for his reward already. Now was the time to deal with Jennifer MacKay and he knew exactly where to start.

Chapter 83

Ethan stopped the water and stood dripping in the shower an instant before reaching for the towel. He'd been back in San Francisco twelve hours, but his mind was still in Montana.

The sting operation at the barn had gone smoothly. Amadeus—a Silicon Valley millionaire by the name of Harvey Patterson—was now in custody and cooperating with the authorities. He didn't seem to know a whole lot about the operation, however. The Woodroughs had been prudent.

Patterson had first heard of the barn on the dark web—a completely unregulated side of the internet used for illegal activities. Whether one was looking for a case of RPGs, sex slaves, or heroin in bulk, the dark web was where the search started. Nowadays, a few clicks were all it took to purchase a human being. The only requirement was money, and Patterson had plenty of it.

After registering on a site specialized in matching perverted needs with specific service providers, Patterson had been contacted by phone and assigned the alias Amadeus. At the end of a two-week vetting period, he'd been contacted a second time with GPS coordinates and a meeting time. Upon arriving at the rendezvous, he'd been placed into a van with no windows and had been driven to the cabin in the woods to meet his victim.

According to Patterson, he'd only sexually abused the woman—who had of course been eighteen—but it had been enough to gain the trust of his hosts. Before leaving the dungeon, he'd been given access to a direct line to place his future orders. From that point on, he'd also been allowed to drive himself to the cabin without chaperones. He claimed to have no idea who the men behind the operation were, however. He'd met the same couple of guys every time he'd shown up at the cabin, but he'd never heard any names mentioned.

Ethan slipped into a pair of jeans and walked to the kitchen. He took a bottle of water from the fridge and headed for the living room where he grabbed his laptop lying on the coffee table and sank into his couch.

The FBI had discovered that the cabin actually belonged to a Cayman Islands-based corporation whose ownership couldn't be traced. Even if Patterson or another client had tried to figure out who they were dealing with, looking up the property's title would have delivered no useful information. The Feds were now working with their Mexican counterpart to expose the entire distribution network. The whole thing was out of Ethan's hands and he could focus all his brain power on catching Casanova. That's what the staged press conference had been all about. The latest move in a game of chess that had started nearly two years earlier. A bait for Casanova to swallow.

In Ethan's book, the connection between the Woodroughs and Amanda's killer was established, but the press-conference bait would only work if the killer was also somehow associated with the sex-trafficking operation. If he weren't connected to it in any way, the press conference was unlikely to be of much use… But if he were involved, on the other hand, the bust would very likely piss him off no end. And there was little doubt Casanova would hold him responsible for it. The whole plan was based on the hope that Casanova would try and retaliate against Ethan once again. Just like his Cowboy persona had a year earlier.

Since the Cowboy had gone after Amanda to get to him, there was a good chance Casanova would single out Jennifer this time around. Casanova had been at the cabin during the holidays, and he'd seen how close Ethan was to his assistant. That made her a prime target.

Jennifer didn't know it, but she was being followed by two FBI agents wherever she went. Theo's team had also identified a beachfront property they believed was currently being rented by Casanova. The property was under FBI surveillance 24/7 and if Casanova somehow managed to snatch another victim, he'd be arrested the instant he brought her to the house.

But Ethan would have never agreed to Theo's suggestion of using Jennifer as a bait if he hadn't had his own guarantees that no harm would come to his assistant. In addition to the FBI's measures, Ethan was tracking Jennifer's every move by GPS. Hers was one of the four phones he'd asked Suzy to track for him, and one of the two Suzy had already hacked into, the other one being Blake's. She was still working on hacking Matthew's and

Clive's accounts, however. This wasn't an ideal situation, but Suzy had promised she'd have the other two for him in the coming hours.

Ethan booted his laptop and retrieved Theo's email from his inbox. The email contained attachments with copies of the IDs Casanova had used to rent the properties in which he'd tortured and killed Naomi Berhan and Stephany Pierce.

Ethan opened all the social media he could think of and started searching for the names on the IDs: Percy Stevenson and Paul Richards. Within fifteen minutes, he'd found Percy's Facebook and Instagram accounts but nothing for Paul Richards.

Percy's accounts showed no sign of activity in over a year. Not particularly surprising given that the account's legitimate owner had died in a traffic accident fourteen months earlier.

Ethan then searched Pinterest, Twitter, and a few smaller sites for accounts associated with either name but to no avail. Paul Richards appeared to have no social media presence whatsoever.

Ethan was about to give up on his idea when a thought crossed his mind. He started digging a bit deeper and eventually found a closed Facebook account under Paul Richards' name. Now, *that* was interesting… Could Casanova have opened this account to legitimize his persona in case Naomi Berhan looked him up? If it were the case, it would have been wise of him to close the account as soon as Naomi Berhan was in his grip.

Ethan next turned his energy to Percy Stevenson and soon uncovered a closed Facebook account under that name as well. Unfortunately, the profile pictures associated with the two accounts were locked inside Facebook's secured servers, and Ethan lacked the skills necessary to hack them. But he knew someone who could…

He picked up his cell from the coffee table and dialed Suzy's number. "Hey. Where are you with the two trackers you promised me?" he asked, not bothering with another form of greeting.

"I'm just about done. Come in an hour and I'll upload the code to your phone."

"Great! I'll be right over. Tell me, how tough is it to peek inside a closed Facebook account?"

"Depends what info you're after," replied Suzy stoically.

"I want to see the profile pictures associated with two closed accounts."

"That's easy. Give me the names on the profiles and I'll have the pics for you by the time you get here."

Chapter 84

Casanova gave the room a circular look and was satisfied with what he saw. Everything was ready for Jennifer MacKay's arrival. The wooden bench he'd built especially for her was one of his best ones. He could flip it from a horizontal to a vertical position at his whim and could even suspend the woman by her feet if it struck his fancy.

The walls of the cozy little torture chamber weren't soundproof, but it didn't matter. The house was so remote that nobody would ever hear her screams, no matter how loud they got. And there would be plenty of screaming… He could guarantee it.

Standing in the middle of the room, he closed his eyes and took a deep breath. He held it a few seconds and slowly exhaled, opening his eyes as he did so. This was part of the ritual to put himself in *the zone*. The place of extreme focus from which he would operate the snatch. For this wouldn't be a Casanova move. There would be no seducing the bitch first this time around. He would kidnap her and bring her here, to the middle of nowhere. And then, he would take his sweet time with her.

He retrieved his phone from his pocket and turned it off. From this point on, he would tolerate no distraction. It was showtime.

Chapter 85

Jennifer was sitting in front of an untouched cup of coffee in her favorite bookstore. Across from her, Tabatha was reading a poetry book while sipping on a caramel macchiato.

Ethan was finally back in town and Jennifer's vacation would soon be over. She'd taken the whole week off, but it was already Friday morning and Monday she'd be back at the office with him. She didn't feel ready for that.

Five days had passed since the FBI had discovered a secret basement under the Woodroughs' barn, but Jennifer still felt sick to her stomach when she thought about the two women who had been found dead in the underground cell.

According to their autopsies, they'd died of dehydration sometime between December 26 and December 28. Which meant they'd been alive at the time Jennifer and Ethan had arrived at the cabin and for probably a day or two afterward. This angered her so much… but she couldn't blame herself; how could she have known?

Her phone vibrated and she was surprised to recognize Clive's number on the caller ID. She gave Tabatha a quick glance, but her girlfriend hadn't noticed anything. After a quick circular glance at the faces around her, she retired to the ladies' room to read the text.

We need to talk. Can you come to my hotel?

Jennifer hadn't been in Clive's room yet, but she knew where it was. She walked back to the table where Tabatha was still absorbed in her book. She didn't seem to have even noticed Jennifer's absence. "I need to go to work, Ethan just texted me. He needs me for something urgent. Sorry about that, Tab. I'll see you tomorrow."

"Now?" said Tabatha, already getting pissed off.

Jennifer just shrugged and was on her way after another circular look at their neighbors. An unnecessary precaution, most likely, but she'd had the weird impression of being watched lately.

She thought about Tabatha as she exited the bookstore and decided there was no need to tell her anything.

Chapter 86

E than had just parked his car in front of Suzy's shop when his phone rang.

"We have some action at the beach house," Theo said.

Ethan's heart jumped. "What kind of action?"

"Nothing too exciting yet so don't work yourself up. Casanova spent the day putting some equipment together in one of the bedrooms."

"What kind of equipment?" Ethan asked.

"Can't really tell. We're watching the house through partially closed blinds via a drone-mounted camera hovering over the sea three hundred feet away."

"You're joking, right?"

"We can't install microphones or cameras inside the house without a warrant, Ethan. But our measures are good enough. We'll know if he brings a woman to the house."

"He's still inside?"

"No, he left a couple hours ago. But relax, we have a team following his car. If he snatches someone, we'll catch him red-handed."

"Could your guys see his face?"

"No, he was wearing sunglasses and a baseball cap, so they didn't get a good look."

This was good news overall, but Ethan felt no relief, quite the contrary. They were closing in on Amanda's killer and he wouldn't start breathing normally again before the man had been arrested or shot dead.

"What's the address? I want to be there when your guys move in."

"That's not gonna happen, man. I can't do that," said Theo, and he sounded like he meant it.

"The fucker killed Amanda. I have the ri—"

"Not this time, Ethan. This time you sit on the sideline and let us do our job. You're way too emotionally involved to be allowed on the scene."

"If you fuck this one up, I'll never forgive you. You know that, right?"

"I know," answered Theo, in a matter-of-fact voice.

"Let me know as soon as you have news," said Ethan as he hung up the phone. He wanted to be there. He wanted to sink his eyes in the killer's when they arrested him. But it didn't look like it was going to happen.

His mind jumped to Jennifer. He started the tracking app and immediately located her. She was downtown: walking, based on her pace. He wanted to talk to her, make sure she was okay.

He dialed her number. It rang a few times, but the call eventually went

THE GIRL WHO WENT NOWHERE

to voicemail. He tried three more times before finally giving up, a sinking feeling in the pit of his stomach.

He then dialed the number Jennifer had given him as an emergency contact in the city: Tabatha's.

"Tabatha? This is Ethan Archer. Is Jennifer with you by chance?"

"She's not with you? She left for the office almost two hours ago," answered Tabatha.

"She was going to the office? What for?"

"To meet you. She got your text," Tabatha said. Worry had crept into her voice.

"Alright. I must have missed her. Tell her to call me if you get a hold of her." He ended the call. He didn't want to worry Tabatha unnecessarily, even though he had plenty of reasons to be worried himself.

He'd never sent any text to Jennifer which left two options. Either someone had cloned his number and sent a text impersonating him, or Jennifer had lied to Tabatha. He favored the second option but mostly because it was the least terrifying of the two.

Chapter 87

Clive's room was on the third floor of the hotel, by a large window at the end of a hallway. It was 3 PM and Jennifer wondered once again what Clive wanted. They hadn't planned to see each other today. Instead, she'd intended to spend the afternoon, and most likely the night, with Tabatha. But now she had the feeling her plans were going to change.

She knocked on the door and waited for a response as Clive's neighbors were walking inside their room with arms full of shopping bags. No response came. She waited for them to shut their door and knocked again. This time the door opened wide.

Before she had a chance to react, the two prongs of a Taser made contact with her sweater and she felt herself falling forward, her muscles unresponsive, locked by the electricity running through them.

She watched powerless as the man she knew to be Amanda's killer received her in his arms and dragged her inside the room.

She heard the door closing as he laid her down on the bed. She was just starting to regain some control over her muscles when she felt a prick in her arm and a liquid flowing into her veins.

The dead eyes of Clive Thomas staring into hers were the last thing she saw before losing consciousness.

Chapter 88

"Do you have the trackers ready?" asked Ethan, as he entered Suzy's shop.

"Yeah. Give me your phone," replied the blue-haired woman.

He handed her the device and followed Suzy to her high-tech den where she plugged the phone into a computer. She then sat behind a keyboard and started typing at a pace far exceeding what Ethan could manage on the best of days.

"Done!" she said, unplugging the phone and returning it to him.

He immediately loaded the tracking app and confirmed that Clive and Matthew had been added to the menu. He clicked the radio button next to Clive's name and the map re-centered around a pulsing green dot. It took Ethan a second to realize he was staring at a map of downtown San Francisco. Clive was in San Francisco? What was the ranch foreman doing in the city? Ethan didn't like this a bit.

He clicked the button next to Jennifer's name and a red dot starting pulsing virtually on top of the green one. The two of them were in the same building—a hotel!

He immediately dialed Jennifer's number, not bothering to answer Suzy's questioning look. It rang a few times but eventually went to voicemail once again. This was a nightmare.

He rang Theo back and the agent answered almost immediately.

"Are your guys with Jennifer?" asked Ethan urgently.

"No, but they're close. She's in a downtown hotel, one of my men is waiting for her down in the lobby."

"Do they know what room she's in?"

"I doubt it. They couldn't have followed her inside the elevator without looking suspicious."

"She's with Clive Thomas! Your guys need to get in there right away, Theo! This stinks to high heaven!" Ethan could feel sweat dripping from his armpits despite the cool temperature in the shop.

"I'll call you back," said Theo, hanging up.

Ethan stood in the middle of Suzy's command center looking dumbfounded for a second. He'd never put his money on Clive. Although in hindsight, a rancher was a pretty good Cowboy…

If anything happened to Jennifer, Ethan would never forgive himself. But surely Clive wouldn't kill her in a hotel room. Under both his Cowboy and Casanova personas, he'd always murdered his victims in secluded locations, away from prying eyes and ears. He couldn't kill her in the middle of downtown San Francisco… This wouldn't be satisfying to the psychopath.

"Is everything okay?" asked Suzy, who was still staring at him.

He just shook his head, unable to speak.

"Anything I can help with? I pulled the Facebook profiles' pics you requested…"

In the heat of the moment, Ethan had completely forgotten about those. "Show me," he said halfheartedly. He already knew who would be on those pictures: Clive Thomas.

Suzy clicked on a folder and opened a few files. They were all screen captures of the closed Facebook accounts and looked exactly the same as any active Facebook page. But Ethan couldn't believe what his eyes were seeing. The same man was posed, smiling, in every single picture, but it wasn't Clive…

Ethan's cell rang at that moment and he answered immediately. "Did you find her?"

"No, but we found Clive Thomas. He'd rented the room under his real name, so we simply asked the front desk. We also found two phones and a purse in his room," answered Theo.

"Did you talk to him? What did he say?"

"He said nothing… He's dead, Ethan. He was stabbed in the heart."

"Are your guys still tailing the man who rented the beach house?" asked Ethan without missing a beat.

There was a pause on the line and he knew it wasn't good news.

"They lost him in traffic," answered Theo.

Ethan took a deep breath. "Describe the purse and the phones to me."

The agent began and Ethan quickly interrupted him. "The purse and the second phone are Jennifer's. Listen to me carefully, Theo. Casanova is Matthew Woodrough. You must put an A.P.B. on him immediately, he has Jennifer."

"How do you know that?"

"I'm staring at the deleted Facebook profiles he created to attract two of Casanova's victims," answered Ethan impatiently.

"I'll put an A.P.B. on him, but if he's bringing her to the beach house, we'll catch him. Have no fear."

Ethan had plenty of fear. "Give me the address, Theo. Now!"

The agent caved and gave him the address to the rented beach house.

Ethan ended the call and recalled the tracking app on his mobile. He clicked the button corresponding to Matthew, but no dot appeared on the screen. "Why isn't this working?" he asked Suzy urgently.

"He turned his phone off. You can't track it if it's not on," she said, sounding sorry.

Ethan wanted to scream.

Chapter 89

Ethan was behind the wheel heading to the isolated house when Theo called him for the third time of the day.

"It looks like it's a go," said Theo.

"What do you mean?"

"Our perv just drove back to the house in an SUV with tinted windows. He parked in the garage but this time he's not alone. There's a woman with him."

"How do you know?"

"The drone saw her through the blinds."

"What does she look like?" Ethan was holding his breath.

"Hard to say. The sun is setting and the lights are still out inside the house. She's not a platinum blonde, but she could be anything else. We can't get too close with the drone or else he'll notice it. These things aren't quiet."

Theo fell silent for a moment and Ethan negotiated a tight turn while maintaining as much speed as possible; he couldn't afford to slow down.

"What's going on, Theo? What are you seeing?"

"Nothing right now. I've just lost the video feed, the connection wasn't great to start with and now it's completely gone. I need to rely on the agents in the field to relay the information."

"Great! What's your E.T.A.?"

"I should be there in five minutes."

Ethan sighed heavily. He hated the whole darn idea. This had been such a horrible plan. What had they been thinking?

"The agents on site don't see anything either. It's too dark inside the house right now," said Theo, after a while.

"That's not good! He could be killing her as we speak!"

"What do you want me to do? Burst through the door without a warrant or probable cause and see him get away with it on a technicality?"

"Yes. I think that's exactly what you should do," replied Ethan. "If Jennifer is in there, I'm more interested in getting her out unscathed than arresting the bastard by the book."

This was the absolute truth. Ethan was actually hoping Matthew Woodrough would get away with it on a technicality. He would be ready for him if it happened.

A car came flying in the opposite direction out of a tight curve and invaded Ethan's lane in the process.

He swerved and nearly lost the control of his vehicle but managed to correct his trajectory at the last second and stayed on the road. It had been a close one.

He spent the next few minutes with his foot flooring the accelerator while awaiting news from Theo. His pulse rate was increasing with every passing second of radio silence.

"We have some light. Looks like it's coming from the master bath," said Theo suddenly.

"What do you see?"

"Nothing yet… Wait a minute, looks like we have someone lying on the bed."

"Is it the woman? Is she restrained?"

"Can't tell… Yes, it's the woman! The man is coming out of the ba—

Shit! Where did he go?"

"What's going on?" asked Ethan, passing three cars at once before swerving back into his lane way too close to oncoming traffic.

"Here he is. He'd walked to a corner of the room, now he's back in our field of vision. He's walking towards the woman. Yes, she's restrained. Looks like she's got tethers binding her to the bedframe and now he just slapped her. We're going in."

Ethan heard some commotion on the other end of the line and then it went dead. Waiting for news that would take a while to come, he prayed to God that his intuition was wrong.

He was getting close now. At this speed he'd get there in another ten minutes. And then what?

Theo called him back as the house appeared in his headlights.

"It's not our guy, Ethan. We fucked up."

"What happened?"

"We walked in on a low-budget porn production set. The asshole making the movies rented the house with a fake ID because some of the girls are underage. We have no idea where Matthew Woodrough is."

Chapter 90

The drive from downtown San Francisco back to his rental in the northern part of Napa County took Matthew nearly two hours. That was thirty minutes more than he'd expected, but no one could control traffic. The isolated ranch house was lost in the middle of the wine country. He usually favored beachfront properties for his playtime since women found them romantic, but he'd opted for something different this time. Habits weren't a good idea in his line of work; they got you caught, and Casanova couldn't afford that.

He hadn't passed a vehicle in over five miles, but he still parked the car inside the garage and made sure the door had come all the way down before opening the trunk. Why take chances?

He pulled the large suitcase out of the trunk and rolled it all the way to the bedroom he'd prepared for his twisted games. In addition to the wooden bench he'd designed himself, he'd purchased a commercial contraption where a sexual partner could be attached and bent to whichever degrading position Matthew desired. The equipment had been designed for people into S&M, but it was also a rapist's dream come true.

He opened the suitcase and pulled the folded body of Jennifer MacKay out of it. The woman was still sleeping, but probably not for much longer, based on the amount of anesthetic he'd used. He'd had to guess her weight, but the fact she was still breathing suggested he hadn't been too far off.

He briefly debated whether to attach her to the bench or to the S&M contraption but decided he was better off going with the bench at this time. Its metal shackles would make for a more vivid impression when his guest would finally wake up. Should he strip her naked before binding her to the bench so she would wake up in the dark wearing nothing but her Eve costume? An interesting idea but he decided against it in the end. It would be more fun to tear the clothes off her body once she was awake and stinking of fear. He closed the shackles around her wrists and ankles and headed back to the kitchen. The whole thing had made him hungry and he was going to need some energy for when the cunt woke up. It wouldn't be much longer now.

He prepared himself a sandwich and started snacking in front of the TV without paying much attention to what was happening on the screen. In his mind, he kept picturing the indescribable fun he was about to have with the woman strapped down in the bedroom at the end of the hallway. He heard a cracking noise and listened intently. The sound didn't repeat but he went to check on his guest, nonetheless.

The house was dark, but he didn't bother switching on the lights as he headed for the bedroom. His entry needed to be perfectly staged in a way that would maximize terror in his victim. And from times immemorial humans were afraid of the dark. An invisible enemy you could hear coming was ten times more terrifying that one your eyes could see.

"Did you miss me?" he whispered as he entered the dark bedroom.

"One could say that, yes." The voice of Jennifer was coming from the direction of the bench but didn't have the tinge of terror he'd expected.

He walked to the wall and flipped on the switch.

Despite the shackles pinning her to the table, she didn't look the slightest bit scared, which caused him great frustration. She had to be faking that bravado. Nobody could be this relaxed under these circumstances. It didn't matter anyway. She wouldn't keep it up very long. The act would drop the minute he'd thrust himself inside her.

"It must have been a shock when you saw me in that hotel room… pun intended," he said, slowly approaching the table. He was taking his time, like a cat toying with a mouse stuck to a glue trap.

"Yes and no, Matthew. I'd felt electricity flowing between us at the cabin already, you know. You were trying to be discreet, but I could tell you were interested," she replied, smirking.

She was starting to get on his nerves with her smartass comments, but he did his best to hide it. He wouldn't give her the pleasure to see that she was getting to him.

"It's too bad you Tasered me right away, we could have had a drink and reminisced on the good old days," she said, a twinkle in her eyes. The woman was insane, there was no other explanation.

"But cowards like you don't take chances with women like me," she continued. "Tied down to a table is the only way you'd ever be able to handle me. Because let's be honest, since it's only the two of us, in the end you're really not much of a man, are you?"

He smiled a humorless smile as he reached the table and sunk his empty eyes into hers.

"I bet it's also your sense of inadequacy that pushed you to go after Amanda Archer. Ethan was smarter than you and you just couldn't take it, so you went after his wife like the coward you are. And even then, you simply couldn't handle her on your own, you needed Avery to do the heavy lifting for you. Because you could never have picked her up in a bar. Someone like you could never have seduced someone like her."

"You're mistaken, little girl," he said. He was close enough to feel her breath on his face now. "I did it to cause the maximum amount of pain to your prick of a boss and it worked like a charm. He went off the deep end for the better part of a year. Only recently did he start recovering. Just in time to deal with the traumatic death of his beloved assistant."

He gave her a feral smile to which she answered with a wink as she headbutted him. He heard the bridge of his nose cracking on impact as he jerked his head back.

"You little cunt. That wasn't smart. That just bought you hours of agony. By the time I'm done with you, you'll beg me to end your pathetic existence," he said in a snarl, while wiping blood off his nose.

He heard someone whistling behind him and turned around just in time to receive Ethan Archer's fist square in the jaw. He felt his teeth shatter as he was driven off his feet and landed heavily on the ground. Archer was on him before he had a chance to get back up. Kicking him in the head as if it'd been a football. Matthew passed out an instant later.

When he regained consciousness, he was strapped to the wooden bench and on his belly. Archer was walking around him like a vulture circling its future meal. Jennifer was sitting on the edge of the table a few inches from Matthew's face, her legs dangling. She was enjoying the show.

"I've had so much time to think about this instant," said Archer. "I spent so many nights contemplating what I'd have done to Angus Avery if I'd gotten my hands on him before the cops did. I simply couldn't believe the bastard had gotten such an easy way out. It was so unfair. He needed to suffer the way Amanda had suffered—"

"Do you see where Ethan's going with this, Matthew?" interrupted Jennifer.

"Give him a little credit, Jennifer. Matthew Woodrough's not the brightest crayon in the box, but even he can get the point I'm trying to make. I want to thank you, Matthew. Thank you for sending me the video and letting me know you were still alive. Thank you for being so predictable that you'd decide to once again go after the woman closest to me. And thank you for picking such a perfect spot for our reunion. Somewhere nobody can ever hear your screams."

Matthew was angry, but he wasn't scared. Psychopaths didn't feel fear and he was a psychopath… He'd known this a long time. He felt no shame for it, either. Why would he? Nature had made him this way. It wasn't his fault if he was stronger than the others. The strong lived and the weak died. That was just the way the world functioned. Survival of the fittest.

"But then I decided torture wasn't my thing," continued Archer. "And killing you wouldn't be satisfying either. So, of course, this raised the question of what would be a suitable punishment."

Matthew turned his head just enough to look at Archer hovering above him.

"After much consideration, I decided that sending you to jail was probably the best option after all."

Matthew smiled, a bloody smirk showing holes where three of his front teeth had been. The prick was disgraceful, he wasn't even man enough to kill his wife's murderer. Prison didn't worry him. They had nothing on him beside kidnapping. He'd be out in a couple of years at most.

"But then I changed my mind again," continued Archer. "Jail isn't a place for somebody like you. People like you don't learn from their mistakes, people like you can't be rehabilitated. You might even manage to convince your fellow inmates that you're a decent guy. No, that wouldn't do at all," said Archer, shaking his head. What was he getting at?

"You get a kick out of controlling your victims, making them realize that they're at your sole mercy. So I thought some more, and finally found a fitting punishment for a rapist such as yourself." Archer had pronounced the last words very seriously. His smile had completely disappeared. What the fuck was he talking about?

"But your punishment requires some preparation, probably a few days actually. Good thing you've rented this house for a while; I won't have to look for another place to hide you while I iron out the details of your penance."

Matthew saw Archer approaching, but from his vantage point tied up on the table he couldn't see the man's hands hidden behind his back. Suddenly, Archer disappeared completely from his field of vision and he felt a prick in the back of his neck. A few seconds later, everything went black.

Chapter 91

Ethan was silently observing Jennifer from the corner of his eye. Three days had passed since he'd rescued her from Matthew Woodrough's grip and the two of them were sitting at their respective desks, waiting for Theo's arrival. Jennifer had already been interviewed once by the cops, but Theo wanted her to clarify a few points for him.

They heard knocking but the FBI agent didn't wait for a reply before entering the office. "Good afternoon, Miss MacKay," he said, shutting the door closed. "Ethan," he added, nodding towards his friend. He then headed to Jennifer's desk and placed her phone and purse in front of her.

"Thank you, Agent Hansen—this purse was a gift and is dear to me. And thanks also for stopping by and not making me come all the way to the Federal building for this," said Jennifer. And she looked like she meant it.

"It's my pleasure. I'm glad everything worked out in the end, even though things didn't go quite as expected."

"You can't be as glad as I am."

"Can I get you some coffee?" asked Ethan from the coffee maker.

"Yes, thanks," said Theo. "I can't believe you're having Miss MacKay back at work already after what she went through. What kind of a boss are you?"

Theo had been talking to him, but Ethan knew the agent's attention hadn't left Jennifer. He was surreptitiously watching her.

"Please, call me Jennifer, Agent Hansen. And Ethan isn't as big a slave driver as you'd believe. I'm here because I want to be. I don't feel comfortable alone in my apartment right now."

"I think I understand what you mean. Though I can't begin to imagine what you went through."

Seriously? You really think she's going to fall for your psychology for dummies bullshit? thought Ethan.

"I know you've already been interviewed by the Napa County Sheriff's Office," Theo continued, "but I need you to tell me once again in your own words exactly what happened after you reached Mr. Thomas' hotel room."

Jennifer smiled and retold the story she'd already recited a couple of times.

"I knocked on the door but nobody came at first. A minute or so went by and the door finally opened. I was surprised to see Matthew Woodrough answering the door but before I could say anything, he shot me with a Taser and I lost control of my muscles."

Theo was nodding empathically while taking notes, which seemed redundant since he was also recording the conversation.

"My legs felt like cotton and I collapsed, but he caught me before I hit the floor and dragged me to the bed where he laid me down beside Clive's body. It was horrible. I couldn't move and he'd purposefully positioned me so that my face would be inches away from Clive's."

"Clive was the person you were supposed to meet, the one you'd come for, correct?"

"Yes, the text message inviting me to the hotel had been sent from Clive's phone. The thought someone else could have written it never crossed my mind…"

"It wouldn't have crossed my mind either," said Theo. "Can you tell me why Mr. Thomas would request your presence to his room?"

"As I've already mentioned to the sheriff's deputies, Clive and I were having an affair. I'm not ashamed of it, but I'd appreciate if you could keep this part quiet. Gwendoline Thomas has already lost her husband. She doesn't need to know he was cheating on her on top of it."

"I can't promise anything, but if at all possible, I'll keep this information confidential. What happened next?"

"I felt a prick on my arm and I lost consciousness. When I finally woke up, I was in a large suitcase in the trunk of a moving vehicle."

"How did you know you were in a suitcase?"

"I didn't yet at this point. I realized that's what it was when I managed to break free."

"How did you break free, Jennifer?"

"I could tell how the suitcase was supposed to open so I put my back against the lid of my prison and pushed with my hands and knees against the opposite side. Eventually the locking mechanism gave in and I was out. I felt the car slowing down immediately, and I assumed Matthew had heard the sound of the breaking lock."

Jennifer paused an instant to take a sip of her coffee, not making eye contact with Ethan at any point. Good girl.

"What happened next?" asked Theo.

"I searched for a weapon and I had just grabbed the tire iron when the trunk opened up. When I saw Matthew Woodrough towering over me, I didn't even think and swung the tire iron at him. It hit him square in the face."

Jennifer looked paler and her cadence had increased. She was giving a great performance.

"He fell to the ground and I got out of the trunk and started running. I didn't know where I was, but I was surrounded by grape vines. I kept running, turning around from time to time to see if Matthew was behind me but he wasn't. I reached a winery eventually and told the employees to call the police right away. You know the rest, I believe."

Theo nodded. "I have one more question for you, Jennifer. You reached the winery about three hours after you were kidnapped, but the drive from the hotel shouldn't have taken much more than ninety minutes. Do you have any idea why? Any idea where Matthew might have taken you after the hotel?"

"No, I'm sorry."

"Any idea where he was taking you when you managed to escape?"

She just shook her head.

"Well, I believe that's all the questions I had for you."

"We still have no clue about his whereabouts?" asked Ethan.

"No. We found his car abandoned on a Walmart parking lot, but no trace of the man. The suitcase was still in the trunk, though. Good thing you keep yourself in shape, Jennifer. Those were some locks you managed to break."

She smiled meekly. It had been a jab, Theo's way of calling bullshit on her story, and Ethan had no doubt Jennifer knew it, too.

"You need to catch the bastard, Theo," said Ethan, doing his best to fake anger.

"We have all the cops in the country looking for him. We'll get him."

"I'm sure the bastard is also behind the Christmas killing spree at the cabin," said Ethan

"What makes you say that?"

"Simple logic. We know he was involved in the sex trafficking since he came after Jennifer the minute we announced on TV that I'd been the one responsible for dismantling the operation…"

"And?" Theo was apparently not following.

"And it's not a stretch to imagine that Matthew wanted to get rid of his associates and take control of the operation to maximize his own returns."

Theo looked at him skeptically. "I'm not sure it's as obvious as you make it sound. These were his close relatives—his father, his uncle, his cousin. And what about the kid? You're going to tell me he was a sex trafficker, too?!"

"I don't have an answer for the kid," admitted Ethan, "but the man's a psychopath, so who knows…"

"And what about the killer who shot Sheriff Bradford and the retired orphanage director? That definitely wasn't Matthew Woodrough, was it?" said Theo.

"I'm sure Matthew contracted him to throw everyone off his trail. The ghost did a few very visible hits while Matthew took care of most of the killings inside of the house."

"Maybe." Theo sounded unconvinced.

"Because you think it would make more sense to have another serial killer in the lot? We're running out of suspects here, Theo. Clive is dead, so that leaves us with Blake Jones, Gwendoline, Emily, and the Travises. What would be the odds that one of them is behind it all?"

"Not very high. I'll give you that," said Theo reluctantly. "Especially since it's been confirmed that the branding iron belonged to Matthew. He had it since he was a kid. The brand he left was actually meant to be read as an M, for Matthew."

"Who told you that?" asked Ethan.

"Gwendoline. She says her cousin had found the broken iron in a discarded pile of junk when they were kids and used it to brand his initials on the pets and wild animals he would trap. Already as a kid he was quite a mess."

"That's a piece of intel we could have used a couple of years ago," said Ethan. "Was she protecting him?"

"I don't know, but I doubt it. Her husband was just killed by the bastard and she's not taking it well."

"Did she know Clive was in San Francisco?" asked Jennifer, blushing slightly.

"No. They had a fight a week ago and he left without saying a word. She says she's been without contact since. But of course, her phone records say otherwise. The two of them talked almost daily during that time. We'll push the issue later. The woman has just lost her husband and she has a daughter to care for so Melany's cutting her some slack for now."

Theo took his leave shortly after and the two of them watched him get back into his car before Jennifer broke the silence. "Do you think he bought my story?"

"No. At least not all of it, but he can't figure out why you would be lying."

"He might in the near future…"

"He probably will, but it will be purely conjectural. He won't go out of his way to build a case against you either, especially since he'll know I'm the one behind the whole thing."

"I'm done scoping the place, by the way. I drew the path we'll need to take. And I did my research, your hypothesis was correct, they'll go for it."

"Great! Then I suggest we move tonight. I'm sick of playing jail warden."

Chapter 92

Ethan and Jennifer walked into the Napa Valley rental around 10 PM to find Matthew sleeping. He was tied up to his own bench, a shock collar wrapped around his throat. The device had proven useful to keep him under control during his daily meals and visits to the restroom.

Ethan had been the killer's warden over the past week, expressly keeping Jennifer away from the house. He didn't want her to take more risk than was necessary. Tonight was a different story, however. This was a two-person job. One for which Jennifer had volunteered without him even asking.

Staring at Matthew in his restraints, his mouth silenced by the same S&M ball gag the bastard had meant to use on Jennifer, Ethan wondered if he shouldn't just kill him here and now and be done with it. There were definite risks associated with what he had in mind for him, and Ethan wasn't entirely comfortable with the grotesque aspect of the punishment. When he'd expressed his idea to Jennifer for the first time, she'd stared at him incredulously for a moment before warming up to it. She'd then assured him that it was a fitting sentence for the psychopath who'd raped and tortured so many women. The fact Woodrough had meant to add her to that list had probably made her slightly biased.

For an instant, Ethan pictured Jennifer tied up to that bench the way he'd found her three days earlier. He'd reached the house a mere fifteen minutes before Matthew and Jennifer. Just enough time to conceal his car behind a grove of trees down the road, pick the lock, and find a suitable hiding place.

He could have kissed Suzy when she'd showed him how to recall a phone's location history. Matthew's phone had been off, but its last location had been captured and that's all Ethan had needed to find the house. In three minutes, he'd been able to confirm that the address belonged to a rental property in Napa Valley. One nowhere close to the beach house the FBI had under surveillance. He'd kept the information to himself, however. He'd even let the FBI storm the wrong house. He had to… just in case he was wrong.

From his vantage point inside the room's closet Ethan had watched Jennifer emerge from her drug-induced slumber. He'd slowly approached her, careful not to make the slightest sound for fear of alerting Matthew who'd retired to the living room. She'd come out of her anesthesia with Ethan's hand on her mouth. He'd spoke reassuring words to her ear, letting her know that she was safe, that she would soon be free. He'd then instructed her to start making noise as soon as he'd regained his hiding spot. The plan had worked. Matthew had been completely caught off guard.

Ethan snapped out of his reverie as Matthew woke up, suddenly alert to the presence of his jailers. Ethan approached him, syringe in hand, and grabbed the killer's arm.

"Today's the big day, Matthew. You're finally getting out of here. You've been looking forward to it, I bet?"

The psychopath just stared at him blankly; there was no fear in his empty eyes. He didn't know what fear felt like, but he could still experience pain. That would do.

Ethan injected Matthew with an anesthetic used for minor surgical procedures, which placed him under what doctors called twilight sedation. In this state, he'd remain more or less awake but would be perfectly cooperative and would have absolutely no recollection of what had happened to him while under the influence of the drug. The effect was almost instantaneous. Matthew Woodrough suddenly relaxed and closed his eyes. Ethan removed the gag and placed a tiny piece of LSD in his mouth. The dose had been carefully calculated to wear out by the time the anesthetic would.

They then freed the prisoner from his restraints and walked him to the car where Jennifer sat in the back with him. She held the shock collar's remote in her hand just in case the sedative wore off faster than anticipated, but the precaution didn't prove necessary. They made it to their location with a very cooperative serial killer in tow.

"Okay, walk exactly in my steps," said Jennifer to Ethan. "And make sure Matthew doesn't follow us too closely. Unlike ours, we want his face to be on as many cameras as possible."

"You're positive the cameras aren't being monitored?" asked Ethan.

"Not at night. Why would they?"

They walked to a service entrance and Jennifer unlocked it with a key she'd swiped from a maintenance guy. She'd managed to steal his whole set of keys, copy them, and return them to his pocket without him ever noticing a thing. Men were so easy to manipulate...

Once inside, Ethan stuck closely to Jennifer while Matthew followed them at a short distance, his gait unsteady, not unlike that of a drunk man.

They reached their destination ten minutes later. Jennifer pulled another key from her back pocket and unlocked a series of gates. There were no cameras in this section, and they walked freely, pushing Matthew in front of them. Jennifer unlocked the last gate and Ethan told her to remain behind as he accompanied Matthew to the middle of an open space. The moon was nearly full above their head.

He removed Matthew's pants, placed another set of keys covered with the killer's own fingerprints in one of the pockets and tossed them under a dead tree standing a few feet away. He then grabbed a spray bottle from his backpack and liberally spread his wife's killer with the liquid, focusing on his legs and ass. He then ordered Matthew to lay down and take a nap. The killer was only too happy to oblige.

Ethan rejoined Jennifer inside and locked the gate behind him. They then waited, watching from a viewing window, for the anesthetic to wear off. It took nearly two hours, but eventually it did.

They watched Matthew sit up on one of the few patches of grass that strewed the otherwise bare dirt ground, slowly taking in his surroundings. He then stood up on shaky legs and took a few steps towards the fence. But there was nowhere for him to run. When the precarity of his situation finally dawned on him, he started screaming for help. That's when Jennifer released the lock on the other gate.

Chapter 93

E than was parked in a residential area outside the city when the call he'd been expecting all day finally came through.

"Theo! What a good surprise," he said, answering the phone as the bell of a nearby church rang 9 PM.

"You've seen the papers, I assume." Theo was clearly not in a joking mood.

"I've seen some papers…"

"Stop kidding around. You know very well what I'm talking about. Matthew Woodrough was found dead at the zoo this morning. In the gorilla exhibit!"

"I read something about that," answered Ethan evasively. "Do we know what happened exactly?"

He heard Theo take a deep breath before answering, "No! *We* don't! That's why I'm calling you, so you can fill me in."

"Give me some details and I'll see if I can come up with a theory."

"Stop being a jackass! I know you're behind this. I've no idea how you got Woodrough to willingly walk into the enclosure and get himself raped by a 400-pound gorilla, but I know it was you."

Theo had been his best friend for over ten years and knew Ethan far too well to not suspect him, but the agent had absolutely no evidence to support his gut feeling. The toxicology screen would reveal that Matthew had taken acid prior to entering the exhibit and nothing else. The specialized anesthetic Ethan had used wasn't part of the substances coroners screened for… They were also very unlikely to detect the female gorilla pheromones sprayed all over the dead man's ass.

Woodrough had tried to fight the male gorilla off, but it had been a serious mistake. In the end the killer's screams had been too much even for Ethan. He'd gestured towards Jennifer and the two of them had left Casanova to his fate. Despite the morbid nature of the show, Jennifer had stayed with Ethan the whole time. But he hadn't been particularly surprised by the woman's resilience. There was a lot more to Jennifer MacKay than what met the eye.

"How the fuck did you do it, Ethan? Please tell me. This is mind-blowing, even coming from you."

Ethan knew that, deep inside, his friend didn't really want to know the truth. If Theo uncovered evidence of what had really happened, he'd have no choice but to arrest him and he didn't want to do that. "The bastard was MIA for over a week. Every cop in the country has been looking for him. What makes you think *I* found him?" said Ethan. "And surely the zoo has cameras... Did you check the tapes?"

"Of course, we did. Woodrough appears to be alone, but it just means you knew where to stand to avoid the cameras," said Theo, struggling to keep anger out of his voice. "I hope for you that you were extra fucking smart about this, because if you left the slightest piece of evidence, the cops will find it and you'll get twenty to life. I hope it was all worth the risk?"

"You're my best friend, Theo, so I'm going to answer your question. Let's assume for a moment that I somehow managed to catch the asshole who raped, tortured, and murdered my wife. The piece of shit who kidnapped Jennifer and tortured and murdered countless other women. In that hypothetical scenario of mine, would it have been worth it to take matters into my own hands despite the risk of being caught? Fuck yes!" Ethan hung up before his friend could reply.

He understood Theo's position, but he wasn't in a mood for a sermon. Ethan had done what had to be done. There had never been a choice in the matter. Woodrough needed to pay for his crimes and now he had.

He took a sip of lukewarm coffee that did little to warm him up. He'd been sitting in his car for hours, waiting. Probably for nothing. He'd been here several times over the past week, but he'd had no luck so far.

Ethan's fortune turned forty minutes later when a tall white man walked out of a house a hundred feet from where he was parked and got into a black S-class Mercedes. The asshole was doing well for himself.

Ethan let the driver of the Mercedes turn the street corner before starting his own car. He followed him at a distance all the way to San Francisco's Tenderloin district. The destination was no surprise to Ethan; that's what he'd been expecting.

The man parked his car in front of two hookers standing on the sidewalk and got out for a chat. Five minutes later, Ethan was following him on foot through the streets of San Francisco's sleaziest neighborhood.

The pimp was making his rounds, checking on the girls working for him, collecting his dues from each one of them. Ethan had been tailing him nearly thirty minutes when the pimp walked to a hooker wearing a tight leather jacket and a skirt short enough to show the garter belt holding her fishnet stockings. She wore nothing underneath the jacket.

Ethan was across the street fifty feet from the woman, but she was facing his direction and despite the distance he clearly saw the look of resigned fear flash on her face the instant she noticed the pimp heading towards her.

He stopped by her side, puffing on a cigarette. They exchanged a few words and she handed him cash, but the man shook his head as he placed the bills in his jeans' pocket. Standing in front of a sex shop, seemingly checking the merchandise, Ethan watched from the corner of his eye as the pimp grabbed her by the arm and headed down the street.

Ethan watched them disappear into the closest back alley and silently approached the intersection. Partially hidden by a dumpster, the pimp was standing against the wall, a stone's throw from Ethan. The woman was crouched in front of him, sucking on his dick while he held her by the hair to affirm his authority.

The pimp's phone rang to the tune of a gangster rap song, and he answered the call as the woman continued her forced labor. The pig came while on the phone and thanked the hooker still crouching in front of him by pushing on her forehead hard enough to make her lose her balance.

She landed on her back but quickly got back on her feet and walked out of the alley, brushing off the dirt she'd picked up in her fall. She walked right past Ethan who was standing on the other side of the dumpster but didn't see him.

He waited for the man to finish his call and approached him without a sound as he was pushing his now flaccid appendage back inside his pants. The pimp looked up at Ethan standing six feet in front of him, gun pointing at his chest.

"Remember me?" Ethan asked.

"Shoot me, and you're a dead man."

Ethan ignored the remark. "This is for April. Don't say you weren't warned," he told the man as he depressed the trigger. He fired three more times for good measure before wiping the fingerprints off the weapon.

"You can have your gun back now," he said, dropping it in the dead man's pocket.

Chapter 94

Ethan was home watching a movie on a Friday night when his phone chimed with an unfamiliar sound. It took him a second to realize what it meant. He'd nearly forgotten about the tracker.

Two months had passed since Matthew Woodrough's death, and the police had found nothing linking Ethan or Jennifer to the incident. They hadn't even been questioned by the authorities. The case was now closed. Matthew Woodrough had voluntarily entered the gorilla exhibit while on acid and had paid the price for his own stupidity. That was the official version. Nobody knew where the killer had found the set of keys he'd used to let himself through the zoo's gates, and no one cared. Theo wasn't buying the story, but he'd only brought up the subject that one time. The two of them simply avoided the matter when they saw each other, which hadn't happened very often over the past few weeks. It was a good thing Theo hadn't heard of the pimp's death, because if the FBI agent had put two and two together, the strain on their friendship might have reached a breaking point.

Ethan grabbed his phone and tapped on the tracking app. It wasn't the one he'd used to track Jennifer's and Matthew's cell phones. This one was equipped with a proximity alarm set to ring if the tracker got outside the city limits. It was that alarm that had gone off a minute earlier.

On the screen, the tracking dot was moving fast on the freeway and seemed to be heading for the airport. This was to be expected. He grabbed his laptop and logged into his Delta Air Lines account. He didn't want to be on the same flight so he booked a ticket for one departing at 6 AM the next morning. That would also give him a chance to confirm that the tracker was heading where he thought it was.

Upon landing in Montana the next day, Ethan immediately turned his phone back on and opened the tracking app. The tracker was no longer emitting, but he knew why. He searched its location history and marked the coordinate of the last signal received on a map. He then rented a four-wheel-drive vehicle and headed straight for the Madison mountain range, the tracker's last known location. Surprisingly, the roads were clear of snow and he reached his destination ninety minutes later. He hadn't quite arrived, but it was as far as the car would go. He'd have to rely on his feet for the rest of the way. He parked his vehicle on a trailhead parking lot and went to the trunk to retrieve a backpack, a warm winter jacket, and a pair of hiking boots. He'd come prepared this time.

There was a single other vehicle on the parking lot, and he suspected he knew the owner. He unfolded a topographic map on the hood of his car and drew a path he thought would lead him where he needed to go. He was fully expecting to lose cell reception a few minutes into his hike and would have to rely on his freshly acquired navigational skills to get there. He'd been preparing for this for some time and was confident he could reach his destination using the map and his brand-new compass.

He'd only gone up a hundred feet or so when he started encountering the first patches of snow under the trees. A mile later, he was hiking in ankle-deep melted slush, but that didn't last long. As he went up the mountain, the temperature steadily dropped, and he was soon treading on frozen snow and patches of ice.

He lost his footing a couple of times and fell flat on his face once, but he eventually made it to the mountain wall where the GPS tracker had vanished. This particular tracker didn't rely on cell phone coverage and had therefore functioned all the way to that point, but its signal couldn't pass through the thousands of tons of granite currently sitting over its head.

It only took Ethan a few minutes to find the cave's entrance hidden behind a boulder covered with thick shrubs. Without the tracker, Ethan could have walked right by it a hundred times without ever suspecting a thing. This wasn't the entrance they'd shown on TV, the one that had been found by a couple walking their dog, but Ethan was convinced it led to the same cave. It had to. And unlike the main entrance, this one couldn't be more than a mile or two from the Woodroughs' cabin.

He placed his headlamp around his forehead but didn't turn it on as he entered the cave. He didn't want to alert anyone to his presence. He was forced to switch it on ten yards later, however. The darkness had become so thick he couldn't even see his own hands in front of him. He set the flashlight to night vision and a warm red glow soon lit his way. He reached a large room shortly after and encountered his first difficulty. Three tunnels departed from the room and he had no idea which one to follow. He hadn't even brought a spool of cord to uncoil along the way, a handy trick to find your way back in such places. Maybe he wasn't as prepared as he'd thought.

Before he had a chance to make up his mind on which path to follow, he heard a low growl coming from one of the tunnels. He'd completely forgotten about the wolves, a mistake he was going to pay for dearly.

In the red glow of his head lamp, he saw a massive black wolf emerge from the tunnel, soon joined by four more. They advanced towards him, baring their fangs and emitting threatening sounds. Ethan grabbed the hunting knife he'd secured to his belt, but the weapon was unlikely to save him.

He heard a weird guttural sound that vaguely resembled a human voice and the wolves relaxed. All signs of hostility had vanished. That's when his headlight caught the two silhouettes standing at the tunnel's entrance. He'd never seen the man before, but he knew the woman very well.

"What are you doing here, Ethan?" asked Jennifer MacKay. "How did you find us?"

"A GPS tracker in the purse I gave you. Aren't you going to introduce me to your friend, Jennifer? Or would you rather I called you Myriam?"

Chapter 95

Myriam Woodrough had realized very young that something wasn't right with her family. The atmosphere of unease that fell upon a room every time her father or uncle walked in and the subdued attitudes of their wives had been early warning signs, but the full realization had finally dawned on Myriam when she'd started noticing similarities between her father and her brother.

Archibald Woodrough had never showed any love or even warmth to his children. Just like Allan had never demonstrated an ounce of compassion towards anyone, least of all his sisters whom he bullied relentlessly, often to the point of tears. His bullying had turned into something more disturbing when Gwendoline had hit puberty. Terrified by her brother's inappropriate behavior, Myriam had gone to her mother, but the woman had simply shut her up. Vivian Woodrough had always dealt with problems by acting as if they didn't exist. After failing to rein Allan in as a kid, she'd completely given up on trying to manage her son by the time he'd turned twelve.

But no matter how creepy Allan's behavior had become, it still paled in comparison to that of their cousin Matthew. That one was so disturbed he was in a league of his own. At thirteen, he'd already gotten himself expelled from school for coldly choking a classmate unconscious during a fight. Myriam was convinced Matthew would have killed the boy if a teacher hadn't intervened.

During family gatherings at the Montana cabin, Matthew could spend days trapping small and medium-size animals for the sole purpose of torturing and killing them. Taking himself for an artist, he would always sign his work by carving his initials in the poor creatures' flesh using his favorite knife. This practice had lasted until the day he'd found a broken branding iron at the ranch. From that point on he'd started searing a capital letter M on the animals' skins while they were still alive. An even more delightful way of torturing the unfortunate critters. The practice drove Myriam to tears, but she wasn't about to tattle on her cousin. She not only feared his reprisals but also doubted her father and uncle would even care. The rot permeating Matthew was in their blood, too.

Living among her kin, Myriam had felt like a zebra amidst a pride of lions. Often, she would fantasize about losing her whole family to some type of disaster, such as a plane crash or a fire. She and Gwendoline would be the sole survivors. With everybody else dead, the girls would be adopted by a normal family and would no longer have to live in fear. But the act of God never came. Instead, the veneer of normality covering Myriam's existence shattered to pieces two months after her ninth birthday.

The Woodroughs had gathered at their cabin in Montana to spend Christmas there, and Myriam had been surprised to not find the Travises welcoming them upon arrival. She loved sweet Mrs. Travis and her husband, but the two of them had apparently been given the week off. This wasn't a common occurrence, and Myriam had wondered about the reason behind their absence. Her father never did anything out of kindness. If he'd sent the two away, he had an agenda.

Archibald's motivations became clear two days after Christmas. Myriam was lying in bed asleep when a sound woke her up. A squeaking sound coming from Gwendoline's adjacent room. She'd gone to enquire about the origin of the noise and had found Gwendoline in her bed, Allan thrusting atop her. Her sister was sobbing quietly in the pillow he'd placed on her face. Myriam wanted to defend Gwendoline, but she was afraid her brother would end up hurting them both. She made up her mind in an instant and ran to fetch her father. Even he wouldn't stand for this kind of thing.

She went straight to his bedroom but found it empty. She ran downstairs, but he wasn't there either. That's when she noticed the light coming from the barn. She grabbed her jacket, put on her shoes and headed for the building.

As she approached, she heard whimpering and other sounds she couldn't identify. On her guard, she went to the window and peeked at a spectacle she would never be able to erase from her memory.

A little boy was lying down on a mattress that had been thrown on the floor. It was the orphan Sam Clifford had brought over with him that afternoon. Myriam had spent two hours playing in the snow with the kid and Emily. And now the boy was crying in their barn in the middle of the night. Crying because her father was doing unspeakable things to him while her uncle and the orphanage director watched with delight.

Before she knew it, she was running through the woods, trying to put as much distance as possible between her and this nightmarish place. She had no idea where she was going. Her only plan was to get away and never return.

But she'd run from one nightmare only to fall into another, for she was soon being chased by an invisible enemy. Like everyone in the area, she'd heard the rumors, but Myriam had never believed them. Ghosts didn't exist. Monsters didn't exist. But then the beast caught up with her…

The beast emitted a guttural growl as his enormous paw covered her mouth. She tried to scream, but to no avail. She saw it reaching for something behind its back and its other hand came up, holding a strange-looking knife. Its blade was darker than the night.

In that instant she realized this wasn't a beast either. No beast could do this to a child. There was only one creature capable of such atrocities. She no longer had any doubt about the nature of her aggressor. It could only be a man.

As her teary eyes watched the blade fall towards her throat, she decided she had no regret. Running away in the middle of the night might not have been the best of ideas, but it was still better than staying there.

The blade never reached her throat, however. Instead, she heard a cracking sound as the man planted it in the ground inches from her right ear. He then got up and she slowly turned her head to look at the knife whose blade was rammed to the guard into a rattlesnake's head. The reptile had died instantly.

This was how Myriam had first met the man who would raise her as his daughter.

The man had brought her to the cave she would soon call home and introduced her to his son and daughter. She'd immediately wondered where the kids' mother was but had been unable to breach the language barrier to ask the question. Months later, she would learn that the woman had died giving birth to her daughter.

Although definitely human, the cave dwellers' appearance was very peculiar, and Myriam struggled to place them in any ethnic group known to her. Under the thick bison pelts they wore outside the cave their hairless bodies were as white as chalk. The boy looked to be around twelve and his sister was maybe six or seven, but their father's age was a mystery. There was a deep wisdom in his eyes, but his skin showed no wrinkles or other signs of aging. Whether it was due to his youthfulness or to a life spent avoiding the damages of UV light, Myriam couldn't tell.

They spoke a language made of guttural sounds that Myriam couldn't even begin to pronounce. To her ears, the words sounded fused to each other and nearly void of vowels. Unable to communicate with her hosts other than by gesturing, the first few weeks in the cave had been trying ones. Yet she'd never felt the desire to leave. She'd had nowhere else to go, of course, but this wasn't what had made her stay. She'd stayed because of them. She didn't need to understand their words to see how loving they were to each other, how much compassion they showed her.

The cave's perpetual darkness had by far been the toughest thing to get used to. At first Myriam had been mesmerized by her new companions' ability to roam seamlessly along the dark hallways. For weeks she'd relied on them to guide her from one room to another in the giant granitic maze they called home. But she'd come to discover that the darkness was seldom total. Glowworm colonies were endemic to the cave and spread along the walls of almost every room and tunnel. In locations where their population reached a certain threshold, their bioluminescence conferred a twilight atmosphere to their surroundings. Even in places where their numbers were limited, the creatures provided enough residual light for trained eyes to orient themselves.

It was by following a path lit by the glowing critters that Myriam's new family had led her deep inside the cave to a small underground river that passed through parts of the cave and eventually outside. There, they'd collected fresh water and caught enough fish to feed the four of them. But the river wasn't the cave's only source of food. Different varieties of mushrooms and edible moss grew on the walls of certain tunnels too.

With the cave providing for all their basic needs, they sometimes spent days inside the mountain without emerging to the outside world. When they did venture out, it was always at night and usually covered with some sort of animal pelt. The expertly-crafted fur coats not only protected their bodies from the cold but also made them look more like animals to anyone who might observe them from a distance.

These night-time excursions were always a learning experience. Her new father would teach her to move without a sound, hide in plain sight, erase footprints in the snow, find food, water, warmth, and everything else one needed to know to survive in the wild.

Myriam had spent months of her new life wondering who these three people were who'd become her family. Where did they come from and how long had they been living like this? It had taken her nearly a year to master their complex language well enough to start getting answers to some of her questions.

The three referred to themselves as Krrers and they were the only survivors of what had once been a flourishing tribe. Despite the paleness of their skins, her new family wasn't of Caucasian descent but Native

American. A conclusion Myriam had already reached on her own based on their knives and arrowheads made of flintstones, their tomahawks, and the wooden bowls they used to eat from and collect berries.

When Myriam had finally been able to enquire about the fate of the children's mother, she'd been taken to a chamber she'd never visited before. Much larger than average, the room was an ossuary where hundreds of skeletons rested in small niches carved into the rock walls. That's when she'd realized her mistake. The tribe hadn't spent years in the cave; they'd lived here for generations. She started asking more and more questions about the tribe's origins, but the answers were always incomplete. From what she was able to put together, her new people had always been cave dwellers.

Cave dwellers spent most of their lives outdoors, only coming inside their caves at nighttime for protection from the cold and predators. The Krrers had been no exception, but their lifestyle had drastically changed the day a warring nomadic tribe had entered their territory. Hunted down by an enemy far superior in number, they'd retreated deeper inside the cave system that had always protected them.

For weeks they'd been hiding inside the cave during the day, only venturing out at night to find food and other necessities. This had been a temporary measure meant to last through fall when the invading tribe would no doubt be migrating for winter. But the invaders hadn't moved on. Instead they had settled in the Krrers' territory and forced them to remain hidden underground for months in a row.

The months had turned into years, and one day an earthquake had buried the cavern's only entrance under tons of boulders, effectively trapping the Krrers inside their subterranean shelter.

Relying exclusively on the cave's ecosystem, the Krrers had survived underground for a period Myriam estimated somewhere between ten and fifty years. Eventually, one of their children had stumbled upon a second entrance and provided the tribe with a way out of the cave. This newly discovered entrance was located a mere mile and a half from the clearing where, centuries later, the Woodroughs' cabin would be erected.

Myriam hadn't found records of the earthquake, which meant it had taken place prior to the arrival of the first European settlers in the early 1800s. Based on the number of skeletons in the ossuary and her understanding of the tribe's history, Myriam suspected the cave had actually been sealed sometime in the late 1500s.

She wasn't sure whether this period of forced seclusion inside the dark cave had been the catalyst for the transformation, but one thing was certain: the Krrers had undergone a form of microevolution over the centuries they had spent isolated from the world. Their night vision was far superior to the average human being and the light of day had become painful to them. In comparison, Myriam's eyes weren't nearly as performant as theirs in the dark, even after years spent underground alongside them. Further evidence that the Krrers had followed their own evolutionary branch was provided by their incredibly white complexion. Years of avoiding sunlight had made Myriam's skin as pasty as normal Caucasian skin would ever get, but it was still far darker than that of her adoptive family.

All in all, Myriam had spent eight years living inside the cave. But she would always remember her second year among the Krrers as the best of her life. Her friendship with her adoptive siblings had grown stronger with every passing day and she particularly enjoyed the company of her newly found sister. But the blissful happiness wasn't meant to last. The two girls were playing a hide-and-seek game under a starlit sky when a mountain lion had claimed the life of the little Krrer.

Myriam had watched her father bury the girl's remains in a mixture of dirt and caustic ashes to strip the flesh from her skeleton. The cleaned bones had been retrieved from the soil a few months later, but against Myriam's expectations they hadn't been brought to the tribe's ossuary like those of the girl's mother. Instead, they'd been placed in a small alcove beside the skeletons of other children. Children who would keep her company for the rest of eternity. Myriam had first assumed these were the bones of other tribe members, but she'd been wrong. Her adoptive father had collected the small skeletons from shallow graves dug all around the Woodroughs' cabin. These were the victims of the Woodroughs' gruesome sex-trafficking operation. Children that had been placed into the hands of her psychopathic family by the very people who were supposed to protect them in the first place: Sam Clifford and Sheriff Bradford. For years, Myriam's adoptive father had watched the Woodroughs' sordid operation from a distance. Powerless to stop the monsters, he'd done the only thing he could for their defenseless victims: he'd given them a real sepulcher.

Myriam had known all along that one day she would leave the protection of the cave. Her thirst for discovery could never be quenched by remaining in the underground refuge that had sheltered her all these years. She needed much more intellectual stimulation than what the woods had to offer.

Knowing that her departure would break their father's heart, she'd spent many hours talking about it with her Krrer brother. She'd delayed her decision as long as she could, but in the end, she simply had to go. She was seventeen when she left the two people she loved the most on this earth and rejoined the outside world.

Dressed in clothes she'd stolen from campsites, she reentered civilization with pockets full of silver extracted from the veins marbling the rock walls in the central part of the underground complex. It wasn't long before she'd sold enough of the precious metal to finance an apartment, a wardrobe, and a new identity.

She hadn't spoken much English in the past eight years, but she disguised her lack of practice under a rather poor Scottish accent. It seemed fitting given the paleness of her skin.

Over the years, she'd spent thousands of dollars on red hair dye to maintain the looks of her new persona: Jennifer MacKay. Time had also refined her Scottish accent. Playing the part of a foreigner was also a convenient way to explain her lack of past and absence of family in the US.

The cave's nearly unlimited supply of silver had given her the means to undertake anthropology studies to try and understand the hidden tribe's history while volunteering in countless animal shelters and even zoos. Her Krrer father had taught her to respect and love the animals with whom she shared the planet, but she wanted to take things a step further. She wanted to help them survive in a world that had become hostile to them.

A few years later, she'd taken a job as an animal trainer and had found that she was a natural. She was soon hired by a studio in Hollywood where she'd spent years working with countless animals. Dogs and cats had of course represented the bulk of her work, but she'd been lucky enough to work with tiger cubs and even a grizzly bear.

By then, she'd managed to convince her Krrer brother to leave the cave, too, and after a few years spent rooming with her, he was now living on his own under the assumed identity of an Icelandic immigrant.

His departure had nearly killed their father, but the man had understood this was the best thing for his son. The tribe was nearly extinct and there was no reason for him to remain in the woods where he had no hope of ever finding a romantic partner to share his life.

Myriam had tried to convince their father to join them in the city, but his refusal had been categorical. She hadn't insisted. The cave was all he knew. That's where his ancestors, his wife, and his daughter rested. That's where he'd spent his entire existence. He couldn't envision any other life than the one he had.

She still went to visit him at least once a month and on one of her trips she'd been surprised to find him surrounded by five wolf pups who followed him around wherever he went. They belonged to a breeding pair who'd had the misfortune of crossing paths with Sheriff Bradford. The pups had been too young to survive on their own, so her father had adopted them. He had no idea how to handle the pups, of course, so Myriam had moved back to the cave for a few months to help him raise and train the young wolves. Under her care, the pups had quickly grown up and become an integral part of her father's existence. Satisfied their training was complete, Myriam had returned to her life as Jennifer MacKay.

She'd been back in her San Francisco apartment only a few days when the Cowboy had started to make some noise in the media. When it was leaked to the papers that the psycho branded his victims with two capital-letter A's, Myriam hadn't thought much of it. But when the actual brand had been shown on TV, she'd immediately realized the cops' mistake. They were reading the brand upside down. The A's were actually the Woodrough W. Matthew's signature. Her psychopathic cousin had finally graduated to the ranks of serial killers.

She'd spent days agonizing over what to do. She knew she should go to the cops, but she simply couldn't. Jennifer MacKay didn't really exist, and the authorities wouldn't take long to figure that out.

Eventually, she'd decided to go to Ethan Archer, a private investigator she'd seen on TV and who'd been consulting for the FBI on the Cowboy case. The good-looking detective clearly enjoyed the spotlight and was as arrogant as they got, but if his reputation was accurate, he might be able to help.

Equipped with a fabricated story and a manila folder containing newspaper clippings of the Cowboy's murders, she'd walked into Ethan's office where he'd immediately offered her a secretarial position.

Before she had a chance to clear the misunderstanding, his phone had rung to announce that the body of his wife had just been found buried on a beach.

She'd made up her mind and decided to stick around long enough to tell Ethan about Matthew, but by the time he'd returned to work a week later, an arrest had been made and the Cowboy had officially been killed in prison.

Unsure of herself, Myriam hadn't dared mentioning to Ethan that there might have been a mistake. That his wife's killer might still be at large. Having no urgent engagement calling her elsewhere, she'd elected to play secretary to Ethan Archer for a few weeks to see how things developed.

The Cowboy hadn't resurfaced, but she'd kept playing the boring part of Ethan's assistant simply to keep an eye on him. The arrogance she'd seen him display on TV had completely vanished with his wife's death, and he'd entered a self-destructive phase that worried her. She'd been surprised to find herself genuinely caring for the guy, despite the temper he manifested in his frequent outbursts. Before she knew it, a year had passed, and she was still working for him. That's when she had bumped into her birth sister in a bar.

It had been twenty-two years since they'd last seen each other but Gwendoline had recognized Myriam all the same. Ever since she was a kid, Myriam had always rested her chin in the palm of her hand and massaged her ear lobe between her index and middle finger when deep in thought. This was the silly habit that had betrayed her, the quirk her sister had immediately recognized.

Gwendoline had walked up to Jennifer MacKay, asking if they knew each other. Myriam had faked incomprehension, but Gwendoline hadn't believed her. She'd blocked her exit shortly thereafter and confronted her bluntly. Myriam had immediately lost all interest in denying the truth. She'd always loved Gwendoline and had thought about her many times over the years. Above all, she felt guilty for having abandoned her sister to their degenerate family.

They'd spent hours talking that evening and had met again the following weekend. They had so much to discuss.

Gwendoline had been completely unaware of her relatives' shady business until a year and a half earlier when she'd walked in on a conversation between her brother and her father. The discussion had been about pricing matters pertaining to a thirteen-year-old girl. Gwendoline had feigned incomprehension, but Archibald hadn't bought her act. Instead, he'd explained in gruesome detail what would happen to her daughter if Gwendoline were to ever speak of what she'd heard with anybody. She'd been living in fear ever since, and the stress had affected both her health and her marriage.

In turn, Myriam had filled her sister in on the atrocities she and the Krrers had witnessed around the cabin. It wasn't long before the two sisters had decided that the world would be a better place without their relatives in it.

Epilogue

Jennifer looked at Ethan silently for a moment. Clearly, she hadn't been expecting this.

"I see you finally connected the dots. Good for you," she said eventually. "I suspected you might be tracking my phone. That's why I turned it off the second I left for the airport, but it looks like you had a back-up plan…"

Ethan shrugged. "I couldn't rely on the cellular network in the mountains anyway. So who's this?" He nodded towards the man.

"My adoptive brother. He goes by Silas in the outside world. I could give you his real name, but you wouldn't be able to pronounce it. I'm sure you have many questions for me, Ethan, but for now they will have to wait. Silas and I have a funeral to attend."

Ethan followed them through a maze of dark tunnels all the way to a chamber the size of a basketball court. Hundreds of small niches had been carved in the rock walls, each containing an entire human skeleton assembled into a neat little pile.

Ethan watched Jennifer and her brother fill an empty niche with the bones of the man he'd only known as the ghost. He suspected Jennifer was crying but the red glow of his headlamp didn't provide enough light to confirm his suspicion.

The next day, Jennifer took him to a natural hot spring in the middle of the woods. The spot was deserted, save for the five wolves that had followed them around, eying Ethan suspiciously. Jennifer had guaranteed they wouldn't hurt him and this time he believed her. She clearly knew a lot more about wolves than she'd led him to believe.

She'd already answered most of his questions, but there were still a few things he wanted to ask her.

"I assume you killed Senator Woodrough, correct? You were out of town that weekend…"

"I did. Using intel Gwendoline had been able to obtain through Emily," she said, stripping down to her bikini and getting into the warm water.

"Emily was in on it?" asked Ethan, surprised.

"No, she wasn't. But she's close friends with Gwendoline and she'd mentioned her father would be in Vegas that weekend for some political event. Once we knew where Allister would be and the hotel he had reserved, the rest was easy. The fact he frequented gay bars to pick up younger men wasn't much of a secret in the family. And since he was going to be in Vegas, it was easy to infer that he'd probably be seeking company. All I had to do was follow him around discreetly and sit down next to him at the bar. He did the rest."

"He never noticed you were a woman?" asked Ethan, standing beside the hot spring. The ambient temperature was in the forties and he wasn't in a hurry to remove his clothes.

"Not until it was too late. You should have seen his face when he ripped open my shirt and saw my boobs constrained by Saran wrap..."

"But he didn't know before that?" Ethan couldn't understand how anyone would take Jennifer for a man.

"I was dressed as a guy, wore a wig, no makeup, and I was in a gay club. I could have fooled *you*, Ethan," she said, collecting water in her cupped hands before slowly letting it pour between her fingers.

"Why did you brand that A on his chest? Was it a clue for the cops?"

"No. It was meant for Matthew. We wanted him to know a killer was onto him, make him nervous, but it was probably too much to hope for from a psychopath like him."

Ethan nodded. He was pretty sure she was right about her cousin. The psycho had probably found the challenge exciting.

"Tell me something, Jennifer, how did you manage to convince all these people to go along with your plan to eradicate the Woodrough name? Did you hypnotize them?"

"What do you mean, all these people?" she asked defensively.

"I mean Gwendoline, your adoptive father, and let's not forget Clive... It's not usually that easy to get people to help you commit first-degree murder."

"It was never *my* plan, Ethan. It was a team effort between my father, Gwendoline, and myself. And we only wanted to eradicate the psychopaths in the family, not necessarily the name. It wasn't our fault if all males displayed signs of the disease. Clive wasn't in on our scheme initially. Gwendoline was forced to tell him the truth halfway through when he discovered a satellite phone hidden in her suitcase. That's how we secretly communicated between each other and with my Krrer father on the outside despite the lack of cellular network. I'd even given my father four replacement batteries for his. The cave doesn't really come with electricity..."

"And Clive went with the idea? Most people aren't so keen on becoming accomplice to mass murder."

"That's because most people don't have to live in close proximity to a bunch of child-molesting rapists and psychopaths. In the end he went with it for his daughter's sake. Once he learned the truth about the family he'd married into, he was terrified for his kid."

"A valid point, I suppose… But what was he doing hiding in that hotel in San Francisco?" he asked, finally stripping down to his boxers and entering the surprisingly warm water.

"Gwendoline sent him to protect me from Matthew. We all knew it was only a matter of time before Matthew tried to hurt you through me, and Clive was there to make sure my cousin didn't get to me before we got to him. Unfortunately, Matthew must have seen Clive shadowing me. He probably thought we were having an affair and decided to use it to his advantage to lure me into a trap. I don't think Gwendoline will ever forgive herself for sending her husband to his death."

"Why did Gwendoline stay working with Archibald and Allan all these years? Why didn't she leave the house and never come back the day she turned eighteen?"

"I know it will probably seem strange to you, but until recently, Gwendoline didn't know on a conscious level that her relatives were monsters. I think it was a kind of self-preservation mechanism. One day, her brain found itself at a junction. It could either be driven crazy by the repeated trauma she'd withstood as a teenager at the hands of Allan, or it could simply forget all about it and act as if it had never happened. Her mind picked option number two. She locked the traumatic memories in a part of her brain and threw the key away. She'd nearly forgotten about the whole thing until I told her why I'd fled the cabin that night."

"She'd forgotten about being raped repeatedly?" It sounded so unlikely.

"She wouldn't be the first one, Ethan. It's a well understood phenomenon. Ask any psychiatrist. When I first told her that I'd seen Allan raping her that night, she just stared at me incredulously. The memory came back to her like a tidal wave an instant later and she couldn't stop crying. The rapes had stopped when she'd turned sixteen and Allan had always acted as if nothing had ever happened. She'd resented her brother and the rest of the family her whole life, but having buried the trauma in a corner of her mind, she'd never understood why until I finally reminded her."

"She had no idea about the sex-trafficking business either?"

"She found out by accident a year or so ago after overhearing a conversation between Allan and Archibald. She didn't dare flee with her family for fear of reprisals, but she started snooping around and eventually discovered the secret room in the barn's basement. She really freaked out after that. Things were much worse than she'd imagined."

"She's the one who stole the stuffed bunny we found in Archibald's pocket, I assume?"

"Yes. She went to the cabin by herself two weeks before Christmas. She went down to the basement and retrieved the bunny from the psychos' keepsake pile. The messages sent with each body were to let the others know why they were being punished. They needed to know this wasn't the act of a random killer but justice for their crimes. They needed to know they were next on the list," answered Jennifer, reaching out of the water to pet one of the wolves that had lain down near the spring's edge.

"So, killing a cat was all Gregory had done to deserve his fate?" Ethan asked, still highly uncomfortable with the premeditated murder of a twelve-year-old. He knew it had been Gwendoline's idea, but Jennifer hadn't done anything to change her sister's mind.

"Gwendoline had seen how he behaved around his cousins and the whole family knew about his passion for torturing animals. This was exactly how Matthew behaved as a kid and we all know where that led him."

"Maybe with professional help, the kid could have gotten better…"

"You don't believe that, do you? You've studied enough behavioral psychology to know better, Ethan. My father witnessed Gregory killing Mr. Travis' cat and threatening Clara that he'd do the same to her…"

It took a second for Ethan to realize the father Jennifer referred to was the ghost.

"And you know he would have done just that if given the chance," she continued.

He knew she was right. He'd seen the way Gregory had looked at Clara on Christmas Eve and the way the girl had reacted to him. He wanted to believe that the kid still had a chance, but there was no science to support that belief. In his extensive studies, he'd never heard of a psychopath getting better. Psychopathy was nearly impossible to cure because psychopaths weren't clinically insane in the first place. They were perfectly aware of their actions and how wrong they were. They simply didn't give a shit. Matthew Woodrough was a textbook example of how much pain these individuals could inflict on others without the slightest remorse.

"I bet Matthew escaping the cabin must have thrown a wrench in your little plan," said Ethan.

"Yes! That was… unexpected. We thought we had everybody trapped, but we were wrong. After his escape we had to act quickly. We knew he'd come back with the cops. Not that he gave a shit about the fate of any of us, but he'd have looked guilty if he hadn't alerted the authorities. And for once he hadn't done anything wrong."

"Why didn't you start by killing him? He was arguably the most dangerous one of them all."

"Aside from the senator whose death was meant as a message to the others, we wanted to kill them in a specific order. Matthew and Archibald had the most to pay for and they were supposed to be the last ones to die."

Despite the chilling air, the spring's temperature was starting to make Ethan uncomfortably hot. He stood up and sat on the edge of the spring with only his feet dangling in the water. Jennifer was staring at him silently.

"Why are you looking at me like that?" he asked.

"I'm just wondering what you think of me now that you know what I'm capable of."

"I think you and I aren't all that different after all. I'm not sure I could have killed Gregory, but had I known what you knew, I'd have dealt with all the other scumbags without a second thought," he said, before adding, "and the way you plotted it… that shows style!"

She smiled. "My turn to ask questions now. How did you even start suspecting me? I took every possible precaution, I delivered an Oscar-worthy performance, how in heaven did you figure it out?"

"Since you think you're so smart, maybe I won't tell you and just let your superior brain have a crack at the mystery."

"You know, Ethan Archer, I could have the wolves tear you to pieces right here, and nobody would ever be the wiser."

"Murder isn't the answer to everything, Jennifer. But since you so kindly asked, I'll tell you. The realization dawned on me slowly. Over the weeks we worked on the case, you did a number of seemingly unimportant things. But once I started putting all of them together and noticed they fit my hypothesis; I knew you were behind it all."

"That easy, hey?" She sounded unconvinced.

"It's hard for me to explain how my mind works but I believe I first started suspecting you the day I tried to go for help and was attacked by the wolves. Obviously, I had no idea they were your pets at the time, but you failed to wave me goodbye at the window as you'd said you would and it got me thinking."

Jennifer gave him a skeptical look.

"You seemed genuinely concerned about me going out there by myself," he continued unfazed, "but instead of seeing me to the door, you decided to stay in your room because you were supposedly sick of the others' company. That was fair enough, but if you were truly concerned about my safety, you probably would have been at your window waving me goodbye as you'd said you would. Since I was pretty sure you *were* concerned about my safety, I started wondering why you hadn't waved me goodbye and the most logical explanation was that you had something better to do. At the time I had no idea what it might be but when I was attacked by the wolves in the woods and they left me unscathed, I started wondering…"

"Wondering what?"

"I was almost certain someone had called the wolves off. I knew it couldn't be you, but what if you'd been able to communicate with someone outside the house to let them know I was coming? That would have explained both the need for you to get away from the others and the fact you hadn't been at your window to see me off. You couldn't wave me goodbye because you were busy letting your accomplice know that I was on my way and wasn't to be harmed."

"Very conjectural of you, but surprisingly accurate." She looked dumbfounded.

"It was all hypothetical at that point, you're correct. But then I saw you slipping upstairs when Matthew escaped on the snowmobile and my theory started to look a lot less farfetched. Were you once again going to your room to communicate with the man I was now calling the ghost?

"Once I hypothesized you might be the ghost's accomplice, I started wondering how it could all fit together. That's when the pieces started falling into place. If you truly were one of the killers, you couldn't be at the cabin by chance. You were there by design, which meant Gwendoline was in on it, since she'd been the one inviting us over."

"She'd invited you, not me..." teased Jennifer.

"Right! I could never quite understand why she'd come to me in the first place... For a while I suspected that she'd just hired me as a decoy, thinking I'd never figure out she was the one who'd sent the blackmail letter. But it wasn't a satisfying explanation. The answer to that riddle became obvious once I started suspecting you. Gwendoline had brought me in because it was the best way of inviting you to the cabin without raising suspicions. The blackmail letter was just a decoy. Something to give you a reason to be at the cabin between Christmas and New Year's."

"Correct," admitted Jennifer.

"At that point, I needed to find more evidence of Gwendoline's involvement before venturing further down my speculative rabbit hole. Once I started reflecting on her actions, I soon did. I was fairly certain the poison had been given to Gregory in his hot cocoa and Gwendoline was the one in charge of preparing the kids' beverages. But what finally convinced me of her guilt was her behavior the morning of Vivian's suicide. A gunshot had just been fired in a house where two murders had already been committed, but Gwendoline left her daughter by herself in her bedroom while she came to enquire about what had happened. If she'd been worried about a killer running loose, she'd never have left her kid unprotected. The fact she did suggested she had no reason to be worried about her safety. Which meant that she was familiar with the killer's agenda."

Jennifer nodded her approval. She even looked sincere this time.

"And finally," continued Ethan, "Gwendoline came to knock on my door asking questions about the blackmailer that first evening after Matthew returned with the cops. The timing of her enquiries was particularly odd given half her family had just been murdered. But of course, the purpose of her visit was simply to distract me long enough so that you could slip out of the house without me stopping you. Why did you want to get out so bad, by the way?"

"I wanted to see my father one last time before he died," answered Jennifer, her voice cracking.

"But you didn't, did you? You couldn't have had time to go all the way to the cave and back."

"No, I didn't. Clive came after me and convinced me it was a bad idea. My disappearance, even for a couple of hours, would have raised too many questions I didn't want to have to answer."

Ethan remembered seeing the two of them walking back towards the house. At the time, he'd even suspected Clive of having eyes for Jennifer.

"Anyway, that's some impressive deductive work, boss," she said, faking admiration. "But how did you figure out I was Myriam?"

"Since I was reasonably certain Gwendoline and you were accomplices, I started wondering how the two of you knew each other. You and I had worked together for a year at that point and I hadn't picked you for a contract killer masquerading as a secretary. Therefore, I assumed you knew Gwendoline on a personal level. I'd been brushing up on Myriam's disappearance and so it was only natural that I started wondering if the little Myriam was truly dead or possibly working with her sister on sawing a few branches off the family tree. Myriam's IQ was off the chart and I had come to realize, albeit a bit late, that you were yourself a lot smarter than I'd first given you credit for."

It was Jennifer's turn to get out of the hot spring. She sat beside Ethan and one of the wolves immediately came to place its head in the crook of her neck.

"But if you were Myriam, where had you been hiding all these years? A nine-year-old doesn't disappear and survive in the world without help from an adult. Someone had helped you disappear. Could that someone be helping you again from the outside? Was that someone the ghost who'd killed Sam Clifford and tried to kill Sheriff Bradford?"

"Could you stop calling him the ghost? Just call him my father, please."

"Alright, I'm sorry. What I was about to say was that it became pretty obvious the wolves sided with your father after they killed the sheriff. And I remembered hearing on the news that wolves had chased teenagers out of the cave without harming them. Were these the same wolves that had herded me back to the cabin without leaving a scratch on me? And if they were, why had they gone after the kids in the first place? Were they protecting the cave? I had noticed your fascination for that cave. You started receiving news alerts on your phone shortly after it was discovered and were glued to the TV every time it was on the news. I'd found your obsession a bit weird at the time, but it wouldn't be weird at all if you actually knew the place. Was it where Myriam had gone to hide after fleeing the cabin all those years ago? Had she been rescued by a man who inhabited that cave?"

"Had she?" asked Jennifer teasingly.

"That's what the evidence suggested, my dear Jennifer. The first few murders hadn't seemed to impact you much when they occurred, although I saw your eyes glistening after Vivian's death—"

"That one wasn't planned," interrupted Jennifer. "We'd never meant for her to die. But I guess the stress of the situation got to her. That and maybe the guilt of having stood idle while her son raped her daughter and her husband ran a sex-trafficking operation…"

"I didn't understand why her suicide impacted you at the time, but I clearly remember thinking you had nerves of steel because the other murders didn't seem to have the slightest impact on you. Until the sheriff's death, that is. After that you became sad and visibly depressed."

"It had nothing to do with the sheriff!"

"Obviously… You were mourning your father who'd just been shot by the sheriff. Do you know how he ever managed to escape with a belly full of lead?"

"My brother helped him."

"Silas was also involved?"

"No, our plan scared him to death. He was against the whole idea and wanted nothing to do with it, but he couldn't help worrying about us. While my dad kept an eye on the cabin, Silas secretly kept an eye on him. When he witnessed my father getting shot, he went to his rescue. That's the extent of my brother's involvement… that and the last arrow."

"The one with the *'Wrong door!'* message attached to it? This wasn't part of your initial plan, was it?"

Jennifer shook her head. "No. I had to improvise and expedite Archibald's execution after Matthew took off. I knew we were running out of time, so I came up with the idea of the second power outage. I unlocked the cabin's side door so my dad could flip the breaker and I sent the message to my father's satellite phone. But he was too weak to do anything at that point, so my brother did it for him."

"I assume it was you who stabbed Archibald at the base of the neck? You did it just before joining me outside, correct?"

"Right again, Sherlock."

"You really are a talented actress."

"And I would have gotten away with it too, if it weren't for you meddling kids!" she said, quoting the famous Scooby-Doo line.

"You almost did. You only slipped up a couple of times."

"When?" she asked, sounding doubtful.

"You knew the cabin was in the Madison range before I even had the address. I bought your explanation at the time, but that was definitely a slip-up."

"Okay, maybe it was. But that was the only one."

"The blade you used to kill the senator was also a mistake, if not technically a slip-up. You used a flint blade to avoid being caught by his metal detector. Who has access to a flint blade nowadays? Contrary to what Theo seems to believe, you can't find a flint knife on Amazon. The average killer would have used a ceramic blade to avoid detection, but the use of flint tied the weapon to the flint arrowheads used by your father."

"Stop gloating, Ethan. I'm embarrassed for you. Instead, tell me who killed Allan since you're so smart. Was it Gwendoline or was it my dad who came from the outside?"

"Like I'm going to fall for that one… *You* killed him, of course. You claimed to have a migraine and were rubbing your temples, eyes shut, a minute before the lights went out. Your eyes were shut because you were going to need your night vision at its best to move for the kill. As soon as the light were out, you went to Allan's glass and poured the cyanide in it before returning to your seat. I saw you moving in that cave without any light, Jennifer. Your night vision is significantly above average."

"So you weren't convinced by my attempt at resurrecting him after he'd drunk the poison?"

"You mean the excuse you used to get your hands on him after he was already dead to hide the vial of poison in his own pocket?"

"Fine, you got me again. This is fun!" she said, but the smile quickly disappeared from her lips.

Ethan suspected she was thinking about her father and how her scheme had ended up costing him his life. In an attempt to distract her, he said, "But I had one piece of hard evidence that proved beyond any doubt that you were hiding something from me. Do you want to know what that is?"

She took the bait and nodded, intrigued.

"The phone records you gave me…"

She looked at him, smirking. "What about those records?" she asked, clearly knowing what he was about to say.

"They'd been conveniently sanitized to remove all phone calls to and from Mexico."

"How do you know that? The forgery is undetectable."

"Not if you have a copy of the real records to compare to… When you told me it could take you a while to obtain the records, I went to another source who got them to me within a couple hours. I had already seen the Mexico phone number appearing on Allan's and Archibald's records before you handed me your forged documents."

"That's cheating!"

"You obviously didn't want me to know about the sex-trafficking operation, but I can't figure out why."

"Isn't it obvious? I did it to protect Gwendoline and Emily. They had nothing to do with their fathers' shady dealings. I didn't want the Woodrough name dragged in the mud because they were the ones who would have suffered from it, them and their kids."

They got out of the hot spring completely and dried their legs on a towel Jennifer had brought. Then they dressed and headed back towards the cave, the wolves leading the way.

"They make for really intimidating bodyguards. I could get used to that," said Ethan, taking in the surrounding woods.

"No, you couldn't."

They walked in silence for a few minutes.

"What now?" asked Jennifer, and Ethan knew she wasn't asking about dinner plans.

"You tell me."

The End

Marc Daniel

After spending significant amounts of time in Ohio, France, and Montana, Marc is currently living in Houston with his wife and three dogs.

When he's not writing, cooking dinner or playing with his dogs, Marc enjoys woodworking, going to the theater and escaping the city to reconnect with nature.

Contact information:
marc@marcdaniel-books.com
www.marcdaniel-books.com
www.facebook.com/groups/MarcDanielReaders
@MarcDanielBooks

Printed in Great Britain
by Amazon